Australian author **Ally** [...]
and strong coffee, porc[...]
sunshine, beautiful notebooks and soft, dark
pencils. Her inquisitive, rumbustious, spectacular
children are her exquisite delight, and she
adores writing love stories so much she'd write
them even if nobody read them. No wonder,
then, having sold over four million copies of
her romance novels worldwide, Ally is living
her bliss. Find out more about Ally's books at
allyblake.com.

Michele Renae is the pseudonym of
award-winning author Michele Hauf. She
has published over ninety novels in historical,
paranormal and contemporary romance and
fantasy, as well as writing action/adventure as
Alex Archer. Instead of writing 'what she knows'
she prefers to write 'what she would love to know
and do'. And, yes, that includes being a jewel thief
and/or a brain surgeon! You can email Michele at
toastfaery@gmail.com, and find her on Instagram:
@MicheleHauf and Pinterest: @toastfaery.

ALWAYS THE BRIDESMAID

ALLY BLAKE

TWO WEEK TEMPTATION IN PARADISE

MICHELE RENAE

MILLS & BOON

First published in Great Britain 2024
by Mills & Boon, an imprint of HarperCollins*Publishers* Ltd,
1 London Bridge Street, London, SE1 9GF

www.harpercollins.co.uk

HarperCollins*Publishers*, Macken House, 39/40 Mayor Street Upper, Dublin 1, D01 C9W8, Ireland

Always the Bridesmaid © 2024 Ally Blake

Two Week Temptation in Paradise © 2024 Michele Hauf

ISBN: 978-0-263-32139-5

09/24

This book contains FSC™ certified paper
and other controlled sources to ensure responsible forest management.

For more information visit www.harpercollins.co.uk/green.

Printed and Bound in the UK using 100% Renewable Electricity
at CPI Group (UK) Ltd, Croydon, CR0 4YY

ALWAYS THE BRIDESMAID

ALLY BLAKE

MILLS & BOON

This book is dedicated to Sharon who, when I shared a meme about a girls' weekend away during which you do nothing but go to your separate corners and read, said, "And we are doing this when?"

CHAPTER ONE

CHARLOTTE GOODE STOOD in the shade of a pale pink castle-shaped wedding cake the size of a dolls' house. While the bride, Leesa, not two metres away, gawped back at her, eyes glassy, mouth wide with shock.

No wonder, for the bride's eye-wateringly expensive dress, with its vintage lace bodice, and voluminous layers of imported French tulle, was dripping in great globs of rich, gooey mud-brown cake and pale pink buttercream frosting.

The remains of which were stuck to the nooks and crannies of Charlotte's fiercely clenched hand.

For mere moments earlier, Charlotte had shoved her hand deep into the guts of that fairy-tale cake and grabbed a hearty fistful—in much the same way the bad guy in Indiana Jones and the Temple of Doom *had reached into that guy's chest and come out with his bloody beating heart—before hoicking back her hand and letting the cake fly...*

Charlie shuddered, attempting to rid herself of the shocking memory.

It had been two years since that fateful day. Her Momentary Lapse of Reason, she called it; to everyone else it had become #cakegate.

Two years since Charlie had stepped into her infamous era. Whether it was the optics of such a manifestly opulent wedding, the fact that Leesa, the bride, was the daughter of a US senator who'd gone apoplectic in the aftermath, or that one perfect photo of the aftermath, their perfectly meme-able faces in twin shocked expressions, for a minute *#cakegate* had trended higher than *#distractedboyfriend* and *#today-yearsold*.

Whatever one called it, she'd become a laughingstock, poison, and unemployable. The life she'd worked, and tried, and hustled so hard to build had ended up in pieces at her well-shod feet.

She looked at her feet now—lifting them from the armrest of the lumpy couch on which she lay, and giving them a wriggle, before ducking the chipped black evidence of a hasty home pedicure back out of sight.

She puffed out a breath, and tried, for the thousandth time, to think of some way she might have fixed things.

What if she'd not been so hasty as to resign from her role as junior event coordinator at the iconic San Francisco Bay Library? What if she'd refused to agree to their demand that she not contact the bride to apologise? What if she explained that she'd had a really good reason why she'd done what she did. That she'd been aiming for the groom, and missed.

Charlie groaned, and squeezed her eyes shut tighter, knowing it wouldn't have helped. For despite all that, she'd done something rash, and unconscionable. And in the end she'd only had herself to blame.

Hence the fact she was scrolling cat videos and nibbling at the bowl of stale mixed nuts balanced precariously on her chest while slouched back on the lumpy cane couch in her parents' sunroom in a house on picturesque hilltop Myrtle Way, in the Sunshine Coast hinterland.

There, *that* ought to distract her from #cakegate. The fact that after leaving home and vowing never to return, she was back living in her parents' place.

Her parents' place.

Charlie kept calling it that even though in actual fact the place had been vacant for years; the captured-in-time furniture, peeling wallpaper, funny smell in the laundry, and overgrown front garden were proof of that.

For when her father had died a number of years back, leaving behind a large collection of jackets with elbow patches and Charlie's habit of looking over her shoulder in case he was still there shaking his head at her in grave disappointment, her mum had hightailed it to the UK the day after she'd buried him. Like a rubber band stretched to its limits that had finally snapped.

"Are you sure?" Charlie's mum had said over the phone when Charlie had managed to track her down in the wilds of Scotland, where she was living these days, to make the mortifying "is it okay if I crash at home for a bit?" call. Her memories of the years spent in that house as snarled as Charlie's own.

After giving her mum the shiniest possible version of becoming an unemployable punch line, Charlie had said, "You know I'd not ask if I had any other choice—"

"Of course, honey," her mother had cooed. "Warning, I have no clue what condition the place is in after all this time. There's nothing owing on the place, the one good thing I can say about your father, but there may be a smidge of land tax due, and a few things that need fixing to make it habitable. But stay. Or sell the thing, and come on over here. There's no room in the caravan, but you'd love Edinburgh. Or, do as I planned, and let the earth eat it alive. Heck, burn it to the ground if that's what you want!"

What pleased Charlie was to take advantage of rent-free shelter, while curling up in a ball till she stopped feeling sorry for herself. Turned out that didn't happen overnight. For living in a falling down, debt-ridden house that she'd vowed never to set foot in again wasn't all it was cracked up to be.

So, she'd shaken herself off, stripped the bed, organised power and water like a proper grown-up, made a deal with the council to pay the eye-watering back taxes bit by bit, and started over. Again.

For Charlie was nothing if not resilient. She'd been knocked down—and, far more importantly, gotten back up again—more times than she could remember.

Only this time it had taken her rather a lot longer than usual to dust herself off. She was hopeful it was proportionate to the event, and not some indication that there was a finite number of times a person could get knocked down before it became just too hard to get back up again.

Then, like some portent of doom, Charlie flinched as an *actual* knock came at the front door.

She squinted up the hall, through the dust motes glittering in a beam of afternoon sunlight.

Eighteen months she'd been there now, and nobody had knocked. Likely because it meant braving the wildly over-grown front drive. There was also the fact she'd not exactly done much in the way of friend-making since she'd come home. Why bother, when she wasn't planning on sticking around. She just needed something—a spark, a sign, a kick in the pants—and she'd be back. Fierce and fighting fit. Till then, scrolling funny cat videos held great appeal.

Another knock. This one a little louder.

It was probably someone selling solar panel plans. Or maybe a tradesperson letting her know her hot water might be cut off for a few days, as yet another house along the street had been knocked down to make way for some contemporary hilltop mega-palace.

For the place on Myrtle Way, for all its drawbacks—distance to the nearest big city, inconsistent Wi-Fi, back steps held together with termite poop—was situated in the prettiest place on the planet.

The road itself wound along the peak of a band of verdant hills, leading to a number of small but popular tourist towns filled with quaint shops and even quainter people. But it was the view east that was the real money shot—a bright blue dome of a sky above layers of rich layers of green undulating forest rolling toward the deep blue distant twinkle of the Pacific beyond.

The gentrification of the area since she'd left was unsurprising. The speed at which it had was enough to give a person whiplash.

Another knock.

Wow, they were *really* keen. Their stickability was next level. It reminded her of...

Heat rushed up Charlie's neck and her belly felt all pins and needly as the aftermath of #cakegate came swimming at her all over again. In the weeks that followed she'd had to battle emails, phone calls, people stopping her on the street to take selfies. And once her address was out there, knocks at her door at any hour.

The breaking point had been an interview with a potential employer, smiling at her as if he'd met her somewhere before. Until something clicked, his eyes widening as he realised who she was. What she'd done. His disappointment had felt like a knife through the heart.

Thank everything good and holy this place was backwater enough that the whiff of #cakegate hadn't followed. But if it found her again, she honestly had no clue what she might do.

Knock. *Knock. Knock-knock-knock.*

Enough was enough.

Cursing the gods of mischief and mayhem who seemed to have taken a liking to her from birth, Charlie tossed her phone to the couch, pushed herself to standing, and padded up the hallway to the door.

A quick check of her T-shirt sporting the mean old guys

on *The Muppets* told her she had put on a bra that morning. The messy bun atop her head, and the fact she likely smelled like coffee and a medium to low current level of self-care were what they were.

Then, with a fortifying breath, she whipped open her front door.

To find a man mountain blocking the sun on her wide front veranda.

Even facing away, looking up the curving driveway past the overgrowth, toward the hidden road beyond, it was clear the guy was no door-to-door salesperson. Or a tradie for that matter. Too well-dressed in his slick brown boots, dark jeans, and peacoat a smidge too warm for the subtropical climate.

Too tall, too. Was that a thing? Could a person be too tall to take on a door-to-door job? For the man was mighty at well over six and a half feet and built to match.

Even his hair was a lot. Thick, gloriously tousled, the colour of rich dark chocolate. So soft-looking her fingers curled into her palms.

It was the weirdest thing. Her entire body seemed to be in the midst of some kind of chemical reaction. As if it was trying to tell her something. Had she stood up too fast? Been bitten by something on her walk down the hall?

All that in the space of two seconds.

For then the man turned.

Time seemed to slow as sunlight rained over him, dappled and bright, creating a halo of white gold around his spectacular face. Sparks glinted off black-rimmed glasses, shards of golden light picked out a sharp jaw covered in neat stubble, a straight nose, the outline of the most beautifully carved lips curving into a slow smile—

"Charlotte?"

Memories flickered and flashed, tumbling frantically over one another—rope swings, hide-and-seek, shooting-star watch parties. Picking wildflowers to make potions. A secret space in the small dank nook under the back porch of her house to hide in when her father, or his parents, were being particularly…them. A tumbled mess of laughter, daring, tenderness, rebellion, togetherness, confusion, anger, and the deep ache that comes from falling out with a friend—

Charlie rocked on her feet, as if something had reached in and dragged her through a gap in the space-time continuum.

"Beau?" she said, her voice catching.

It was. It was *Beau Griffin*. The boy next door.

Only he was not a boy anymore. For this Beau was a man. A big stunning manly man. With facial hair and bone structure and shoulders she had to move her head to measure.

Beau huffed out a soft laugh, and shook his head. As if he was as surprised to find her in her parents' home as she was to see him on their front veranda. A crease curved in just the one cheek, lines fanning out from the edges of his glasses behind which resided eyes she'd at one time known better than her own. Eyes the colour of peanut butter. Of autumn leaves. She may once have written a *very* secret poem saying as much.

Thankfully, some seed of self-control burst inside her. Which was a small miracle, considering her history of giving into urges that erred on the side of self-destructive.

"Beau!" she said again. Then, "Beau Griffin. It's been *forever*."

Not quite, though. For she remembered the date, the day, what they were both wearing. The awful fight they'd had the night before. How she'd had to cross her arms so tight across her chest in order to stop the shakes when he'd driven away to take on the phenomenal early scholarship he'd been awarded, and not looked back.

How her father—a "renowned doctor of chemistry" to anyone who asked, as opposed to mildly successful high school science teacher—had moved in behind her, and hissed into her ear, asking why with all the advantages she'd been given—aka being his daughter—*she* couldn't be *more like Beau.*

"It's so good to see you!" she said, feeling *totally* fine about all that now. Then she reached out and gave his arm a chummy smack, and her hand bounced off what felt like wool over solid concrete. *That* was new.

"I thought," he said, brow furrowing over his glasses, "I'd heard you were working overseas?"

And didn't that just set off a swirl of feelings inside her, imagining he must have googled her or secretly stalked her social media at some point.

Then, as if it had been lying in wait, #cakegate poked out its head. Had he seen the memes? Or heard the song someone had made that had gone viral for a half second, using the gasps and chair scrapes and clanking plates as percussion.

Her whole body felt as if it was curling on itself as she waited for the follow up. The weirdness that always came next. Hell, if she saw *disappointment* in Beau Griffin's eyes she might never recover. But nothing more came of it, and she relaxed a very little.

"Mm-hmm," she said. "I'm crashing here for a little bit. Passing through really. And you? Working hard doing something amazing I bet."

Last she'd heard *he* was in Sydney, fronting a groundbreaking team of engineers working to invent some renewable, green clean energy battery, or engine, or something, that was going to save the world. For yes, she had cyber-stalked him a while back, before she realised it didn't make her feel any better about how things had gone down.

He lifted a hand to the back of his neck, a classic Beau move, giving him the air of a tortured poet. "Busy enough. Though I've just… I'm taking some time off right now."

She might have asked, *Time off from what?* or *Why?* but there was the fact that he was looking at her mouth. Like, *really* looking.

Then his hand lifted from its position hooked into the front of a pair of awfully flattering jeans and both she and her inner monologue had no words as he reached up. His fingers hovered an inch away from her jaw, his thumb hooked as if he might brush her lips. While his gaze was so focused, warmth spread through her like liquid sunshine.

Then, in Beau's voice yet not Beau's voice for it was lower than she remembered, deep, with a husky edge, said, "You have a small flake of something on the corner of your mouth."

Sorry, what now?

Charlie's tongue darted out, catching a *not small* flake of peanut skin that had been stuck there. The entire time.

All the strange warmth that had been dancing through her zoomed straight to her cheeks as she wiped quickly at her mouth, to find it *covered* in peanut salt. Looking down she found yet more salt, *more peanut flakes,* glittering her boobs.

She brushed herself down, frantically flapped her shirt, then started to laugh. Cackling, really, for the first time in what felt like eons. Till her stomach hurt.

"You have no idea how much I needed that," she said, once she was recovered. Then she looked up at him, arms wide, and said, "Truth is, I'm a hot mess. How the heck are you?"

"I'm…fine," he said, as if, despite all evidence to the contrary, he'd needed that moment to be sure. Then, "Surprised to see you. Thrilled, that it was you who opened the door, but surprised."

"Thrilled, you say?"

The crease in his right cheek grew a little deeper, and even while the smile never quite reached his eyes, her knees all but gave way.

"I was beginning to wonder how many more times I should knock before it bordered on too many," Beau said.

Charlie braced a hip on the doorjamb. "Oh, it was definitely too many. I was ready to set the dogs on you."

When he looked over her shoulder, down her parents' front hall, as if expecting a horde of Dobermans to come at him, she added, "Metaphorically," and got another half smile for her efforts.

As an inconvenient bloom rose inside her, Charlie wrapped the old wrap tighter about herself.

"Was there a reason for the knocking?" she asked, rather than the zillion other questions knocking about inside her head.

Why are you here? How have you been? Where have you been? Are you okay? Like, really *okay? What happened to us? Are you married? Kids? Do you ever think of me? Of us? Do you ever wonder if the adventures we had before the whole weird "falling out" thing might end up being the best times of our lives?*

Something flashed behind his eyes, making her wonder if he, too, was choosing which of a dozen questions to start with, before he went with, "How are your parents? Are they still about?"

Parents. Meaning he must not know about her father. She'd always imagined that while she and Beau had not spoken in years, her father had found a way to stay in contact over the years, for he'd seen Beau as the child he'd believed he deserved. The fact that she'd been wrong about that loosened something inside her.

"Dad passed away a while back," Charlie said. "Mum is travelling the Scottish wilderness in a campervan with her *lover*, Alfredo."

Beau lifted his chin in a nod, as if that all tracked. What he didn't do was offer up any condolences over her father's fate. Which she appreciated. For Beau understood that she'd have struggled to accept it. In fact, he was the only person who ever truly would.

She did him the same courtesy. She'd already moved overseas, having nabbed a green card in the visa lottery, when Beau's parents had died. Her mother had called to tell her—gas inhalation in their kitchen, classified accidental, evidence suggesting both were likely too high to even notice.

His parents. Their house. Oh, no.

Before she could second-guess herself, Charlie leaped out onto the veranda, grabbed Beau's arm, her hand sliding into the crook of his elbow the way it had done a thousand times before, and used the element of surprise to spin him so that their backs were to the place where Beau's childhood home used to be.

For it was one of the most recent to have been torn down. Wrecking balls and bulldozers. The whole nine yards. It had been quite the show.

While it had probably a good thing, considering its macabre history, a gargantuan sharp-edged beast of a structure had begun to be constructed in its place. And while Beau's childhood had been more chaotic than hers, even downright frightening at times, foundational memories could be complicated. She knew.

"Charlotte?" Beau said again, an all too familiar note of indulgence in his voice.

"Mm-hmm?"

"Is there a reason we're looking at your rubbish bins."

"Yep."

Chances were, he knew about the house, right? Though, from the road it looked the same as it always had—big brick pillars covered in moss and wild jasmine, the gate long since gone, long driveway dipping past shrubs and lush trees blocking any view of the house settled into the gently sloping hill-side at the rear.

But still he waited. Big to her small. All still stoicism to her constant fidgets. Patience to her restlessness. So warm and strong. So *Beau*.

A deep psychic ache rose up inside her then. The years she'd missed, even when he'd still been around. Wondering what she'd done to make him pull away, hating not knowing where they had gone so wrong.

So, yeah, maybe *grabbing* the guy hadn't been the best move.

Then Beau made a sound. Or maybe he flexed beneath her gripping hand. Either way she looked up to find his gaze questioning. When his mouth did the quirk thing, the cheek bracket bracketing for all it was worth, she let go as if burned.

And moved away from him, keeping his attention in the bin direction, which was probably what she *ought* to have done in the first place. *Clicked her fingers. Look over here!*

Then she said. "I have to tell you something."

"Okay."

"Your house… Your *parents'* old house—it's no longer there. And now they're building some modern monstrosity in its place. All sooty wood, cantilever architecture, with the charm of a weapons facility. It's as if the new owner has the hots for *Grand Designs* and hopes to blow out their hare-brained budget in the name of owning their very own Mojo Dojo Casa House."

Beau's eyebrows slowly rose. Then he turned, as if to see for himself.

In a panic, Charlie grabbed him by both arms this time. Holy hell, the man was made of concrete. "I just—" She stopped to clear her throat. "I didn't want you to head over there, unprepared."

And as he looked at her, once again the memories just

flooded on in. She, his great defender. Taking on school bullies, sneaking him food when it was clear he'd gone without, forcing him on adventures to distract him from whatever went on behind his front door that made him look so haunted all the damn time. His friendship giving her quiet assurance that she was worthy of it.

Until the summer she turned sixteen, and their friendship had gone up in smoke.

"May I?" he said, a hand reaching to open his jacket.

Realising she still held him, she let go. Stepping back, she put her hands in the back pockets of her short cut-offs so that she'd not grab the guy again. Sheesh!

Beau reached for his phone, swiped it open and held up a picture of *her* front porch. A strange package thereupon.

Charlie looked around to find no such package. "I don't understand."

"This is why I came knocking. And knocking some more. My builders received this message yesterday saying some bathroom fittings they had been waiting for had been delivered. Only this was the image the delivery company sent as proof. Only it's not my new front porch, it's yours."

His new front porch?

Charlie's gaze swung past his big shoulders to the trees blocking the view of the house next door. "I don't understand. Your house was sold after your parents—"

She bit her lip. According to her mum, debt collectors had swept in and picked it clean before the bank sold it for a pittance. A series of renters had moved in and out before her mother left and any connection to the house next door had been lost.

"I recently repurchased the place," Beau said.

Charlie, moving back into the safety of the doorway, watched him look toward the house next door, the sliver of his face she could see unreadable.

"Recently?" she pressed. "Meaning you bought it…in order to *knock it down*?"

He turned back to her, then. A rueful smile on his face as he said, "I suppose I did."

And again she noted that the smile didn't quite reach his eyes. In the old days that would have been her sign to drag him up a tree so that they could spy on her other neighbour, or under the back porch for a game of speed Uno.

Now she had nothing for him but, "Wow."

"You haven't considered doing the same?" he asked.

"Me? No!" she said, her hand leaping to her heart before she dropped it back to her side. For one thing, what with her situation and back taxes, *she* didn't have the funds to fix the dodgy wiring, or look into the water stains on the ceiling, much less rebuild an entire house.

As to selling up? She *could* do that. Reinvest, move on. Her mother had even given the green light to burn the place to the ground. Yet she, the queen of burning it all down, was holding back on making a decision. Something keeping her put for the minute. And she wasn't quite ready to unpack what that might be.

Beau, on the other hand, appeared totally cool with having razed his childhood home.

Beau, who'd been the sweetest little kid on the planet; the kind who'd step over an ants' nest and never take the first turn. Who, even when he'd begun to make a name for himself, winning every national science championship there was, had hosted online Dungeons and Dragons games from the local library computers, because he was too shy to do so in person. Teen Beau had been more of an enigma, even before things had gone pear-shaped between them.

But he'd always been forgiving. Of her, when she pushed too hard. Of the kids at school who pegged them both as outsiders and treated them as such. Of his parents, despite what they'd put him through.

Clearly, she'd been mistaken.

When she realised they were both just looking at one another again, and her skin began to warm, Charlie said, "Sorry. I never saw that package in the photo. Maybe check with the delivery guys?"

He blinked as if pulling himself from his own fog of memories, then said, "Will do."

Then, when Beau looked to the driveway, as if making to leave, Charlie found herself saying:

"And who do I call if I want to complain about the week of cold showers I was just forced to endure?"

That time the crinkles most definitely reached his eyes. Happy warmth flooded through her, reminding her how deeply satisfying it had been, all those years ago, to make this guy smile.

"Plumbing is all done," Beau assured her with a tilt of his head, "so any cold showers you take from here should be by choice." And was his voice a little dry? The kind of dry that scraped down a woman's insides leaving a scratchy feeling in its wake. *Her* insides. She was the woman.

"If I get any more mystery packages?" she found herself asking.

After a beat, and a long breath in, Beau said, "Let the builders know."

The builders. Not him.

Charlie swallowed, and nodded. "Sure. Of course." Then she stepped back and reached blindly for the door handle. "I was in the middle of something," aka scrolling cat videos, "and I really should get back to it. It was really nice to see you, Beau. Hope all goes well with the monstrosity!"

Beau's mouth was open when she shut the door.

Charlie spun and leaned against the door, her head falling back to thunk against the wood.

Once she was sure enough the guy wasn't about to knock again, she pushed off the door and tiptoed back down the hall to the sunroom. Where she sat on the lumpy cane couch, grabbed a cushion, hugged it to her chest, and stared into the middle distance.

So that was Beau Griffin. The once upon a time gentle to her wild. The sense to her daring. Twin stars revolving around a near-permanent state of imminent danger, keeping one another from flinging out into the void. All grown up.

What was his plan for the house next door? Was he going to sell it? Rent it out? Or keep it for a vacation home? Surely, he wasn't moving back in. Not that it mattered. Not him, not his house. It was nothing to her.

It was enough to be on the lookout for that one great spark of inspiration that might get her out from under the #cakegate fugue. After which she'd be out of there! Faster than lightning.

She would find some place new. Some place entirely devoid of memories to make her mark. For while life might *try* to knock her down, the memories tripped her every damn time.

CHAPTER TWO

A MINUTE LATER Charlie's phone buzzed.

Her heart stuttered when for a half second she wondered if it might be Beau. Beau who didn't have her number, and who'd made no effort to give her his even after she'd given him the perfect opener.

Rolling her eyes at herself, she pulled herself back to sitting in order to read the messages.

Helloooooo!!! Is this Charlotte Goode???

She read it again—her form of dyslexia meaning she often had to read things multiple times for them to sink in—and counted three exclamation marks *and* three questions marks. Whomever they were, top points for enthusiasm!

When more messages came through, *bing-bing-bing*, she clicked on the text-to-speech mode to speed things up, and listened as the dismembered voice said:

"My name is Annie! Martine Jones gave me your number! She told me what you did for her, and OMG, she could not have raved more!"

Martine was a recent and pretty decent client. For in her hustle to make money to pay back taxes and you know, eat, she'd kind of accidentally started a fledgling new venture. A hobby, really, that could thankfully pay her bills. She'd been

loath to call it anything more than that just yet, for surely that
would be baiting the #cakegate gods.

A month after coming home, her mum had called, saying
one of Charlie's second cousins, Rosie, who she'd apparently
once played under a garden sprinkler naked with as a kid,
was getting married. Rosie's maid of honour had broken her
nose in a skiing accident, and Charlie's mum had suggested
Charlie could fill in.

It had no doubt been her way of getting Charlie out of the
house, as if she could sense her continued reticence even
from far, far away. Also because Charlie was event-trained
and available. Win-win!

For much the same reasons, Charlie had agreed. And
whether it was she had no skin in the game, or she'd so needed
to do something where she felt useful again, it had been the
best fun. Easy. Exciting even, putting out real-time spot fires
before they could flare up.

Her cousin could not have been more grateful. While wedding guests, who'd heard the story of all she'd pulled off in
so short a time, had asked for her business card in case they
could use her in *their* wedding party.

Cousin Rosie—a career counsellor who had not paid her
a cent—had leaped in, gushing, "She's worth every penny!"
with a conspiratorial wink.

And that's how *Always the Bridesmaid*—Charlie's kind
of, accidental, money-maker—had been born.

Her phone buzzed again.

I would love to meet with you, to see if there's a chance
that you could squeeze me into what must be an insanely
packed schedule.

Brace yourself: there will be three hundred + guests, and
it's in six weeks!

You would be literally SAVING MY LIFE!!!

Charlie coughed out a laugh at *insanely packed schedule*. She wished. Only not out loud. No point getting too excited about what it might one day become, for it could all come tumbling down just as quickly.

But it was nice hearing such things in her father's house. In fact, she turned up the volume, lifted her phone and played the next messages, in case a certain ghost might by some chance be listening in.

The way you stopped her nephew from spiking the punch, genius!

The dad jokes you pull out every time she tried on her dress, knowing her dad wouldn't be there.

Forget the numbers and the crunch time. The brilliance of what you do is none of that matters for you'd be all mine! My very own professional bestie!

A professional bestie. She'd never thought of it that way. But if Always the Bridesmaid *was* ever big enough to demand a mission statement that'd be close.

Then the idea of being anyone's bestie only brought up thoughts of Beau Griffin. How tight they'd been, how important to one another. Until they weren't. She'd been too confused back then, too hurt, too sixteen years old to confront him. To ask what it was about her bestie-ness he'd found so easy to live without. But now?

"Argh!" she growled. Then, "You know what? Screw it."

She looked at her calendar to find she was due to meet up with Isla—a client who was fretting about her choice of wedding dress, and needed some cheerleading—the next day.

She texted back, but not before checking her spelling three times.

Free tomorrow morning?

Within a minute a meeting place was booked.

Charlie replied to a few questions from her bookkeeper, Julia, via voice notes as she walked up the hill toward the café the next morning. Always the Bridesmaid wasn't exactly big enough to require such help, but Charlie's dyslexia was.

Her condition hadn't been picked up until rather late, around halfway through primary school, as she'd hid it behind being precocious, asking a lot of questions when the words made no sense, being the most helpful. Anything to distract people from thinking she was stupid. Incapable. Lazy.

She got enough of that at home.

Once diagnosed, her mum and teachers had done their best to help her navigate it, but her father blocked them at every chance. *No child of his required learning assistance.*

Only as an adult, in fact the year she'd spent in San Francisco, had she had the means, and the courage, to find her own dyslexia therapist. And it had changed her life. She'd discovered her brand of dyslexia wasn't merely swapping numbers and letters, it was also the likely reason behind her excellent memory, and the fact that reading body language and knowing how much personal space to allow for were not her forte.

The flipside? Give her a problem and she'd find a way to solve it. It was her superpower.

She had been getting a handle on things, and acknowledging that so many of the things she'd struggled with were *not* her fault, when #cakegate happened.

Leaving her therapist had knocked her as much as losing

her apartment, her employment, the version of herself she'd worked so hard to become.

When Always the Bridesmaid had become a thing, and she'd found Julia's details in a hobby business forum. After the second, super-long, excited email from Julia, Charlie had braved up, called her and let her know that due to her dyslexia, she just couldn't function that way.

Julia had paused for a beat and said, "How would voice messages go?"

Needless to say, Julia was a blessed relief.

Charlie walked past the Clock Shop, the old windmill, boho cafés, and handmade toy shops, listening again to the dozen messages Annie had sent her that morning. Picking out the highlights:

Three hundred plus guests.

Six weeks.

Money no object.

Taking the final message with a grain of salt, an event that size would still be a step up from the mostly local DIY weddings that Always the Bridesmaid had worked thus far. In fact, it was leaning a *little* close to the kinds of event she had assisted in organising during her San Francisco Library days, but whereas a few months ago it might have brought her out in hives, she felt ready.

In fact, it felt like just the right time.

Hadn't she been waiting for a sign? A spark? A kick in the pants? Then Beau Griffin had turned up on her doorstep, looking all windswept, and solid. Like the ghost of summers past, reminding her of who she used to be—how bolshie, and fierce, how nothing could stop her.

She breathed out in relief as she finally reached the meeting spot—the Pretty Kitty Café. Only to head inside and find…actual cats. Everywhere.

"Hand sanitiser over there," the emo girl on reception intoned, pointing to the other side of a glass partition where the patrons and cats hung out together. "Don't leave your glass unattended as they will knock it over. You can pick up any cat, bar Jerry." She pointed to a picture tacked to the glass wall; a half tiger, half house cat looking menacingly at the camera.

Something beyond the image caught Charlie's eye. She refocused to see a woman in a fluffy pink top, holding a fluffy white kitten, and madly waving her hand.

And all remnants of any chipper feelings Charlie had been harbouring about this meeting fled as dread poured into its place.

For "Annie!!!" turned out to be Anushka Patel.

While Charlie had lost any appetite for celeb gossip after #cakegate, there was no avoiding Anushka Patel—an ex-reality TV dating show star turned radio drive time cohost, who famously dressed like a Manga character, and had become an actual postfeminist icon after infamously dumping her football star boyfriend for refusing to read *Twilight*.

Three hundred guests Charlie could do.

A wedding in six weeks Charlie could do.

That level of media interest, of public interest, Anushka Patel had shining upon her day and night, simply by existing? No, nope. No way in hell.

When Anushka waved for her to come in, it was either do just that, or spin on her heel and make a run for it. The least she could do, as a professional bestie and all, was meet with the woman, and let her down gently.

"Charlotte!!!" Anushka cried, the triple exclamation marks absolutely implied.

Holding her breath against the cloying scent of kitty litter and flea powder, Charlie narrowly avoided stepping on a kitten as she made her way to the hot pink booth in the corner. "Annie as in Anushka?"

Anushka waved her spare hand at Charlie, glitter seeming to waft from her person, before yanking her into a tight one-armed hug. "I know. Sorry. I never type my real name. Hacking, you know."

"Totally," said Charlie. Though thankfully her moment in the sun had been hot enough to burn, but had burned itself before hacking had become a thing. And she'd really prefer to keep it that way.

Anushka made smoochie noises at the kitten before placing it on the floor at her feet, then sat, and stared at Charlie as if feeding off her energy.

"Gosh, you're pretty," Anushka said in her famously breathy voice. "And I *know* pretty. Most of us on the kinds of shows I've done are 'makeup and good colourist' pretty. But a forties gumshoe detective would give up his career over your peepers."

Charlie blinked eyes she'd always thought made her look a bit like a Disney chipmunk, as she slid into the booth. "I have cellulite, if that helps."

"Oh, that helps a lot."

"Now," said Charlie, when Anushka took in a breath. "Before we go any further—"

"No!" said Anushka, her face downfallen. "Please don't say no. I *need* you. I've felt so much better the past day, since we spoke. Now I can't imagine going ahead without you."

Charlie wondered if Anushka was waving catnip under Charlie's nose. You need me? I'm just that capable?

But no. The risk that someone looking to Anushka's wedding for clickbait would put two and two together was too great. And while risk might *once* have been her middle name, she had to be more careful now. Unsure how many more failures she had in her.

"I'm really sorry," Charlie said, flinching when something furry brushed by her ankle. "My schedule simply won't allow it. But I'd be happy to refer you to my wonderful associate, Julia."

Yep, Julia the bookkeeper. For Julia had agreed to take on the bookkeeping at a vastly reduced fee if she could learn the ropes, so that she might "move up in the organisation." Julia had taken on a couple of clients down Byron Bay way, while Charlie charged a finder's fee for basically doing nothing, and it had gone just fine.

"Julia lives a couple of hours away, but is wonderful," Charlie assured her. "Perky, tough when needed, so organised it's terrifying—"

Anushka held up a finger, then grabbed a pen—glittery, pink, with a pompom on top—and paper—pink with sparkly edges—and said, "I'm sure anyone you recommend would be lovely. But I am a gut person, and my gut tells me I need you. Only you."

Anushka slid the piece of paper across the table, and Charlie's gaze fell upon a figure that made her eyes widen so fast it was miracle her eyelids didn't turn inside out.

"Anushka, I'm not sure what it is you think I do, but for this number you'd be right in requesting unicorns to ride in on, a honeymoon in space, and out-of-season flowers in your bouquet."

A skinny grey cat leaped onto the table, and Anushka lifted her milkshake with practiced adeptness as she said, "I don't want all that. I want you."

Charlie kept looking at the number, her eyes burning from not blinking, in case when she did the number might change.

It was serious money. The kind of money a businesswoman who was aware of what her experience, bravado, and capability were worth might demand.

It hit like a punch to the gut how deliberately she'd been undervaluing herself.

Damn you, #cakegate.

And damn Richard, her ex, the #cakegate groom, the one she'd *tried* to throw a handful of squished cake at, and missed.

She'd not originally been on the roster for that event, but he'd known she worked there. Meaning he could have convinced his wife-to-be to have the reception somewhere else, just in case. But that wasn't Richard's way.

The gods of mischief, and stomach flu, decreed that she be called in at the absolute last minute to take over from a sick colleague once the reception was already underway. She'd been on cake duty, literally watching the thing, making sure no one came too close, when she felt someone move in behind her.

How do you like me now? he'd muttered, his voice filled with caustic pride.

No more than I did when I left you, she'd shot back, her heart thudding in her throat as she'd looked around for someone to take her place.

At which point he'd called her a filthy liar, and a fool, for she would cry herself to sleep that night, realising just how wholly she'd screwed up in letting him go. Then he'd called her a word only one other man had ever called her. And even then he'd only done it once, before he'd kicked her out of her home.

"You've gone terribly serious all of a sudden," said Anushka.

And Charlie snapped back to the present. "You've surprised me, which I'm sure was the point."

Anushka batted her lashes Charlie's way.

"Tell me about your fiancé," Charlie blurted, needing to shake off the shakes that had started in her hands and would soon have her wanting to curl into a ball if she didn't stop them. Besides, if she was truly considering this, best make sure the guy wasn't a serial killer, prank show host, or yet another ex.

In Charlie-land, things that seemed too good to be true usually were.

"Of course!" said Anushka. "I can't believe I didn't start there. This is Bobby." Then she slid her phone across the table, and leaned her chin on her hand, her expression softening so that Charlie could all but see the cartoon hearts popping over her head.

The photo showed Anushka clinging happily to a man with curly brown hair, deep brown eyes, moustache, nice smile, a tad shorter than she. A bright red race car in the background.

"Your Bobby is *Bobby Kent*?" The rise at the end of Charlie's sentence was due to the fact that while Anushka was a press magnet, Bobby Kent was an absolute superstar. Australia's best ever Indigenous racing car driver, he was even more of a media magnet than his fiancée.

Anushka nodded. "Isn't he adorable?"

Charlie nodded, while thinking she couldn't do this. More to the point, she dared not.

Dammit. Truly. Would #cakegate loom over her forever? Maybe. Maybe her hopes for finding her way to eventually something wonderful were crazy. Maybe she was destined to stay slow and steady, if she wanted to go through life without people looking at her with such—

"Disappointment," said Anushka.

Charlie blinked.

"I mean," Anushka went on, "they've never explicitly made me feel that way, his parents. They just love their son so very much. I want them to feel sure that I am good for him, while also being my true self. And while I honestly do not care what my wedding day looks like, or tastes like, or sounds like, so long as I'm standing by Bobby, it would be helpful to have someone who's unassailably on my side. You know?"

Charlie knew all too well. And she was *good* at it. She always had been, thanks to Beau Griffin. He'd been her patient zero—dragging him into madcap adventures, distracting with speed Uno, making sure he was fed, watered, and supported.

She might have taken the long way around, but when forced to pare back, to do something spare and honest in order to make ends meet, this was what she'd fallen into. Being a professional bestie.

Charlie made to open her mouth to say, "Hell yes!" when Anushka cut her off.

"There's one more thing."

Of course there was.

"That fee," Anushka said nodding toward the sparkly pink note gripped in Charlie's hand. "It covers hiring *you* as my maid of honour, and a *you* for Bobby as well."

"I'm sorry?"

"Bobby's friends are wonderful, but they're all like him—used to being looked after. Bobby needs a good, honest, solid best man who can cut it with the Kents, keep Bobby's friends on the straight and narrow, and work happily under your purview."

A best man?

And there it was—the foot that had been sticking out, ready to trip her this whole time.

She didn't *know* any men in the area. Well, there was Bryan, her clinically shy mechanic. And Phil, the local grocer who was eighty if he was a day. The closest she came on the daily were the builders at Beau's place next door who she sometimes heard chatting and laughing if she kept her front window open. One might have been named Macca?

Beau's place. Beau.

She knew Beau.

No. Don't be ridiculous. For one thing, when she'd given him an opener to keep in touch, he'd totally ghosted her.

Hadn't he said he'd taken some time off? her inner monologue piped up.

Irrelevant, she shot back.

For what did that mean? A week? A day? Chances were he was back in Sydney already, twerking engine nuts, or whatever it was that he did.

Yeah, no. Not a chance.

A chance. That's what this felt like. A second chance. Heck, it was more like her seventh. It was a big one, at the very least. A chance to prove to herself that she could do this. That she deserved a shot, at least.

All she had to do was take on a job she could do with her eyes closed, stay in the background, and her life might just change.

"Can you give me a day?" she blurted, before she could change her mind.

Anushka bounced gently on her seat, as she suddenly had two new kittens in her arms.

"No promises," said Charlie.

Anushka shook her head. While grinning as if certain it was fait accompli.

A day. A day to do what? Wander the streets of Maleny holding up a Wanted Best Man sign? See if there was an agency from which she could source such a specific person, someone solid she could trust to represent her in what might be the biggest moment in her career thus far?

Someone like Beau.

No! Besides, she had no way to contact Beau even if she wanted him. She *could* pop her head over the rose bushes, and see if any of the builders might give up his number.

No, she didn't want him, just someone like him.

Not that she *wanted* someone like him. She merely had a use for him. Nope, that didn't sound any better, even in her head.

She shook it off, or tried her best. While knowing now she'd thought it, it would burrow its way in. Like one of those frogs that went underground, for years sometimes, waiting for rain, at which point up it would jump ready and raring to breed.

Great, now we'll spend all afternoon imagining breeding with Beau Griffin, her inner monologue chuffed.

Enough! she shouted inside her own head. *Focus.*

For it wasn't just the money. It was the contacts. Word of mouth was everything in her business. *Her business.* For that's what Always the Bridesmaid was. Not a job. Something she'd created from nothing.

"Now, let me buy you something sickly sweet and pink to celebrate."

Anushka smiled as she waggled her fingers at a passing waiter, and the stress lines Charlie had missed at first glance, now stood out like footprints in wet sand. As if she'd been holding herself together with hope and positivity for so long she was collapsing in on herself.

Charlie didn't need a day.

If Beau had been the ghost of summers past, then Anushka was her ghost of summers present. And if anyone learned anything from *The Muppet Christmas Carol*, it was that those ghosts knew their stuff.

She'd find a best man.

She'd put Always the Bridesmaid on the map.

Just like that, Charlie Goode's moxie was back.

CHAPTER THREE

BEAU GRIFFIN WAS known for being a man prepared.

Existing in a constant state of readiness, having already run every possible scenario in his head—a skill learned during a childhood spent avoiding the Department of Child Services—was a big reason behind his company's rapid success. It had also been the only way to survive growing up in the house on Myrtle Way.

Only now his ability to make even the smallest decisions had up and left. Eggs for breakfast or muesli? The blue shirt or the other blue shirt? More to the point, what did it matter?

Not great timing, considering the passion project he'd been working on his entire life—the Luculent Engine—was going through its most rigorous review yet, and the architecturally challenging house he'd pushed to have built as soon as possible required decisive choices quickly made.

It was the final reason why he'd decided to take time off, to see the build through to its bitter end. The reason he chose to focus on, at least.

"How's it looking?" Matt—Beau's business partner and best friend—asked through the speaker in Beau's watch. Matt who was back in Sydney, holding up the fort, when considering the past few months, it should very much have been the other way around.

"Much the same," said Beau, standing in the backyard just beyond the edge of bomb site that was his old backyard, hands on hips, gaze on the jutting corner of the gargantuan framework leaning ominously over the giant muddy footprint gouged out of the land.

All the personality of a weapons facility came at him in Charlotte Goode's matter of fact way. And despite how strangely disquieting it had been, seeing her again, he found himself huffing out a laugh.

The house, he reminded himself, bringing his attention, unhinged as it was of late, back to where he wished his focus to remain.

And yet Beau's gaze shifted left, to the wall of thorny rose bushes that created a barrier between their two yards. Echoes, shadows flickering gently in the depths of his mind—a grazed knee, a hand reaching from a higher branch, overlapping front teeth in a wide grin, long dark auburn hair peppered with pollen. A secret handshake, complete with spit and dirt under the nails. A safe place to wait out a storm.

He deliberately dragged his gaze back to the house.

Thoughts of Charlotte Goode leaning against her doorjamb looking lush, and insouciant, and hectic could wait. Or better yet, they could quietly go away. For he'd not come back to this place in search of what seeing her had unearthed in him; a visceral reminder of the time before his childhood home had been summarily wiped from the earth.

He'd come back looking for…what? Clarity? Closure? The key to his current unravelling so that he could turn the thing and find his way back? He honestly had no idea.

All he knew was that Matt had lost Milly—the mother of his kids, the right hand to his left—to cancer—several months before and nothing he said or did made sense anymore.

They'd been great friends, the three of them, since they met at university. As Matt and Milly paired off, got married, had kids, their family became Beau's family. Dinners at the coffee table, finger paint on the walls, laughter and quiet luxury and arguments that never went deeper than surface scratches. A family so polar opposite from the one he'd grown up with as to be laughable.

Milly's diagnosis had come out of nowhere, the disease taking her with such ferocity, ravaging her, the woman Beau considered a sister. It had sent Beau into the kind of tailspin Matt hadn't had the luxury of indulging in, considering the two little ones he had to stay strong for.

It could have imploded—his long friendship with Matt, their company Luculent—taking down all they'd built with it. Except they saw how close they came, and they spoke of it, honestly, constantly: Beau's lack of drive, his faltering focus; Matt's loneliness, and fury, and his determination to get his and Milly's kids, Tasha and Drew, through as unharmed by it all as possible.

Till even Matt had had enough, telling Beau to take some time off—get some perspective. Give himself a break. Luculent had been Milly's as much as it had been theirs, and it was at an all-time high—their engine in review, the world itching for more like it, faster, better. The pendulum would only hold on so long before a downward swing.

Beau was told to figure out what he wanted.

He stared up at the house as if it might have the answers.

It loomed greyly over him and gave nothing away.

"Can you see better now, how it might end up?" Matt asked.

Beau could not. Perhaps because when designing the place, his instructions had been simple: *Make it unrecognizable.*

It *should*, he believed, look less imposing once it was painted, clad in all the designer extras that would "soften the exterior" according to his architect. Once the landscaping was complete and the backyard looked less like the psychological cleansing it so clearly was.

"Beau?" Matt's voice called.

Beau came back into his skin only to feel as if it no longer fit right. It had been that way for months now. As if he contained too much blank space, filled with unseeable, unknown feelings, wanting out. Far too close to how his parents had felt before medicating their way to oblivion.

"It'll be big," he said, dragging his eyes back to the edifice.

Matt laughed. "No surprise there. You do nothing by halves, big dog. It's just not in you."

Speaking of big dogs, Beau whistled and Moose bounded out of the brambles that now seemed to fill the gorge at the rear of the property. Ears flapping, tongue lolling, covered in filth, the dog sniffed Beau's hand, then bounded off again.

Noting the burrs in Moose's smooth brindled coat, he thought, *Cobbler's pegs? Lantana? Blackberries?* He'd better get someone on it or else the neighbours would be on him.

Though the fact that his neighbour was Charlotte Goode had him shifting on his feet.

He might not have been surprised to see one of her parents open the door the day before, but Charlotte? Looking soft and rumpled, chunks of auburn hair falling by her cheeks. All long bare legs in cut-off denim shorts. Loose neck of her old *Muppets* T-shirt showing the delicate triptych of moles along her left collarbone.

The last time he'd seen her was the night before he'd left. She had been in a goth phase; nose ring, lipstick the colour of blackberry wine, long hair cut short making her eyes appear huge. Despite how changed she'd been even then from the girl he'd grown up with, she'd been so... *Charlotte* he'd almost changed his mind.

"Mate?" Matt called.

Beau reached into his back pocket and pulled out his phone, switching off the Bluetooth and holding it to his ear in order to keep himself present. "Sorry. I missed that last bit."

"In dreamland?" Matt asked.

Beau didn't demur.

"That's how we make the big bucks," Matt joked, even while both were well aware that Beau wasn't dreaming in that way these days. "When do you think it'll be done?"

By that, Matt meant, *How long will you be gone?*

"A couple of months," Beau said. "A little less."

"All good, mate. Just, make the most of it. Okay? Your escape to the country."

"It's hardly the country," said Beau, even as he turned and looked out over the valley to the distant beachside towns dotting the coastline.

Matt said, "Anything that's not Sydney might as well be the moon, as far as I'm concerned."

Beau laughed as he knew he was meant to do. "When it's finished, you'll have to bring Tasha and Drew up for a look. You might just change your mind."

"Sounds like a plan. Now, I'd best be off. Five more minutes of work, then it's dad time."

"Give the kids a hug from me."

"Always," said Matt, and Beau heard the note in his voice. The grit, and the tremor.

He could only hope that giving Matt space, and trying to find his way back to what they'd built, he was truly doing the right thing by them both.

"We'll talk later," said Beau.

"Of course, brother." With that, Matt rang off.

Beau slipped his phone into his back pocket and took a slow turn, looking over the land he owned. Acres of greenery, fresh air, sky, dirt. And a view that should make everything else seem inconsequential.

What did he want?

He breathed deep, as if it might come to him. Some thought or seed of understanding he could grab a hold of.

He felt the early evening sunshine, crisp and warm on the

back of his neck. Watched Moose bound after a pair of small yellow butterflies. And listened for anything, anyone that might tell him one thing that might make sense of things—

"Beau!"

Beau jerked out of his reverie, as he glanced up to find Charlotte Goode shoving her way through a gap between two rose bushes.

Only in lieu of the bare feet and ragged clothes from the day before, she looked spectacular in a diaphanous top, tight jeans that hugged her long legs, and spiky high heels. A collection of thin gold chains swished elegantly across her collarbone as she moved.

No longer the fierce little kid, or vehement best friend, or gangly teen who'd bloomed overnight into some strange glowing creature who'd made him feel strange and tongue-tied and out of his depth. Yet in the time it took her to pick her way over to him, swearing under her breath, swatting at a bug that flew at her face, he could see echoes of them all.

For a man who had always been so adept at compartmentalising, watching Charlotte pick her way across his yard brought on a wave of nostalgia so wholly disquieting he rocked on his feet.

"Stop," he called, his voice louder than he'd meant.

The adrenaline racing through bloodstream easing as she stopped, her foot mid-step, her arms still swinging. Her gaze met his, questioning.

"You shouldn't be here," he managed, in lieu of, *I can't have you here*, which was what he meant. So he didn't look like a total head case, he added, "Not in those shoes. It's a worksite."

Charlotte looked down and lifted a stiletto heel as if it hadn't occurred to her that traversing piles of detritus and dug up ground in such a getup might not be ideal.

"Anyway," she drawled, as if the head-case thing was obvious, but no deterrent. "The work trucks were all gone when

I got home. Then I saw movement back here, through the sunroom window. Thought, I'd better check to make sure it wasn't a robber."

"A robber."

"I know. Look at me being all neighbourly." She smiled, a flash of white teeth blinding him momentarily. "Did you get your package?"

"My package."

Her head tilted, her gaze narrowing. "The reason you came a knocking on my front door yesterday."

Realising he couldn't keep repeating the ends of her sentences, he gathered himself and said, "Right. Turned out the delivery mob realised it was the wrong place not long after dropping it off. They'd already collected it and taken it back to the warehouse when I came knocking. It will be redelivered tomorrow."

"Wow. Well, great. Crisis averted! Go you."

Hardly. Beau wasn't an engineer in name only. He'd manually stripped more engines and put them back together in new ways than he could remember. Yet, the builders had taken one look at him and sent him on the "important" mission to track the package down. He was prepared to be sent on more "important missions" over the next few weeks, as they endeavoured to keep him out from underfoot.

Which was fine with him. Keeping busy would mean less thinking time. Or, to be more precise, less time spent troubling over the fact that he was struggling to think much at all. For a guy whose entire life had been built on his ability to innovate, that was a precarious space in which to exist.

"So," said Charlotte, "this is the house."

She'd put her hands on her hips, her top lifting to show a sliver of warm tanned skin on her belly. The flash of a sparkle at her navel making him wonder if the goth might have lingered, after all.

Unprepared, *unshielded*, a frisson shot through Beau, a shard of heat and discomfort. Like a last breath of adrenaline. Or something other. Either way, he looked away, joining her in looking up at his build.

She muttered something under her breath along the lines of, "Wow!" before she looked out toward the Pacific. "Remember how this curve of Myrtle Way was nothing but odd ramshackle houses. None of us had aircon, or town water. Just buzzing bees in summer and frosty windows in winter and those wildly beautiful views. The fact that it's becoming all hoity-toity holiday homes and snazzy gentrification feels highly personal."

She turned back to him, then. And the frisson was back. He put it down to the shock of seeing her face—but now her eyes were more knowing, cheeks sharper, lips fuller. When his gaze moved back to her eyes, he saw something shift over her face, as if she was cataloguing the changes in him, too.

Though the way she breathed—in deep, out hard—tugged at him in a way he wasn't in any place to negotiate.

Then she blinked once, breaking the trance, lifted her chin, and said, "That's a very white hat you have there."

Taking a moment to catch up, Beau lifted a hand to his head, where he did indeed sport a white hard hat. Unlike Charlotte, who when he wasn't paying attention had begun once again picking her way across the dug-up lawn, arms out in balance, high heels wobbling, the chunks of hair that fell from the loose way she'd tied her hair swinging by her cheeks.

When she leaped over a pile of rocks in shoes that had not been engineered with leaping in mind, Beau's heart, which until this point, had stayed out of things suddenly lurched painfully.

Arm out, he once again said, "Stop." Then, "You've entered a construction site. A hard hat is mandatory. As are flat, enclosed leather shoes, if not steel-capped boots. If you'd come via the front of the house you'd have seen signs expressing as much."

The front of the house. The way of strangers and acquaintances. Not long-time neighbours, one-time best friends.

"I can go back," she said, pointing over her shoulder. "Come in that way?"

Beau let his hands slowly drop, fully aware how extreme he must seem. Didn't stop the discomfort gripping him any time she moved. "Will you source the requisite safety gear on the way?"

"Nope."

"Then I don't see how that would help."

"Good point." She cocked a hip, one hand thereupon, the other waving at his head. "Aren't they meant to be yellow. The hats?"

"Depends on the worksite. On this one it's blue for carpenters, brown for welders, yellow for general labourers."

"And white is for...?"

"Supervisors. Engineers. Visitors."

"Hmm. So you big wigs can show those blue-collar guys who's boss," she said, taking another step. As if she couldn't help herself.

He was the rule follower, who respected cause and effect, simplicity and clear instructions. While she'd been restless, intensely empathetic, compulsive, and far too stubborn to do as she was told.

When she took another step, and landed on a stone, her ankle turning, his heart twisted in and over itself as if she'd wavered on the edge of a cliff.

He put it down to the fact that his entire system was up the spout. His usual steady balance in flux.

Until her gaze flew to his, pure crackling energy in those soft moss green eyes, and the frissons he'd felt earlier were mere warm-ups to the electric shock that fizzled down his spine. And he knew that it wasn't all him.

Which was somehow far worse.

"Can you just not?" he growled. "There are hidden dangers everywhere. The lumber is precarious."

Her gaze widened, till they rivalled any Disney princess. "I'm sorry, did you say you have *precarious* lumber?"

He pointed to the stack of old wood before her, rusty nails jutting every which way, and the other pile stacked on the fenceless balcony jutting high above them.

"I see," she said, her mouth twitching. But at least she'd stopped moving.

"So, stay where you are, please. In fact, move back to that nice soft patch of grass. I'd hate to see you get hurt."

And there it was, the underlying truth of what was surely a grand overreaction on his part; the realisation that those under his protection, his care, were in fact in perpetual danger, whether he was on the case or not.

He'd somehow made it through his entire childhood believing he'd been the one to keep total disaster at bay. His vigilance, his unrelenting good grades, his stability—they'd given him a sense of control that had alleviated the state of permanent terror he'd come home to find his parents unconscious, or worse.

When he heard they'd died, while the pain had been sharp, a great burden had lifted. The threads of worry and guilt that had underpinned his ambition had relaxed.

And he'd become complacent.

Then Milly had fallen sick. And he'd not been able to do a thing to help her.

Now here was Charlotte Goode, the wild child next door. Who'd never thought before she acted. Never backed down from a fight. Who'd climb a tree, or cross a stream, or spin with her eyes closed, never once mapping out how it all might go wrong beforehand.

Not that Charlotte was under his purview.

She wasn't even in his life anymore, so much as in his backyard.

And yet...

"I hereby promise not to sue if I stub my toe," she said, hands lifting in surrender. Her voice was teasing, but her gaze was ripe with assurance. Letting him know she'd been messing with him, but was now done.

For while years had passed, and their friendship would never be what it was, once upon a time she had known him. Known what he'd battled. And had had his back.

He nodded his thanks, and his next breath out was a little easier.

"So, Beau," she said, after a few loaded beats.

"Yes, Charlotte."

"It's Charlie now, actually. That's what I go by. These days." She glanced away, as if there was a story there, before she looked back at him, daring him to say different.

For some reason, he felt himself smile a little as he said, "Is it now?" As if the all Charlotte-induced bursts of adrenaline had made him a little giddy.

"It is. Now, yesterday, when you came a knocking on my door, you mentioned you'd taken some time off."

Seemed his adrenal glands weren't yet done. His chest squeezed as he waited for her to ask why. What could he possibly say? *My friend died. After which I became burdened by the weight of existential dread which also left me so untethered it's terrifying.*

Instead she asked, "Time off from what exactly?"

Relieved, he said, "Right. My partner and I run a company called Luculent. We design, test, build and roll out clean alternative power sources. Magnetic, solar, perpetual motion. New technologies as yet unnamed. For travel, industry, city grids. If it requires power and we can help make it clean, we'll try."

"Wow. Did you get that off the brochure?"

"The investment prospectus, actually."

"Ha. That's superhero stuff, Beau. Though Batman wouldn't bother with the hard hat."

"Only because it wouldn't fit over his ears."

She laughed, then. A bark that seemed to surprise even her. Then she tapped a finger against her mouth. And he realised, belatedly, that she was being awfully nice. She was buttering him up. For what, he couldn't even hazard a guess.

"So, this time off, how long might that be?"

A day? Forever? He'd quite like the answer to that one himself.

"The build has another two months. Perhaps a little less. But how about you just tell me what it is you want," he said.

Funny, considering he'd just spent the past half hour staring at a half-finished house he owned but wasn't sure he understood, asking himself the same question.

Then she narrowed her eyes at him and nodded. "First, would you agree that I played rather a big part in setting you up for your amazing superhero career?"

It was Beau's time to laugh, the sound escaping his lips before he felt it coming. "In what way?"

His mind once again went to the last night they'd seen one another.

In all the years they'd known one another it had been the first time he'd ever been in her bedroom. First time in over a year that they'd said more than a couple of words to one another. He was telling her about the scholarship, and that he was leaving the next day.

Charlotte had paced back and forth, shaking her head, arms flying as she said a lot of nothing. Before she'd stopped, looked at him and said, "Go."

"Go?"

"Take it. Take the scholarship. But do not take it for granted. Soak up every moment. Show them who you are. Knock 'em dead. You deserve it, Beau," she'd said, as if she'd known he craved her blessing.

Then she'd pulled him in for one last tight hug, kissed him hard on the cheek, long enough that he'd felt the touch of a tear sliding onto her lips, then given him a shove out her bedroom door and shut it behind him.

"Well," she said, "for one thing, you'd never have been able to afford your first car had I not made those tutoring posters and tacked them up all over town. The same car you drove away in, when you left. Would you say, then, that you owe me?"

"I owe you?"

"Correct. *And* you're taking time off. What does that look like for you? Like a day here and there? Or are you on a full-on sabbatical?"

Beau lifted a hand to his neck and squeezed. "Why do I get the feeling you're about to offer me a time-share on the moon?"

Her mouth twisted, her nostrils flaring as she breathed out hard. "Okay," she said, "can I run something—?"

She stopped as her gaze caught on the rustling leaves on the other side of the yard; Moose burst from the bushes and came lolloping up the hill.

After that, everything seemed to happen in slow motion. Charlotte's surprised face. Her hands lifting to protect herself. Moose's massive front paws landing on her chest.

He saw her teeter, pictured her falling backward like a felled tree. Too far for him to catch her, he having told her not to come any closer. His vision shrank to a pinprick, till he heard her laugh.

His vision cleared to find her on her backside, legs akimbo, her face moving side to side to avoid Moose's tongue.

Beau moved in, attempting to heave the dog away and earned a tongue to the nostrils for his efforts.

"Who the heck is this beautiful boy?" said Charlotte, leaning in to rub at Moose's ears and scratching under his collar as he tried to slobber her to death.

Beau managed to stand over Moose, legs locked around the dog's waist, while Moose looked up at him as if it was his happy place.

"That would be Moose. He belongs to a friend."

Belonged. For he was Milly's. She'd adopted him when she first fell sick, as a distraction for the kids. He'd grown big, fast, and was the single thing Matt had not been able to handle once she'd gone. So Beau had swept in and taken the dog off his hands. The very least he could do.

"I'm looking after him for a while."

"Are you sure that's wise?" she asked, leaning back on her hands and squinting up at him. Moose's whole body wriggled, the swish of his tail connecting hard enough to bruise.

He'd never *had* a dog. Or a cat, or a goldfish for that matter. His parents had been so high most of the time they'd not had the wherewithal to look after him, much less a pet.

He eased off, letting Moose free. The dog, sitting now, looked up at him as if awaiting instruction. As if butter wouldn't melt. Until Beau made a grunting sound that the dog understood as release, and set off, sniffing a path across the patchy back lawn.

"We're still figuring out how to coexist in a way we both find comfortable."

Her eyebrow rose.

He rose one right back.

She blinked, as if in surprise that he'd mirrored her sass.

Then she held out a hand. He reached down and grabbed it, wrist over wrist, fireman style. And heaved her to standing.

She looked strong, all that bristling energy taking up space, but there was nothing to her. As if it was all bluster. Meaning he pulled a little harder than necessary and she let out a whoop before landing.

He held her hand till she settled. It felt small to his big. Unknown. New. It felt like something else, too. Warm, soft, as if it fit just so in his. It felt like relief.

Considering it had been months since he'd felt much in the way of anything at all, his palm began to sweat, his fingertips losing feeling, the whole of him enveloped in a kind of breathless, airless tightness.

Thankfully, with a gentle clearing of her throat, Charlotte peeled her hand from his. She used it to fix her hair, before stepping carefully away, putting distance between them again.

This time when her eyes met his, there was determination therein. "Would you like to have dinner? With me? At my place?"

He opened his mouth. Closed it again.

"That is, if you're staying nearby."

He saw a moment open up between them, then. A chance to pull back, to set up boundaries he'd thought he'd managed to secure the day before. But she'd stomped over them the moment she pushed through his rose bushes.

But the way she looked at him—a mix of hope, nerves, and bolshie vulnerability—was so very, *very* Charlotte that he found himself saying, "Moose and I are staying in a holiday rental in Maleny till the house is finished, or until Moose eats something crucial and we are forced to leave."

"Nice. So, come over, okay. I'll feed you. My mum was a great cook, do you remember? I'm close. Come and tell me more about your magic engine, and your plans for this place. If you're going to be knocking about here for a couple of months, let's not make this weird."

She was right. It had been weird. Only not for any reasons

she might imagine. It was all him. He wasn't sure if his company would be nice. Or if *nice* was what *he* needed right now.

Yet he found himself saying, "What time?"

Her smile was so sudden, so incandescent, it left him feeling as if he'd been hit over the head with a mallet.

"Let's say seven." Then she began backing away, carefully so as not to freak him out, while also giving him no chance to change his mind. Then she was at the rose bushes, and gone.

The sudden lack of her left behind a fresh, sharp kind of quiet, a shallow emptiness that he was certain had not been there before she'd arrived. He pressed into the centre of it, a hard place behind his ribs, then turned to look out over the view once more. Breathing through it as he watched the blue of the softening sky bleeding into the blue of the sea.

Dinner at Charlotte's, he thought to himself, only to find it did not feel weird at all.

As for the rest?

When he breathed deep, there was a moment when he thought he could *almost* catch it. The scent of roses, and greenery, and salty air. And something else. Not a memory, but something close. The one thing that might grab all the disparate parts of himself and bring them back together.

For whatever reason, the fates had decided the only chance he had of finding it was by coming back here.

CHAPTER FOUR

CHARLOTTE WRIGGLED A feather duster at spider webs in the hall, switched on table lamps, fluffed cushions and tossed throw blankets she'd brought out from her bedroom. Marvelling at how little it had taken to make the place feel cosy.

And felt a frisson of guilt at just how long she'd been wallowing. As if living in and amongst her father's things in her father's house was just the right level of punishment for how effectively she'd imploded her own life.

When the truth was she had a roof over her head, was making headway with the back taxes, and her business was steadily growing due to word of mouth from people who believed in her.

She'd not said it out loud for fear a big foot might descend from the clouds, Monty Python–style, and squish her. But she was saying it now: she wanted the Patel/Kent gig.

The guest list would put her business in front of a whole new kind of clientele, and the money would be life-changing.

She could pay off the back taxes in one go, *and* afford to fix the house up a little. Nothing like the monster homes going up around her, but enough to make sure the roof wouldn't collapse, and the dodgy electrics wouldn't burn the place down. In fact, as soon as she'd allowed herself to imagine it, the ideas of how she could zhoosh the place up had been near overwhelming!

She might even have tugged on the loose hallway wallpaper to see how easily it might come off—not very, meaning the hallway was now a disaster. But she could fix that. Then she could safely rent it out, or maybe sell up. She could use the funds to help her relocate to some place that didn't remind her of her father at every damn turn.

And why not Edinburgh, as her mum had suggested? She might even have googled the place a little. It looked beautiful. Wedding-friendly, meaning she could take the bones of her business with her. A nice distance from both here and California. And she could see her mum again.

The *possible* risk of Always the Bridesmaid being tarnished, or even brought down by the spectre of #cakegate was outweighed by the benefits. At least that's what she told herself as she added dressing to the summer salad that would go with the salmon she had in the oven.

Except she was getting ahead of herself. It wasn't in the bag yet.

She'd had no luck finding a man, much less a best one. Then she'd glanced out her side window and seen Beau looking up at his house, all big, and handsome, and solid, and there, and she'd known...

Well, she'd known he was *literally* her only option.

Without him, the rest wasn't going to happen.

Beau Griffin, her ghosts of summer past, was back for a reason. And this, she had decided, was it.

She started as a knock came at the back door. As, for all her renewed enthusiasm, she was nervous as hell.

She and Beau might have been best friends as kids but that was all very much in the past. Despite how charming she'd tried to be, his smiles *still* hadn't quite reached his eyes.

Licking lemon juice from her fingers, Charlie moved out from behind the kitchen bench and through the small dining nook to open the permanently unlocked back door. She wasn't even sure if it could lock.

The thing creaked as she pulled it open to find Beau, two bottles of wine in hand. Which was excellent.

Not so excellent was the fact that while she'd de-glammed, stripping off her girl-boss duds and changing into baggy jeans with a tear in the knee and an oversized Reputation Stadium Tour T-shirt, Beau had done the opposite. He'd clearly had a shower and washed his hair, evidenced by the finger tracks through his dark hair. He'd also changed into a royal blue long-sleeved T-shirt and clean jeans, both of which clung so lovingly to the shape of him she wasn't sure where to look.

"Hi," she said, her voice offering up a stupid croak.

"Hey," he said back. And even though, behind his glasses, his eyes were wary, the burr in his voice had something climbing her insides like quick-grow ivy.

Till he said, "Only one of your lights is working." He stepped back, gave one of the spotlights a wriggle.

"It's all good! I've got it," she said, turning her back to hide the unhelpful rush of blood to her face as she waved him inside. Yes, the place was falling down around her but it wasn't her fault.

When she rounded the kitchen bench, she saw him duck as he entered, as if by habit. Whereas in the past he'd have stayed hunched over, stooped from the hours he spent on his school laptop, now he stood tall. Comfortable in his skin. As if, having gone away, he'd grown into himself, knew his worth, and owned it.

"Charlotte," he said, his gaze taking in the yellow Formica kitchen, the small sunroom with its cane furniture, the well-scraped wooden floor. "It looks exactly the same."

"You think," she said, not all that keen on thinking on just how *the same* it felt to her much of the time, too. "But since I'm only squatting here for a little while longer, till I get my ducks in a row, there didn't seem any point in going all home decorator on the place."

So there.

"Oh, and it's Charlie."

He glanced at her, his expression serious. Quiet. So *Beau* that her stomach gave a flutter. Only not Beau, for too much time had gone by for her to claim any knowledge of the man at all.

"I think I mentioned earlier that I go by Charlie now."

For *Charlotte* had spent a fortune getting her hair foiled and professionally straightened every six weeks. She'd worn pencil skirts and business shirts. She distracted everyone with all her might to hide her dyslexia so that she might fit into a world she'd imagined would never let someone like her in.

Charlotte had also lost her mind and thrown a handful of cake at her ex-boyfriend—a leech of a human being who used his new bride as a human shield—and missed.

Charlie, on the other hand, dressed how she liked, wore her hair how she liked, and after her game-changing conversation with Julia now told every client right up front that she was dyslexic. Charlie was a work in progress, which was a good thing.

"Regretting your decision to knock your place down?" Charlie asked, waving a hand at the ancient wood kitchen counter, the cork floors.

"Not for a second."

She mock-gasped, hand to her heart. "Harsh!"

And he smiled. A flash of perfect teeth. He must have had braces at some point, after he'd left. The twisted eyeteeth now in perfect symmetry. Less a cosmetic decision she suspected than a way to wipe away his childhood.

It hit her then, the fact he'd never tried to get in touch her after he'd left—had it been his intention to wipe her from his childhood, too?

"Gimme," she said, shaking off that maudlin thought, and clicking her fingers toward the wine in his hand.

"Suitable?" he asked, turning so she could see the labels, top-notch South Australian Sauvignon Blancs.

"It'll do." She offered up a sassy shoulder shrug. Then, "No Moose tonight?"

"Not tonight. I wasn't sure you'd appreciate him lumbering about, destroying the place."

She looked around at the furniture her mum must have picked out decades before. It might actually have helped.

Then she fixed her T-shirt, after it slid a little off her shoulder, and Beau's nostrils flared. His neck pinked, too. And Charlie once again felt a flicker in her gut. Only this time there was no mistaking what it was. Awareness.

While gratifying—for when wasn't it gratifying to realise someone who gave you tummy flutters felt the same way about you?—she decided to chalk it up to trying to find their new tonal balance. Because awareness, attraction—considering their history, considering *her* history—was not an option.

What she needed him for was far too important to mess up with any of that. And she was not going to screw this up. Not this time.

For once she gave the whispers at the back of her mind air to breathe. They took on the voice of her father, her first roommate, an old boss, and her ex—sheesh, looking at it now, it was if she *gravitated* toward such people—and they told her the myriad ways she'd likely fail. And used it to cool her jets.

She'd feed Beau, get him feeling all warm and full, then she'd hit him with her plan.

"Sit. Dinner is nearly ready." She waved a hand toward the small round dining table she'd set with actual linens and her mother's good china, wanting to set a professional tone. Only now it looked like the perfect set up for an intimate date.

"Can I help?" Beau asked, *not* sitting. Instead he leaned against the kitchen bench, arms braced, hands splayed. The sleeves of his shirt were pushed up to his elbows, revealing strong brown forearms roped with veins. And had he always had such long fingers, such elegant hands?

"Nope," she said, gaze quickly lifting to his face, which was really no better. Because, he had turned out lovely. A crystal cut jaw softened with dark stubble, warm dark eyes, strong straight nose, kissable mouth now slightly open.

When she realised hers was mirroring his, saliva pooling beneath her tongue, she snapped it shut.

"Sit," she ordered. "Please." Thinking of the way he kept telling her to *stop!* in his backyard that afternoon. Had it been about the precarious lumber? Or had he felt a need to keep her at a physical distance then, too?

He smiled at her, while frowning at the same time. As if he was thinking the same. Or maybe he was thinking about something completely different. As for him, those kinds of feelings had *never* been a part of their relationship.

Whereas for her, it kind of had.

She was fifteen when she'd first felt that flutter in her belly where Beau was concerned.

She'd been standing in the high school hallway, getting some books from her locker, when a couple of the "cool" girls had walked past, giggling; one saying she'd just come from the gym, where Beau Griffin of all people had spent the lunch break shooting hoops.

"One after the other," the girl had said on a breathy sigh. "Like his life depended on it. His shirt and shorts were all sweaty, you know, sticking to his chest, his thighs. Whoa, Mumma. Where has he been all our lives?"

Charlie remembered the head rush, the dry mouth, the way her pulse had beat behind her ears, how her fingers hurt from where she'd gripped the door to her locker. Remembered thinking, "Oh, no." Knowing, in some deeply instinctive place that things would never be the same again.

A rap of Beau's knuckles on the table as he curled his long

legs beneath snapped her back to the present to find her heart
beating a little harder now.

Whereas a regular person would pull out their phone, scroll
a little to fill the silence, Beau looked out the window, tested
the napkin, breathed the scents from the kitchen. All with
such quiet confidence, and stillness. Warmth seeped into her
restless bones like a balm.

He'd always been the unruffled to her unquiet. The temper to her temper. Until he hadn't. And the loss of him had
felt like a missing limb.

A timer binged and she leaped out of her skin.

Muttering to herself about staying focused, and making
good choices, and keeping her head, she grabbed her oven
mitts, pulled the old pan from the oven and slid it onto a
wooden cutting board.

The oily base had slightly browned, the thyme appeared
crispy, the cream and lemon glaze were glossy and gorgeous.
Perfect.

She'd take it as an omen. She was a capable, self-govern-
ing woman with a dream. Screwing up was *not* her default.

She had this…

"That," said Beau, a half hour later as he put down his knife
and fork, "was phenomenal."

Napkin to his mouth, he looked to her. His gaze glinting
in the firelight. Because, yes, she'd lit candles. And now the
image of that face, all warm eyes and heartache-inducing
gorgeousness, was now burned into her retinas for all time.

"What do you think our parents would make of this?"
she asked, knowing she might as well have dropped a small
bomb between them.

"The two of us having a candlelit dinner?" Beau asked,
swiping his finger through the last of the sauce before licking it off his finger.

"It's not *candlelit*," Charlie managed, before leaning forward to blow them out, plunging the room into a dusky intimacy.

Feeling a little overly warm no doubt due to the lingering humidity of the day, she lifted her wine glass to her mouth to find it empty. Oops.

"It's a business dinner," she announced, leaning back farther so as to find some space that didn't have him in it.

"I wasn't aware."

Right. Once conversation had turned to his very not wild university days, to how she'd gone about winning the green card lottery, it had been lovely to fill in the blanks, she'd not quite gotten around to the reason *why* she was liquoring him up. And herself, by the feel of it.

It seemed the time had come!

"I have a proposition for you, Beau. One I am certain you will find most diverting."

"Diverting?" he repeated, a smile in his voice if not his eyes.

She'd have to do something about that. Distracting him away from the dark clouds that followed him was her special skill. And while, by the sounds of it, his life had turned out great, by anyone's measure, it felt crucial that she find a way to do so again.

But first…

"So, Beau Griffin, have you ever been a best man?"

Well, *that* got a reaction. His jaw ticked, and his head jerked back. While for some time he said nothing, the muscles in his neck did rather magical things.

"Or a groomsman," she nudged.

"In a wedding?"

"That's where you'll usually find them."

After another long pause, he said, "Once."

"And how did you find it?"

"I'm not sure I understand the question."

She wriggled on her chair. "Did you enjoy it? Were you

any good at it? Were you a follower or a leader? Did you have any particular role? Have you been hankering to have another go?"

He lifted an eyebrow in confusion.

"Okay, let's start with whose wedding was it?"

Again with the long pause. Then, "Matt, my business partner." Then, after a beat, "And my friend, Milly." This time he clenched his jaw tight enough she could hear his teeth creaking.

So, there was a story *there*.

"*Ex*-business partner?" she wondered aloud.

"Current. Why?"

No reason, she thought even as his hand gripped his wineglass hard enough she feared it might break.

What she said was, "The reason I ask is that I have been offered an opportunity. A business opportunity. A pretty significant one. Only it comes with strings that I'm hoping you might be able to…pluck."

The hand gripping the wineglass flexed as if electrocuted. He took a moment to find his words, which turned out to be: "What kind of business might require me to…pluck your strings?"

Hand to heart, Charlie said, "Not *my* strings."

"You want me to pluck *someone else's* strings?"

"*Metaphorical* strings," she elucidated, madly flapping her hands at the universe. Which also helped dissipate the tingles that had shot through her at the thought of all that plucking.

"A bit of background," she said.

Then, in as few—and least likely to accidentally create a double entendre—words as possible, Charlie explained how Always the Bridesmaid had come about, how it worked, her vision as to how it might grow.

She left out #cakegate, because why complicate things?

"That's inventive as hell," he said. "Good for you, Charlie."

The pause before *Charlie* was telling. He'd listened, and respected her request, even while it must have felt strange to him. It made her feel all light and fluffy inside.

She put own her empty wineglass and reached for the glass of water. After draining it she said, "Thank you," while flushing to her damn roots.

Then he said, "I'm just not sure where I come in."

And in the lamplight, her new name on Beau's tongue still bouncing about inside her head, it felt right to offer up some unvarnished truth.

"I had to work, really hard, for any opportunities I had. All the while having to jam my toes in closing doors, climb over impossibly high walls to even get a shot. But this...this is *mine*. I created this while *crashing here* for the past eighteen months. And now someone has stumbled onto what I offer, and given me such a sense of clarity as to what it might one day become."

Beau listened. Even if it made no sense to him, even it was beyond the scope of his own experience, he truly listened. As if he wanted to understand her.

She'd read a meme once, saying something along the lines of "don't talk to me while I'm rubbing my eyes as I won't hear you". That was her ex, Richard, in a nutshell. Even before he'd played his ultimate role of villainous groom.

And she'd *accepted* it. For he'd not yelled at her, never hit her, or called her names. In fact, he'd let her make all the choices; where they lived, what they ate, as if he trusted she'd get it right. Mistaking his laziness for regard, it had taken her far too long to realise how exhausted she was carrying the entire load of their relationship. That he'd "let" her take care of him while he did nothing but flatter her battered self-esteem.

The moment she'd seen it, his brand of manipulation turned on a dime, proving him as ugly as her father had ever been.

Not Beau. His gaze was warm and engaged, his body relaxed, not a fidget to be seen. As if every word she'd ever had to say had its own inherent worth.

Her throat got a little tight. Charlie made for the finish line. "Anushka Patel is that person for me. And, the only way I can take her on as a client is if I also supply a best man."

It only took a second for Beau to join the dots. He shifted, his eyes widening behind his glasses as he leaned back. "You mean *me*?"

Charlie nodded. "And we can negotiate a fair rate for your time."

"Surely you have other men you can ask."

"Other *men*?"

It was a fair question, but just thinking about Richard, about some of the choices she'd made in the past, made her nerves feel all crackly and raw.

"True," she said, "I forgot about the hockey team locked in my basement. Or, if none of them are amenable, there must be an app for this kind of thing?"

Beau said nothing. Loudly. The years between them suddenly feeling as wide as they were deep. But she had one shot at this, so she went for it.

"Here's why you're my number one choice. You ready?"

"Doubtful," he murmured.

"You're available."

Thankfully, he laughed. For a heady second, Charlie thought it might even have reached his eyes, but it was probably the lamplight reflecting off his glasses.

"And you're the right vintage," she added.

"Vintage?"

He lifted a hand to his neck. And she remembered sitting a few rows behind him in assembly, after their falling out, watching the way he massaged his neck, the way his hair fell over his fingers, and feeling as if she might die if he ever stopped.

"Age-wise," she said, sitting up straight, and silently hissing at her inner monologue to take control of itself. "And you'll look the part."

At that, his hand stopped massaging, and his eyes found hers. Direct behind his glasses, no reflections. No glints. So many questions. His voice was a little rough as he asked, "How so?"

Was he really going to make her explain? It seemed he was.

"Well, you're…tall," she said, "which is nice. For a best man. And you're tidy. You don't hunch, or fidget overly much. And clothes don't look terrible when you wear them."

"Clothes don't look terrible?"

She flapped her hands at him, as if it was self-explanatory.

At which point his mouth did that "one corner lift" thing it had done when he'd been standing on her front veranda, looking at her as if she was a happy surprise. The thing that pressed a curve into his cheek. Add the stubble, the slightly too long hair, the way he took up space, all big shoulders and broad chest and…

Hell. Her pulse was racing now. Her lungs struggling to fill. Then her lady parts got in on the action. Heat pooling low, aching. Too many parts of her were reacting now, trying to calm them down was like playing Whac-a-Mole. As if, having seen *no action* since #cakegate, the first chance they had they were preparing to revolt.

"Look," said Charlie, squeezing her eyes shut tight, "I need someone who can follow my instructions, who will understand that I am the boss. Who'll understand that this isn't some party, that it's meaningful for me. Someone I can rely on. Someone I can trust to…"

Her words dried up. Oof, she'd not expected this next bit to be so hard. But in remembering Beau hopping into his bomb of a car and driving off into a future without her, she might as well have stuck her head in a bucket of iced water for the effect it had.

She swallowed, looked him in the eye, and said, "I need someone I can trust to be there when I ask." She let her hands flick out to the sides, then float to her lap. "I know this is a big ask. And despite what we were to one another as kids, we are basically strangers now. But I've found in life that if you don't ask, you don't know. So, this is me. Asking."

Beau said nothing. But she could feel him thinking, at least. Weighing up her request in that thoughtful "look at all sides of the argument, play out every eventuality" way he had about him.

Thankfully, being Beau, it took about five seconds, before he said, "What would it entail, exactly?"

"I don't have that worked out as yet, but I imagine meeting the groom and the other groomsmen socially as to establish rapport. A suit try-on or two. Rehearsal dinner, bucks' night, but perhaps not. Depends on what they need from us. Then the big day. It's less than six weeks away, meaning it would all be done and dusted before you're done here."

That was all she had.

Now everything she wanted depended on what he said next.

He said, "Sure. Of course. Why not?"

She pressed her chair back with a scrape and stood, more energy coursing through her than she'd felt in months. "Are you serious? You will actually be a pretend best man at the wedding of a person you do not know for me?"

Shut up, Charlie! Just say thank you, then maybe have him swear a blood pact.

By then Beau had pushed his chair back and also stood. He tossed his napkin to the table and said, "It seems so."

Charlie felt as if a pair of hands grabbed her by the waist, lifted her from her chair and propelled her around the table then, for suddenly she was leaning over Beau, flinging her arms around his neck and hugging the life out of him.

They'd had *no* personal space as kids. Always bumping shoulders or linking arms as they traipsed over hill and dale of their backyards. Feet tangled as they lay in her backyard, star gazing, hands colliding as they dipped into a shared box of popcorn while snuggled beside one another in the break in the fence at the local drive-in. She'd sat on his lap as he'd taught her how to drive, long before either had a license, for Pete's sake!

But this? Charlie came to from her burst of adrenaline to find her head buried in Beau's neck, drinking in a heady mix of fresh cotton, and warm male skin, and something light and citrusy. His hair tickled her temple. His stubble scraped her cheek.

Only then did she notice his arms strong and warm around her back.

It had been so long since she'd held someone. Or been held. With abandon and trust. Not measuring how long it should be before she let go. Which was why Charlie stayed there a beat too long. Several in fact.

Her body a comma curled into his. The heat of him burning through her clothes, till his heart beat in syncopation with her own.

Her inner monologue cleared its throat, waking her from the heady fog. And she pulled away, pushed more like. Once clear, she tugged at her T-shirt and attempted a smile.

"Thank you," she managed. "I mean it, Beau. This will be life-changing."

In a good way for once, she hoped with all her might.

"Happy to help," said Beau, running a hand through his own hair till it was more than a little mussed. Then rolling out a shoulder, as if trying to shake off the same warmth that was still moving through her, too.

When Charlie found herself looking at him, for no reason other than she liked doing so, she shook her head and said,

"Look, I've kept you far too long. How about I box you up some leftovers. For tomorrow night. Or for Moose."

"That'd be nice."

Charlie hotfooted it into the kitchen, her skin still tingling like crazy, her blood going more than a little haywire. Because he'd said yes. Because she might actually pull this off. And because being in Beau's arms had felt like heaven.

Her hands shook as she fussed about finding the right-sized Tupperware. Only to spin from the cupboard to find him at her sink, their dirty dishes piled up on the bench as he rolled up his sleeves a little higher before slinging a tea towel over his shoulder and turning on the hot water.

"What are you doing?"

"You cooked. I clean. That's how it works, right?"

Not in her experience. But since her parents had never put in a dishwasher, she wasn't about to say no.

Once she was done wrapping, she snuck the tea towel from Beau's shoulder, catching his eye as she snuck around him, the dark glint, the slight lift at the corner of his mouth, before she took over drying.

"Anything else I can do?" he asked. No doubt noting the wonky cupboard door over the stove, the water stain on the ceiling.

Grateful for the help washing, but very sure she could look after herself otherwise, she all but manhandled him out the back door. Everywhere she touched him, his arm, his back, she could feel the shape of him, the give of hard muscle, the warmth seeping through his clothes, imprinting itself on her palms.

On the back landing, he glanced up at her broken light.

"Ignore it," she commanded.

He looked back, his face danger close, as he shot her a quick smile. "It would take me two minutes."

"And yet, it's not your problem. It's mine. I like it that way."

His smile dropped away. Later, when she was alone, trying to shut the back door so that it didn't fly right open, she might kick herself. But right now, she needed to finish this evening with Beau agreeing to help her with the Patel/Kent gig, and that was all.

At the bottom of her rickety back steps, the very ones they used to hide under as kids, he looked back.

"Thank you for dinner."

"And thank you for agreeing to help me out. You have no idea how grateful I am."

"I have some idea," he said, before he strode toward the rose bushes.

And if by that he meant the effusiveness of her hug, well damn.

"Beau!" she called when he was halfway across her backyard. "You don't live there anymore, remember. Build site. No hard hat. Many dangers."

He lifted a hand, then spun forty-five degrees and headed up the side of her house. And was gone.

Charlie watched the space, even though she couldn't see him. Feeling as if he'd grabbed a hold of a loose thread in her jumper, unravelling it, and her, as he went.

Charlie squeezed her eyes shut for a moment, before she spun back inside the house. She went straight for her phone, grabbed it and texted Anushka. So freaking exhilarated was she, she didn't even check for typos.

The perfect best man all lined up. We're in!

Seconds later a spate of emojis exploded into her messages. It was done. The ball rolling. No going back.

A mix of relief, and mild terror fought it out inside her, as Charlie realised one way or the other, the safe, *slowly slowly* pattern she'd fallen into was all about to change.

CHAPTER FIVE

BEAU COULDN'T RIGHTLY say what had convinced him to agree to Charlotte's harebrained scheme. For he wasn't in any place to be a person's so-so man much less one's best.

A mix of things, most likely. A need to fill his empty days with more than "fake missions" from the builders. A throwback to the way he'd always ended up bundled along on her "adventures." Surprise that she was living in her father's house.

Charlotte had always been a force of nature; she changed a room simply by walking into it. But as far as he could see, she'd done nothing to update the place since moving in. It was a time capsule, and not in a good way. For while she and her mother had always been tight, Charlie and her father could not have been more at odds.

The man had called Charlotte names, constantly. Picked on her for being a minute late, for laughing too loudly, for scraping a knee. And he constantly brought up Beau's grades, then asked for Charlotte's results, knowing they'd not measure up in his eyes.

As a kid he'd thought of Professor Goode as being a bit of a storybook ogre, but looking back the man was a pitiful bastard who'd systematically tried to tear his daughter down. Likely because no matter how hard he tried, to the outside eye he never made a dent on her.

But Beau knew that wasn't true. For it was his shoulder she'd cried on.

He remembered the day she'd told him about her dyslexia diagnosis—how excited she was to have a reason to give her father for being "dumb." Only it had made her father even more enraged, for how dare a child of his not be naturally brilliant? After that she'd given up on even thinking about going to university.

Till then it had been their joint plan; for him to take a gap year and work, so that they could head to uni together. A plan he'd been the one to break.

When she'd asked for his help, could he say anything but, "Of course"?

Then she started sending him voice messages at unearthly hours of the night, links to draft schedules colour-coded in bright pastels with sparkly graphics, created by someone called Julia, and text messages he imagined her reading three times before sending, the way she had as a kid.

Charlotte: Schedule okay with you so far?

Beau: Yes.

Charlotte: If there are any conflicts, the sooner I know the better.

Beau: It's fine.

Charlotte: Your enthusiasm is infectious.

And:

Charlotte: Adding a suit fitting for four o'clock next Tuesday.

Beau: I am in possession of suits.

Charlotte: And yet. Groomsmen match.

Beau: Then how will people know that I am the "best" one?

Charlotte: Prove it.

He got on board with:

Beau: My electrician tells me you traipsed through the rose bushes this afternoon.

Charlotte: Dobber!

Beau: He said you weren't wearing a hard hat. Or covered shoes.

After that came a voice message: *Did he not tell you that I found a recipe for banana muffins that is both dog and human friendly? And since bananas contain both magnesium and potassium and...some other thing that is brain-calming, I thought it might be good for Moose. And by way of Moose, Moose's babysitter. But you weren't there so I gave them to your builders, and if you're going to be all "wear a hard hat next time" about it, then that's the last banana muffin you'll ever see from me.*

Lastly, a final text:

Buckle up, buttercup, tonight is the bride and groom meet & greet. A club in Noosa. Dress pretty. My place at six. I'll drive.

He wondered if he could slink back to Sydney, tell Matt he was all better, and forget the whole thing.

That night, after checking on the build, Beau knocked on Charlotte's back door, only for the thing to bounce on its hinges and open right up.

"Charlotte?" he called.

No answer. A frisson of something dark and slippery slithered through him.

Louder, he tried, "Charlie?"

"Come in!" she called. "I'll be a minute!"

A deluge of relief followed. Enough that he wondered if it was too late to pull out.

For telling her to stop walking through a construction site filled with hazards because he was terrified that everyone he cared for might die on his watch was on him. Fretting over her busted back door and broken back light was surely a step too far.

Then he made his way into the kitchen, noting the curling edges of a seven-year-old calendar on the wall, the frosted glass cabinet filled with her father's coffee mugs. And he knew he was exactly where he ought to be.

Which, considering the past few months, was not a small thing.

Charlotte's head popped out of a room in the hallway so Beau wandered that way. She held up a finger, motioned to the phone at her ear, as she said, "Isla, listen to me. Your bridesmaid dresses are not *puce*, they are dusky rose. And they are gorgeous. The next time your mother-in-law tries to undermine your choices, imagine me kicking her in the ankle just before the mother son dance."

Her eyes caught his, and he gave her a thumbs-up.

Her mouth stretched into a quick dazzling smile.

Then her gaze dropped as she gave him a quick once-over. Her gaze paused on his chest, his thighs, his neck. When it met his one more, the bob of her throat and the way she tucked her hair behind her ears made it clear he was up to scratch.

Lucky, because he'd actually put effort into getting ready that evening; shaving, shining his shoes, had the rest of his clothes couriered from his apartment in Sydney. He wanted to represent her ably. And if it meant he got to experience that look in those eyes, well that wouldn't be entirely terrible, either.

A minute later Charlotte rushed down the hall.

"Okay, let's do this!" She began riffing names of those they were to meet that night—bridesmaids and groomsmen, their relative family situations, jobs, relation to the bride and groom.

Not that he heard a word for his brain was filled with the sight of her in her knee-high black boots, short black dress over white button-down, her hair in a crown of braids wrapped about her head with curls springing free at her temple and neck.

She gave wholesome milkmaid meets Wednesday Addams, and for a man who'd never thought he'd had a particular type, he knew in that second he'd been wrong.

He cleared his throat. Looked anywhere but at her. Reminded himself this was Charlotte. *Charlie*. A very old friend. For whom he was doing a favor she deemed important.

They'd never been the other thing.

Yes, he'd had "crush type" feelings at one time, but he'd very much kept them under wraps. Choosing to focus even harder on his studies and take up basketball after reading a research article that suggested exercise was a healthy way to redirect such things.

"What?" she said, and Beau realised she'd stopped halfway up the hall, her hand in her bag, her expression wary. No doubt because he was staring at her like he'd been hit over the head with a mallet.

"All okay with Isla?" he asked, spinning a finger in the air before herding her back up the hall so they could head out the front door to the car.

"Sure. Maybe. Her mother-in-law is a dragon. My role there with that client is to make the mother-in-law hate me so she leaves Isla alone."

"Is that normal?"

She shot him a grin over her shoulder, and he felt it in his gut. "Always the Bridesmaid is hardly normal. We're not wedding planners, we look after the jobs no one else wants, or the ones they didn't know they needed. We traverse the emotional landmines. Mitigate the 'in the moment' dramas. Have the hard conversations with members of the outer circle so that the bride and groom can enjoy their big day."

"Sounds consuming."

"It's much easier when you don't have skin in the game. I'll drive!" she said as she let him out the front door.

He watched to make sure she locked up. "I'm happy to drive. My car's out front."

"And I'm the boss of this show. I want everything to be as easy for you as it can possibly be so that you do not regret agreeing to help for a single second."

Too late, he thought, then watched as she noticed the car parked next to her dented Cooper S.

"Are you kidding me?" she asked, her eyes wide, voice giddy as she walked toward his car as if she was being beamed. Her fingers air-traced the sleekly curved bonnet. "What is this thing?"

"This is Lucky. A prototype. Concept car. One of a kind. Cars like this are usually no more than a chassis on a rotating platform at a car show, but Lucky is the next step. She currently runs on our patented electric engine; but she's been built to swap straight to the Luculent Engine we have in the testing pipeline right now."

Lucky and the Luculent Engine were his passion projects. The creations he'd nurtured from seed to fruition since he'd first envisioned the tech a decade ago. The engine was the last thing he'd seen to completion before Milly passed, before his muse tossed its hands in the air and said, *Everything ends anyway, so why bother?* The thinking so redolent of his parents, it bothered him.

"Do you let *Moose* hop in this thing?"

Beau nodded.

"Wow. That's…brave. Can I drive?" Charlotte asked.

Beau tossed his keys skyward, watched as her eyes lit up, before he caught them again. "Not on your sweet life."

He went around to the passenger door, gently moved her out of the way, and pressed a button on the key so that the passenger door swooped open like a wing. She jumped back, into him, an impressed oath falling from her lips.

Even in her high-heeled boots, the top of her head just reached his nose, meaning he had no choice but to drink her in—the scent of hair, some botanical aroma, and that warm sweet something that was purely her.

He ushered her inside the car.

Once she was settled, he jogged to the driver's side door and slid inside.

Lucky's design was Matt's field, but he'd kindly built it so Beau didn't have to twist himself up like a pretzel in order to fit. The interior details were clean and elegant, vintage throwbacks mixed with proprietary clean tech that made other designers salivate with envy. The colour—a dark bronze—was Milly's favourite. Making Lucky, to their minds, the perfect Luculent vehicle.

Beau turned her on, ran both hands over the wheel, before easing the car down the curving driveway, avoiding the overhanging greenery along the way.

"Oh, wow." Charlotte laughed beside him. "I'd forgotten that you did that."

"Did what?"

She lifted her hands and copied the way he'd traced the steering wheel. "Remember? You'd do that with your first car, giving thanks she started at all."

He ran his hands over the wheel again as they reached the front gate, lifting the memory from the recesses of his mind. The cracked leather under his hands, the flicker of bitumen through the small hole in the floor. The car in worse shape than he'd hoped, his mother having found the first few hundred dollars he'd saved and using it to buy dope, meaning he'd had to choose a car held together with duct tape.

Should he be doing this? Could he?

He flicked a glance toward Charlotte, to see her snuggling into the sports seat, eyes closed, beatific smile on her face.

He could do this. In fact…

After checking both ways were clear, he shot out onto Myrtle Way so fast Charlotte whooped.

A little under an hour later, they'd parked the car on a side street in Noosa.

"Will Lucky be safe here?" Charlie asked, eyes worried, clearly having become rather fond of the car.

"She'll be fine." Beau pressed his thumbprint to the key, locking the doors and setting the security features.

Their publicity team had also made a good case for organic interest, so having the Luculent badge on display was the least he could do for his company while doing nothing at all.

Charlie waited on the footpath, smiling as he joined her, then they began walking in tandem down the road, taking in the distant sound of gentle waves and the briny scent on the air.

When Charlotte's hand slipped into the crook of his arm, Beau started.

Taking it for distress, she quickly removed her hand and stepped away. When the truth was her touch had sent an electric shock right through him, and rogue sparks still skittered through his system.

"Sorry," she said, shooting him a quick glance. Then, "It's a dyslexia thing."

He lifted an eyebrow in question.

"When I was living in the States, I found this amazing dyslexia therapist. She believed it affects my spatial awareness, and how I read body language. It explains the way I used to manhandle you."

"I think I'd remember being manhandled—"

"It was constant!" she said, giving a little skip down the footpath. "I was always sliding my hand through your elbow. Hugging you. Curling my feet around yours. I could barely leave you alone."

He remembered. His parents had moved into that house, an inheritance from a grandparent he'd never met, when he was seven. The first time he'd seen Charlotte she'd been up a tree. After a few minutes spent casing him as he sat below, she'd leaped down, grabbed him by the arm, held a finger to her lips, then dragged him into the brambles down the hill to show him a veritable field of small yellow butterflies that must have just shed their cocoons.

At first it had been a shock, all that energy, and friction inside his space. But soon he'd come to expect her easy affection. Then to crave it. For he got none of that kind of thing at home.

Before he could stop himself, Beau held out the crook of his elbow. "Come on, then."

With a surprised smile, Charlotte stepped back in, sliding her hand into the nook.

"Now, test time," she said, as they slowed their pace down the footpath. "Who are we meeting?"

"We're *meeting* people?"

Laughing, Charlotte rocked closer, giving him a shove with her hip. "Come on. I've sent you enough voice messages about tonight. You must have been dreaming their names."

He could hear her voice in his head: Anushka and Bobby. Anushka's bridesmaids, her cousins Phyllida and Jazmin. Bobby's groomsmen, work mates Jeff and Lenny. But he looked to the sky as if he might find them there.

"Stop playing," she said. "You're making me nervous."

And he could feel it in her, that infectious Charlotte energy. The restlessness of her steps, the way her fingers wrapped tighter around his arm.

"Okay. No more games," he promised.

She shot him a quick look, as if she thought he might have meant something else by it, before she looked straight ahead and said, "It's not far."

What had she been thinking he meant? He'd been imagining the Uno pack she kept in a metal box under her back steps, so worn down they knew the cards by the creases and tears. Or had she been thinking of the one time they'd played something entirely different.

The summer before his senior year, not long after he'd taken up basketball in order to sweat off the way he'd begun to feel about her, she'd found them some new friends. Kids she worked with at the vintage vinyl record store.

He didn't have much in common with them, as none were interested in what they might do after school bar get their license and swap fake IDs for real ones. But he liked that they liked Charlotte. How they looked to her, saw her spark. How relaxed and happy she seemed.

One afternoon they'd met up at the local playground with chips, picnic blanket, and Frisbees. Their laughter that had gone on into the evening after one of the guys brought out a bottle of gin that had them all coughing and falling over one another well into the evening.

Beau hadn't touched the stuff, not after seeing how his parents would drink till they passed out. But Charlie had, swigging and laughing with the rest of them.

Once the bottle was empty, someone suggested a game of spin the bottle.

He remembered, with such clarity, looking up, his gaze inexorably finding Charlotte sitting directly across the blanket. Her eyes were on him, wide and diamond bright.

His chest had boomed so hard under the power of that look he'd thought it might burst. Only he had no idea what she was thinking, or feeling. Only that their gazes had caught. Tangled. Linked at some multidimensional level. The moonlight obfuscating so much, but not everything. Not the way his heart had thundered in his chest, or the rise and fall of her chin as if her breaths had not come easily enough.

Only she'd been drinking. So how could he, or she, be sure?

So while he'd have given just about anything to have his bottle land on her, to be able to lean over that blanket and press his lips to hers, even once, when the bottle had spun, he'd reached out, grabbed the bottle, walked it to the nearest council bin, and let it drop.

As if the lot of them had been feeling the tension, and were glad to be rid of it, they'd fallen about, laughing in relief. And they'd moved on to something else.

While he knew that letting fate decide whatever happened between them that night would have been all kinds of wrong, afterward he and Charlotte were never quite the same.

His final year of school, his studies had consumed him. They had to, if he had any chance of earning a scholarship to pay for the engineering degree he had his heart set on. While she'd begun spending every afternoon working or hanging out at the record store. Until one day, when he passed her in the hall at school, she'd not even noticed him.

"This is it," she said now, when they reached a dark brick building with fluorescent flamingos and palm trees twice Beau's size decorating the facade. Stepping back to catch his eye, her hand still gently resting in the crook of his elbow, she said, "You ready?"

"Anushka and Bobby," he said. "Anushka's bridesmaids are her cousins Phyllida and Jazmin. Bobby's groomsmen are Jeff and Lenny."

Her resultant smile was worth every moment of discomfort that led up to it.

Hours later Charlie leaned her forehead against the mirror in the passenger seat of Beau's space car. The cocoon of the ergonomic seating and the quiet hum of the electric engine acted like some kind of relaxation app, all but rocking her to sleep.

It might also have been that after the buildup to the night, she was exhausted due to her lingering concerns regarding risk versus reward associated with Anushka's offer, as well as wondering whether Beau would find anything in common with a bunch of reality TV stars and F1 motorheads.

She needn't have worried.

After the round of introductions, during which Charlie made it clear that she was the boss, and Beau was a very brilliant, very wonderful, very much appreciated old friend doing her a favour, Anushka had asked what Beau usually did with his time. When he'd explained he was cofounder of a company called Luculent, Bobby the F1 driver and his "car mad" friends had lost their minds.

Beau had done her proud, listening more than he spoke,

which was pure Beau, and when it was his turn to speak, he'd been erudite, funny, and warm.

And anytime she caught his eye, checking in to see if he needed rescuing, he'd given her a look as if making sure *she* was okay.

If that had made her heart go all a flutter, it was only because she was usually the one doing the checking. It was the crux of her job, after all. Her relationships, too, if she was honest with herself. Richard had seen her coming from a mile off.

"Penny for your thoughts?"

Charlie blinked, then shifted to face Beau, to find his long fingers resting lightly on the wheel, at ten and two. Such the rule follower. It made her smile.

He shot her a quick glance, his brow furrowing in question, before his gaze moved back to focus on the dark winding road.

Remembering he'd asked her a question, Charlie said, "Nothing much. Stream of consciousness, mostly." Then, "Starting with what a revelation *you* were tonight."

He laughed, the sound deep and husky. "Am I detecting a hint of surprise?"

"Uh, yes! You weren't exactly a chatty Cathy when we were kids. Too much going on up here." She pointed to her forehead.

"While you never stopped talking," he said.

"I had a lot to say. Lucky for me, you were such a good listener. Still waters ran deep."

They still do, she thought. She watched as the moonlight flickering through the trees overhead washed over his face, kissing his strong features, playing over his glasses like a movie. Then said, "My panic decision to ask you to help was truly inspired."

A smile hooked at the corner of his mouth, and it did such nice things to his already nice face that she shifted on her seat.

"Anyway, in case I forget to say so later," she said, stifling a yawn. "Thank you, for exceeding my expectations."

"Stop," he said, "before my ego spins out of control."

"Okay," she said, then went back to looking out the front window.

After a few moments, Beau said, "I can't imagine what it must be like having to navigate all of that on your own."

"That was nothing. That was friends at a party—stress level minimum. The wedding day—that is war games in fancy dress. It's the Wild West."

"You love it, though," he said, and it wasn't a question.

"I really do. Even the truly unexpected moments, where I am the only one between complete disaster and hilarious wedding memory, are mostly fun." When her thoughts went to #cakegate, she was actually surprised. For it actually had been a couple days since she'd even thought about it.

"What about you?" she asked. "What do you love most about your job? Apart from driving around in a sexy rocket car?"

He laughed then, a soft chortle that felt surprisingly intimate. Then took quite a lot of time to say, "There's a lot to like, actually."

"Such as?"

"It's ours, for one. Meaning we've been able curate the shape of it. The scope. The size. And our roles within. I get to be hands-on, to spend time on-site playing with materials, and seeing how our designs come together. Our name is an invitation that gets me in front of great minds. Our setup means I can hole up in my studio, sketching out ideas day and night."

"Wow. That's my dream to be that autonomous. To have that level of respect in my work."

She'd thought she'd been on her way in her last job, but with time and distance, and after how readily they'd cut her free, she had to admit she'd been dreaming. Stuck in a rat race, dancing to other people's tunes. Which just wasn't…her.

"If I had all that," she said, "I'm not sure I'd ever want to take time off."

A full minute went by, during which Charlie somehow found herself imagining Beau wiping a grease-stained hand across his sweaty brow, those long fingers working at something deep inside an engine, before he said:

"The best part? Building it alongside close friends. Matt, my business partner, he and I did our degrees together at university. Milly, too."

Matt and Milly. "As in Matt and Milly for whom you were best man?"

His hands shifted on the wheel, gripping a little harder as he said, "The very same."

"Aw. That's so nice. And what was that like, their wedding? Big? Intimate? Destination? Did you do anything terrible to Matt at the bucks' party? Was Milly a total bridezilla? I met enough of those working events in San Fran. Funny, since starting Always the Bridesmaid, all my brides have been lovely."

Another reason why working for herself was such a kick. She could choose what behaviour to accept. And never get herself in a situation where she worked for someone who wished her ill. Which seemed like the baseline, really.

When she realised Beau had not answered her pepper of questions, she looked over at him to find his hand was squeezing his neck, hard. "Beau?"

"Can we not?"

Charlie blinked. "Not…?"

"Talk about the wedding."

"Oh, sure." Charlie nibbled at her lip, keeping mum for a

good fifteen seconds, before saying, "Unless there's something about it. I ought to know what would affect your ability to do the job—"

"Milly died."

Charlie flinched, a small shocked sound shooting from her lips. For a while she'd picked up that there was something amiss. But she'd *not* seen that coming. "Oh, Beau. I'm so sorry. Back then?"

Please no. If she'd asked him to be best man after that…

"A few months ago," he managed.

Which was not better. "May I ask how?"

Was asking even the right thing? Trapped in the cocoon of the car, the soft sounds and gentle sway and darkness outside lit only by the headlights made it feel okay. As if they were the only two people in the world.

"Cancer. Fast. She and Matt… They were just right for each other. Both blisteringly smart, and open, and for whatever reason they took me on, too. Business partner. Best man at their wedding. Godfather to their two kids. And—"

He stopped. Breathed out hard.

"Hey," she said, reaching out to rest a hand on his shoulder, before pulling back. Hearing her therapist's kind voice— *Body language, personal space.* "It's okay. We don't have to talk about it."

His eyebrows rose. "I think that horse has already bolted."

"Yeah, it kind of has." Then, "Is *that* why you're here? Why you're taking time off?"

"The simple answer is yes."

"You're grieving," she said, and that something amiss, the way his smiles never reached his eyes, when in the past that had been one of her favourite things about him, now made such sense.

He said nothing. But he didn't need to.

She'd looked up the five stages of grief, after her father

had died, trying to work out what she *ought* to be feeling. The anger bit she got. Anger with him, with her mum for sweeping them off to the United Kingdom, where her family were from. With herself for not letting his words wash off her back like the formless venom they were.

If she were guessing, she'd say Beau was somewhere in bargaining/depression spectrum. For surely tearing down his parents' house was connected. Had he truly grieved their loss? Her mother hadn't seen him at the small funeral, or heard anything from him when the house had sold.

Not that she was any expert when it came to facing up to the wounds of one's childhood. Hell, her father's office remained untouched by her, or by her mother. Anyone wandering past it might think it a shrine, rather than an example of how excellent they both were at pretending out of sight meant out of mind.

Beau slowed and turned his car into her driveway, then let the engine hum to a stop. And the interior lights slowly turned on till a golden light shone over them, making the space seem smaller.

She wanted to say thank you, again, *and* that she hoped he'd feel better soon, but both seemed such inconsequential ways to sum up what she wanted to tell him.

So instead, she leaned over to kiss him quickly on the cheek.

Only he must have seen her move, as he turned at the last, and her lips brushed the corner of his mouth. The rough scrape of stubble and the soft give of his lips sent shards of embarrassment and liquid heat rushing through her. And yet she stayed, the both of them rigid with surprise.

When the embarrassment bit outweighed the other, she pulled back, said, "Well, good night!" then started jabbing at the door, trying to find her way out.

Beau's door opened and he slid easily from his seat.

Charlie's leg jiggled madly as she waited, and when her door winged open she shot outside in a gaggle of legs and bag and hair in her eyes.

Beau stood by the car, hands in the pockets of his suit pants, looking tall and solid, cool as a cucumber. He also had a small smile at the corner of his mouth, as if her flutters were amusing.

"So," she said, not daring to see if the smile reached his eyes. Instead, she looked at the sky, the trees rustling in the night breeze. "Thanks again for tonight. You were amazing. And this is going to be such fun! And I so appreciate your help...yep." She clicked her fingers at him and finished with, "I'll be in touch with next steps."

Beau lifted a hand to his heart. "I'll feel every buzz."

Charlie stared at him, feeling the buzz herself. All over. Flickers, sparks, making it hard to stand still.

Then she realised he meant his phone. In his pocket. When it buzzed. With her incessant messages.

"Great, great, great!" she said, sounding like a hyperactive hen. Then, "And thank you, for telling me about Milly."

Shut up! her internal monologue insisted.

I can't!

"Please let me know if I push too hard, or ask too much. I can be like that; a little over gung-ho when I get excited about things. I mean, you know me."

"I do," he said, as if he did. Still. Not merely that he *had*, a really long time ago. When they were both unformed, both so young. But that he saw her now, as she was.

"Okay," she squawked. "Well, good night."

She could have stepped back, waved, slipped inside the house. But she felt as if she were floating outside of her own skin, watching herself from above as she stepped in, lifted a hand to Beau's chest, tipped up on her tiptoes and kissed him on the cheek again.

This time she hit her mark.

The brush of his soft stubble against her cheek brought her back into her body with a slam. Till she could feel everything. The flutter of her lashes against her cheeks, like butterfly wings. The scent of his skin in her nostrils. The feel of him under her hand, which had landed on his chest.

When she pulled back, their eyes met. No smile there still, but there was no room between the sparks of heat, and silvery moonlight, and history that seemed to swirl therein.

"Good night, Beau."

"Good night, Charlie."

Then with one last long look, he shook his head, and jogged around the front of his car.

She lifted her hand in a wave, then somehow made it to the door on legs that didn't feel quite right. He waited until she was inside before he drove away.

As she washed off her makeup, got into her pj's, and brushed her teeth, her mind went over the night again and again.

Her arm in his as they'd walked to the club. The way he'd kept her hand when they'd gone inside, so that he could shield her from the swarm of bodies. How charming and on song he'd been with her clients, making her look so good.

And now she understood that glint of grey he carried with him, now she knew that he was grieving, deeply, for a friend. Was it wrong that it only made him more appealing?

Not that it mattered. For outside of his work on behalf of Always the Bridesmaid, Beau Griffin's "appeal" was irrelevant. Soon his house would be finished and he'd head back to his real life—one of luxury cars, and big business, and "close friends" she'd never know.

Or would he? He'd not said what his plans for the house were when he was done. Was he planning on renting it out? Keeping it as a holiday home? Was he even planning on going back to Sydney? What if he stayed? Then they'd be proper neighbours all over again.

No. No, no, *no*!

His plans mattered not a jot. For *she* was leaving. On her own terms, and good ones, this time. Not kicked out of home by an unsatisfied man who'd used her as a mental punching bag, not "vowing never to return," or being chased out of town, out of a life she'd thought she finally had a handle on, because she'd made such a colossal error of judgement.

Leaving, starting somewhere fresh, some place with no intrinsic baggage, would be the opposite of screwing up, or self-sabotage, or reacting to her situation. Making it the very best thing she could do for herself.

It was after midnight when she finally fell face down on her bed, then climbed under her bedsheets. And while her mind raced in circles, most of them around Beau Griffin, by the time she did fall asleep, she slept like a rock.

CHAPTER SIX

BEAU DIDN'T MAKE any unnecessary trips to the house over the next couple of days. Though what constituted *necessary*, he couldn't honestly say.

Instead he stayed near the rental. Did a little sudoku, scrolled funny cat videos. He took Moose for a walk, then another, doing as had been suggested and putting a little less pressure on himself where the dog was concerned. Trying the same for himself, he passed up his usual hot black double shot espresso and tried a decaf almond "milk" latte in a holistic café in Montville, and quickly decided it wasn't for him.

All of which was done in the effort at not thinking quite so much about Charlie.

Charlie. When had he started thinking of her as such? Hearing Anushka rave about her. Or when he'd gone into town, found the record store she used to work at, and the guy behind the counter had recognised him, saying, "Hey, aren't you Charlie's Beau?"

Or was it when she stepped up, leaned in, and kissed his cheek.

For all the times they had been all over one another as kids—wrestling, arm in arm, snuggling under her back stairs on cold winter nights—*Charlotte* had never done that.

Now he couldn't stop replaying it, over and over again in a hypnotic loop. The way her eyes had gone wide and soft all at once. The way her fingers had curled gently against his chest. The way she'd breathed deeply, as if gathering the scent of him. The feel of her lips, soft and pliant, lingering. The small sound she'd made, as if kissing him had given her relief.

Then, when he dragged himself out of the loop, he'd think of Milly. Or, to be precise, he'd think of Matt at home missing his wife. Somehow getting through each day, taking care of their kids, with help from Milly's devastated mum, all of their hearts in shredded ribbons.

While he was going to nightclubs, laughing, making friends with race car drivers, swaying to music he'd never heard, Milly never would again.

One thing had nothing to do with the other. He knew that. Didn't stop the grit that gathered inside him with every turn of the story. When it became too much, in need of a distraction, he opened his work email for the first time since going north.

Only to find it was lighter than he might have expected. As if it was being deliberately curated by a concerned business partner, who had more than enough on his plate than to be adding that.

He'd opened an email to tell said business partner such, when Moose jumped up, a great paw landing on the laptop and sending an email that went something like "ncjosabuisari albiuwer".

Beau ruffled the dog's ears, before gently pushing him back to the floor. Where he panted happily, before rolling on his back for a tummy rub.

A minute later Beau's phone rang.

"You emailed!" Matt announced, as if trumpets and revelry would be an appropriate accompaniment.

"Moose emailed," Beau explained, giving Matt a moment to actually read the thing.

"Worrying," said Matt, "if that had been you. And yet, it was from your email address. Meaning unless the dog has learned your password, you had checked in."

Beau sat back in the too small chair at the too small desk in the corner of the too small nook in his summer rental, and remembered how nice it felt to be in one's own office. Honestly missing the converted warehouse in which Luculent resided for the first time since he'd left.

Not the setup, or the white noise of staff busy at work, but those early days when they'd first moved in and he'd been able to make the space exactly what he needed it to be in order to *think*. To imagine, to create, without the weight of time, or money, or guilt, or worry hanging over him.

He pictured one of the huge bedrooms in the new house on Myrtle Way. At the rear, leading off the large open plan living area—it had large windows with a view over the hills, plenty of room for a couch, large coffee table, walls of bookshelves, a desk facing the window, a drafting board in the back corner, even a telescope.

It would be a highlight, for whomever ended up living there.

"Were you looking for something in particular?" Matt asked, cutting into an image Beau was building of *him* sitting at that desk, a blessed sense of calm coming over him as he looked out over that view. "Not that I'm rushing you."

"I was," said Beau. "I was…going to do some catching up."

"Okay," said Matt, his voice now a little giddy. "Want me to catch you up instead."

"Have at it."

Matt breathed out hard, then peppered Beau with bullet points, as if he'd been collecting them. The Luculent Engine had made it through phase one of independent testing. They were getting political blowback from the usual places, members who were sympathetic to fossil fuel providers. Another offer had been made for Lucky, double what they'd been offered last time.

"Tell them they're dreaming," Beau said.

And Matt laughed. Even though they were both pragmatic enough to know that leaking the story would give their rep as much of a boost as taking the money.

"How's the house coming?" Matt asked when he'd exhausted his bullet points.

"Come up and see."

"Is it still a bomb site?"

"Very much."

"Then not yet."

"Fair."

A beat of silence pulsed between them. One in which both wished to ask if the other was okay, both knowing the real answer was no...but improving. Whether they would improve in the same direction, Beau couldn't promise. Not yet.

"If you'd like to let my inbox off the leash, I'd be amenable," Beau said. And meant it. A week ago that would not have been possible. But now he could at least do that.

"I'd like that very much. Now prepare thyself for the deluge." With that, Matt hung up.

As threads of their conversation curled about inside his head—things said, things left out—Beau leaned back in the chair and the thing nearly toppled.

"The sooner the house is finished the better," he growled.

And Moose, thinking he was talking to him, nuzzled against his hand. Beau patted the dog back, while realising that Matt already knew something he'd not even considered.

In leaving, there had been a chance he might not go back at all.

Unlike Anushka Patel, most brides couldn't afford a wedding planner on top of the cost of everything else, so leaned on Charlie as a kind of "choose your own adventure" helper.

Some bought pre-negotiated packages such as attendance at three pre-wedding events, such as gift registry, first wedding-dress fitting, hens' breakfast, plus six phone calls, and twelve hours of pure bestie energy on the big day.

Others worked on hourly rates, calling on her when needed.

She even had a text message subscription service, via which brides could ask her anything, anytime, no question too small, no worry too trivial. It had been Julia's brilliant idea, her amazing bookkeeper-slash-backup-bridesmaid who'd been helping her set the thing up. And it was growing consistently, month on month. It was this last one that might even tide her over during the transition period when she left.

For example:

Q: My MOTHER IN-LAW did not disclose an ALLERGY to shellfish until today, THREE DAYS OUT from my wedding. In Hobart, on the water, with a full fresh-catch menu. What do I do?

A: First thing—breathe. Second thing—you're getting married in three days! Third thing—text me the details of the reception location, your caterer, and your MIL's favourite dinner. It will be sorted. Love, Always the Bridesmaid xxx

Of course, things didn't always go quite so swimmingly.

Charlie sat at her kitchen bench, staring at her laptop, while pressing fingers into her temples as she tried to block out the whir of concrete cutters coming from the house next door.

After the mega success of meeting Anushka and Bobby and their wedding party, she should have known karma would make amends. And it did, swiftly, using Isla the mega-introvert of the not-puce bridesmaid dresses as its vehicle.

"I'm not sure I can do this, Charlie," Isla had cried over the phone that morning.

"You can do anything. And anything you can't do, I'll do for you. Well, anything bar marry your guy."

Isla had laughed, then burst into a deeper set of sobbing tears.

"Okay," Charlie had said, "let's go back over the list we made of things we can do to make this not feel so terrifying."

"Well…" Isla sniffed.

"Well?" Charlie encouraged.

"There was one thing."

Elopement.

Apparently, after they'd rung off Isla had called Justin, he'd come straight home from work, they'd packed their bags and left to get married. Isla's mother-in-law had refused to pay the final Always the Bridesmaid invoice, and was threatening legal action to recoup the down payment.

As if she needed a sign of how precarious her situation really was, how careful she had to be, the light above Charlie's head crackled, flickered, and turned off. Then popped on again. Right as a piercingly high whine of construction equipment shook her window.

She could go over there and ask what time they might finish up so she could make some work calls without having to shout. But she'd done so a few days before, chocolate chip cookies in hand, only for Beau's project manager to stop her at the rose bushes.

They'd apparently been "told" not to let her through. "Unless you're in the appropriate safety gear," he said, accepting the cookies with a smile.

Charlie could have taken it as Beau trying to keep her safe, but her gut knew it was more than that.

He didn't want her there.

Since the roses had always been a rather pathetic excuse for a fence, he'd had to create an invisible way to make it clear that while they were working together, she no longer had unfettered access to his life.

As if his radio silence hadn't made that clear.

For after what had been an amazing night out, by all metrics, the only contact they'd had was her calendar updates regarding the Patel/Kent nuptials, and his thumbs-up. Which was *normal*, for people with a casual working relationship.

Only this was *Beau*. And so she couldn't let it lie.

He was upset with her, for pushing too hard about poor Milly. It must have been so difficult to speak about, and she'd pressed him till he felt he had no other choice.

Or it might have been the kiss.

Yes, it was on his cheek, and it had been a chaste thank-you kiss. But the way she'd leaned into him, the way her hand had curled into his shirt so that she'd had to tidy it up a little before stepping back... What had she been *thinking*?

She'd been *thinking* that she liked the way he looked at her these days. She'd been thinking that he was brilliant, and kind, and a little bit broken, and how that combination called to all the parts of her that had felt abandoned for so long. She'd been thinking that he had washed her dishes the other night without being asked.

She'd been *thinking* that for the first time in a long time she felt at ease, happy, hopeful. And that having Beau Griffin in her life again, even for a short time, was turning out to be a little bit of magic.

She let her face fall into her hands, and tried really hard not to let the words *dumb* and *stupid* make their way through the whirr in her head.

Then, as the screech of the concrete cutter hummed to silence, someone next door turned on the radio, and the *Wicked* soundtrack began playing at full blast.

Without another thought, Charlie shot off the kitchen stool and out the back door. She got halfway across her yard, before she backtracked and grabbed a pair of yellow gum boots her mum used to wear when gardening, shucking them on as she made her way to Beau's.

When she pressed her way through the rose bushes there were no workmen to be seen out back. She heard the clang of a Ute tray closing in front of the house, an engine gunning, then the *Wicked* soundtrack softening as the truck left.

Meaning she stood in Beau's backyard, alone.

It had been a few days since the "chocolate chip cookie" debacle, a few days more since she'd found Beau there in lieu of the imaginary "robber" and Moose had all but knocked her for six. And a lot had changed.

The yard had been cleaned up some. A flat patch graded in preparation for some kind of landscaping. The back facade had been painted a lovely warm cream. And the glass had gone in downstairs—an entire wall of it in soft smoky grey that reflected the view beyond.

"*Oh*," she said, the delighted sound coming out before she could stop it. While for some time the place had looked so imposing, so hard, she could see how it might, in the end, reflect, enhance, and become one with the land around it. Not fighting it, or taming it, but existing together. Each bringing out the best in the other.

And her head of steam dissipated as if a cold change had swept over the valley.

"Charlie?"

Wincing at having been caught trespassing, Charlie turned to find Beau picking his way down the side of the house in a T-shirt, old jeans, work boots, and his ubiquitous hard hat. He had a smear of dirt on his neck, a graze in the knee of his jeans, and sweat patches all over his shirt, the fabric clinging to him in a way that turned her mouth dry.

"I came to ask your guys if they might turn the music down a smidge, but either my timing was excellent or I scared them off."

"Not a fan of *Wicked*?" he asked, with no hint of all the tumult she'd spent the past few days imagining him roiling in.

In fact, he looked chipper. Healthy. Refreshed. All the more gorgeous for it.

"Are you kidding?" she said, dragging her mind back to the subject at hand. She belted out a few terrible notes of "Popular." "I'm just not sure it goes all that well with a concrete-cutter accompaniment!"

He smiled. And did it just reach his eyes? Yes! There was a definite glint in those warm, autumn leaf depths. Her heart did a happy little jig against her ribs, till she told it to calm the heck down.

Which was never going to happen when Beau suddenly seemed to clock the "outfit" she'd grabbed off her clean clothes chair after her shower that morning, knowing she'd be working from home—a Miss Piggy tank top, frill pink gingham cotton pyjama shorts, and once-yellow gum boots.

He gave her outfit the quickest possible up and down, and yet she felt as if he'd run his hands over every inch of her skin his gaze had touched. And when that gaze once again met hers, he looked at her in a way that meant, when she got home, she'd be putting her head in the freezer.

"I freaked you out the other night," she blurted.

He stilled, then used the back of his hand to wipe a bead of sweat from his brow. And said nothing, because he was a listener and she was a talker, meaning she had no choice but to follow through.

"By kissing you. Twice. On the cheek, yes, but still that must have felt as if it came out of nowhere. Even though it didn't, because I am so grateful for what you're doing for me. Then I pushed you into telling me about Milly, when I'm sure that was never your intention. And I want to apologise for both."

He lowered his hand to his hip, grit coating the creases in his knuckles. Stylish guy Beau was quite the thing, but manual labour Beau was making her knees turn to liquid.

"You have nothing to apologise for, Charlie. In fact, it un-blocked something inside me."

"The kiss?"

He tilted his head in a manner that felt wholly indulgent, and her dry mouth felt so parched she had to swallow, hard.

"The conversation," he said, his voice hitting a deeper note. "I've been feeling a lot of feelings, and had nowhere to put them. Not wanting to bother Matt, and not ready to talk to a stranger about it all."

"And I'm neither!" she said, her voice bright.

"You are most definitely neither. So, while it wasn't my intention, it helped."

"I'm...glad." Understatement alert. For she was quietly giddy. First that she'd *not* screwed things up, also that she'd actually been a force for good. She really was getting her mojo back!

As to who she was to Beau now? Neither of them, it seemed, was in any place to fill that blank space.

Beau smiled. "While you're here, do you want a tour?"

"Sure," she said, curiosity piqued. Then looked around. "No Moose?"

"Left him at the rental with something called a Kong? Filled with peanut butter. The local grocer recommended it when he saw how much dog food I was buying."

"Phil! Isn't he the sweetest? He was my backup if you said no."

Beau, clearly picturing Phil on his special stool behind the counter, his one working hearing aid, his tufty silver hair, deadpanned her. "Is that right?"

"Mm-hmm," she said, the picture of innocence, marvelling at how light she felt, when five minutes earlier she'd been all rain clouds. "Now show me around."

Only Beau glanced at the top of her head, which still in its messy shower bun was, of course, "hard hat" free. And she deflated like a nicked balloon.

Beau held up a hand, "Can you... Just wait here a sec." Then he held out a second hand, doubling down, untrusting that she'd not follow.

Charlie threw her hands out to the side as she watched him step over rocks and old bricks and disappear back around the side of the house.

When he returned, he held a large black gift bag.

"For me?" she asked, when he held it out to her.

Beau nodded, eyes gleaming behind his adorably smudged glasses.

Flutters of anticipation and surprise dancing inside her, Charlie looked into the bag to find...

A hard hat. In a bright pale peach. And her heart squeezed so hard she had to let out a breath.

Slipping the hat from the bag, she looked to Beau. Speechless for once in her life.

"So, you can come over anytime," he explained, "to stickybeak, or bring the guys baked goods, or put in requests if you prefer *Hamilton*, or *The Muppets*," he said, with a quick flicker of his eyes to her top. "And so that I can sleep better at night."

He'd been thinking about her, when not with her. Worrying, even. And while there were a thousand ways she could have brushed it off, made a joke, lightened the sweet tension curling inside her, she couldn't. Even while it was so unusual for *her* to be the one being looked after, and it felt disorienting as all hell.

Because now she knew about his grief. The shadow trapped inside him that surely touched all other areas of his life. Including her. Meaning she had to take extra care.

So she pulled the hat from the bag and sat it on her head, with a, "Ta da!"

"May I?" Beau asked, then moved in close to shift the hat so it sat more firmly on her head. "There. Better."

When his eyes dropped back to hers, he blinked. He looked from one eye to the other, as if trying to read whatever was written there. Then his gaze dropped to her mouth. And stayed.

The urge to lick her lips was agonising, but she didn't want him to get the wrong idea. Or the right idea. That she'd been thinking about him when she wasn't with him, too.

Because what good would that do?

"Now I'm properly decked out, are you going to give me the grand tour or not?" she said, a small miracle the words came out at all.

Beau nodded, and blinked furiously, his jaw tight, his cheeks a little pink. Then he held out at an arm, and said, "After you."

Rolling her eyes at the sky, and muttering to herself to keep it together, Charlie picked her way around piles of detritus to look through the downstairs glass.

"It'll remain open-plan," he said, moving in beside her, but not too close. Which was fine with her. "There'll be a kitchenette at the rear, bathroom, so it might be a granny flat, or office space. Options."

Options for whom? she suddenly wanted to know. Needed to know with a ferocity that surprised even her. But after the strange tension of the past few minutes, she decided not to press.

Next he pointed out space for the wine cellar, and a laundry/mudroom. The foundation for the ice bath. Sauna. Gym.

"No dungeon?" she asked, lifting up onto her toes as if she might then find a secret trap door.

"We tried, but the foundations were too hard."

"Don't you hate that?" Then, as she'd held off as long as she could, she said, "A gym is a pretty nice add on for a holiday place. Or a rental. Unless…unless you plan to sell the place?"

Despite his family having not owned it for the past decade, that felt wrong somehow. As if, in some secret place inside her, after Beau had left, and while she'd been overseas, she'd taken some small comfort in the Griffins and the Goodes being connected by their rose bushes still.

Then Beau lifted a hand to his neck and said, "When I set to knocking the old place down and building anew, that was the part I focused on most of all."

"And now?"

His gaze met hers, the muscles in his raised arm bunching. "Now I'm not sure. The closer it gets, the less I like the idea of other people getting the benefit of what we're building here. At least at first."

"So, at the end of the build, a few weeks from now, you might stay on?"

Stop! Her inner monologue woke up. *Stop pushing him. What he does with the place is none of your business. If all goes well, a few weeks from now you can pack your bags and flee! So leave the man alone.*

Then Beau breathed in, his gaze still locked on hers. "I don't know. Maybe."

"Hmm," she said, her breath light. "I mean, you could. But keep in mind the Wi-Fi signal is touch and go. Everything *city* is a good hour's drive away, at least. Then there's your very fancy, very important, very well-paying job, which happens to be in Sydney, meaning it'd be a hell of a commute. And—"

I won't be here.

Charlie gulped. Chuffed she'd managed to cut herself off before blurting out that last part. For she had nothing to do with his reasons to stay, or to go. Just as he had nothing to do with hers. If their being here at the same time had a purpose, surely it was to find some kind of closure.

"And I'm *not* sure that tearing down your parents' house and building something in its place actually wipes out the horrors that happened here."

Beau's arm dropped, and he looked up at the mighty house looming over them. "While I'm not sure that living in a museum dedicated to the worst of your childhood is any better."

Charlie's jaw dropped. "Wow, burn."

His gaze moved back to her, eyebrows raised. "Am I wrong?"

"For one thing, as soon as I can afford to get out of here, I will."

"Is that so?"

"Yes," she shot back. "It is entirely so. It's *why* Anushka and Bobby's wedding was important enough for me to rope you into the thing. And *why* making myself at home here hasn't been a priority."

"Mmm," he said, so noncommittal she ached to press back.

Instead, rolling out her shoulder, Charlie glanced over the rose bushes to the familiar skyline of the house next door. The house that carried the echoes of her father in the bookshelves in the sunroom, the jackets in his bedroom cupboard, his office, completely untouched. While the vegetable and herb gardens that had been her mother's salvation had been reclaimed by the earth.

And all the arguments she felt backing up in her throat turned to dust.

She let her face fall into her hands. Then remembered the hard hat, righting it as it began to slip. "Aren't we the pair?"

"What's the saying—wherever you go, there you are."

"Isn't that the truth?"

After a few long moments, Beau said, "It wasn't entirely horrible." And she knew he meant his childhood, because of her.

She moved a little closer and bumped him with her shoulder.

And he bumped her back.

"As for this house," she said, moving out from under the cantilevered balcony and into the yard, where she might be able to find air not infused with his warmth, his scent. "I may have been a tad disparaging at first. For it's definitely less like a weapons facility than I first imagined."

Beau, who had followed, gave her a warm smile.

"Great! Okay! Well, I have stuff to do, so if you could let your guys know to keep the radio down a decibel or two, that'd be great."

"Will do."

She took a step back, and tripped off the edge of the balcony foundation. Beau reached for her, but she righted herself just fine.

She pointed at him as she backed away. "If the next time I come over you have a roll of bubble wrap fashioned into overalls, that's where I draw the line."

He held up both hands, palms out.

After which, she turned and clomped back to hers.

And if she put the hard hat in a special place on the corner of the kitchen bench, then so be it.

CHAPTER SEVEN

IN BETWEEN BEAU'S suit try-ons and lunch in Noosa with Anushka and her soon to be mother-in-law at the fancy restaurant of the chef who was catering the event, she had back-to-back weddings with other clients on the weekends.

Keeping Robin's handsy cousin Stu occupied—a cinch. Keeping Gladys's tipsy Pastor Ron away from the punch before the backyard wedding—not as easy, but done. Each bride sent off happy, and relieved all had gone well.

High on her run of success, and a little on the fact that so far none of Anushka's circle had looked at her and said, "Hey didn't you throw cake at a bride once?", on the next cool free afternoon Charlie took a trip into town to pick up fertiliser, seedlings, seeds, mulch, and a few gardening tools.

For the frames of her mother's veggie and herb gardens were still there, and the thought of bringing them back to life that had been seeded by Beau's rather pointed comment about how she was living in a morbid museum had grown with each passing day.

Sure, it might not eventuate by the time she left, she might not get to reap the benefits, but in the same way Beau was leaving his mark on the house next door, she wanted to sprinkle her brand of joy on this place, too.

It was near dark by the time she'd softened up the soil, weeded the beds, added soil, watered, and planted a few seeds. Just enough light to stand back and take some photos to send to her mum. Who'd sent her back an eggplant emoji, which Charlie could only hope referred to the veggie garden.

A cool breeze swept in from the valley, as Charlie cricked her back. Looking out over the view, to where the moon gleamed down on the distant water, Charlie saw the first stars twinkling in the sky.

Feeling loose and warm and rather pleased with herself, she washed her hands, grabbed a throw, spread it out on the back lawn and lay down on her back, watching as the sky went from mauve to deep blue to black.

It was pure muscle memory that had set her down in the exact spot she and Beau used to do exactly this. Sneaking outside at some ungodly hour, long after their parents had fallen asleep, ostensibly to count shooting stars. But mostly to talk about school, about how they imagined their futures might be. Knowing, from experience, the next day would be better for it.

The rustle of the rose bushes, followed by Moose's doggy snuffle were the first signs she was about to have a visitor, the vibration of Beau's heavy boots on the ground as he neared was the next.

"Boots off," she said, "hard hat, too, if you're wearing it. This is a safety-free zone."

She saw him pause, out of the corner of her eye, before doing as he asked. Then Moose's face filled her vision as he licked at her chin. Laughing, she patted the ground beside her, and after a few turns in the soft unmown grass, Moose lay down with a *harrumph*.

"Where have you gone?" she asked, then looked overhead to find him staring at her back porch, the light above it so weak she'd not even bothered to turn it off. "You are obsessed with that thing. I will get to it. It's on a long list of exciting DIY projects I have decided to take on."

He looked back at her, and even upside down, and frowning; he made for a fine view.

She went back to looking up at the stars.

"I'm assuming the other half of that blanket is for me," said Beau as he neared.

Had she deliberately lain on one side, just in case he found her there? She'd known he'd been about, had seen him head down into the drop at the edge of his backyard, garden sheers in hand, as if he was going to attempt to tackle the lantana himself.

"Whoever calls dibs," she said.

With a soft laugh, Beau dropped to the blanket beside her. She felt the heat of him, the bulk, shift the air around her as he laid his big body down. He smelled of hard work, dirt, and botanicals. And something other that she was beginning to recognise as pure Beau.

"Remind me of the rules," he said, and a frisson of delight sparked inside her, that he remembered this had been their thing, too.

"We can't leave till we've both seen a shooting star."

"Found any?" he asked.

"Not yet."

And after a few quiet minutes spent revelling in the brush of the wind, the hum of distant frog song, it became dark enough that if she squinted just right, she could just make out the pale ribbon of the Milky Way.

"You won't see *that* in the city," he said. Convincing himself it was a plus of living here, *staying* here, or convincing her?

"Do you remember the time, we were around fourteen, when you tried telling me that shooting stars weren't stars at all, that they were big rocks, or space junk, burning up as they entered Earth's atmosphere?"

"Because it's the truth."

Charlie laughed, the press of it hard against her ribs. "But not the *point*."

"What was the point?"

This, she thought. *Us being together.*

"The point, dear Beau, was the beauty and ferocity and vastness of the universe making our problems seem a little less all-consuming."

"Mmm," he said, his voice a growl in the darkness, and Charlie's skin raised in goose bumps.

"So, I hear you had lunch with Bobby this week."

"I did. Hope that's okay?"

"Of course! Outside of my needs, you do you, boo."

Anushka had called Charlie to gush over how Bobby had a total boy crush on Beau and wasn't that the sweetest thing ever. And Charlie had wholeheartedly agreed, while also having to stave off a raging case of pride that Beau was out there, making friends and doing nice things for himself. As if the depression/bargaining might be easing up some. And it was her doing.

"And am I meeting your needs?"

Her needs?

Oh, he meant regarding the gig! "Yep. Sure. You're doing great. I'll let you know if you're not, don't worry about that."

"Okay." Then, "How long does this usually take?"

"To see a shooting star? Why so impatient?"

He moved around beside her, his foot knocking against hers, sending what felt like a belt of shooting stars up her leg. "I've been pushing Sisyphus's rock up a hill all afternoon, trying to clear out the scrub out back, and if I lie here too long my back will seize up and I'll be walking funny tomorrow."

Laughing, Charlie pulled herself to sitting, and Beau did the same.

She looked sideways to find him watching her, not the sky. "I could have told you that you need a pro to clear lantana."

"You knew I was out there. I saw you watching."

Oops.

Had his voice dropped a little as he asked, "So why didn't you tell me?"

The answer—because then she'd have missed out on watching him walk up and down the hill, getting sweatier and messier as the day went on.

"Most of the men I've known haven't appreciated my advice, or opinions, or skill set when it came to such things."

Beau took that in. "Then most of the men you've known were fools."

She leaned back on her hands, let her legs stretch out in front. And said, "True that."

Beau, after watching her for a few heady moments, did the same. His bare foot brushing hers. She knocked it back. And once they'd settled, their little toes touched, though neither said a thing about it.

"You've mentioned a few times now that you're keen to head off," he said.

"As soon as humanly possible." Though it had been her mantra for months, this time it felt a little hollow.

"Then why come back at all?"

Whether it was the cloak of darkness, or mention of the men she'd known, or the fact that this was the place they'd talked about their big fears, she found herself telling Beau about #cakegate.

Her heart was thudding in her ears by the time she got to the moment Richard had slunk in behind her. Leaving out his choice words, she jumped to when she came out of a fog to find she'd thrown cake across the room. And yet, in reliving it, she felt as if she was back there, right in the middle of it, Richard's gaze bright with shocked delight.

"Does any of that ring a bell?" she asked.

Beau, watching her in that quiet way of his, shook his head.

So Charlie grabbed her phone from where she'd sat it on the edge of the throw, googled, and pages of images glowed brightly on the screen. She scrolled down till she found the infamous video.

The vision was shaky, zoomed in from the back of the large room. Heads bobbing in and out of view, focus shifting before the bright pink castle cake came into view.

"Phones had been forbidden," she said, "left in baskets at the door, as the rights had been sold to an online wedding site. But naturally someone had not complied. Meaning the only footage is this. After Richard had thrown his bride in front of him."

She watched Beau's face rather than the video, not needing to see it to know exactly which part it was up to. His expression remained impassive, until the security escorted her from the venue, at which point his nostrils flared and his gaze shot to her.

"What the hell did he do?" Beau asked.

"Hmm?"

"The groom. He said something. Or did something. It wasn't just that he was there. I know you, Charlie. You've faced down monsters with phenomenal grace your whole life. What did he do?"

Charlie swallowed. Tried to brush it off, the way she had in those first few months. Until a need to get it out of her, like an exorcism, had the words spilling from her mouth.

Beau's jaw grew tight, his eyes fierce behind his glasses, as she told him what Richard had said. How he'd called her a screwup. And far worse. In her place of business, where she'd worked so hard to build herself up into something more. Until she'd snapped.

"Wait," he said. "Did no one stop to ask why? Did no one assume you had good reason to do what you did?"

Charlie blinked. "Ah, no." In fact, it had never once occurred to her that they should. "He's an asshole, yes. But I still should never have done what I did. The worst part—it was reactive and dramatic and utter self-sabotage. Everything my father always accused me of being. I remember feeling as if he was watching. Feeling as I was screaming, in my head, *See! You were right!* And now it's going to follow me my entire life."

She turned her phone toward herself and turned off the screen.

While Beau looked out at the distant sky.

Having told her side, fully, for the first time since the whole thing began, she felt terrible, and relieved, in equal measure.

Whatever happened from here would happen. So long as he didn't say he could now no longer go ahead with the wedding, anything else she could handle. She hoped.

Then, voice low with a note of feral that had her insides curling, he said, "Where does he live? What's he most afraid of? Any allergies? I'll sort him out."

And she laughed. A quick bark, then more. Guffaws that brought tears to her eyes. Tears she'd not cried at the time, her entire body rigid with shock.

Then, when she was done, she looked at him.

"He doesn't matter," she said, and found that she meant it. Lately she was beginning to see the difference. "Karma will get him in the end. While look at me! The mistress of my own domain. Sure, the electrics are shot, and I walked down the hall this morning and I felt as if I was tipping sideways, meaning the place probably needs to be restumped. I've dropped every cent I've made so far with Always the Bridesmaid in keeping it from falling on my head. But it's better, not being there. Not being that… Charlotte. Stripped back I've had to be…me."

"From my point of view, there's nothing at all wrong with that."

She smiled. Then looked up at the sky. Because if she looked at Beau, the way he was looking at her, she might just cry.

A minute later Beau said, "There."

Charlie leaned in and followed the point of his finger to catch the tail end of a bright shooting star, shimmering back to darkness. Then she laughed, the joy of it fizzing her. "It never gets old, does it?"

"No," he said, "it seems it does not."

When she turned to smile at him, his face was tipped to hers. They were so close, their noses nearly touched. And the heat in his eyes was so patent he felt it hit her cheeks in a warm glow.

Then he reached for her, his hand hovering near her cheek. When she didn't demur, his fingers moved to tuck her hair behind her ear.

Alarm bells sounded. A riotous clang.

Don't do this. He's hurting. He's confused. He's breaking things and remaking things and isn't entirely sure why. Things are finally kind of okay. Don't mess things up.

Or perhaps they were celebratory bells. A rousing cheer going up inside her. That after being separated by oceans, and time, having lived lives that had challenged and forged them in new ways, they'd found their way back here. To one another. For the shortest of times, before the universe was set to fling them apart again, but still.

Then, as Beau breathed her in, his gaze roving over her face, his fingers on her skin, she knew it wasn't closure she'd been yearning for since the moment he knocked on her door.

It was this.

Charlie lifted her head and his hand moved with it, now cupping her jaw, his thumb moving to trace her cheekbone, the edge of her mouth. His gaze followed, drinking her in, taking his fill. As if he, too, felt the press of time.

Where he touched her, she burned. Where he didn't, she ached. And when his gaze found hers, his mouth curved into an understanding smile.

She lifted her hand to his face, her fingers sliding against his jaw, the rough stubble sending splinters of electricity down her arm. And a small moan escaped the back of his throat.

He touched her with such tenderness, and such restraint, it was too much. And not enough. She felt like she was floating, and tipped her forehead to his in order not to float away.

Then, finding a note of bravery, she might not have had had she not told him her truth, if he'd not given her reason to trust him with it, Charlie lifted her head and pressed her lips to his.

A kiss.

She was kissing Beau Griffin. Something she'd dreamed of more times than she dared count. Pining for him, confused by him, missing him.

It was the lightest of things—a brush of lips. Then another. All the while time seemed to stand still. Her blood turning sluggish, as her fingers traced his jaw before delving into his thick hair. Touching him, learning him, committing him to memory lest she wake to find this was a dream, too.

And the kiss. Oh, the kiss!

It was slow, delicate. A gentle touch and release as they learned one another's shape, warmth, feel, taste. Like a flower that blossoms once a year right on midnight, utterly precious, utterly wondrous.

But she knew it could be more.

Needing to be closer, to wrap herself in him, she moved up onto her knees. In complete sync, Beau's arm gathered her around the waist hauling her over him, so that she straddled him. Her hand slid up his back, under his shirt, the sheen of sweat and hot skin and steely strength made her weak.

But he had her. Gathered her to him, holding her close,

her body curled against his. All movement, and rolling bodies. And sliding touch.

Then his tongue traced the seam of her lips, opening her to him, and everything changed. The world went dark, and light, and sweet, and lush. Heat rolled through her in waves as her body turned both limp with need and as light as if it was full of sparkles.

Then Beau breathed out, her name a whisper against her lips. An ode. An incantation. As he kissed his way along her jaw. Her head fell back as he pressed sweet drugging kisses to her neck.

The words he was saying, words of want, and heat, and need, melted together till she no longer heard them, only felt them. A rising tide of lust inside her, burning her alive.

Then a loud *woof* broke through the fog, and another, and Beau's lips paused at the edge of her top. One hand in her hair, the other hooked under the strap of her bra.

Charlie opened her eyes to find herself on her knees, Beau's hard thighs beneath her, her head back, the stars a glittering spray across the sky.

She stayed a beat, trying to find her centre, before she slowly dropped her head to find Beau breathing deep, his lips damp, his eyes diamond bright.

Then Moose huffed a breath in their faces, and they disentangled quickly, as Moose woofed around the stick in his mouth.

Beau reached out and grabbed the thing, wincing at the slobber on his hand, before he tossed the thing across the yard.

"Saved by the dog?" he murmured and Charlie laughed.

While she'd been thinking what a fine thing it might have been if this was a day he'd left the lovely Moose at home.

But no. This was better.

A kiss was wild enough. A kiss wasn't *that* big a deal. People did it all the time!

In fact, maybe it had been inevitable. All that history, and Beau going through what he was going through, and Charlie with the whole Richard and #cakegate debacle. It was a lot. A kiss might take the edge off, without completely messing with the nice thing they had.

She glanced to Beau, who was running his hands through his hair. His brow furrowed as if he, too, was thinking hard. Then he heaved himself to standing, all athletic grace for a man his size. It was enough to set her heart to racing again. When he looked down at her, he let out a great sigh, before holding out a hand to help her up.

As she took it, her breath leaving her as he lifted her to her feet, she cried, "Look!" as a spectacular shooting star curved to life behind his shoulder, perhaps the best she'd ever seen, its tail a blinding mix of colour across the sky.

Magic in the air, and hormones still raging through her body, for a second Charlie considered asking Beau to stay. For dinner. And then?

Beau said, "Well, we've both spotted a shooting star; rules say it's time for me to leave."

And she swallowed her invitation back. "You always did have a thing for the rules."

And yet there they stood, for a few long seconds, as if there was too much to say, but neither knew where to begin. Then, when Moose came bounding back with his stick, Beau started walking backward toward the rose bushes.

"Don't forget, you have another suit fitting next week," Charlie called.

"I won't forget," he said, still walking backward, as if he wasn't quite ready to see her face for the last time that night.

Which was how Charlie felt herself blurting, "I have a wedding on this weekend. Quite a cool one in fact. Takes place on a train. And I have a standing plus-one, if you'd like to come?"

Beau paused. Taking his time answering. Oh, no, he was looking for some way to let her down, wasn't he? Concerned she thought the kiss meant something more than what it was.

"Think of it as a dry run," she said. "So you can see what it is that I do on the day," she added, wishing she'd led with that.

"Fine," he said, his voice cavernous in the darkness.

And for the first time she wished both her back lights were working so she could see his face. See if he looked pained, or if he was smiling that half smile. See if the light reached his eyes.

Then she was glad of the darkness when she remembered, "It's an overnighter. Do you have anyone who can look after Moose?"

"I have someone."

"Great! Saturday morning. Wear a suit. Pack an overnight bag. Pick me up at ten a.m. in the sexy rocket car?"

Beau's laughter danced across the darkness and Charlie crossed her arms, holding it close.

"See you then, Charlie," Beau said, then he and his dog were gone.

CHAPTER EIGHT

BEAU LEANED AGAINST the bar, the glass in his hand only three quarters full in consideration of the rocking of the train.

While around him wedding guests guzzled and nibbled and got generally sozzled, as the grandly appointed carriage shuttled them south to where they would soon all disembark, witness the wedding, then hop back on the train where the real party started.

At least that's how Charlie had described the order of ceremony, before she'd ducked away to look after her client, Ginny, leaving him with nothing to do to distract him from thoughts of her.

For that's where his thoughts had lived since their evening star gaze, tipping from the sweet salty taste of her, the heat of her skin, the way she curled into him with such abandon to incredulity as to the events that had sent her careening back home. His equilibrium up the spout.

After spending months feeling little but apathy, he now had a surfeit of energy to deal with. He had to put it somewhere. That somewhere turned out to be poring through applications for future works plans as submitted by Luculent's junior engineers. Making sure to support those to whom he was obligated, where in Charlie's case that had not happened at all.

His phone buzzed. His blood heated, thinking it might be her. Instead, he was blessed with a photo of Mike, the electrician, sitting beside Moose on his couch, watching *Turner and Hooch.*

Beau downed his iced water, the last thing Charlie needed was her date getting tipsy, and ordered another. Not that he was her *date.* He was shadowing her, learning from the master, in readiness for Anushka and Bobby's wedding in three short weeks. For all that his role would be a one-time gig, he found himself truly curious to see how it all went down.

An hour later, as the well-lubricated guests poured from the train and onto the platform where the wedding was to take place, Beau took up a spot at the rear, meaning he was in prime position to see the wedding party's big entrance.

But all he saw was Charlie. Her dress appeared more sparkles than fabric, her hair in slick waves, her lips a dark luscious pink; she looked ready to tempt a mobster to go straight. Or a priest to turn rogue.

Her confident gaze swept over the crowd, as if making sure they were all behaving, until it found him. And there it stayed.

He felt his heart buck against his ribs, his skin felt a little tight, and his extremities began to cool as if all his blood had rushed somewhere more important.

He lifted a hand to his heart, intimating an arrow had hit, right there. It earned him a twist of a smile, and the most subtle of eye rolls, before she slid her eyes back to the front and for the next several hours, gave everything she had to her bride.

Once they were back in the bar carriage, she slid through the room like silk—passing out tissues, sneaking away drinks from those who'd had their share, keeping the fathers of bride and groom—whom Beau had been told did not get on—laughing and relaxed. It was no surprise, having been the original receiver of her fixed attentions as a kid, yet watching from the outside, she was a sensation.

When she caught his eye late into the night, he lifted his

drink in salute. She motioned to see if he needed her and he shook his head. After a beat, she excused herself and made her way through the crowd toward him.

"I'm parched," she said as she slid into the gap he made.

The waiter slid her the iced water Beau had just ordered for her.

"Wow. You're a natural. If you ever wanted to give up playing with cars for a living, being at my beck and call might be a great backup option."

He lifted his glass, clinked it against hers, and they watched one another as they drank. He wondered if he looked as flushed as she did. If his pupils were as large. If she could see the same thoughts in his eyes that he could see in hers.

"Have you picked up any ideas?" she asked. "For when it's your turn?"

"The best man stands beside the...bride, right?"

She laughed, then glared. Then, sighing, looked around, as if she'd not yet had the chance. "This is pretty amazing, don't you think?"

"It really is."

The carriage was packed, a three-piece band played '90s boy band songs in a classical manner at the far end, and everyone rocked in gentle tandem with the movement of the train.

When she looked up at him again, it was like some magnetic force was drawing them both there. Beau felt a *boom-boom-boom* behind his ribs, as if a gong had been struck.

Then something caught her eye across the bar, and she winced. "Sorry, gotta go."

But then, after a beat, she tipped up onto her toes, slid her hand along the back of his neck and kissed him. Hard. When she pulled away, Beau leaned in, chasing her mouth, to kiss her again. Softer this time, a tender promise.

"Marking my place," he said, before she sighed, then disappeared into the crowd.

Only for the *boom-boom-boom* to continue. Like a drumbeat. A harbinger.

No, like a ticking clock.

Hours later, once the wedding guests had retired to their sleeper cars, Ginny—eyes rimmed in watery kohl, lipstick long gone—pulled Charlie into a hard hug.

"You are a professional angel," Ginny said.

"I'm better than that. I'm a professional bestie."

Ginny's eyes widened. "OMG, that's exactly what you are. Whereas your guy, he's a professional sweetheart. My dad loves him. Maybe more than he loves Callum."

"Okay, time for bed."

"I will never forget this. I will never forget you."

Charlie, who was pragmatic enough to know that her part in Ginny's story was a mere heartbeat, peeled Ginny's grip from her arm, and transferred it to her husband's. Callum, for whom this was clearly nothing new, mouthed *thank you*, before guiding his happy teary bride to their wedding suite.

Then with a huge sigh, she turned to Beau who was sitting in a booth, checking his phone. He turned it around to show her a photo of Moose asleep on Mike the electrician's bed.

"I'm going to regret this," he said, "aren't I?"

Charlie, who'd been counting down the minutes since Beau had marked his place, shrugged. "Oh, I don't know. It's been a pretty good night so far."

Beau slowly lowered his phone, before peeling himself out from behind the table. He stood before her, looking like a million dollars in what had to be a custom suit, the way it made the absolute most of every glorious piece of him. This long tall drink of heaven.

The lights dimmed, a sign they were the last ones left. And Charlie yawned, then rocked on her feet in a way that had nothing to do with the train.

Beau laughed softly. "Come on, Sleeping Beauty. Time to get you to bed, before you collapse on the floor."

Then he held out his hand, and when she placed hers there, he entwined his fingers with hers. Then led her out of the bar carriage and down the gently swaying hall past the sleepers till she found their room number.

When she pulled her key from her clutch, Beau was standing danger close. She could sense his breaths, feel his pulse. Her own heart was beating like crazy by the time she managed to open the door to find a big, neat double bed looking back at her.

She slammed the door shut, and turned to block the way.

"Is there a problem?" Beau asked.

"No. Yes. Sorry. I was told I'd been given a twin room, in case it turned out I needed an assistant for such an un- usual job."

"Charlie," Beau said, gently moving her to one side. Then he opened the door. After a beat he said, "That's our luggage against the wall, so I guess this is our room."

He moved inside so she had no choice but to follow.

"There are semi-recliners, halfway down the train," she said. "I've slept in stranger places than that, so I'm more than happy to take one for the team."

Beau turned, the room getting smaller just by him being in it. "Charlie."

She swallowed. "I just don't want you to think that I in- vited you along to…" She glanced at the bed.

"I hadn't thought as much, but the more you point it out, the more of an elephant in the room it seems to become."

"Right." Good point. "So do you want first shower?"

"You look like you're about to fall asleep where you stand, so you go first."

Great. She was vibrating with memories of his kiss, and visions of the bed before her, and in his eyes she looked tired.

She went to give her zip a head start. Reaching with her

right hand, then her left, only to find the tag was tucked in too deep.

When she growled in frustration, Beau asked, "Are you okay?"

"Yep." She tried twisting the neck a little toward the front. No luck there, either. She breathed out, exhaustion creeping up on her fast. "Do you mind?"

Beau looked at her a moment, his nostrils flaring, his eyes dark behind his glasses, before he gave her a short nod.

She turned, and moved her hair out of the way. When Beau's hands touched the back of her neck, she shivered. Enough that he waited a moment, before his fingers found the zipper tag and slid it down, slowly, so that she could feel the warmth of his fingers curling down her spine.

When his fingers hit her lower spine, her dress fell forward. She gathered it at her front, and turned to send him a quick thank-you, only to find him already moving around to the other side of the bed.

He stood facing the window for a long moment, his hands on his hips, his body taut, before he rid himself of his jacket and removed his cufflinks with such spare elegance her heart hurt.

"Ginny wanted me to pass on her thanks for the time you spent with her dad," Charlie said.

Beau stopped, his shoulder turning slightly, but his face remained turned away. "Turns out Ginny's dad is the reason we are here, for he is a train spotter. I now know all there is to know about every train that ever was."

Charlie winced. "You weren't on the clock. You didn't have to do that."

"Did it help you?"

"*Me?* Well, yes actually."

"Then that's *all* there is to know."

Charlie hadn't invited him to come, expecting anything to happen. She'd just wanted to be with him. As often as she could, before their time ran out. Then, the entire day, knowing he was near, she'd felt as if her blood was filled with bubbles.

And now, knowing he'd put himself out for no reason but to make her day easier, knowing how he kissed, how often she felt his eyes on her through the day, she couldn't remember why she was making this so hard.

Before she could think herself around in another circle, she let her dress fall forward, the shimmering fabric landing in a heavy *swish* at her feet. By the way Beau's shoulders tensed, the way he stood rock still, she knew he'd heard.

Then he looked up, his gaze catching hers in the reflection in the train window.

Time seemed to pause, as if teetering between their past and future. A crux on which everything would change. Irrevocably. Forever.

Beau turned, slowly. His jaw was like granite, his eyes crystal bright, as he took her in. Naked bar a fine beige G-string and silver high heels.

"Charlotte," he said, his voice cavernous, and she didn't correct him. For hearing her name, in that voice, it felt like a promise.

He was too far away, all the way over on the other side of the bed. So she knelt on the edge, and crawled her way to him. Which had seemed like a good idea at the time, as she'd not expected the mattress to be so soft.

When she reached him, she lifted onto her knees and instantly toppled forward. Thankfully, he came out of his fog in time to catch her.

He gathered her to him, his arms around her back, while her hands pressed against his chest. She felt the steady beat of his heart. Felt his strength, and his restraint. Breathed in to find he smelled like a woodland grove and some deeply masculine note that made her head go woozy.

"Earlier," he said, his eyes determinedly on hers, rather

than all the naked skin below. "Earlier, when I said that I was marking my place, that was not with any expectation—"

"Do you want to kiss me again, Beau?"

His hands slid up her back, gathering her hair at the nape of her neck. While his body, hard, and ready for her, pressed against her chest. And she wasn't sure he had a clue either thing was happening.

"I do," he said. "I want to kiss you more than I need air."

"Then kiss me," she said.

He didn't need to be asked twice.

With a growl he ducked his head and pressed his mouth to hers. No gentle exploration this time. Where their first kiss had been soft, and sweet, and like fresh honey and starlight, this was pure fire.

His tongue swept into her open mouth as they shared lush open-mouthed kisses. Her hands were in his hair, his arms hauling her close. Bodies pressed together, as if they could not get close enough.

Then he let her fall back a little, enough that she gasped, as he slid an arm behind her knees, then lifted her into his arms. It was a hell of a move. Made even more impressive when he turned and lowered her to the bed, before lowering himself over her.

She grabbed him by the back of the head and kissed him. And kissed him. And kissed him.

Until she was no longer inside her own body. She was a kiss. She was roving hands and delicate sighs and limbs curled over limbs. She was rising heat, and liquid pleasure.

Then he shifted, his thigh pressing between hers, and she broke the kiss to gasp. Sucking in breath, her eyes shut tight as she bore down into the sensation. Her blood was so high, her nerves so wrought, she felt like she could come at any moment.

As if he knew it, as if he could read her every breath,

every gasp, the way she tugged at his hair, and writhed beneath him, Beau pulled back. An inch, enough. And her eyes
fluttered open.

No, come back, she thought, and shifted down the bed,
reaching for his backside, still clad in suit pants. How was
he still dressed when she was all skin and heat?

He laughed, then moaned as he pinned her to the spot.
When she growled at him, he silenced her with a kiss. A
kiss so sweet, and deft, and perfect she melted into the bed.

"There's no rush."

But there was. She could feel it. Time slipping away. His
house, Anushka's wedding, her freedom.

"Speak for yourself," she said. Taking his moment of distraction to let her knees fall out to the sides. He sank against
her, a hiss leaving his mouth, as he nestled into the cradle
she'd created, a perfect fit.

He lifted a hand then, and brushed her hair from her face.
And the way he looked at her, she wasn't sure she'd ever felt
so seen. Or so exposed.

She lifted up to chase his kiss but he pulled back.

"Charlotte," he said, his voice rough. Ragged. Then, on a
whisper, "Charlie."

And she squeezed her eyes shut tight. And let her head
drop to the bed.

He lifted over her then, the muscles in his arms bunching
beneath his shirt, then he nudged the tip of his nose against
hers. She nudged back, all but purring as their faces bussed
one another, in dreamy gentle strokes.

He took off his glasses, and placed them on the small table
beside the bed. His lashes were imposingly long and beautifully tangled, his eyes the colour of a drift of autumn leaves.

"Were you always this gorgeous?" she asked.

He smiled at her, said, "Nah," then began to move down
the bed.

He rained kisses over her jaw, down her neck, across her décolletage, before swirling his broad tongue around her right nipple, then her left. Moving on before she was ready. Keeping her hovering on the edge of the best kind of agony.

When he settled in, moving a hand over one breast while feasting on the other, for long lush minutes, her hands went to his shoulders, squeezing, frantic.

When he nipped his way down her side, before scraping his teeth over her hip bone, her hands moved to his hair, gripping, tugging, directing. She felt him smile against her belly, then he slid down her neck, between her breasts, over her navel before hooking it into her G-string and not even pausing before he dragged it down, down, down.

His arm was long enough to rid her of the thing, without having to move from where he was, his breath washing over her centre, a warm rush that had her trembling, writhing, wanting his touch. His tongue. Wanting him.

In her half-conscious state, she felt him move to the end of the bed, his knees gently hitting the floor.

She looked down her body, to find his gaze taking her in, a mix of wonder and hunger on his face, before his eyes lifted to hers. Dark as midnight and glinting with desire. Keeping her gaze, he lowered his mouth and breathed against her, a cool stream of air, before laying the gentlest of kisses at her centre.

She sobbed. Then bit her lip against her sound.

Then he slid his hands beneath her backside, and lifted her to his mouth and for the next several minutes, or eternities, she could not have said which, Beau Griffin marked his place and then some.

Sunlight glowed a weak watery gold, as it rose outside their train window. The sound of the carriage, a gently *clackety-clack*, matched the subtle sway of the bed.

Charlie, her head on Beau's chest, her thoughts running a mile a minute, tried to match his sleeping breaths, but they were too deep, too strong, and she had to suck in a deep breath so as not to faint.

"What is in your hair?" he asked, his voice rumbling beneath her cheek.

She lifted her head, her breath catching at the sight of him—dark hair rumpled, stubble a dark shade across his jaw. "Did I wake you?"

She'd been awake for some time. Partly because she knew she'd have to be up soonish, to get ready for the post-wedding breakfast. And partly because her mind was a tumble.

For she'd slept with Beau Griffin. Knowing how important it was to get through the next few weeks with zero drama. Though the sleeping part had been the least of it. And the non-sleeping parts might well add up to the very best, most glorious, night of her entire life.

When Beau ran a hand over her hair again, then looked at his hand, she said, "Gel, hairspray, glitter. I would have washed it last night but my roommate had other plans."

His gaze moved from his hand to her face. And he breathed out and said, "Hey."

"Hey."

"Sleep okay?"

"Hardly at all."

Laughing gently, he stretched, his chest lifting her, the muscles in his arms bunching in a way that had saliva pooling beneath her tongue.

And despite her jokey tone, she felt a wave of fragility wash over her. For Beau Griffin in the morning, glasses free, after only a few hours' sleep, looked the way a guy in an ad for some expensive hotel might look. Whereas, by the way his gaze kept going back to her hair, she must have looked as if she'd slept in a cave.

She made to roll out of bed, but Beau curled his arm around her and brought her back to his chest.

"Stay," he said.

"I can't. I have to go to breakfast soon."

"Stay," he said again, and for a minute she thought he meant stay, as in don't move out of the house next door to my house so we can play neighbours, with benefits, forever.

But then his hand dropped to her back, his broad palm running down her spine, shifting the sheet that had pooled over her backside, so he could trace a finger over the curve of her cheeks. She blushed, knowing *stay* meant go another round.

"Is this really okay?" she asked.

He lifted his eyebrows.

"Us. Here. This."

He seemed to truly consider her question for a moment, which had always been one of her favourite things about him, before saying, "I reckon it's better than okay."

"Okay, good, I was just checking." Then, for good measure, because she'd never been able to hold her tongue, she added, "We don't have to put a label on what happened. We can chalk it up to circumstance. All that romance in the air. One bed. It was bound to rub off."

Beau stopped caressing her and instead put his arm behind his head. Then he lifted his spare hand and crooked a finger.

Charlie, heart racing now, crawled a little higher up his body, the light smattering of dark hair covering the hard planes of his chest scraping against her over-sensitised skin. Once her face was level with his, he took her chin between his fingers and looked deep into her eyes.

"You know I had a crush on you, right? In senior."

Her eyes bugged. She felt it happen. "You did not."

"That final year of school, watching you make new friends, thinking constantly about that damn game of spin the bottle, kicking myself for not picking it up and placing it down so it faced only you—I was the poster boy for teen torture."

Charlie blinked at him, for none of that tracked with her experience. For one thing, she'd been the one with the crush. She'd thought he must have picked up on it, too, and that was the reason why he'd pulled away. He was too kind to tell her it was one-sided. And then…

"What game of spin the bottle?"

Beau gave her a look. "Are you kidding me right now?"

She shook her head, wracking her brain, but nothing came.

It had been a rough summer. Things with her dad had been escalating, taking on the job at the record store a final straw in his eyes. Empirical evidence that she'd amount to nothing. She'd cut her hair, pierced her nose, started wearing eyeliner and torn tights to school. And begun drinking.

When the drinking had led to true forgetting, not just the dyslexic kind, she'd given it up. Had this game happened during that time?

She shook her head, realising she was focused on the wrong thing.

Beau had *had a crush on her*. He'd told her so in a way that intimated that this wasn't just some hook up for him. But it had to be a hook up. It couldn't be anything more. For that would carve focus away from all that she was trying to achieve, for herself, on her own terms.

And yet here she was, in bed with Beau. Since it would take more willpower than she had to promise herself it wouldn't happen again, she needed to set the tone. Whatever happened from here, things had to remain as they had been between them before last night.

Before the kiss under the stars.

Before she'd kissed him on the cheek, swooning like a woman to whom this was all so much more than a hook up could ever be.

Argh!

"Look," she said, curling as his fingers began their exploration again, "last night was fun. But I really do have to get up. Breakfast is in an hour. After which the bride and groom will be dropped off, while the rest of us stay on the train as it turns around and takes us back home. You're most welcome to join us. Or find a quiet spot to… FaceTime Moose. Whatever takes your fancy."

She avoided his eyes, certain he'd feel let down by her manic backtracking. While he was being brave, and sweet, and open. A big deal for a guy going through all that he was going through.

None of which changed anything for her.

She quickly slipped out from under his arm, and didn't bother to cover up as she padded across the room and ducked into the en suite, for the night before he'd seen it all. Kissed it all. Hell, the man had licked her up and down and sideways.

In the bathroom, she leaned against the door, closed her eyes for a few moments, and re-recalibrated. Wondering how many more times she'd have to do so before their job was done.

Knowing what the answer had to be—as many as it took.

CHAPTER NINE

"So, we're two weeks out from the big day." Charlie caught the eye of a passing waiter and motioned for a bottle of water and two glasses, then mouthed her thanks.

"I know!" said Anushka, bouncing on the seat in the café.

Charlie's leg was bouncing, too, as she wanted to get home and get cleaning.

After leaving Beau in their sleeper car, she'd become a woman on a mission. Her goal, to use the train ride back to tap the wedding guests for any DIY home fixer-upper tips, so that when she got home, she could hit the ground running while she was still here. Turned out cleaning the place out before stripping the wallpaper got the most votes.

Her new goal was to spend every spare minute doing just that. Then, when she was ready to leave, she could do so knowing she'd left the house in a better place than how she'd found it.

If it meant avoiding Beau all day, avoiding what would no doubt be a look of disappointment on his face that she wanted to keep things cool, win-win.

The drive home from the station in his sexy rocket car had been quiet. As if once they'd stated their positions, neither had more to say on the issue.

When he'd pulled up outside her front veranda, angling the car light so she could see her way safely to the door, she'd held her overnight bag to her chest, readied herself to uncurl herself from the car, thank him for his help, then bolt inside.

Super mature, but effective to her cause.

Instead, when she'd alighted the car, he'd reached for her hand and swung her against the car. His hand delving gently into her hair. His jaw working, his eyes dark, and fierce. As if he'd managed to give her the space she wanted all day, but had hit his limit.

She could have slipped away, and he'd not have stopped her.

But no. Heart racing, lady parts rejoicing, ramparts crumbling at their first test, she'd dumped her bag at her feet, lifted to her toes, pulled Beau's head to hers, and kissed the man for all she was worth.

So much for keeping things cool. Her lips had been swollen, stubble rash covering her cheeks, for a good day.

"And how's it all going?" Charlie asked Anushka after gulping down her glass of water.

"Great. So, so great. I can't even with the greatness!"

Charlie cocked her head. "You do realise that I'm the one person you don't have to pretend for."

Anushka drew in a small breath, then let rip. About a swan situation. About her mother, a woman of humble means, having a breakdown at not being able to contribute. About a pimple that wouldn't go away. About Bobby's decision to change the groomsmen's outfits after seeing Beau in a suit. Anushka winced at the last. "Is that me complaining about you?"

"It's my job to fix any annoyances. Shall I have a word with Beau?" Beau. Saying his name, even *thinking* his name, had her remembering his touch, his reverence, his skill.

"Oh, no!" said Anushka. "It's the first request Bobby has made regarding the whole thing. In fact, having Beau around has him completely engaged. I think he has a little crush."

Get in line, Charlie thought.

"Can I make a suggestion, regarding your mother?"

Anushka nodded. "Please."

"Let's find some way she *can* contribute. Giving a speech at the rehearsal dinner. Or ask her if she has a favourite song to play at the reception."

Anushka beamed. "Good gods you're good at this."

"That's why they pay me the big bucks."

Anushka laughed. Then slumped. "It's stressful being *the bride*," she said air quotation marks in play. "Right?"

Charlie smiled.

"Have you ever…? Or *are* you? Married? I assumed you and Beau were a thing, but… No? Yes? Wow, I can't believe I don't know this about you."

"No," Charlie assured her. Then, "Always the bridesmaid, remember?"

And while she knew that while the nature of the relationship between bride and professional bestie had a hastened sense of intimacy, and that one day she would be a mere heartbeat in Anushka's story, too, she found herself saying, "Though someone did offer once."

"Do tell!"

"Well, okay. I was living, working, overseas, and didn't know *anyone*. Then I met Richard…" She swallowed. "He was outgoing, had a lot of friends, and made it clear he adored me. He was also kind of hapless, you know? Had this—what I thought was charming—air of…needing looking after."

"Which is what you did," Anushka said, her voice gentle and kind.

"Big-time."

Standing up for those who couldn't, or just shouldn't have to, stand up for themselves was the one special skill her father had gifted her. One that made her feel good about herself, no matter what was going on in her life.

"By the time I realised how unbalanced the thing was he

must have sensed my restlessness. And proposed. In the end it was that, the thought of taking care of someone who refused to do the same for me, forever, made me feel…exhausted. And sad, you know?"

"Mmm. How did he take it?"

"He traded up."

Made sure his wedding reception took place in the building in which I worked, and called me just about the worst thing you can call a woman.

Anushka sat back. "Oh, that all makes so much sense now."

"What does?"

"Well, #cakegate, of course."

Hearing that term coming from Anushka's smiling mouth, Charlie flinched so hard her brain knocked against the inside of her skull.

"Oh, gosh," said Anushka leaning forward, her expression concerned. "You've gone terribly pale. Are you okay? Oh, no, it's because I mentioned #cakegate?"

Heat crept up the back of Charlie's neck, and into her cheeks. She bit her lip in order to stop herself from asking Anushka to stop speaking.

But if Anushka knew… What was this? Some long game? A public hazing? Was she about to lose the best working opportunity she'd ever been gifted?

"I don't understand," said Charlie, in a stage whisper. "If you know about…that, then why am I here?"

Anushka had the good grace to look sheepish.

"I was hiding out in California a couple of years ago, after the whole '*Twilight* breakup' nonsense went viral. Which was absolute rubbish, by the way. I mean I loooooove *Twilight*, but any man of mine can read whatever the heck floats his boat, as can I. I was there when #cakegate went down, found myself caught up in it like anyone, then realised I was feeding the machine that had stalked me."

"Then, when Martine told me all about this amazing woman who had made her wedding an absolute dream, your name rang a bell. And when I put two and two together, it felt meant to be. The two of us, rising from the ashes together."

Charlie sat forward, her forehead in her hands as she tried to recapture her breath.

"Oh, no. Oh, Charlie. I'm so sorry. I had no clue this would be such a big thing. It seemed gauche to bring it up when we didn't know one another. But now we're such friends. Aren't we?"

"Anushka, if anyone else knows—"

"They don't!" she said, crossing her heart. "At least not by my telling. I promise. Though second chances should be far easier to come by in my opinion. Falling down is easy. Picking yourself up, and dusting yourself off, and trying again, that's the real story here. But I get that it's not mine to tell."

Charlie finally looked into Anushka's sincere eyes. She *knew*. She knew about Charlie's screwup, and had hired her anyway. No, hired her *because* of it.

Charlie pushed her chair back, walked around the table, and bent down to give Anushka a huge hug.

"Friends?" Anushka asked, her voice hoarse against Charlie's ear.

"If you like it or not."

When Charlie sat back down, Anushka said, "Shall I order us each a glass of bubbly? I feel like after that we deserve one."

"Sure," said Charlie, laughing, mentally putting off painting the hall till tomorrow. "That'd be great."

Once the bubbly was ordered, Anushka sat forward. "Now, back to your Beau. He really is such a good guy. Please tell me you're not merely two beautiful old friends who sparkle every time you look at one another. Please tell me you're secretly hot and heavy."

Charlie laughed, even as images of Beau, hot and heavy, slipped into her mind again. For despite her attestation what had happened was due to one bed, and romance in the air, it simply wasn't true.

She'd wanted him. She'd craved him. Her high school crush nothing on the feelings she harboured for him now.

"And remember," Anushka said, her smile mischievous. "Now that we are such good friends, I'm the one person you don't have to pretend with."

Thankfully the bubbly arrived, giving Charlie a moment to collect herself. She lifted her glass in a toast. "To good guys."

Anushka lifted her glass. "To the women who deserve them."

Glasses clinked, the women both drank well.

Then Anushka said, "When the two of you get hitched, I will be matron of honour. It's only fair."

When Charlie choked on the bubbles, Anushka nearly fell off the chair laughing.

The next afternoon Beau met with Mike the electrician and Rob the master carpenter, who'd kindly come back to add a few extra outlets, and design the wall-to-ceiling bookshelves he'd imagined for what would now be a home office in the big back room at the house.

Leaving them to chat, he moved out onto the jutting concrete balcony, taking care, as while the "precarious lumber" had been removed, the railing was yet to be installed.

There, he glanced across to Charlie's place, hoping for another glimpse of her grappling with her back garden or tossing what looked like papers, and old clothes, into the skip that had appeared there the day after they'd returned from the train trip.

The train trip that was like a burr under his skin. A fever that would not abate. Nor would the desire to go to her, to force her to look him in the eye and tell him again it was nothing but "romance in the air" that had her letting her dress fall to the floor before crawling across that bed, to him.

Then, as if he'd willed her into view, she was there, dragging an old wooden ladder before wrangling it into place against the side of her house. She gave it a wriggle with her garden-gloved hands, then, satisfied, climbed the rickety contraption in old yellow gum boots that might as well have been clown shoes for all the grip they had.

All while wearing the hard hat he'd given her.

He laughed at the sight, while his chest felt as if it had caved in on itself, just a little, as if his heart had squeezed itself into a ball.

All of which quickly morphed into a squeeze of sudden pain when the ladder wobbled. He watched, helpless, as Charlie gripped the gutter with her forearm, one foot swinging off the ladder, before it settled again.

Then, after adjusting her hard hat, she started blithely pulling clumps of leaves from the gutter, as if nothing had happened.

It was enough to get Beau's feet moving, back inside, down the freshly sanded internal stairs, out the sliding glass doors of the granny flat, and across his yard. He was jogging by the time he reached the roses.

The urge to call her name as he closed in, to insist she get the hell down from there, built in his throat like a roar, but he knew that could be the thing that sent her tumbling. Then he whipped off his own hard hat, letting it drop to the ground, before reaching the ladder and holding on, his palms sweating, his head spinning with all the things that could have gone wrong.

Charlie, clearly feeling the sudden lack of wobbles, looked down, saw him, and smiled. Pure sunshine. It was nearly enough to clear out the chill that had settled in his bones.

Then the smile quickly turned into a frown. "What are you doing?"

"The sane thing; keeping this death trap steady so you can do whatever it is you decided had to be done."

She opened her palm, showed him the clump of dank rotting leaves she'd pulled from the gutter, then let it go, wet mush raining down on his head.

"Nice," he said. "Real mature."

"Mature is highly overrated."

Beau's chin lifted, and his eyes found hers, remembering that was a thing she used to say. Right around the time he'd started liking her in a whole new way. When the other kids at school had started pairing off, swearing, smoking, getting into trouble, and the two of them were still in their safe little bubble.

Only now, watching the pink rise in her cheeks, the way she swallowed, hard, Beau wondered if in fact he'd *not* been alone in feeling their friendship shift and change.

Then Charlie broke the spell, rolling her eyes. "Are you really going to stand there while I do this?"

"Yes, Charlie, I'm really going to stand here, and keep this ladder steady, while you clean your gutters."

Her voice was steady, and a little quiet, as she said, "You're not the boss of me."

His smile was irresistible. His own voice low as he said, "Sometimes it feels like someone should be."

Her eyes flashed. "And you think that is you? Why? Just because we slept together?"

And there it was. The real argument that had them both so heated up. Beau smiled up at her, sweet as pie, as he said, "I'd never dream as much."

She paused then, as if she'd built some narrative inside her head, and he'd gone rogue. But Beau was not having this conversation while she was half hanging off the side of a ladder that looked to be held together with trusted nails and mildew.

"As you are well aware, *Charlotte*, I have nowhere else to be. I can stand here all day. So, we can argue, or you can do what you set out to do."

Her eyes narrowed at him, before she turned back to the house and did her thing.

After a few more minutes, when she'd cleaned all she could clean without moving the ladder along, Charlie made her way down the rungs. Her backside, encased in cut-off shorts, frayed cotton dangling against her thighs, swished back and forth as she did so. Deliberately? He'd put money on it.

When she reached the bottom rung, she turned, not willing to give up the high ground. "What did you imagine was going to happen, when you came over here in such high heat?"

"Do you really want to know?" he asked, slowly releasing the ladder to find his fingers stiff.

She shook her head, as if hearing it she'd have to accept that he was out there in the world, caring about what became of her. When, from the bits she'd shared along the way, was something she'd not felt all that much.

He understood her reticence. That pressure that came from meaning something to someone, or vice versa. Add their history, how important they had been to one another's very survival once upon a time, and this tension that had been brewing between them didn't run on a singular dimension.

But neither did it have to be as complicated as she seemed determined to make it.

"We had sex."

Charlie blinked, her mouth dropping open ever so slightly, making it appear entirely kissable.

"Not just sex," he added, his voice rough. "Great sex. And I believe I made it clear that if you were amenable, I'd be open to having more great sex with you in the future."

Her throat worked, the pink blotching her cheeks had little to do with exertion. And she said, "You're not meant to talk that way."

"Says who?" he asked, laughter taking the edge off the tension riding him even now.

Her arms flung out to the sides. "I don't know. Past me?"

"I think it's time we put past Charlotte and past Beau firmly where they belong."

"In the past," she said on a sigh.

"As for present Beau and Charlie. Can we agree that what happened had nothing to do with *romance in the air* and everything to do with the fact that I am 'bonkers level' attracted to you. And if the way things unfolded is any evidence, you feel the same way about me."

Far too many emotions than he could count raced over her face—but he did catch stubbornness, desire, relief, and apprehension.

Then she lifted a finger, pointed it at him, and said, "So long as you can assure me you're not imagining anything that might go beyond the next few weeks. Because I am leaving. As soon as the house is tidied up, and my finances are squared away. I don't have the bandwidth to take on something that might…turn messy when it's all said and done."

Beau shook his head, even while he knew that for him it was too late to think in such terms. For Charlie had a habit of sweeping him into the whirlwind of her life and when she let go, the landing was never much fun.

It would hurt when they parted. Just as it had hurt when they'd parted last time. But he'd survive it. He always did.

"Would you like to hear what I'm imagining?"

She lifted a shoulder. "Why not?"

He moved in again, this time bracing his hands on either side of her shoulders. "I'm imagining kissing you, as often, and in as many places, as you will allow. But for that to happen, I need a little reassurance that you won't put yourself in danger, unnecessarily. Because nothing messes with my libido more than imagining you breaking your sweet neck."

Something he'd found himself doing since they'd come back home. Any time he heard a crash next door, or heard her car engine roar before she shot off down the road. The thought of her, hurt, caught like a burr in his fur. Not painful as such, but there, tugging when he moved wrong.

Charlie's eyes widened, then softened, as it occurred to her why his head was so ready to go there. Milly's spectre seemed to hover between them a moment before fading away.

"I'm wearing your hard hat," she said.

Beau lifted a hand and moved it so it sat a little farther back on her head. "If a bird flies over and drops something on it, then you'll be glad you did."

She looked down at her hands in their oversized gloves, then at her gum boots too big for her feet, the splintered ladder rung on which she stood. And her shoulders slumped.

Then she lifted her eyes to his and said, "Anushka knows. About #cakegate. She's okay with it, she says, and that she'd not told anyone. And yet..."

Beau let out a hard breath, as the implications sank in. "That's why you needed to clean your own gutters using a rusty ladder."

"Seemed as good a way to shake off the terror that I'm this close to getting what I want and it still all might be taken away."

He reached for her and she leaned in, wrapping her arms about his neck. He lifted her off the ladder and carried her to safety before he set her down. She looked up at him, this wild, beautiful, stubborn, mess of a human.

While he knew his level of concern was excessive, to him it was a real thing. And while she wasn't exactly cliff diving, or playing Russian roulette, her presence made him feel a level of low-key tumult he could not deny.

Now, when he was finally coming out the other end of months of such inner turmoil. Now, when he was sure he never wanted to feel that way again.

"Beau?"

Beau glanced over his shoulder to see the back of Mike's hard hat on the other side of the roses.

"Coming," he called. Then, to Charlie, "I have to go. Can I see you soon? Or do you have to replumb the house?"

"I do not."

"No? No roofing that you're desperate to get on top of?"

"Not today," she said with a sweet smile. "I will finish the gutter, and I will take care doing so. And when I'm done, I'm going to have a long hot shower, and wash off this grime." Then, "Care to join me?"

With a growl in his throat, one for himself as much as for her, Beau leaned down, bending Charlie back so that she had to hold on tight. Then he kissed her throat, the bare skin just below, before lifting her up just enough to find her mouth.

All of it, any lingering concern, the fact that she was fixing to leave, right when he was putting in measures that gave him an option to stay, dissolved in the heat of that kiss.

When he pushed his way back through the rose bushes a minute later, he looked back to see her lining up the ladder, this time her bare feet gripped the ladder, the gardening gloves were tucked into the back of her shorts till she had purchase.

The peach-coloured hard hat remained.

Beau, watching the leaves rustle in the forest in the valley beyond, looked up when Charlie's back door squeaked.

She stood on the landing and stretched her arms overhead.

Then she slipped her shirt over her head, dropped it at her feet and went inside. A second later her back light switched on.

Beau laughed out loud.

Then called, "Nearly done?" to Mike, who was finishing packing up.

"Yep. Anything else you need, or if Moose needs a baby-sitter, give me a buzz."

Beau shook his hand, then ushered the man out the front door as fast as was humanly possible.

A minute later, as he jogged up Charlie's the back steps, he looked to that weak single light, doing little to light up her big open backyard.

He brought out his phone, and sent Mike a quick message. All the while knowing he wasn't about to win any favours. But if it meant he slept better that night, and all the nights after, he was willing to take the hit.

He picked up the shirt Charlie had dropped, and followed the trail—bra, shorts, gardening gloves—then followed the sounds of running water till he found what must have been Charlie's bedroom. Faded green quilt with pink stitching crumpled on the bed, a pair of mismatched pillows. Clothes draped over a single lounge seat in one corner.

Steam pouring from an open en suite door.

Then a hand appeared, holding the peach hard hat, before she tossed it to the bed, her hand trailing becomingly back into the bathroom.

Beau stripped faster than any man in the history of strip-ping, and strutted into the bathroom so fast she screamed. Then laughed, raucously, as he hauled her into the shower.

And there the laughter stopped. Making way for sighs, and gasps. The slide of slippery hands and slow wet kisses. Losing themselves in one another. Till the water turned cold.

After drying off, they'd wrapped themselves in blankets and padded out to the kitchen to eat the best leftover pasta of

Beau's life. Then dug into a chocolate torte she'd whipped up that morning, devouring it with a pair of mismatched spoons, while telling stories of heartbreaks and bad dates, embarrassing gaffes and moments that made them feel proud.

Then she walked him to the front door, hand in hand, before he'd turned her to the wall, one hand braced beside her head, his thumb stroking her neck as he kissed her. His other hand peeling the blanket apart, leaving just enough room to slide his hand between her legs. The sweep of his tongue in her mouth mirroring the slide of his fingers, till she gasped against his kiss, and shuddered under his touch.

With one last kiss to her forehead, he left, heading back to his rental and his goofball of a dog.

Wondering how the hell he was going to get over her a second time.

CHAPTER TEN

"Is this necessary?" Beau asked, more to himself than the dance studio at large.

"Mate," said Bobby, bouncing from foot to foot, rolling out his neck, as if he was about to engage in a little light cage fighting rather than a dance lesson. "If I have to be here, then as my best man, so do you. That's the deal."

Beau was fairly sure the deal had more to do with being on the outer with Charlie, yet again.

For when, the night after their "shower," she'd discovered Beau had had Mike fix her back porch lights, the things now illuminating her backyard so it looked like daylight, she'd called, and not to say thank you.

"Seriously?" she'd said by way of hello.

Beau, who was taking a dog behaviour lesson he'd organised through the local vet, said, "I think the term you're looking for is thank you."

He mouthed sorry to the instructor, who rolled her eyes as if it was clear why Moose was unmanageable.

"For what?" she shot back. "Thinking me incapable?"

"Of being an electrician without a license, hell yes."

A pause, but only so she could rev herself up again. "Did you not hear me tell you that the men I've known haven't been all that interested in my advice, or opinions. Or...what was the other...skill sets!"

"I am interested in all those parts of you, as well as many

other parts. I can even name them if you'd like. Starting with the freckle next to your left—"

"Beau," Charlie had growled.

While the dog behaviour instructor's eyes went a little wide at that one.

Beau took a few long strides away. "Charlie, I know that you are highly capable. I also know you well enough to know that despite your opinion being wrong on this one, you were stubborn enough to try."

And the thought of that happening, when he wasn't there…

Another long beat slunk by before she said, "I just… I spent the past year and a half hearing my father's voice following me through the house, telling me I was kidding myself thinking I could start again. Then, a while ago, it stopped and I'd gotten used to imagining doing all these things to the house, even though I'll likely get around to like three percent of them."

Beau held a hand to his forehead. "I understand. I won't do it again. But I can't promise not to come at you with slides, and graphs, and pie charts if I know I'm right."

At that she'd laughed, before ringing off, and his relief had been immense.

That had been three days ago. And what with work pouring into his inbox, work he was finding himself looking forward to again, time felt as if it was speeding up with the wedding ten days away, and his house all but done.

"Clap-clap," called the instructor, clapping her hands at the same time. Dust motes swirled in the streams of sunlight pouring through the old arched windows of the dance studio.

Then she looked to the two men—Beau, at six foot four, towering over both her and Bobby—and narrowed her eyes, as if she was up for the challenge.

Bobby leaned toward Beau. "You thinking what I'm thinking?"

"That she's wondering if I can lift you over my head?"

"Exactly."

Then—

"Sorry we're late!"

Beau and Bobby breathed out in unified relief, and turned as Anushka burst into the studio wearing a bright pink leotard, fluorescent yellow tights and blue leg warmers. She dumped a huge tie-dyed duffel bag on a bench by the door, jogged over to Bobby, and leaped into his arms for a kiss.

That all happened out of the corner of Beau's eye as his gaze remained trained on the bench, where Charlie sat, shucking off her shoes and frowning at her phone.

After a few moments she placed the phone face down, took a moment to collect herself, then pressed herself from the bench and walked their way.

Beau could hear Anushka chattering about how they'd gotten lost, then stopped for a drive-through milkshake because she was so dehydrated, but it was all background noise.

For all he could see was Charlie. Her hair pulled back in a loose bun. A cropped black tank top, a long black skirt that sat low on her hips and swished around her ankles as she walked. She looked beautiful, and fragile. And tired.

He swallowed against a lump in his throat as it occurred to him that even if he was able to hold her ladder for her now, fix all her broken lightbulbs, there would always be more. And he'd not be around to see them.

"Hey, stranger," he said as she walked up beside him, avoiding his eyes.

"Enough chatter!" the instructor called.

Anushka jumped, leaping into the space beside Bobby, who grabbed her hand, kissed it, tucked it into the crook of his arm. While Beau and Charlie might as well have been on opposite sides of the room.

The instructor, Mariana, positioned the couples into a correct dance hold. Lifting hands and placing them where they ought to go. Squaring shoulders, tipping chins high. Moving feet into position with a sharp kick of a dance shoe against the instep.

She hummed happily at Anushka and Bobby, then tsked at Charlie and Beau, before pushing their torsos closer together.

"Music!" said Mariana, before she tapped over to an ancient boom box and a song broke out. Some sultry French number, all snare drums and hazy trumpets. "Now we dance!"

"What do you reckon?" Beau crooned as he pulled Charlie a smidge closer. "Do we go with the 'Macarena'?"

Bobby snickered, and Anushka shushed him. While Charlie's gaze finally flickered to Beau.

"Oh, hi, look who showed up."

She narrowed her eyes at him, then looked away. Beau pressed a gentle finger under her chin and moved her head back to face him. When her eyes found his again, he nodded. *There.*

"Move. Feet. Glide!" Mariana called.

Eyes on one another, Beau swayed with the music, unsurprised to find Charlie fought him the whole way.

"Why exactly are we here?" he asked, when no more instructions came their way.

"Moral support?" Charlie said.

Beau looked to Anushka and Bobby who were watching them with big smiles on their faces, before quickly looking away.

"They're matchmaking," Charlie chided.

"It would seem so. Should we tell them we're doing okay without them? For proof, I can tell them about the freckle on your left—"

Charlie smacked him on the chest, then left her hand there.

Beau took his chance to pull her closer. "Is it the light thing?"

"Is what the light thing?"

"The fact I've not seen you in three days."

"I've been busy."

Beau swung her in a circle. Whooping, in surprise, she gripped his shoulders, before looking to him with wide eyes when he went back to swaying.

When he said nothing else, she filled the silence with, "It's kind of the light thing. But not in the way you think."

Beau swept them a little farther away from the wedding couple, who were showing Mariana a move they wanted to incorporate into their wedding dance routine. And again, left silence for Charlie to fill.

"I was upset. But I also knew your intention was never to best me, the way my dad always had. Meaning my righteous indignation lasted about thirty seconds before I saw your actual intention. Which was looking out for me."

She looked to him then, her soft mossy green eyes bright with vulnerability, as she said, "Yes?"

"Yes."

She blinked several times in quick succession. "I've never had anyone be that person for me before. I can't get used to it, Beau. It's just… I can't." Her intimation being that she'd miss it, miss him, when this was all said and done. "But you won't stop, will you?"

"Won't stop, can't stop," he admitted.

And she gave him a look that seemed to say, *Watch out, Beau Griffin, you know not what you want.* And while he'd thought exactly the same thing not all that long ago, now he wasn't so sure.

"It seems we are at an impasse," said Beau as he pulled her against him. With a sigh she leaned her head against his chest. He wondered if she could feel it, the thunder and lightning crashing inside him.

In the recent past that level of feeling usually heralded a

bout of high anxiety, but this felt less like existential dread, and more like…life. The flint of snapping nerves, the chemistry of warming skin. Part and parcel of being around Charlie.

The music stopped, mid-song. Beau felt Charlie flinch against him. He took his time slowing the sway, wanting this moment, her body molten against his, to a last a little longer. Forever if possible.

"That was brilliant!" Anushka called out from the other end of the room. "Did you guys work out any moves? We came up with a couple of bangers. We may yet look like newborn giraffes, but it'll be a blast."

Mariana looked unimpressed, as she stood by her boom box, wiping down her hands with a wet wipe.

"We have to go," said Anushka. "Couples massage time. Wanna join?"

Charlie looked to Beau, and lifted an insouciant shoulder. *Yes?* she mouthed.

Beau, eyes wide, shook his head infinitesimally. *Noooooo.*

Charlie laughed, then quickly wiped a finger under one eye, as she said, "Not for us."

"Okay. See you later!" Anushka tucked her arm into Bobby's, and they were gone.

Beau and Charlie made their way over to the bench where Charlie shucked her thongs back onto her feet.

"What next?" Beau asked.

And Charlie looked into his eyes. It was a big question. Go forward, step backward, either way knowing there was an end point coming.

"Coffee?" she asked, deliberately misunderstanding.

Which was fine with him.

He reached out an arm, offering refuge, and with a small smile, she stepped in. He wrapped her tight, laying a kiss to the top of her head. The scent of her—warm, delicate, a hint of heat—was like a balm. It soothed weary limbs. Mended broken hearts. Lit up broken souls.

He also felt the end rushing at him now. Only this time, since he saw it coming, he could prepare. Well in advance.

"Time to go!" Mariana called, and they both flinched. "Next students due soon."

"Yep!" said Charlie, putting her arms around his waist, and tucked in tight to one another, as both were soaking up every moment they had left, they ambled out of the dance studio together.

It was the week before the wedding and with Beau on-site keeping the builders honest, his house had come together more quickly than expected. It was, for all intents and purposes, habitable.

Which was great, as Charlie could stickybeak without need for gum boots or hard hat. Though considering the things she'd done with Beau while wearing that hat, it would have a very special place in her heart forever more.

Then, right as she started thinking that maybe, just maybe, it would all go as smoothly as could be, Beau announced Matt and his kids—Milly's kids—were coming to visit.

Anushka, having found out about the completed house, and Beau's friend's imminent arrival, had insisted they have their final wedding war meeting double up as a housewarming, and convinced Beau to give her a budget to "spiff the place up."

Which she did. With panache. In three days the place was decked out with art on the walls, the kitchens and bathrooms fully fitted out, lux couches and solid tables, and beautiful natural decor in every room, until it was as far from a weapons facility as a space could be.

While Beau drove to the airport to pick up the guests of honour who, he assured her, *were excited to see for themselves what I love about the place*, Charlie sat on his balcony, spiralling. Even more than she had with "the light" thing. Or the "sleeping together" thing.

For while she might be dyslexic as heck, she could read between the lines just fine. If Matt was as smart as a business partner of Beau's must be, he was coming to bring his boy back home.

It was laughable really. There she'd been, imagining the day she had the house ready, money in the bank, standing by her front gate, a hand to Beau's stricken face as she told him it had been lovely, before she hopped into a taxi and was swept away.

Romantic—and karmic—as she made it sound, she wasn't delusional. They had become so close, so fast, she was so used to having him near, that it would be fraught as all hell. She may have retired to the shower to ugly cry over it more than once.

But what had *not* occurred to her—as Beau had forged a connection to his new house, the town, the locals who had fallen for him here—was that he might be the one to leave her. Again.

While Beau drove to the Sunshine Coast Airport, to pick up the guests of honour, Charlie curled up in a big outdoor chair on his upstairs deck, making her way through her second glass of bubbly. While Phyllida and Jazmin, Anushka's bridesmaids, ran about in circles, stressing and generally getting in the way, Anushka was a seasoned general, ordering Bobby's groomsmen to hang the chunky outdoor string lights just so.

And then there were voices from front of the house.

Beau was back.

Charlie quickly uncurled herself from her chair, and stood, not quite sure where to put her hands. For they were shaking; nerves, panic that she might do something, say something, that would force events that hurt her in the end. It wouldn't be the first time.

Then Beau was there, accepting cheek kisses and shaking hands, as he led his friend through his beautiful home, with its wide hall, high ceilings, and bright clean lines, its warm wood and vintage accents. A wave of feeling came over her—a mix of nostalgia with some glimpse of the future, as if she was watching him through a time slip.

With every step, she waited for him to look up. Readying herself for the catch of his eyes, warm and bright behind his glasses, the half smile that would tug at his mouth, the certainty that he was happy she was there.

Then a pair of small humans bolted past him—one with curly blond hair flying out behind her, the other dragging a blanket nearly as big as himself.

"Uncle Bobo!" said the girl. *Tasha*, Charlie reminded herself. "Where's Moose?"

"Wherth Moothe?" lisped the boy. *Drew*. Who, blanket in hand, thumb wedged in his mouth, reached back to take Beau's hand.

Beau, who was listening to Bobby tell a story about some statue he'd stopped Anushka from buying on his behalf, slowly crouched down, so as to give his attention to both.

A fist closed around Charlie's heart. It was so swift, and so punishing, she had to brace herself so as not to crumple.

That was when Beau's gaze found hers. He lifted his spare hand in a simple wave and smiled. A smile of joy at seeing her. And something else. Understanding as to why she was outside, on her own.

Before she gave herself away completely, Charlie made to head inside, when Beau stood and called Matt's name. And the illusive Matt, business partner and best friend, the one whose marriage, whose wife, had sent Beau down this path of self-reflection, came through the kitchen door.

A smidge shorter than Beau, he was dressed down in a Henley T-shirt, scarf, and khakis. The guy was easy on the eyes, and widowed some eight months. Charlie was suddenly afraid Jazmin and Phyllida might attempt to eat him alive.

Beau said something to him, while twisting Drew and now Tasha around in circles at the ends of his hands, and Matt glanced outside. Pinning her with a focused gaze.

Gripping her now-empty glass of bubbly, she had second thoughts about the floral strapless dress she wore. Wish she'd forgone the diamanté barrette. Or toned down the bright pink lip.

But this was a *party*. Anushka and Bobby's, as well as Beau's. So, stuff it. Stuff 'em all.

She squared her shoulders, as Beau stepped out onto the balcony, his eyes leaving hers only long enough to take in the decor, the fairy lights, how clean the place was.

"How was this even possible?" he asked.

"Anushka," said Charlie with a shrug. "Phyl and Jaz tried their best to unhinge the afternoon, while I sat back, drank bubbly, and watched. It's been a treat."

He slid his hand to her waist, pulled her close and bussed a kiss to her cheek. Murmuring against her ear, "That's my girl. Smarter than the rest by a country mile."

His girl. *His girl.* The urge to laugh, hysterically, bubbled up in her throat. While at the same time she melted into him, because that was how she rolled.

"Now. Charlie." Charlie jumped as Beau's voice shifted into mad mode. "I'd like you to meet my business partner, Matt Van Patten. Matt, this is Charlotte Goode."

"Hey, Matt," she said, reaching out a hand. "How was the flight?"

"Did you not see the two ratbags who are my travelling companions?" Then, looking around, "Actually, have you seen my two ratbags?"

"I've got them!" a female voice called.

And Matt relaxed.

"Great. Sorry." He wiped his hands down the sides of his jeans before taking her hand. "Charlotte, hello."

"You can call me Charlie," she said.

"Charlie," he said, with a quick smile. While his eyes, sharp and bright, judged her with all the judging a sharp-minded, business-savvy, nice-looking widower in his early thirties could muster.

"Beau!" That was Anushka who was flipping his kitchen cupboards open and closed. "Cups for the kids? Do you have a preference?"

"Excuse me," said Beau, shooting Charlie an "I'll be right back" smile, then glaring at Matt before he ambled inside. He was all loose-limbed and relaxed, the king of his castle. Making her think, *Surely, he couldn't give this up?*

"So, what do you think of the house?" Charlie asked, dragging her gaze back to Matt. And if Matt noticed the effort that took, he kindly didn't show it.

He looked back inside where the small group were chatting and laughing and lounging about, then out at the view with its smattering of white clouds lit silver by the moonlight.

"It's…phenomenal."

The thread of surprise beneath the words made Charlie sure her take on his visit was correct.

"I hear he has you to thank for that," said Matt.

"Me?"

"The last-minute changes he made—such as the wood panelling out front, the polished floors, the linen wallpaper? I got the feeling this place was going to be a monument to the colour grey, till you made it clear he could do better."

Charlie's gaze snapped to Beau, who was leaning against the kitchen bench, making Tasha laugh as he drank something from a blue plastic cup.

Matt sighed. "Far out, it's good to see him smiling."

She looked back to Matt, to see that his own smile didn't

quite reach his eyes. No wonder—he'd lost his wife, and his best friend had moved away, within months of one another.

Charlie found herself saying, "He's really happy you guys are here."

"Yeah?" Matt laughed, the sound soft. As if he hadn't been sure. As if he was on the fence as to what *his* next move should be.

And she realised then that Matt was no bogeyman, out to upend her life. They were, all of them, trying to get by as best they could.

"He talks about you all the time. He adores your kids. Jury is out on the dog."

Matt laughed softly. "Yeah. Big energy that one."

"It's clear Beau was awfully fond of Milly, too."

Matt blinked, his face crumpling, and Charlie stilled.

"Oh, my God, I'm so sorry. Was that the wrong thing—?"

"No," said Matt, putting a hand on her wrist, then curling it back away when he remembered they'd just met. "Most people are so careful around me, they never bring her up in case it upsets me. As if I'm not thinking about her every moment of every day."

She honestly couldn't imagine. "What was she like? If it's okay to ask."

"Sure. Sure. She was crazy smart. Pretty, too. No bullshit. Way out of my league." When Matt looked in her direction again, his expression had changed. As if he truly saw her for the first time. He leaned against the balustrade and said, "Beau's really talked about her?"

Charlie nodded. "He said you guys took him under your wings when you first met. I get the feeling she made it her mission to civilise him. At first, I wasn't sure I liked the sound of that."

Matt lifted a brow.

Charlie looked to Beau in the kitchen and said, "I'd spent

so many years trying to un-civilise him, to rumple him, get him to lose the pocket calculator and play hooky every now and then. I worried she'd undone all my good work."

At that Matt truly laughed. His head falling back as the sound spilled out into the night.

Beau, hearing it, turned shocked eyes their way. And mouthed, *He okay?*

She gave him a quick thumbs-up.

When he lifted a hand to his chest, in thanks, she knew—her feelings for this man were gargantuan. Great gusty clouds of warmth and adoration and lust. If he left first, or she did, it was going to break her heart in two.

"So that's how it is," Matt said.

And Charlie glanced over to find his gaze moving between her and Beau, his brow furrowed in a way that made her heart hurt for him.

"What? No. I mean... No." Yes. *Big-time yes.* But not for much longer, so not for him to worry about.

"Right. Okay. Sorry. Beau did mention that you're looking to head off pretty soon. Off on some grand adventure?"

"Um...yes. Well, my mum is travelling the wilds of Scotland these days. And I haven't seen her for a while. So, I'm thinking a move to Edinburgh might be just the ticket."

It was the first time she'd said it out loud, and her heart lurched, with equal parts anticipation and panic.

"Your work can transfer there easily enough?" Matt asked.

"People fall in love and get married the world over, so sure. All I'll need is a couple of gigs, to show people what I do, and if it's anything like here, it will snowball pretty quickly. I've been thinking I might even keep the branch here going, as I have an offsider," aka Julia the bookkeeper, "who would be super keen to take it on."

"Love it," Matt said, then he yawned. And laughed. And held up both hands in submission. "Forgive me. I have two kids under five. This is my first grown-up night out in months. On that note I'd better go rescue whoever has them."

He reached out a hand and placed it gently on her arm. "It was really nice meeting you, Charlie. I hope the move goes brilliantly."

"It was great meeting you, too," she said, somehow keeping the smile on her face as Matt headed inside in search of Drew and Tasha.

After which Charlie collapsed back into the chair; a stream of air escaping her mouth as she let her head fall back with a clunk.

She'd been living in a dreamland this whole time. Fusing smart, sweet teenage Beau on whom she'd had a secret crush with *this* Beau. A man who, when he wasn't "taking time off," ran a multimillion-dollar business. A man who had an entire life, and people who loved him, who needed him, a thousand kilometres away.

Not that she'd had any dreams of it all working out somehow—Beau and Charlie, together forever. Except she *had* had those dreams. Years and years ago. And more recently, when she'd not been on top of her thoughts.

Maybe if he were still broken, maybe *that* Beau would be right for her. But he was doing so much better, smiling, enjoying himself, back working, even if from home, each day. And according to the person who knew him best these days, they all had her to thank for his turnaround.

She'd screwed up her chances, by *not* screwing up. It was too deliciously ironic to cope.

The next morning the kids were plonked in front of *Bluey* on a downstairs TV, Moose lying between them, loving the little hands playing with his ears. Matt and Beau sat in the shade of the balcony, looking out over the view.

Matt, groaning as the lifted his feet to the coffee table, said, "Last night was fun."

"Glad you enjoyed it."

"But Bobby Freaking Kent? You might have warned me about that? I think my tongue hit the ground before I had the chance to wind it back in."

Beau laughed, rolling a bottle of cold water over the back of his neck before taking a swig. Then found Matt watching him.

"You seem better," Matt said.

"I am. Not all the way, but getting there. On that I want to thank you, again, for letting me go."

"I pushed you as I remember it. It was what you needed. While I needed to stay. No thanks are necessary."

"I can't help feeling I left you in the lurch."

"Something Milly and I realised, right back at the beginning, that you've never quite caught on to, is that Luculent isn't a company that makes green engines, Luculent is whatever we decide it should be. And I'm not sure any of us can expect to come out of this the same as what we were."

Beau breathed out hard, understanding what Matt was telling him. That for all that he was working again, their little company was still very much in flux.

"I have something else, Luculent-related, to tell you, if you're up to hearing it."

"Something good?"

"Something very good. We've had word. The LE has progressed to final testing."

Beau sat up. "Are you kidding me?"

The majority of patents in their field fell by the wayside long before they even reached this point. Whether by way of safety concerns, sustainability, becoming redundant by the time it was their turn, or pressure from outside forces.

Matt, grinning from ear to ear, shook his head.

Beau leaned over and smacked him on the knee, before both men hugged as if they'd won the lotto.

"I can swing the reports your way—" Matt offered.

"Now. Please."

Matt pulled out his phone, fiddled some, then Beau's phone began to ping.

Meaning he was distracted when Matt said, "So, Charlie the neighbour seemed nice."

Beau let his phone drop to his lap. "That she is."

"You know what I liked even better—how you were when she was around."

Beau picked up the bottle of water, then put it back on the table. "Did she say anything to you about…"

"Edinburgh. Visiting her mum. Starting over." Matt leaned forward. "I tell you this because while I understand that we are feeling our way here, I am a selfish human person who wants you to come home."

Beau looked around at the two-bedroom apartment he'd had fitted out underneath his house. The one he'd imagined Matt and the kids could use. While their entire operation went on without them a thousand kilometres away?

"Yeah," Beau said, frowning at his hands.

"But I guess that all depends," said Matt. "If *you* like who you are when she's around."

Beau ran his hand over his jaw. "Charlie isn't like other people. She's fierce, and protective, and unexpected. But she's also extremely fragile. I'm not sure if I trust that she can do this."

"And yet?"

Beau looked to the man who'd become more than a friend. "I also think she's inevitable."

"Man," said Matt laughing softly, clearly loving seeing Beau on his metaphorical knees. "Been there."

"Worth it?" Beau asked, already knowing Matt's answer.

"Every damn time."

The men sat in silence for a moment before:

"Dad! Dad! Dad!" the kids called in tandem.

Matt looked over and raised a hand to let them know he was coming, before laying it on Beau's back. "It must be the 'Sleepytime' episode. I cry every time and the kids think it's hilarious."

Beau raised his water bottle in salute as Matt went to be with his kids.

Then after a few long beats, he pictured himself walking into the house as he had the night before, only to find it empty, Charlie on the opposite side of the world.

After which he pressed himself to standing before heading inside to watch the kids watch what was his favourite *Bluey* episode, too.

He'd get to the life stuff later.

In the week leading up to Anushka's wedding, Charlie helped a bride write vows in which every line referred to a Harry Styles lyric; took another to a favourite vintage store to pick out an inexpensive diamanté tiara; and spent four hours sitting at the hairdressers making sure yet another bride's hair turned out the exact same shade of honey blond as Rachel in season two of *Friends*.

But she was winding down, having not taken on any new "wedding day" clients after she'd booked Anushka. Meaning when her current list was done, she had nothing to keep her fettered here.

Which of course always brought her back to Beau.

She'd only seen him in passing, since the housewarming. He was busy taking Matt and the kids to the beach, to Australia Zoo, to Montville. Still trying to convince them to "love the place like he did" or his way of saying goodbye?

Then, as rain had started pattering against her bedroom window the night before the wedding, her phone rang.

"Beau?" she said in lieu of hello.

"Do you always answer the phone that way?" he asked, his voice deep, and tired, and her favourite sound in the whole world.

"Always," she said, muting *My Best Friend's Wedding* on the TV on her dresser, and snuggling back into her bed. She held a pillow to her chest in lieu of the thing she wished was really there. "You sound rough."

"I feel rough. I thought Moose was a handful but Tasha and Drew and Moose together are a tornado."

"I bet. Do you think that means they're ready to take the big guy back?"

A pause, then, "We've decided he's staying with me."

"Did *we* now?" she said, imagining Beau putting up an argument as to why that should be. The warmth in her chest bloomed all the more.

"Are you ready for tomorrow?" she asked. "Any last-minute best man nerves? Or questions about what you have to do?"

"Not a one. I'll just follow your lead."

Charlie looked to the ceiling, silently shouting at the gods as to why they'd not made more like this one.

"So," she said, "I guess this isn't a booty call, then. Pity, because I'm here in my sexiest night attire."

"I did just drop Matt and the kids at the airport."

"Oh. Then would you like to come over?"

Charlie heard a knock at the door.

She looked up, then at her phone, then dumped it on the bed as she bolted for the front door. She whipped it open to find Beau standing there, his phone to his ear.

His hair was damp. The shoulders of his T-shirt covered in wet splotches. He looked like a man who'd spent a week with two young kids and a harried single dad. He also looked like he was ready to eat her up on the spot.

The thought of not having him in her life anymore hurt so much she moaned.

He put his phone in his back pocket, his voracious gaze raking her up and down.

"Sexiest night attire?" he queried.

She glanced down at her track pants and faded Dsylexia Sukcs T-shirt. Before whipping the shirt over her head.

After a beat Beau was over the threshold and in her arms, kissing her neck, her cheeks, her lips as he lifted her off her feet and pressed her against the hallway wall.

"The front door," she managed.

He reached back with a long leg and kicked it shut.

"I've missed the hell out of this," he said, pressing his mouth to hers. "I've missed you."

His hands moved to her backside, pulling her against his hard ridge.

"Serves you right for having other friends," she said.

"Mmm," he said, now only half listening as he pulled back to run his hands over her shoulders, his thumbs dipping into her clavicles, then he slid an arm behind her back arching her to his mouth.

Charlie's eyes slammed shut as sensation rocked through her. Feeling, and heat, and the knowledge that she missed him, too. Already. Even now.

"Beau," she said, as the rain began to pour down outside, her hands tugging on his damp hair.

"Charlie," he breathed back, his voice ragged with emotion.

Then not another word was said for a long time.

CHAPTER ELEVEN

THE STORM BROKE early the next morning, leaving Anushka and Bobby's wedding day perfect, crisp, and bright. And while Charlie knew that controlling the weather was outside her purview, since the moment she'd woken up, she'd been quietly freaking out.

"It's all going to be fine," she said out loud to the mirror in the powder room of the Kents' fabulous hinterland estate. "It's all going to be fine."

All the while her internal monologue chanted, *Don't screw up, don't screw up, don't screw up.*

It had nothing to do with the size of the place, the mixing of cultures and families and money and celebrity, the security at the head of the driveway and paparazzi helicopters already flying overhead. For her job was as it ever was—keep the bride happy while fending off any slings and arrows coming her way.

It was the amount riding on the day, *personally*, that had her stomach in knots.

After today she'd have enough money in the bank to have real choices.

After today she and Beau had no reason to see one another, except to see one another.

After today her sole focus *had* to be what came next.

Giggling in the hall outside the powder room drew her at-

ALLY BLAKE   163

tention, before the door swung open and Anushka's bridesmaids, Phyllida and Jazmin, spilled in.

"Hey," said Charlie. "Why aren't you with Anushka?"

One hiccupped, while the other giggled uncontrollably.
Brilliant. They were already tipsy.

"And we're off," Charlie muttered, giving her expression a
good hard nod. Selfishly glad to have something else to focus
on other than the roiling thoughts in her own head.

She ran a hand over her hair, stuck a hand inside the low-
cut neck of her black leather dress to plump the girls, then
checked her teeth for stray lipstick.

Ready, she grabbed her bag, rifling through the thing till
she came up with a pill box. "Take one of these each. It's B1,
which will settle your stomachs. Any allergies? No? Have
some paracetamol and a huge drink of water. Then meet me
in the vestibule in five minutes. If I find out Anushka has a
single clue that you are not on song, I will...unfollow your
Instagram."

Phyllida gasped, while Jazmin covered her mouth, panic
in her eyes.

Done with them, Charlie went to find her girl. A text came
through. She checked in case it was Anushka.

It was from Beau. Whom she'd last seen when he'd kissed
her cheek before slipping back to his own place in the middle of the night.

In case it hadn't occurred to you yet today, you are a phe-
nomenon. Anushka made the right decision, including you.
If you're looking for me, I'll be the one standing next to the
bride...no, groom.

Charlie laughed. Read the thing again, in case she'd mis-
read it. Then again. Needing to wipe a quick tear from beneath her eye.

She went to type back, but her hand was shaking. Add dyslexic spelling and it was best not. Probably a good thing, as her gut instinct was to write a string of superlatives, outlining all the ways she thought him wonderful, too.

Which, at this point in the game, would be nothing short of dumb. The worst kind of self-sabotage. For today was the tipping point between her future and her past—the mistakes, the failures, the big swings, the bigger misses. Get through this, and they would soon be all behind her.

Feeling a twinge of guilt, she slipped her phone into her bag and strode toward the vestibule where Anushka awaited her.

Apart from the slight dampness on the ground, a missing uncle—found—and a trip hazard in the aisle—fixed—Anushka and Bobby's wedding went off without a hitch.

The vows were adorable, the crowd rowdy and engaged, the bride and groom themselves in every way. Anushka in her sparkly mini dress and hair in Princess Leia buns wrapped in daisies looked like a pixie princess while Bobby in his midnight black velvet suit, and well concealed lifts, was a revelation.

For Charlie, the hardest part was standing on the raised dais with Beau just across the way. He looked utterly devastating in his morning suit, like something out of a fairy tale. Making it impossible not to remember how it felt to have his mouth on her neck, his voice against her ear, his hand holding her cheek as if she was the most precious thing he'd ever known.

Making it impossible for her to do her job.

In a desperate effort to keep herself together, she made a subtle motion for him to fix his perfect boutonniere.

The grin she got in return made it all too clear he wasn't to be tricked. He knew why her eyes were on him. He knew how to make her smile, how to make warmth bloom brightly inside her, how to make her feel as if she could do and be anything.

The problem was for her to do the thing she wanted most,

to curate a life of her own, one she was proud of, one she built on her own terms and no one else's, Beau couldn't be there.

Things moved quickly after that.

"Another One Bites the Dust" blared as Anushka and Bobby danced back down the aisle, while Charlie collected the fallen petals from Anushka's bouquet as the bride wanted to craft something from them later on.

During the family photographs Charlie reminded the photographer whom Bobby's mother had chosen, that there were to be some fun ones after the stuffy classics.

Once inside the ballroom for the reception, Charlie made sure to spend time with Anushka's mother, and to tell her how much she loved the poem she'd read during the sermon.

Then came time for the first dance. As promised—and witnessed firsthand during that final dance lesson—Anushka and Bobby were a joyful mess. The routine was a little waltz, a little hustle, a little interpretive movement ballet, with Anushka and Bobby tripping over one another, and not even close to being on time with the beat.

Then Anushka's gaze found Charlie's in the crowd. She clicked her hand at Charlie, mouthing, *Save us!*

Before Charlie even had to look for Beau he was there beside her, hand out, drawing her onto the dance floor.

Only rather than hold her the way he had in their "lesson," he lifted her till her feet rested on his, much to the delight of the crowd.

"So much for letting me lead the way," Charlie murmured, wrapping her hands around Beau's neck and holding on for dear life.

"Everywhere but here. And in the bedroom. And on a construction site."

"My options are shrinking before my eyes." She said it as a joke, but the truth of it was all too real.

As if he saw it in her eyes, some pulling back, or some pain, Beau's eyes narrowed in question.

Charlie, the coward, looked down at their feet. "Am I hurting you?"

"I own protective shoes for all occasions."

As Anushka and Bobby had separated and pulled as many others who would join them onto the dance floor, Beau's movements slowed, till *they* were swaying gently.

"Are we having fun?" Beau asked.

"My goal is for Anushka and Bobby to have fun. My enjoyment is secondary."

"What about my enjoyment?" he asked, spinning her so fast she closed her eyes and squealed.

"Eighth," she said when he slowed. "Seventh at the very most."

He leaned back so that she was looking into his eyes as he said, "I'll take it." And she believed him, too.

How little he asked of her, how solid in his own shoes.

Before she could stop herself, she tilted her head and kissed him, a soft slow caress into which she poured all the feelings surging inside her. He lifted her so that her feet were airborne, and deepened the kiss, as he was doing the same.

He slowly let her feet fall back to the floor, waited till she had purchase, then moved her around the floor with more grace, and caution, and sweetness than she thought possible.

You're okay, she thought. *He's okay. We will be okay.*

She waited for her internal monologue to perk up with some sassy comment to the contrary, but for once it stayed quiet.

When the song ended, and the crowd cheered, she forced the swaying to a stop and said, "I have to check on the cake."

The cake? Where did that come from? She did *not* have to check on the cake. She wanted nothing to do with the cake. What she needed was to breathe air that did not smell like him, so she could get her head on straight. For right now it felt anything but.

"Go get 'em," Beau said, twirling her out to the end of his arm, kissed her hand, then let her go. Then he curled a finger toward Anushka who began to draw herself to him with an invisible rope. Taking up where she left off, without having to be asked.

"You're the best, bestie!" Anushka called out.

Charlie lifted her hand in a wave as she shot off the dance floor.

"My daughter is so lucky she found you," Mrs. Patel said, hugging her as she passed.

She managed a thumbs-up.

"I'm calling you Monday," said a young woman, grabbing her by the elbow and looking intently into her eyes. "From what I hear, you are a genius," said another, "and I must have you."

She kept walking, not in the right headspace to explain that she *couldn't* take them on. That she was leaving. Unless they wanted to get married in Edinburgh? Was it Edin-burg, or Eden-borough? She wasn't even sure how to pronounce it properly, but for some reason she'd decided that's where she was going to start over.

She heard Beau's voice saying, *Wherever you go, there you are.* Then she dropped a shoulder and used it to nudge her way through the packed crowd. Needing air. Breath. And time.

She really needed more time.

But all she got was, *No, no, no, no, no, no, no*, pounding in her head in time with the music. For this couldn't be happening. It wasn't possible that she, Charlotte Goode, wild child, rebel, hustler, lucky to pass English in school, thrower of cake, might actually have found her way to accomplishment in multiple areas of her life, all at one time.

Friendship, self-sufficiency, self-worth, respect in her chosen field.

With Beau Griffin the cherry on top.

No, he wasn't the cherry. He was the foundation beneath it all. For until *he'd* come on the scene, she'd been flailing. Barely holding it together. And now…now she was struggling to picture her life without him in it.

There she'd been thinking how great she was doing, how she was ready to launch herself onto the world, when it had been his influence all along.

Another pair of young women stepped in front of her, and she had to pull up so as not to knock them down.

"You're Anushka's maid of honour, right?" asked one.

"The fake one?" qualified the other.

The sharp tone had Charlie looking up. And while the hairs stood on the back of her neck, she was still on the job, still representing Anushka's interests, not her own.

"I'm Charlie Goode, Always the Bridesmaid."

"Told you, Mika," the first said smugly to the second.

"Heard you, Izzy. You were that wedding-ruiner, right?"

Charlie's mouth popped open, only to find she had no words. For what were words when the piano that had been dangling over your head, the one you'd spent months waiting to fall, clanged as it dropped to an inch above your head.

Izzy, hand on hip, said, "You drove the van carrying the wedding party into the lake."

"No, silly. She gave an entire wedding food poisoning."

Charlie wondered, for a blissful moment of freefall, if she might actually get out of this, when Izzy clicked her fingers. Pulled out her phone, scrolled a moment, then read, "Charlotte Hashtag Cakegate Goode ruins twelve-thousand-dollar dress in cake-tossing assault."

Then she held up her phone, assaulting Charlie with the zoomed-in image of herself, mouth agape, hand raised, crumbs falling from her tightly closed fist. And for a second she barely recognised herself. The foiled hair, the uptight clothes, and her eyes—they looked so tortured.

"We have to tell Anushka, right? What if she does something terrible? What if she ruins everything?"

Charlie excused herself and walked away.

What else could she do? No point in denying it. The cat was finally out of the bag. It was done. Telling them Anushka *knew* was putting Anushka in the middle of what was no doubt about to hit the fan.

There was also the fact that Charlie had felt a sudden overwhelming sense of *relief.*

For it turned out being found out was far less pressure than having so many things in her life going right at once that she didn't know where to turn.

Charlie was sitting on a pile of crates in an alcove outside the industrial kitchen when Beau found her.

"Hell, Charlie. Where have you been? I've been looking for you everywhere."

She looked up. Saw him walking toward her—tall, and beautiful, and draped in moonlight.

"Anushka?" she asked.

"Is just fine. She's saying her goodbyes before they head off. I told her you were putting out a literal fire with your bare hands and would be in touch when she got back from their honeymoon."

Charlie nodded.

"Are you okay? Did something happen? Can—?"

"I'm leaving," she said. "This week."

"To go where?"

"Edinburgh. First to visit my mum, then to find somewhere to settle."

"You mean you're *leaving* leaving? That soon? But what

about the business? What about the house? The…the vegetable garden?"

"I've been clear from the start that that was my plan."

"But I thought—"

"You thought what? That I'd stay? Why? Did you think I was all hot air? Did you not believe I'd go? Did you not believe in me? God, it's the 'fixing my light' thing all over again!"

Beau flinched, as if she'd accused him of a great and terrible crime. Which, she knew, in his eyes she had. Because of all the people in all the world, Beau Griffin had always believed in her most of all.

More than she even believed in herself. But she was on the *right* path now, the path she'd decided on before he'd knocked on her door and upended everything, and this time she was not getting off.

"What happened between the dance and now?"

"What do you mean?"

"Charlie," he said, madder than she'd ever seen him. "Don't."

She deflated, looking down at her feet, her heels kicking against the bottom crate. "Someone…confronted me. About #cakegate. They're in there now telling Anushka—"

"Who already knows and does not care."

"And likely telling anyone else who will listen. Meaning I can't go back in there. I'm done. It's *over*."

"Which, since you are apparently leaving this week, should not matter a jot."

Charlie pressed her lips together, realising no matter what she said, she would dig herself further and further into a hole. The only way out would be to tell him the truth—that she was falling for him and it was messing everything up.

Which wasn't his fault because look at him. It was all on her, because she knew better.

Beau watched her, waiting. Before he huffed out a breath and looked up at the sky. "I wondered what you might do, if something like this were to happen. I even thought you might react this way. That your instinct would be to run. I just… As we got to know one another again, I began to hope that that instinct might send you running to me."

Charlie breathed out hard. A war going on inside her. Team Charlie versus Team Beau. For that's what this felt like. As if she was fighting for her life.

"If you don't face this thing, head-on, own it, explain yourself or don't, but look it in the eye and let it go, it will consume you."

"Really?" she said. "This coming from the guy who, instead of facing his own grief, ran away to his childhood home and knocked the thing down."

Beau's jaw worked, his gaze glinting in the darkness. Then he said, "That's entirely fair."

Fair? That's not how this worked. He was supposed to fight back. To tell her she was wrong and he was right. Hell, she'd take one of his threatened pie charts or slideshows right now, so that she could throw her hand in the air and leave. Feeling vindicated that she had made the right choice.

For even while she stubbornly stuck by her plan, how did she know if it was right? It might end up being the absolute worst. All she had, all she could cling to, was that it was hers.

Beau looked back at her. "Do you *want* to leave?"

"I have to."

"I know you think that, but do you want to?"

"I don't see how that matters."

A beat, then, "It matters to me."

Charlie swallowed. Even her inner monologue was starting to panic, whispering, *Stick to the plan, stick to the plan,* over and over again.

When she said nothing more, he looked at the ground, and lifted a hand to the back of his neck, as he said, "I can't do this, Charlie. Strike that. I can. I did so, for years. What I *can't* do anymore is watch you do this to yourself."

"And what is it that I am doing to myself?" Charlie was very glad for the cloak of darkness, as she felt tears gathering at the corners of her eyes. For Beau was pulling away. Which was what she wanted. Didn't mean she had to like it.

"This," he said, waving a hand at her, before turning it on himself. "I thought it was just in you, that wild *stubborn* streak of yours that always sent you headlong into danger. Now, I wonder if it's deliberate. So that you have a ready excuse for any time things go wrong."

Charlie flinched, his words so close to the bruise in her core she gasped. "Beau?"

"And I get it," he said, pacing now. "I get why you did that. Your bastard of a father expended so much energy telling you how useless you were in the end it was easier to find ways to prove him right. But he was wrong about you, Charlie. For you are a strong, empathetic, ingenious, fiercely protective force to be reckoned with. And you never needed to prove that to anyone but yourself. But if you can't get over that, even now…"

Beau's gaze turned hard. His disappointment so keen Charlie felt it slice right through her. But she said nothing. She just looked at him as if what he was saying made no difference. When it made so much difference, he made so much difference, that it overwhelmed her.

As if he finally saw how fragile she felt, he let his hand drop and looked at her. "After Milly… Losing her like that, it was nearly too much for me. And you… You're… I can't keep worrying if you're going to climb a busted ladder in gum boots, Charlie. It hurts, like a fist in my chest, caring so much all the damn time."

Had he just said he cared so much for her it hurt?

While the thought wound around her heart, again and again and again, Charlie said, "Then lucky for you we are on the same page."

At that a light went out in Beau. She saw it extinguish from his gaze, as if it had been a real thing. A thing she'd put there, that she had now taken away.

After a few long beats he nodded. Then nodded again. "Okay. Okay, then." Then, "Are you coming back in?"

She shook her head. "It wouldn't be fair to Anushka, not if people are talking about me. The best thing I can do, right now, is go. And since my time is up, consider yourself off the hook, too."

She'd tried to sound cavalier, to try to end this someplace that didn't feel as awful as she felt right now. But the way Beau looked at her, all rumpled and beautiful and stony, he knew what she really meant.

Not just that he was free to finish the gig, but that this was goodbye.

When one of the kitchen staff came outside, to toss a bag of scraps into the compost bin around the corner, he paused when he saw them, offered a quick smile, then went straight back inside.

Beau and Charlie looked at one another in silence, saying more by saying nothing than all their words had conveyed. This had been wonderful, life-changing in fact, but it had always been destined to end.

Charlie pressed herself off the crates, and walked over to Beau. She placed a hand on his chest, and lifted herself to her toes to kiss him on the cheek.

Unlike every other time she'd done so, he didn't move a muscle.

"Thank you for your help," she managed. Then, "Good luck. With everything."

Then she walked away.

And while she got her wish, leaving him this time before he had the chance to leave her, the closure she'd thought it might bring was very much not there.

CHAPTER TWELVE

CHARLIE SAT IN the car in the driveway, revving herself up to bring in the fertilizer and packing boxes she'd picked up from Phil at the grocery store.

Instead she sat, listening to the Zombies play on the car radio, and looked at her front veranda. Funny that she thought of it as *her* front veranda now, right as she was getting ready to leave.

It did look nice, though. For she'd weeded the heck out of the thing one afternoon the week before, tearing out dead shrubs, trimming others, sweeping and hosing till it was tidy and inviting.

Then she checked her phone. Something she'd done a zillion times since the weekend. Waiting for some awful message from the Kents. Or a voice note from Julia, in case the news had hit her already.

The one person she was sure she'd not heard from was Beau. And at least there she'd been right. Turned out being right didn't feel as great as she'd always imagined it would.

And yet, when her phone rang, her first thought was, *Beau*?

It was, in fact, a video call from her mum. She quickly checked her face, in the hopes she didn't look as ragged as she felt, then answered.

"Hey, Mum," she said when her mother's face popped up. Her hair windswept, her skin a little burnt.

"Hey, honey."

"What's up? All good with you?"

"Great. Alfredo and I have taken up ocean running."

"It must be, what ten degrees, max?"

"Probably."

"Well, I'm not doing that."

Her mother laughed. "What's that I can see in the back seat there?"

Charlie lifted her pone. "Fertilizer."

"Are you making a bomb?"

"What? No!"

"Don't get so pernickety. I distinctly remember you coming home from the library with the ingredients to make a bomb one time. Poor Beau, the boy from next door, was standing behind you, shaking his head at me, a promise he'd never let it get that far."

Charlie's heart leaped into her throat.

"If not for a bomb," her mother said, "why do you need fertilizer?"

"For your old veggie garden that I replanted."

"Aren't you on your way here in a few short days? If so, who'll look after the veggie garden, then? Best to let it go, honey."

Charlie licked her lips. "Yeah, you're probably right. Thanks, Mum."

"Okay. Well keep me up to date with the packing. Talk soon."

When the screen went black, Charlie let her phone drop to her lap as she sank down deep into her seat.

Best let it go, honey, her mum had said, in that easy singsong way she had. Even after spending twenty odd years with her father, she was so chipper. So free. As if she'd woken up one day and let that go.

As easy as that.

Then she had Beau's voice in her head, telling her to face

up to the choices she'd made. To own them. Maybe what she needed to get out of this funk was a mixture of both.

Own up, then let go.

And something that had been itching at the corner of her head the past few weeks stepped fully formed into her mind as if waiting for its moment.

#Cakegate Leesa had owned her own business, and according to Charlie's occasional Instagram stalking, still did. Before she could overthink it, she opened the notes app on her phone, copied the apology she had written, and edited, and polished a dozen times over the past two years, and this time sent the thing.

If she was going to own up to how she'd gotten to this point, she had to start there.

Next, she sent Anushka a message, reiterating how wonderful it had been to meet her, wishing she and Bobby a fantastic honeymoon and delightful life together.

That time her phone buzzed instantly.

Charlie Goode!!!

She'd have known those exclamation marks anywhere.

I'm so upset with you right now.

Charlie gulped.

A little bird told me you had a run in with a pair of nasty vipers at MY wedding. As of now, they know that if they breathe a word of the thing we will not name, I will be their mortal enemy. But when I get back, we are putting this nonsense to bed, once and for all. You and me babe. Besties forever.

Charlie's throat felt tight as a drum, when her phone buzzed again.

Dear Charlotte,
I was surprised to hear from you after such a long time, but I appreciate you reaching out.

Yes, it was a rough few months. For you, too, I saw. I am in a much better place now and I honestly hope that you are, too.

Richard and I are no longer together. In fact, we've not been together since the day after the wedding, when he explained how you knew one another. And I put two and two together as to the cake toss.

Did you know, he used me as a human shield? What a douche.
Regards,
Leesa

Her phone buzzed again. This time with a voice message from a call she must have missed while talking to her mum.

"Hey! My name is Cherry, I'm a friend of Anushka's. I was at the wedding and she raved about you. And I was hoping we could meet to see if I could take you on. It's a June wedding—"

Charlie turned her phone to silent and tossed it in the glove compartment, as if it were a live snake. For that was a lot to unpack.

The first on the list? Beau.

She'd always thought of herself as the carer of the pair, the one looking out for him. But if he'd been looking out for her, worrying about her, doing what he could to stop her from blowing the two of them up...even back then, it was a wonder he'd given her another chance at all.

Beau, who'd clearly been in touch with Anushka, letting

her know what had happened so that she could leap into action. Working quietly behind the scenes. Making sure she had a support network to take care of her.

Beau, who'd not asked to be swept into her craziness, but once there, must have found he liked it. For he'd kept coming back for more.

Beau. The love of her damn life.

As soon as she thought the words, a rush of something wonderful flowed through her. Something bright, and sure, and true.

She loved him. She loved him so very much.

She loved that he was the listener to her chatter. The solid to her flux. The cool reason to her spit and fire. She loved that he was the arms around her, the whispers in her ear, the protective shoes to her dancing feet. She loved that he was her foundation, and loved that he rocked it, too.

Charlie loved Beau.

Only now that she'd owned it, she did *not* want to let it go.

"So, what now?" she asked out loud. Glancing to the tall shrubs blocking her view of the house next door.

Yes, loving Beau was terrifying. For she was as likely to get it wrong as she was to get it right. But so long as she fixed it more times than she burned it down, it might actually all be okay.

Beau sat on the huge couch in the lounge room leading onto his balcony, big brown eyes looking up at him, a cool wet nose pressed into his palm.

For they had come to an understanding the past couple of days, he and Moose. Mike the electrician had dropped the dog off not long after he'd returned home from the wedding. Beau had stripped down and climbed in to bed, too spent, emotionally and physically, to clean himself up first. When

Moose had nudged his way into Beau's bedroom, climbing onto the end of the bed, Beau had pretended not to notice.

A breeze swept into the room, through the concertinaed windows, bringing with it a "wet forest" scent with a hint of roses. And Beau breathed deep. Deeper than he'd have been able to only a few short weeks before.

Which, considering he'd spent the past few days feeling as if he'd been hit in the chest with a mallet, was saying something.

He remembered saying something as much to Charlie, during that wild conversation in the dark outside the kitchen. About feeling as if he had a fist in his chest all the time.

Because she made him worry.

Because she made him care.

Now, without the *boom-boom-boom* of the Spice Girls playing in the background, and the tightness in the back of his head after not being able to find her for a good half hour, and the scent of vegetable scraps in his nose—now that he had lost her—he was beginning to have a better idea of what that feeling truly was.

The reason Charlie made him feel as he was walking around with a fist in his chest was because he loved her.

He knew he loved her. He'd known it from nearly the first moment he'd seen her again. As if it had been inside him, waiting.

Only loving, for him, had always been tied up with loss. His parents. Milly. He'd already lost Charlie once.

He hadn't been in any place to foster those feelings, to nourish them. He'd wanted to break things, knock down his pain and build something over it to cover the scars.

But Charlie wasn't having it. She went about feeding him, distracting him, giving him projects and companionship, a safe space to heal, just as she always had. In doing so, she'd quietly kick-started his heart.

Given him perspective. Given him time. Eased his pain.

Even after the night of the wedding, her decision to leave, his to stay, it didn't feel quite the same. There was no emptiness, no rage. For his love for her remained. A solid visceral thing. As if it lived in him still, unchanged, never to be lost.

He looked up when a knock rattled his front door.

Likely someone selling energy plans, he thought. Or a kid playing ding-dong ditch.

Until the second louder knock roused Moose from his place at Beau's feet. His claws scrabbled on the polished floor as he bolted to the door. Then sat there, looking at the door, looking at Beau, looking at the door—

Knock. Knock-knock. Knock-knock-knock.

"Coming," he murmured.

Then, after patting Moose in that soft spot at the back of his head, he opened the door.

She was turned away, looking up, watching a flock of birds make patterns in the sky, but he'd have recognised the shape of her anywhere. The shaggy dark auburn hair, the curve of her neck, the fine points of her shoulders, raised slightly as if permanently ready to throw down.

"Charlie?" he said, his voice raw.

Charlie turned, sunlight blinding him a moment as it glinted off something she held in her hands. When it settled, and it was just her, standing before him. And the fist in his chest dissolved so that all remained was his heart, beating a steady tattoo for her.

"I wasn't sure you were going to answer," she said reaching down to rub Moose's ear before the dog padded back inside, job done.

"Yet you kept knocking."

"I can be stubborn, don't you know."

Beau smiled, and leaned in the doorway, not about to make it easier for her. She'd threatened to leave him, after all.

"You could have come in the back way," he said.

"After the way I behaved?" She shook her head. "This felt like a 'formal entrance' kind of moment."

"This is a moment?"

She nodded. "I had hoped it might be. In fact, I have a whole plan to make it so. If that's okay with you?"

"Charlie," he said, his voice rough as hell. "I'm here. I'm listening. Just tell me what you came here to say. I want to hear. I'll always want to hear it."

The smile she gave him held literal hints of sunshine. He'd fight you on it.

"Then here goes. The other night, I freaked out."

"I am aware. I was there."

"Right," she said scrunching her eyes up tight. "So, you were. A lot of things all came at me at once that night. Hopes, dreams, feelings, beginnings, when I'd been so focused on the ending. This...thing I wanted so badly to do on my own."

"What thing?"

"Um, win at life?"

Beau laughed. "And what does that look like?"

"That's the thing. I thought I knew, but it turns out I did not. I saw a photo of myself just after I tossed the cake. Before that moment I'd thought I was on my way to winning life, but in the photo I looked as if, even before it was taken, I was already stressed, and unhappy, and not myself."

"Sounds like a lot."

"It was. None of which is an excuse. It's an explanation, I hope, as to why I behaved so unfairly toward you. When you were there doing me a favour."

She looked up at him, her gaze so heartfelt he wanted to wrap her up and make her feel warm, and safe, and loved. And it was clear she had more to say.

Which was: "If it's any consolation, I read somewhere that

people often behave their worst around those they care about the most. Certain that person will love them no matter what."

"Is that right?" he said, holding onto the fact Charlie had just told him that he was the person she cared about the most. And that she knew he loved her.

That would make what he had to say much easier. Then again, a person would have to work awfully hard not to see that he adored her. And always had.

"I'm so sorry," she said.

"I know. And I'm sorry, too."

She shook her head. "What on earth do *you* have to be sorry for?"

"I'm sorry," he said, moving so he could join her on the porch, because now that she was there, she was still too far away. "For the time we missed that final year of school because I was too scared to tell you how I felt about you. I'm sorry I waited until the day before I left to tell you I was leaving, making you think I didn't worry about how it might affect you the entire time. I'm sorry I didn't tell you that even the possibility of a 'spin the bottle' game landing on you was the best moment of my life. Until that moment."

She blinked furiously, her cheeks pinking, her eyes now sparkling.

"You've had better moments since."

"I can think of a couple," he said, taking a step her way. He lifted his hand, cupping her cheek, gently. Feeling, deep in some entirely non-scientific place inside him, that this moment was the first of the rest of their lives.

And while he knew there would be disagreements, and risk, and that she'd freak again and again, there would also be star gazing, and laughter, and this love of theirs that had no regard for time.

When her eyes began to close, her mouth pop open, he said, "What have you got there?"

"Hmm?"

He glanced at the box she was holding, the one stopping him from being able to haul her into his arms.

"Oh, right. I… Well, I brought you a housewarming gift."

She held it a second, as if the way things had gone just now, she wasn't sure she needed it anymore. But Beau clicked his fingers till she handed it over.

He reached into the gift bag and pulled out a wooden sign. Twee and feminine, all curlicues and shabby chic paint, clearly custom-made from one of the artisans in Montville or Maleny. The letters *MWWF* had been etched into the front.

"*MWWF?*"

Charlie checked them, her mouth moving as she read, even though he knew she'd have checked them three times over. Then, looking up at him, one eye scrunched tight, she said, "It stands for Myrtle Way Weapons Facility."

Smiling, then laughing, loudly, at the awful audacity of the thing, Beau turned to hold it up against the sleek, eye-wateringly expensive reclaimed wood cladding, just above the minimalist. "Here do you think?"

"Gods, no." Charlie reached for it. But he held it out of reach. When she pressed up onto her toes and jumped for the thing, her body bumped against him.

Her eyes flew to his, and before she could slide back to her heels, Beau dropped his face to meet hers. After a beat in which he made sure she knew what was coming, he pressed his lips to hers.

Her sigh was the most wonderful sound. The way she kissed him back, her lips clinging to his, pressed into every tender space inside him. Marking him, for life.

When he pulled back, she looked as dazed as he felt.

"I love it," he said. Then as if was the most natural thing in the world, "And I love you."

She blinked. Then demanded, "Say that again."

The hand not holding the sign slid around her back and drew her close. "I love you, Charlie. I love that you feel things deeply. I love that life was never able to smooth away your spikes. I love that despite the confidence hits you took as a kid, you made a career of making sure those under your charge never feel the same way."

"Beau," she said, reaching between them to grab great handfuls of his shirt, and give him a shake. Her eyes were diamond-bright, her face pure joy. And when she said, "I love you so much I can barely breathe right now," he felt it like an arrow straight to his heart.

"I love you," she said again. "I love you, I love you, I love you! I love you so much I feel like such a fool for not telling you the instant I knew. I love that you are so kind, and clever, and patient, and warm. I love how much you love my cooking, when the truth is I'm not all that great. I love how much you love your friends."

She stopped then, lifting a hand to her heart. For Milly. Who, in her own way, had brought them back together.

"I love how you listen. I love how you think. I love how hard you've worked to meet Moose halfway, and how much Matt's kids love you. I particularly love how much I love you."

Beau laughed. Then pulled her closer still. Into his arms, forever this time.

"Beau Griffin," she said, her eyes darkening, as she curled herself against him. "You really are the best man I've ever known."

Beau groaned. "You really went there?"

"How could I not? It was right there, waiting for its moment. And if we are doing this, for real, it's best you know what you're getting into. My penchant for puns. My heretofore unrevealed love of curing fish. My daily three in the morning trumpet practice—"

Before she could say another word, Beau scooped her up.

She whooped, grabbing him around the neck. Then settled into his arms with a sigh.

"If we are doing this for real?" he repeated.

She lifted her face to kiss him. "Oh, we're doing this."

After which he carried her over the threshold, and into the first day of the rest of their lives.

EPILOGUE

CHARLIE AND BEAU sat on the balcony of their house on Myrtle Way, watching as the cockatoos took their twice daily commute overhead, stopping for a spell in the jacaranda at the rear of the yard, messing with the thing till a carpet of lavender flowers blanketed the grass beneath. Then they were off, following the last vestiges of the autumn sun.

The silvery light of the low-slung moon glinted off the ocean beyond, while the sky around them pinked, the smattering of cloud soaking up the last warmth before the sky seemed to pause, then darken on a single long outshot of breath.

Charlie leaned forward, or as much as she could, considering the size of her belly these days. To think their backyard had been piles of rubble, a danger zone Beau would have called it, his beautiful face so serious, a blink ago. Now it was a beautiful flat field of lush grass, set off by the retaining wall dripping in bougainvillea. Her series of raised veggie gardens stuck out like a sore thumb in the beautifully landscaped grounds, but Beau assured her it was his favourite part.

The fact that there was an actual fence now where the rose bushes had once been had been a…conversation. The symbolic thorny wall that had tried to keep them apart all these years was no more. Though they had replanted one of each variety in planters along the side of the house and walking past them, drinking in the nostalgia, was one of Charlie's favourite things.

A gate had been built into the fence at least, so when the house next door had finished with its refurbishment, and Matt and the kids moved in, they'd have easy access both ways.

Charlie shook her head, marvelling at how much her life had changed over the past year.

After Anushka had come home from her honeymoon, she'd taken Charlie by the ear and convinced to come on her radio show, and take part in a long-form interview about second chances. She'd given her side of #cakegate, talked about what she'd done to move past it, told of how she and Leesa had become Instagram friends, and how Always a Bridesmaid had sprung from the ashes. Thus turning what had been the defining moment in her life to a mere footnote.

Once Matt and the kids moved up, and with her mum and Alfredo coming over from Scotland for a prolonged visit when the baby was born, and with Julia the bookkeeper no longer a bookkeeper, having bought into the business and taking admin and training, there was little time to ponder. To look back.

A good thing, though, as it turned out winning at life was really about living it.

"Moose!" she called, when the goofball of a dog sniffed at her baby carrots.

He looked around, wagging his tail, then bounded off down the hill.

Beau moved in behind her, gently moving to sit in a chair with him when he saw she was rubbing at her lower back. He lifted an arm and she leaned to rest into the curve of his big body. His other hand held the book he'd been reading. Some dense tome with more scientist terms than she cared to learn.

"What day are Matt and the kids getting here?" she asked.

"A week today, I think. He has a couple more things to iron out before, then LE goes into production, then they're on their way. If the house isn't ready, they can stay here?"

"Of course." When the kids arrived, the first thing she'd show them was how to sneak under the backstairs, where she'd already put a large metal chest that held a blanket, a torch, and a new pack of Uno cards.

Even after moving in with Beau, Charlie had continued cleaning out the house next door. She'd taken classes on re-grouting a bathroom, and watched videos to learn how to pull up carpet. Someone had to teach their daughter how to do it.

Beau could teach her how to fix anything mechanical. How to be charming on the phone when you wanted something fixed, as Charlie didn't have the patience. He was like a bear with a sore head if she left him in his home office too long without dragging him out for food, or water, or fresh air, so he wasn't perfect.

But he was to her.

She'd known it the moment they'd met. When he'd stood at the bottom of the tree in his backyard and looked up and found her—crying, inconsolable, knees grazed, filled with anger at the things her father had just called her.

He'd said, "I'm Beau. Is it okay if I just sit here a while?"

And then he'd sat at the bottom of the tree, bending blades of grass into patterns, building forts for ants. There, in case she needed someone. In case she needed him.

"Are we ready, do you think?" she asked, placing her hand over Beau's.

"Probably not," he said easily, "but it's too late now."

True, she thought, snuggling into him with a happy sigh.

"You are going to be the most ridiculously gorgeous dad."

"While you will be the fiercest mum in living history."

"Unless, of course, you've made me too soft. Gooey. All blissed out."

Beau gave her a look that made it clear he believed her fierceness was there to stay, and that was fine with him.

Then, because she was done holding things back from

this man of hers, she admitted, "I just hope that they'll be okay. That other kids are nice to them. And that they find that one great friend. And that they have my gumption, but your judgement. And—"

Beau moved, putting a halt to her stream of consciousness. He placed the bookmark in his book—no dog-earing for him, her beautiful rule-following man—and shifted till her eyes caught his.

Then, reaching for her chin, he stroked the sides of her face before leaning in and kissing her gently on the mouth. When he pulled back, he had the thrill of the fight, the fight for *her*, in his eyes, as he said, "You know what they will have? Guaranteed?"

"What's that?" she asked, so much hope filling her that she could barely contain it.

"They'll have us." With that, Beau kissed her again.

And Charlie knew, in her heart of hearts, that no matter what life threw at them from here, it was going to be more than okay. With this man by her side, it would be wondrous.

* * * * *

*If you enjoyed this story,
check out these other great reads
from Ally Blake*

Secretly Married to a Prince
Cinderella Assistant to Boss's Bride
Fake Engagement with the Billionaire
Whirlwind Fling to Baby Bombshell

All available now!

TWO WEEK TEMPTATION IN PARADISE

MICHELE RENAE

MILLS & BOON

Happy Birthday to you!
You look marvelous.
You shine.
And I'm so glad you are in this world!

CHAPTER ONE

Saralyn Martin had not worn a bikini in twenty years.

The dressing room she stood in was attached to a luxurious bedroom that boasted a king-size bed, all-natural linens and floor-to-ceiling windows that overlooked a white sand beach frilled with emerald palm trees. Luxurious island getaway for one? Check!

With a discerning eye she studied her reflection. Having lived in California the past two decades, she owned many swimsuits, all of them a one-piece. The coverage boosted her oft-lacking self-confidence. Yet, she was here to shake up her life. Step out of her comfort zone. Become a new woman! Bikinis had been the logical choice for this two-week vacation and she intended to wear them daily.

Sucking in her tummy, she prodded at her hips. Bit more flesh there than she'd prefer, but as she faced her fiftieth birthday wearing the new crown of menopause, wasn't she allowed some padding?

Not by Hollywood standards. Fortunately, she no longer claimed Hollywood-wife status.

A sigh dropped her shoulders and her tummy relaxed. *Was* it fortunate that she'd recently divorced her soap opera star husband of twenty years who had been unfaithful for half that time? It had been a year and a half since Brock had left their home at her request. The divorce had been finalized a month ago. He had gotten more than he deserved. The house in Los Angeles, the Swiss vacation home. Their friends—Martha, her yoga buddy, was *such* a traitor! Pieces of her dignity.

Saralyn had to be out of the house by the end of summer. With no idea where she would land, she knew with certainty she did want to leave California and the bad memories it held. With a one-million-dollar settlement sitting in her bank account, she could begin again.

Beginning again was one of the reasons she now stood here in this quiet villa on a private Caribbean island. The other had to do with her career. A should-she-or-shouldn't-she? dilemma that must be resolved within the two-week stay.

Thanks to her friend Juliane's last-minute schedule change, Saralyn had the entire island to herself. Juliane had intended to stay here on a romantic getaway with her boy-friend. This island, after all, was where *Sex on The Beach* had been filmed. She'd been curious to check it out. How-ever, Juliane had gotten a call two days ago confirming she'd earned a seat on a six-month Antarctic research mission that was leaving immediately. An aquatic biologist, Juliane knew a refusal would bar the applicant from ever applying again. After accepting the position, she'd called Saralyn.

It hadn't taken more than a "you deserve this" and a "sunny skies and blue waters" from Juliane for Saralyn to accept the generous offer. The rental fee had been nonre-fundable. And while the divorce settlement had been ear-marked for her future home and retirement savings, she had received the final payment for the memoir she'd ghostwrit-ten, so she could manage any expenses this trip presented.

Today was publication day for that memoir.

Sneering at her reflection, Saralyn silently admonished

the foolish woman who had written the autobiography *Living Paradise*. The author's name on the cover? Brock Martin.

"Just let it go," she told the woman in the mirror. "He's out of your life. Start...a new chapter."

So here she was. Two weeks of blissful blue skies, turquoise waters, white sands and tropical weather. On *the* island. Yes, she had written the story that had been filmed here—she was contractually bound not to tell anyone, including Juliane, about that. And it thrilled her that she finally had opportunity to visit this place that she felt a proud connection to.

But during these two weeks she also intended to figure out her life. Where was she headed? Dare she allow love into her life again? How to even begin dating as a middle-aged introvert? And should she take the offer to ghostwrite another book for a *New York Times* bestselling romance author? Or did Saralyn dare to refuse that contract and instead write her own story, the historical-heist idea that had been nudging at her for years?

"You will figure it all out," she said to her reflection. "I know you can do it."

Nodding in agreement, but not completely feeling the assurance from her mirror self, she grabbed the bright, oversize pink silk scarf from the top of her suitcase and began to wrap it around her hips. Then she paused. Saralyn shook her head. No one here to see her cellulite or notice that her breasts weren't quite so high as they had been a decade earlier. And who needed makeup? She was unattached and alone and intended to embrace that refreshing freedom.

She tossed the scarf to the bed. It had only been a half hour since she'd set foot here. The guide who had driven the water taxi to the island had swiftly walked her through the villa placed but a stone's throw from the beach, pointing out the luxurious amenities—a fully stocked wine fridge!—and various spots of interests, but she'd known the layout. She'd watched the movie five times. The excitement of setting foot on this particular island could not be ignored.

Breezing through the living area, a vast half-circle room that featured curved windows three stories high—every view spectacular—she paused in the kitchen where a discreet black box sat under a cupboard. As she'd learned from the guide, it was a Faraday box. A person could place their electronic devices inside and it would block the island's Wi-Fi. No texts, no phone calls possible. Utter peace.

Clutching her phone to her chest, she eyed the box. While she wasn't a huge scroller, she did like to have it near for texts or calls from her mom. On the other hand, she had promised to check in with her, but only after she'd gotten settled.

"I'm going to do this vacation the right way."

She set the phone inside the box, then pulled her laptop from the carry bag, tucked it in, too, closed it and gave it a pat.

A wood walkway dotted with solar lights led her beneath a palm tree archway that sifted crisply in the light wind as she strolled toward the beach. Stepping onto the superfine, pearl-white sand, she delighted in the sensory warmth, wiggling her toes. Tilting back her head, she took in the azure sky, unreal in its utter blueness, and spread out her arms. The breeze tickled through her long brown hair, not pulled back in her requisite I'm-working ponytail. Her skin prickled as it awakened to the sunshine unadulterated by city smog. And the clear turquoise ocean glittered.

"Thank you, Juliane," she said.

Spying a set of wooden chaises, she wandered over— but before sitting, decided to wade into the water. Warmth splashed her ankles and her feet sank into the wet sand as she stepped in deeper. This felt too good to be real. During their twenty-year marriage, she and Brock had rarely vacationed. They'd used the Swiss getaway once, and he'd invited an obnoxious gang of friends along. Yet Saralyn had written many a story set in such gorgeous climes, with only the internet as her research. The real thing was…breathtaking. Surrounded by nature and no electronic devices to distract her. This was heaven! Only now, as her very being jittered anticipation and utter awe, did she understand how much she needed this escape. Tears ran down her cheeks.

"To a new and interesting chapter of my life," she said.

With a kick that splashed water and a dip to swirl her fingers across the surface, she waded back to shore and settled onto the chaise.

The island, owned by a young billionaire inventor, provided the ultimate luxury experience. Food was delivered every morning via a discreet drop-off box she'd seen when the landing boat had arrived. Juliane had selected the drop-off option as opposed to an on-site chef. Various sporty activities were available, including hiking trails, jet skiing, snorkeling, windsailing, and there was even a badminton court at the center of the island next to an infinity pool. Full Wi-Fi—apparently one could speak commands from anywhere and the AI would understand—a spa, yoga taught via Zoom. Everything was ultraluxe yet blended with the natural surroundings.

Digging her toes into the sand, she closed her eyes to the kiss of sunshine on her eyelids. Sea salt and earthy, verdant tones perfumed the air. "I could get used to this."

For a moment, she processed the sensory warmth, scents, sounds and eventually moved inward to notice her calm heartbeats. Not thundering as they so often did when she was forced to drive the 105 freeway. Over the years she'd become a literal recluse, only driving to places close to home. Saralyn had learned to be alone, even within her marriage.

And you're alone now. On a big island. With no means to leave. Who else knows about this island and could easily visit it while you're here?

Heartbeats picked up pace as her writer's brain concocted anxiety-causing scenarios. What had she done? She'd just relegated herself to a private island, far from civilization— the mainland was a fifteen-minute boat ride—and if anyone did come here she would be like a sitting target. Alone. Unable to defend herself...

Shaking her head, Saralyn chased away the crazy thought. Her brain tended to think the worst, and her body reacted as if it were really happening. She pressed a palm over her chest to calm her rapid heartbeats.

"You're fine. You're a big girl. Nothing weird is going to happen. Just enjoy!"

Today, she'd relax and settle in, probably walk the island later to take it all in. She didn't intend to go schedule crazy. Though she did have a few items on her to-do list. First on the list?

"Figure out what I'm going to write next."

If she accepted the ghostwriting job for the romance novel, she'd receive a paycheck, which she did need to cover basic living expenses. And that was about all it covered.

The other option, if she chose *not* to ghostwrite, would be to finish the historical-heist idea and publish under her own name. That would be a roll of the dice. Could she even sell under her name? Saralyn had been a ghostwriter for two decades, her entire writing career. Writing for others had always suited her introverted self. She enjoyed the journey of the story, handing it in, and walking away with a paycheck. No promoting, podcasts or anxiety-inducing book signings necessary. She rarely received credit for her writing; the author always put their name on the book. The nonfiction celebrity autobiographies she wrote did sometimes give her credit on the copyright page. But she'd never felt the need for that recognition.

Saralyn Martin had always been happiest standing in the background. Unnoticed. A literal ghost.

Until.

The divorce had changed her. She still hadn't figured it all out, but she did know one thing: she didn't want to be a ghost anymore. And that applied to all aspects of her life. But could she do it? Had she the gumption and courage to stand as her own woman and make a career for herself, support herself and, for the first time in her life, *not* rely on a man?

The contract she had been offered to ghostwrite was for another romance. The last story she'd written for the author, set on a tropical island, had been exceedingly successful. *Sex on the Beach* had been filmed on this very island. With no credit for Saralyn.

Yet there was the issue of being able to support herself. Ghostwriting paid well enough but never enough that she was able to save, to get ahead. Her entire writing career she'd been married to Brock and he had supported the two of them. Brock had encouraged her to continue with her writing. It was her creative outlet, a means to thrive. She hadn't been required to bring in a certain income.

There were times, though, she'd felt he may have squelched her desire to make more money, to try her hand at stepping beyond the ghostwriting and seeing how it would go under her own name. The earnings possibilities were far greater than ghostwriting.

Had Brock purposely kept her under his thumb, emotionally and financially? Keep the wife tucked away at home while he philandered? He'd never argued when she'd stepped back from attending a flashy event with him. The man had an ego. And she knew he couldn't abide being married to a woman who made more money than him, or who may have stolen the spotlight with a swing of her silken hair and a flash of her veneers. Or possibly, a woman who may have garnered her own fame through her bestselling novels.

Saralyn could craft a great story. And she had the skill to alter her on-the-page voice to match that of the authors she ghostwrote for. And in reviews, fans lauded the author's ability to craft the ultimate sexy hero. They dubbed him their "book boyfriend" and had even written sexy fan fiction about him.

Saralyn loved to read the reviews. And, yes, she did have a talent for creating a sexy alpha man on the page. Generally, he had dark hair and European features. Muscles for days. And he always knew when to walk around without a shirt on. He was aloof but attentive. Smart and fun. He always protected the heroine. And while he had his own goals, ambitions and dreams, he would walk the world and battle dragons to ensure the heroine was happy. The best men existed on the page.

Might she ever find another hero to walk into her life? Did they even exist in real life? Brock Martin had once been her hero. No longer. And really. Did she *need* a man to protect and care for her?

She shrugged. "I prefer my men on the page. Give me tall, dark and…"

She softened her focus and allowed the elements of an ultimate hero to coalesce before her. Tall, he walked proudly and perhaps with a slight bow to his legs. Something so sexy to her about a bowlegged walk. Arms swinging confidently with his strides, he mastered the earth with each step, the hero returning to claim all that he desired—which was only ever the heroine's heart.

His hair, dark as raven wings or coal dust or even precious black tourmaline would be carelessly finger-raked into a non-style, yet look as though a stylist had spent hours on it. Bedroom hair? Oh, yeah. A loose strand would probably dangle over his sharp but domineering eyebrow. Beneath those brows were eyes forged from earth and stone that caught the sunlight and told stories, so many tales of adventure, trial and heartbreak. The heroine could never look into those whiskey-brown irises without catching her breath and seeing her truth reflected back at her.

A chiseled jawline was de rigueur, along with the perfect amount of dark stubble. Not quite a beard, but never straggly. This man was perfection.

And farther down…

"Oh, yes, those abs." Saralyn blinked, loving the fantasy of bare torso and abs. They were hard. Honed. Tanned. The proverbial six-pack.

Licking her lips, her body softened, relaxing against the wood chaise as the sexy vision approached.

The man who walked across the beach toward her held a string of fish and wore his swim trunks low to reveal the cut muscles that looked hard enough to hone steel. Sweat pearled on those muscles—or no, those were water droplets from the ocean. A merman risen from the depths. Come to seduce her silly with a godlike physique and darkly devastating looks.

Saralyn tugged in her lower lip. The perfect amount of dark chest hair glinted with water droplets. Not too much that a woman would wake in the middle of the night dreaming of bears, and not so little that the sun would gleam on his bare skin. Masculinity defined. And he had…she counted… more than a six-pack. Mmm, wouldn't she like to wander her fingers over those hard ridges?

A brilliant glint sparkled between his lips as he curved a sun-shaming smile.

"Wait." Clutching the chaise arms, Saralyn sat upright. Was she hallucinating? She narrowed her gaze against the

sunlight and then opened her eyes wide. The man was…
real? Couldn't be.

"There's not supposed to be anyone on this island." Never
had her imagination conjured the real thing.

Her heart stuttered. Had her worst fear come true? Alone
on the island—he didn't look like a serial killer come to
claim his next victim. But what a perfect ruse to lure the
victim closer!

No. Chill, Saralyn. He's just one of the staff. A local? Or
a fisherman who had anchored his boat nearby?

Whoever he was, he was stunning.

And she was a pale, middle-aged woman wearing a teeny
bikini.

She stood, grasping for her silk scarf, then remembered
she'd left it in the villa. Shoot! She clasped her hands across
her tummy and nervously slid them upward. Then one hand
slid to her hip where she sported that unasked-for menopausal bonus bulge.

"Who are you?" Body discomfort aside, this wasn't right.
"This is *my* island."

"Is it, now?" A bemused smile glinted in the stranger's
eyes. Dark irises, probably whiskey brown or even earthen
umber. His mouth quirked in a seductive smirk, like a romance hero set to seduce the heroine with his charming
aloofness. "Your island?"

"It is for the next two weeks," she said firmly. How dare
he distract her annoyance with an inhale that flexed his pecs?
"Are you staff? Is that my dinner?" She gestured toward the
fish. "Is that what was meant by 'fresh food delivered daily'?
That's taking things to the extreme."

With another flutter of her palm across her stomach, she
sucked in. Did he notice her tummy? Her pale skin desperately in need of a tan? Why was the sexiest man alive

standing so close to her she could feel her nipples harden and—that was so not what she needed right now.

"Dinner?" He jiggled the line of fish. "If you like. I'm willing to share."

Share? As in— Was he *staying* on the island?

"No seriously. Who are you?" she pleaded. "There must have been a booking mistake."

He offered a hand to shake, which she could but stare at. For as appealing as that hand looked, and it was attached to, oh, such a gorgeous physique, she did wonder if it was coated with fish slime. "I'm the owner of the island."

The...owner? That man was a billionaire who invented things and should—according to her writerly imagination— be wearing a lab coat or even a fancy business suit. Not looking like a sexy version of Robinson Crusoe.

"The owner," she said. "Sorry. I didn't know—but I did pay to stay here. Rather, I'm using my girlfriend's vacation since she had previous— Oh, it doesn't matter. This is *my* vacation. On a *private* island. *Private* meaning just me. No one else."

"That could be one definition of the word."

"There is only one definition of *private*," she protested.

"*Private* simply indicates the island is secluded. Set off from the rest of the busy world. I'll be here for a stay."

"But you... This is supposed to be a private island!"

"You keep saying that but the definition doesn't change. It *is* a private island."

The man showed no sign of understanding or complying with her desperate need to make him gone. "Not if there are two people on it!"

"I have a right to be here anytime I want. It's in the fine print."

"The fine print?" Saralyn had developed a need to wear readers for small text. It was not how she'd expected fifty to greet her. Why couldn't she age gracefully? But no matter. "I didn't read the contract."

"Not wise."

"As I've said, this vacation is my girlfriend's booking. She's the one who did all the paperwork and read…" Had Juliane read the fine print? What did it matter? The man should not be here!

Saralyn crossed her arms over her breasts. Who cared about her tummy bulge and cellulite? This was just wrong. How to relax and find her groove when Adonis wandered the island? And in nothing more than a pair of khaki swim trunks that seemed to fade from sight against his tan skin and enhance every single spectacular muscle on his body?

"No one ever reads the fine print," he offered with a shrug. "But don't worry. I won't get in your way. I use the island when I need it. And…" His heavy sigh gave her anxiety a pause. What did that world-weary sigh mean? "I really need it right now. I'll stay at the chef's cottage on the other side of the island. You won't see me. Unless you want to."

Unless she…? Had he said that with a lilting tease? Cheeky of him. Yet it did prod an intriguing wedge into her plans. Alone on an island with a sexy stranger? Such a trope always appealed in romance novels.

"Well, I don't want to share," she forced herself to say to defeat her failing stoicism. "I want to enjoy this vacation as was intended, alone and…"

Alone and desperate? She wasn't desperate. Just…seeking. But she was thrown. Wasn't sure how to react with all that *man* and pulsing muscle and wet chest hair and gleaming teeth.

"I need to go change." She spun and headed to the villa.

"The bikini suits you!" he called.

Saralyn gestured dismissively behind her as she increased her speed. That he must see her thighs jiggle as she hurried off humiliated her. Once in the villa, she pulled the sliding-glass door shut and then the bamboo curtains. Only when she felt sure he could not see inside did she turn her back to the wall and blow out a breath.

A man who bore the physical appearance of every devastatingly handsome hero she'd ever created had just stepped off the page and barged into her reality. And he didn't seem at all concerned that she was bothered by it!

"This is not going to work."

CHAPTER TWO

THE WOMAN HE might have possibly frightened on the beach earlier was a knockout. Long legs, pale porcelain skin, soft brown hair. David couldn't help but notice how she had tried to cover her stomach, then her breasts. If women knew how most men's minds functioned—soft, pretty girl talking to me; score!—they wouldn't give their random body parts a second thought. Men did admire beauty, but it was the personal connection that really got their systems rolling.

At least, that's how it worked for David Crown. Good conversation and an attractive demeanor? Sign him up!

David had expected a couple to be staying on the island—he'd checked the schedule—and had intended to keep his distance while perhaps one day introducing himself and thanking them for their patronage. He'd not expected... He hadn't gotten her name. Who was that marvelous beauty possessed of a serious need to relax?

Whoever she was, she had just shoved a wrench in his plan to work things out. The escape from reality part had been achieved. Owning this island served as the perfect getaway when the real world got too intense. Of course, his COO had his number and had called when he'd landed hours earlier. Reminding him that he could never completely escape The Dilemma. A decision needed to be made, and soon.

He'd carried a photo of a six-year-old boy in his wallet for weeks. His heart fractured even more every time he looked at the child's big bright eyes. That haunting smile was the reason he'd come here to make one of the biggest decisions in his life. It would happen before he returned to New York City.

But right now he was in curiosity mode. A much better place to occupy than grief. His escape from the real world had been disturbed by the presence of a lovely—yet annoyed—woman.

Of course, he was a man of his word. He'd not intrude on her privacy. Too much. Her face, free of makeup and absent those weird long false lashes most women wore, had gone from surprise to anger to worry after seeing him. He wanted to see it go to happiness.

So he knocked on the glass villa door. The curtains were drawn. He hoped not because of him. The best way to enjoy the island was with the two-story sliding-glass doors wide open to allow the tropics to intrude upon the harsh structure of shelter.

The curtain pulled aside to reveal big brown eyes and a straight mouth. Her hair was tidied into a queue at back and a soft white caftan hung off one bare shoulder. Inadvertently exquisite.

He lifted the plate of fish to show her why he'd come. He was no four-star chef, but he could fillet and grill a fish, thanks to lessons from the world-famous chef he employed.

With a reluctant nod, the woman slid open the door, but only five inches. She wasn't going to make this easy.

Fair enough. David often dealt with business execs and marketing pros who insisted their way was best. He had this.

"I come bearing the promised dinner and an apology."

One delicate dark brow arched on her face.

"My manner was rude and dismissive earlier. I apologize. We should have been properly introduced. And I shouldn't have assumed you would appreciate another person staying on *your* island."

Always let the other party feel they are in control.

She opened her mouth, but before she could speak, he added, "As well…" He splayed out his arms. He'd donned a crazy Hawaiian print shirt, which always made him smile at the wild colors, and a pair of beige cargo shorts. "You must have been utterly aghast to see a half-naked man stalking toward you on what should have been a *private* beach."

"Aghast?" She pressed a hand to her chest and then… chuckled. The dulcet sound zapped David's apprehensions and his shoulders dropped. "I do believe I was. Not so much because of all the abs and chest hair and—" She pressed her lips together and shook her head.

She had been studying his abs? David controlled the urge to smolder at her. He'd been told his smolder was irresistible. A panty-dropper, according to some silly social media site devoted to posting photos of him. So weird that people did that. Like stalking him, only it didn't make him feel threatened so much as creepily uncomfortable about all the comments regarding his physique and what the commenters would like to do with said physique.

"Let's leave it at *aghast*." She stepped aside and pushed the sliding door open; the ball bearings took it to rest on the opposite side of the room where the curve of the building began. "And dinner? I accept the apology." She held out her hand in wait of the plate.

David held it a little closer to his chest. He didn't intend to retreat too quickly. Not when he'd won the apology phase of this interesting scenario. "Might I come inside?"

She took an inordinate amount of time studying the plate and compressing her mouth. To let in the perfect stranger or to grab the food and slam the door in his face?

"I suppose."

Not the most promising invitation. "Well, if you're not sure?"

"You did cook. No reason we can't share a meal."

"Thank you." He stepped inside and set the plate on the kitchen counter, cut from a slab of pyrite-bespeckled lapis lazuli. He'd had the entire villa decorated with earthy tones and minerals and crystals from conflict-free mines. Turning, he offered his hand, which she had refused to shake earlier. "David Crown. Owner of the island, inventor, entrepreneur, philanthropist and genuinely apologetic."

She shook his hand, which was a good sign. "Saralyn Martin. Vacationer, writer and no longer aghast."

"Nice to meet you, Saralyn. The fish is cooling. Shall we share a meal and chat? I can fill you in on some of the island's more secret surprises. Then I promise to leave you to your isolation. It is what you paid for after all."

She went to the cupboard and retrieved plates, glasses and a bottle of wine from the fridge and brought it to the table. "As I explained earlier, I didn't pay for it. My friend wasn't able to use the trip and she knew I needed a getaway. I never let opportunity pass me by. Or rather…" She considered what she'd said. "I won't anymore. All opportunities must be considered. Yes. I like that."

She set the plates on the table, across from one another, and then twisted the cork from the wine bottle. An easy twist. She'd already popped the cork? His admiration for the woman increased.

David moved one of the plates to the left so they could sit closer, and seated himself as she sat in her chair. He dished up the fish.

"That looks delicious and smells—" she inhaled, eyes closed as if smelling a flower "—like coconut?"

"I make the sauce using the coconuts on the island," he said. "All local ingredients."

"Are you a chef, too?"

He shrugged. "I like to experiment when I stay here. There are coconuts, fish, some berries and a generous variety of fruits, ripe for the picking this time of year. Though I suspect Ginger and Mary Ann might come up with something much more interesting."

Her eyebrow arched and her inquisitive brown eyes twinkled at his reference to the television show, *Gilligan's Island*, which had revolved around the lives of seven quirky castaways stranded for years on an island.

"I'm not so sure about their culinary adventures," she said. Their specialty was coconut cream pie. I always wonder about those two."

"How so?"

"Seriously? We all know the glamorous movie star, Ginger, never baked a day in her life. Sweet, wholesome Mary Ann, who once worked at a general store, did it all. Yet more often than not she let Ginger take the credit."

"Mary Ann was a people pleaser."

Saralyn exhaled and caught her elbows on the table, nodding. She'd drifted off somewhere and David felt sure it wasn't to an island populated by a professor, a millionaire and a movie star. One of his favorite old-timey shows to watch as a kid, he knew the characters well. "Do you know why the professor booked his tour on the *S.S. Minnow* that day?"

She gave it some thought. "I don't recall."

"He was doing research for his book *Fun with Ferns*," David provided. "I identify with the professor the most."

"Really? Oh, you did say you are an inventor. I guess I must claim Mary Ann's identity but with an ambition toward being the uninhibited and sexy Ginger." She trailed a finger along the plate before her and eyed him with interest. "What's a young guy like you doing watching television shows from the sixties? Weren't kids of your generation into mutant turtles or Barney?"

"Barney. Ugh. That big purple puppet scared the daylight out of me. But you're not old enough to have watched the original series. Surely you watched the replays as I did?"

"If you're wrangling for my age you're going about it the wrong way."

"I wasn't." He nudged the plate toward her to distract from this conversational curve. One thing he did know about women was they could be touchy about their ages. "Try this?"

"Yes, of course." A few bites and some careful consider-ation. David watched an entire litany of sensory decisions glimmer in her eyes. Remarkable how outspoken she could be without saying a word. Finally, an approving nod. "I don't usually care for seafood but this is…just right. What kind of fish is this?"

He inwardly beamed at the compliment. She was either easy to impress or… Was she a people pleaser like Mary Ann?

"It's a kind of mackerel. I'm glad you like it because fish is it for my culinary skills."

"And this sauce is incredible. I give it four stars."

"I'll take it." He poured wine for them both.

"So, Professor, you mentioned earlier that you had come here to escape." Over the rim of the glass, her intense brown eyes didn't so much prod as seek.

"Did I say that? Well, I did put that wording in the fine print so whenever I feel the real world crushing down on my shoulders I can retreat here."

"What's crushing you? What do you do, anyway? Be-sides own the most perfect tropical escape I've ever visited."

"Have you visited many?"

"Well." She touched her goblet, then shook her head. "But

I have done research. And this is a fine example of private islands. The wine fridge alone has won me over."

"You do research?"

She ate another bite of fish and gestured with her fork. "No, we are on you right now. Your work and what's crushing your shoulders."

She got right to the point and was a careful foil to evasion. Smart woman. Not someone he suspected would easily accept a dismissive reply. Fair enough.

"I own Crown Corp. We invent 'remarkable things to change the ordinary world.'" He quoted the company motto. "I'm the chief scientist slash inventor. I'm also a philanthropist. Have a few charitable foundations. And I'm not known for my cooking."

"Then, no one has tasted your coconut fish."

"I save that culinary secret for my inner circle."

"That means I've already entered the circle." She sipped and gave him a steady stare over the goblet. "Nice."

His circle was small, but he wouldn't mind inviting her into it. And not simply as a friend to review his cooking skills. Those soft brown eyes pulled him in and he wasn't sure if he would drown or float in them. She wasn't openly flirting with him, but some undertone in her voice lured him deeper. Not like most women, he decided. At least, not the ones he'd dated.

"Crown Corp basically runs itself," he said. "I've some very trusted people running the show, but I like to keep my hands on the gears, so to speak. The lab is my usual hangout. I will never remove my inventor's apron and safety goggles. Ideas abound in my brain. Which means the concept of leisure is foreign to me. Usually takes me a day or two to unwind after I arrive here."

"Crown Corp? Is that…the hug blanket?"

"Yes, you know it?"

"Who doesn't? The commercial is on TV all the time. And…don't you donate blankets to children's hospitals and homeless shelters?"

"And women's shelters, and when there's a natural disaster, we ship directly to the relief site. Helping others was the principal purpose for the blanket's invention."

"A blanket that actually hugs a person. That's crazy."

"You've never tried it?"

"No."

Surprising. It seemed his invention had literally blanketed the world, at least according to sales numbers. David was accustomed to friends, acquaintances, even the lady in the supermarket checkout—he liked to buy his own produce—regaling him of its beloved qualities.

And yet, the photo in his wallet reminded him that some things perhaps weren't meant to be shared with the world.

"I know we stock them in the villa." He scanned around the half-circle living area. "That blanket strewn artfully across the couch by the staging team is one of them."

She glanced to the cream-colored blanket which matched the interior's neutral wood, bamboo and sandy tones. "I'll give it a try later." She pushed her plate aside, having finished the fish, and propped an elbow on the table, her attention focused entirely on him.

Thankful she'd dismissed the blanket—he wasn't emotionally prepared to talk about it—he fell into her gaze. What a unique experience. For a woman to look at him like she was interested in what he had to say? Rarely did he talk shop with anyone. Most women he dated nodded absently while he could see their brains rushing to sensational queries like: *How rich are you? Do you really own a private jet? Can I get a photo for my socials? Did that princess really ban your blanket in her country because you wouldn't date her?* And the oft-asked question of late: *What about that trial, eh?*

"So, something with your business has got you seeking escape?" Saralyn prompted.

There it was. The question that stabbed at his too-tender heart. Did she *not* know? He'd thought the entire world aware of his struggles. Of that trial.

"Yes, something to do with the business." He quickly downed the rest of his wine and poured more.

"That question makes you uneasy." She tilted her head, studying him. And not in a surface manner, but rather, she seemed to permeate his very molecules and root about for atom-level truth. That both startled and intrigued him.

"I know we just met," she said, "but I'm interested in the deep delve. It's the writer in me who likes to step into a certain bold space."

"I can sense that."

"You do?" She bowed her head and smiled a little. Surprising herself with her boldness? What a lovely contradiction. "But also… I confess I have an intense desire to take control of my life. Be more assertive. So I'm going to ask the hard question. You can answer or not. What is *it* exactly?"

"Taking control of your life? Have you not had control over it?"

"Not me. You." She gestured with a finger toward him. "You're in the hot seat right now. What's the thing you're avoiding?"

Did she notice the sweat forming at his temples? He didn't like the interrogation, the morbid interest in a private matter. Fine. It was a Crown Corp matter. And mostly, the sensationalism of personal pain.

Yet Saralyn threatened in none of those ways.

He asked, "Promise you'll sit on the hot seat later?"

She considered the question, then nodded.

"Fine. Why am I here? It's to do with the lawsuit."

"A lawsuit? Against…you?"

"Do you not listen to the news?" he asked. "You've heard nothing about the legal travails of Crown Corp and its feckless CEO, David Crown?"

He did not like that label of *careless*. He was always concerned for the safety of others. Crown Corp could not have risen to such success had he not been adamant about safety.

"Sorry." She teased a fingertip around the rim of her wine goblet. "Another writer foible is that I tend to get lost on the page. Seclude myself from television and social media while working on a project. And with the past months…" She looked aside and shook her head. With an inhale, she lifted her head as if renewing her purpose. "I catch up on news now and then."

"Lost on the page." And what had happened in her past few months that she couldn't speak it? "You most certainly are getting on that hot seat later."

"Fair enough. So, a lawsuit?"

David pressed a thumb to his brow. It was much easier when a person knew the salacious details the media put out. Whether they were accurate details or not, at the very least they had a sketch.

"Crown Corp has been involved in a lawsuit…"

It was the reason he had escaped to the island. Not to talk it out, but rather to dive deep and discover the truth of his beliefs and determine if he could walk forward with the same integrity he'd always strived for.

If he didn't give her all the information, the self-proclaimed researcher could look it up and learn on her own.

"Legally, I can't give all the details." Mostly true. Though the trial was over and the transcripts had been released to the public. "Suffice, Crown Corp was cleared. It was an arduous two-week trial. I attended daily. And…" He caught his head against his hands and pushed his fingers through his hair. The tightness at his temples warned of an impending headache. He had to monitor his stress or it would flatten him like a steamroller. "I guess it messed with my head more than I thought it would. I've been snapping at employees lately. Not my style. Dodging the reporters that hang outside Crown Corp. The media has picked up on my distress, hyping me as heartless."

"Oh, my. I'm so sorry."

"I will never understand how the paparazzi seem to spring out from nowhere. No matter where a man goes, they are always there. Anyway, I needed to get away. Breathe this stunning fresh tropical air and get right with my heart."

She nodded. Understanding? "Well, I hope you find what you need while you're here. I can relate to getting right with one's heart."

"Yeah?" He could tell that they shared common struggles as he felt an enticing pull towards her. He saw a chance to turn the tables. "Your turn on the hot seat?"

"Fine. But I'm going to state this quickly, then jump off the seat. Because I'm still processing."

"Fair enough. Why your escape?"

"I got divorced about a year and a half ago. We were married twenty years."

David nodded. That would place her in her forties? Fifties?

"My ex was—rather *is*—a soap opera star. I stood on the edge of the Hollywood lifestyle the entire time, looking in, trying not to stumble on too much glitter. Anyway, I learned he had been screwing women on the side for ten of those years. The divorce was finalized last month. I walked away with enough to buy a house and start over. And he gets a ghostwritten memoir—today is the publication date—telling the world how fabulous he is. Thus, the need to take back my control. To rejoin life. And in the process, I've also to plot out a new book to satisfy my agent."

"Wow. That is some escape-the-world stuff. I'm sorry about the divorce."

"Don't be. It was meant to be. But it is tough to walk through the process of dissolving such a long attachment."

"I imagine so. And the book? I love a good novel."

"Really?" The light returned to her eyes, and that massaged the stab of regret David felt at asking about her escape. "Who is your favorite author?"

"The list is so long. Of course, I'm a King fan. He does average-Joe horror like no other. And Koontz is a comfort read. I also enjoy a good action, heist story. And any mystery that doesn't involve a sweet little old lady knitting or baking cupcakes."

Saralyn's laughter was deep and refreshing. For a woman who sought to take back control, she owned the room with that confident laugh.

"Good call on the mysteries," she said. "I'm actually a ghostwriter. So you'll never see anything I've written on the bookshelves. Or actually, you'll see it, you just won't know I've written it. Another author's name is on the cover."

"No credit whatsoever?"

"Nope. And I don't mind. Or rather…"

She drifted to that thoughtful place again and he decided to let her go with it this time. Because his thoughtful place had become furnished with her soft hair and those telling brown eyes. Perfect bow lips and the smooth alabaster of her shoulders. Could he curl up and lose himself? An incessant desire for connection niggled at him. After so many failed relationships—or rather, they just hadn't been the right person for him—dare he hope for something real?

"I want to step up and be known," she declared. "The time has come to see *my* name on a book. To support myself. So my dilemma is... Should I ghostwrite another story for a well-known romance author? Or do I dare write the novel that's been prodding at me for years?"

"I vote for the novel that's prodding you. But what do I know? Do you need the ghostwriting gig to survive?"

"Yes and no. I'll be fine for a few years, but then I'll need to buckle down and support myself with my writing. And the thing is, can I do that as an unknown with my name on the cover? I'm not sure. Surely, it would pay more than the ghostwriting jobs, but selling is the issue."

"What does your agent say?"

"She thinks I would be a fool to let the ghostwriting gig slip from my fingers. It's a guaranteed paycheck, though I'm not sure I can support myself with it. I've always relied on my husband's income."

"Can you write both?"

"Not well. I'm a one-project-at-a-time writer. It's something I'm going to consider over the next two weeks. I want to leave this island with a sound plan for my future."

"I wish you luck."

"Thank you." She reached across the table, her hand nearing his, and then suddenly pulled back. Had she been about to take his hand? Offer a reassuring touch? His heart thundered to consider such. But she'd caught herself. Good call. He didn't want to disappoint her. "I hope you find the peace you're seeking."

"This island never fails to calm me," he said. "I can loll in a hammock and read with waves sloshing in the background for hours."

"That's on my schedule for tomorrow. Along with a hike around the island to check out all it has to offer. I'm not sure I'm up for parasailing but kayaking and snorkeling could prove promising."

"If you intend to snorkel, you need to sign up on the portal so an instructor can come give you safety lessons and accompany you. It's all in the informational video."

She nodded toward the tablet computer set up on the kitchen counter, which provided twenty-four-hour support, information and guides for those guests who chose to do the completely staff-free experience. "Got it."

David felt the need to add, "I promise to stay out of your way."

"Oh? Uh… You don't need to do that. I owe you an apology, too. I was a bit harsh with you on the beach. Well, you did surprise me. Rendered me utterly aghast." Her smile was so delicious; it attacked her without warning, and he found that intriguing. "But there's no reason we must avoid each other, is there? I mean, I'm not inviting you to move in…"

"I get it. Maybe if you're lucky, I'll give you a spearfishing lesson one day."

"I might enjoy that. Sounds like good research."

"You're going to write a novel with a spear fisher in it?"

"I did that with the last novel I wrote for a romance author. It was set on a tropical island. Exactly like this one, in fact."

"And you're only now visiting one?"

"Yes, well, I'm a homebody. Not big on traveling where there are crowds or…" She sighed. "People. But that's going to change."

He could understand that fear of people, or rather, crowds, and when in lesser amounts, people he did not know. "I do need to point out one thing."

"What's that?"

"You said you want to rejoin life and to be known."

"I do."

"And yet, the place you come to prepare for that is a private island? Seems counterintuitive to me."

"Doesn't it?" Her laughter found a place in his core and spun gently. It wasn't a feeling he wanted to lose. "I'm starting slow. You know that Stella-getting-her-groove-back story?"

"Loved the movie."

"Well." She spread her arms out to her sides. "This is Saralyn *finding* her groove."

David lifted his goblet to toast. "To Saralyn finding her groove."

CHAPTER THREE

A HEAVY SIGH seeped from Saralyn's lungs as she tilted her head back against the beach chaise. It was early afternoon, and after a morning swim and a light lunch, she'd decided to laze awhile before hiking the island. Mentally, her gears were spinning. She didn't have to make the decision regarding her writing career in one day, but weighing her options was necessary.

If she accepted the ghostwriting offer, she'd have to write a ninety-thousand-word romance novel in five months. Hand it in. Cash the check. And be done. No edits because what she wrote then became the publisher's property. From that point, the author whose name went on the book cover in gold foiling—and who took all the credit for writing it on the copyright page—was allowed to do a light edit. From what Saralyn had read of the four published works she'd produced for that author, she hadn't changed more than an occasional name or car color. The gold-foil author earned royalties, got all the publicity and fame, and had even been the author of record when the publisher sold the last book to a movie producer.

Saralyn never complained about her ghostwriting gig. With each contract she got paid enough to live well for about half a year. And she had never been a spotlight seeker. Standing on the sidelines was her jam. The ghost no one had ever heard of or cared about.

Yet this island represented the achievement that she could not claim. The movie of her book had been filmed on this very sand. It was remarkable to be here. To take it all in. But it also reminded that she needed to step up, to grasp a new set of reins and finally take what she desired.

That being the other option, which was to not accept the ghostwriting contract. If she chose not to, her agent, Leslie, had warned she might never get another offer from that publisher. And Leslie had implied that if she was so stupid as to not take the offer, she wouldn't continue representing her.

Tough words to hear after a fifteen-year relationship with the agency. But Leslie had become complacent. She no longer sought writing jobs for Saralyn, she simply sat back and waited for the offers to come to her through publishers who had previously contracted with Saralyn. That oddball idea for the history of the bath that Saralyn had pitched her two years ago? Her agent had sniffed and said she didn't think her present stable of publishers would be interested. Well, certainly they may not be, but weren't there plenty other publishers out there? Why not shop it around? That, and the fact Leslie rarely negotiated for film royalties bothered Saralyn. Yes, her work was take the paycheck, no royalties, move on. But shouldn't she be compensated if it sold for film or screen?

Anyway, not accepting the ghostwriting job would allow her to work on the story she'd been chasing in her dreams for years. The historical heist with a twist. Set in eighteenth-century Paris, her favorite time period and location. She'd already drafted a third of the story. Had written detailed studies for the characters. And she'd worked out the impossible timeline. The twist was killer! The interesting characters beckoned to her. She just needed some time and space to focus and write it.

But writing a novel on spec would bring in exactly zero dollars to her coffers. And while Saralyn had the divorce settlement, she would rely on her writing to pay for groceries and basic living expenses. She would also need a car since Brock had managed to retain all three vehicles in the settlement. Truthfully, she'd easily given up on trying to keep any of their shared possessions. She'd simply wanted out and to remove as much of his unfaithful DNA from her life. Walking away with cash and no shared marital possessions had felt empowering. And it still did.

The future was hers to design. Yet what to do? To continue to ghostwrite or dare to write under her own name?

And what was that delicious scent that fluttered around her like invisible butterflies? She leaned to the side, slapping a palm onto the warm sand and tilted her head to study the trees and foliage behind her that edged the beach. Must be a tropical flower in there somewhere. The urge to bring along her phone so she could look up the flora and fauna had been strong, but...

"Maybe a few days before I leave," she decided. "I do have to take advantage of this hands-on research while I've the chance."

When she'd written the tropical island romance, she had wanted to visit an island to experience the sights, sounds and scents. Honestly, a writer need never leave their chairs for all the sensory details one could find online regarding any thing, place, emotion, etcetera. But she'd begun researching Brock's memoir at the same time. And that had made her physically ill. Escaping to a tropical island couldn't have happened with a queasy gut and broken heart.

Saralyn had discovered more than she'd wanted to learn while researching Brock. As soon as she'd handed in the romance, she'd called a lawyer. At the time, she'd wanted to be discreet. Saralyn Martin was a ghost who was accustomed to standing in the shadows, accepting whatever role she was required to play in her famous husband's life, as long as she was treated well and kindly. She'd always felt that Brock cared about her. Even the last eight or so years when his attention had noticeably waned.

Had it been her fault his attention had wandered? Of course it had. She blamed herself for being so busy with her writing, not paying him enough attention. Call it an introvert's fear of parties or call it not feeling up to shining as brightly as was required of a Hollywood star's spouse. Once she'd had domestic dreams of family, children and the proverbial white picket fence. Saralyn had never fallen into the groove of the rich and famous. After only a few years of their marriage, Brock had stopped asking her to attend functions with him.

Truly, she had written herself into her own disastrous marriage.

Now? She wished she had blasted her research on all the news stations and social media. Let them know Brock Martin was an asshole who had cheated on her for half their marriage. A man who had insisted his wife remain in the background, write in the shadows, never stepping up and into the spotlight. But instead, meek and ghosty Saralyn had wanted to ensure no feathers were ruffled, that she wasn't drawn into the media frenzy, and had quietly settled. And at her agent's nudging, she'd even honored the stipulation that she finish writing her husband's autobiography because she was contractually bound. Leslie lost more points for not standing in her corner on that one.

Brock's memoir, *Living Paradise*, had been released yesterday. With his name in gold foil on the cover and no acknowledgement on the copyright page that Saralyn had written it all. It was a glowing narrative of his two decades on the soap opera scene. No mention about his hidden fixation with hooking up with young Botoxed blondes who he tended to promise a sit-down with his agent. Never happened. But Brock had gotten a few nights of sex out of those nubile ingenues. All of it, Saralyn had learned from going through his texts and emails. Tech-savvy and unbreakable passwords were not Brock Martin's forte.

"You are such a pushover," she muttered. Feeling the heavy weight of her past decisions, she slipped off the chaise and onto the sand, rolling to her back and stretching out her arms. "Can you really stop being a ghost? Do you dare?"

Next week, she turned fifty. Half her life gone. And what had she to show for it? A few rare acknowledgements on some copyright pages and a failed marriage. Not to mention the menopausal pudge that she certainly hoped David hadn't taken note of.

The second half of her life had to improve. It could only get better, right? What she'd said to David in a moment of self-confidence about finding her groove had been exactly right. Saralyn Martin—make that Saralyn Hayes, her maiden name—needed to take back—no, to *create*—her life.

Might finding her groove include an affair with a younger man?

Saralyn spit out the few sand granules that dusted her lips. She was thinking like some kind of romance heroine if she thought the billionaire inventor would have an interest in her.

Though, the way he did look at her…as if she were the only person in the room.

"You *are* the only one in the room and on the island," she chastised her hopeful thoughts. "And he's too young. You don't want to humiliate yourself anymore by engaging in silly fantasies. Just stick to the plot."

A boring, cliché plot. That definitely needed some tweaking.

* * *

David spied the woman lying arms outstretched on the sand beside the chaise. Had she passed out? Been attacked by one of the aggressive island parrots that tended to fly low to a person's head if they were eating? Washed ashore after a vigorous swim had resulted in a poisonous jellyfish sting? There were no jellyfish, but his imagination could not be corralled.

She wasn't moving.

Thinking the worst, he rushed to her side. "Saralyn?"

"Oh, my God, there you are, like some kind of—" she sat up, brushed sand from her thighs and shook her head "—rescuing hero."

"Sorry. Not for rescuing you. You didn't need— It's not every day I find a woman lying sprawled on the sand as if she'd been attacked by wild parrots or a man-eating jellyfish."

"Man-eating— Are there jellyfish in the water?"

"There are not. It's just my inventor's brain. Sometimes it takes an imaginative leap and my body reacts as if it's really happening. Adrenaline."

"Been there, done that. Writer's brains can be the same. I can reduce myself to tears thinking terrible thoughts. But don't worry. I was…"

"It's okay. You don't need to explain. I'm not supposed to be bothering you." He stood yet didn't feel the urge to leave her because…beautiful and interesting woman. And he had her all to himself. Yet he sensed a deep sadness in her posture of dropped shoulders and bowed head. And she had been sprawled in the sand as if a water-starved starfish. "*Is* everything okay?"

That he'd asked surprised him. He did worry after others, but he rarely knew how to voice that concern. Showing empathy was something that made him feel extremely uncomfortable. Did he do it right? Or make it worse? Would it be offensive to offer a gentle touch or handhold? He just didn't know what was proper.

"I'm working on it." She brushed sand from her long, smooth legs. A slide of her palm across her stomach resulted in her sucking it in. "Just trying to figure out the rest of my life."

"Is that all?" He squatted beside her, making sure to keep a few feet of space between them. He didn't want her to feel as though he were imposing on her privacy. "How's that working for you?"

She opened her mouth to reply but her eyes suddenly diverted to what he held. "Do you always walk around with a machete in hand?"

He remembered the blade and sheepishly waved it before him. "I'm collecting coconuts."

"That's a better explanation than plotting my murder."

"No need for that. Your bill is already paid. And I don't have the first clue on how to hide a body."

"Good to know. So, coconuts? I've seen them up in the trees. They are all green."

"Best time to harvest them. They are sweeter when they are young."

"Young and sweet," she said, savoring the words on her tongue.

Was that a hungry look she gave him? And her voice had taken on a deeper, sexy tone.

"Oh." She shook her head and seemed to come back from wherever she'd drifted. "Don't mind me. I slip into plot mode at the worst of times."

"It's because I'm a terrible conversationalist, isn't it?"

"Oh, darling, we haven't had a real conversation yet. Oh, for a soul-deep conversation," she pleaded to what he could only imagine was the universe.

He felt much the same. When was the last time a woman

sat down and talked to him? And really listened? They had shared their reasons for fleeing to the island last night. That had lifted something from his shoulders that he couldn't quite name but felt relieved for having shared.

"I'd like to have a conversation with you," he said. "But I'm aware that I am infringing on your privacy so—"

"Infringe away. I need a break from life planning. Will you show me how you harvest coconuts?"

"I'd love to."

A while later, Saralyn sipped sweet coconut milk from one half of the green fruit David had opened with an expert slash of the machete. He'd shimmied up the gracefully curved palm, like a monkey, and half a dozen coconuts had dropped to the sand after he'd called out, "Fore!"

She'd laughed at the golf reference. He'd explained he hadn't any other way to warn of impending flying spheres.

"What is that beautiful bird song?" she asked as she pried at the coconut meat with a fingertip.

"Some sort of tanager. They are tiny and bright scarlet. A portion of their wings flash emerald. They keep out of sight but enjoy serenading the island inhabitants."

"I could listen to them sing all day."

"A spoon works best." He gestured to her efforts. He'd collected half a dozen coconuts and put them in a woven bag. Wielding the machete, it caught the sun and glinted. "Do you want to try your hand at cutting one open?"

"I think I'll pass. I need all my fingers to type. Thanks for teaching me Coconut Harvesting 101. I'll definitely use it in a story someday."

He plopped down on the sand before her, squatting with his feet planted and his knees by his chest. Again he wore just the swim trunks. It was perhaps his island costume. With the temperate weather, it made sense. And it suited him more than she imagined a business suit might. If this man were to walk into her home office and flash his charming smile at her she would never get any work done.

"Did you know coconuts are considered a fruit, a nut *and* a seed?" he asked.

"I have come across that in my research but had forgotten about it. I take in information, use it, then it gets lost. But…something about it not being an actual tree seems to ring a bell?"

"Right. The coconut palm doesn't have bark or branches so it's not an official tree. I forget what the name is for the perennial. I'm like you. I take in a lot of info, keep the stuff that is meaningful and let the rest go. Though, don't you think it's all in there somewhere? Waiting to be retrieved?"

"Possible." She munched a piece of coconut meat. "If all the research and characters I've used over the years were always fore in my brain I'd go mad. There has to be a vault somewhere in our brains for storing the stuff that is no longer needed."

"So as a ghostwriter does that mean no one ever knows that you're the person who wrote it?" he asked.

"Exactly. I'm contractually bound to never reveal I'm the author. Though in a few cases I am given an acknowledgement on the copyright page. That's more like work-for-hire stuff. I've also written for an ongoing series that includes more than one author. We all wrote under one made-up author name placed on the cover. It was an adventure series featuring a female archaeologist who wielded Joan of Arc's magical sword. She could take out bad guys with a slash of her sword. It was a kick."

"It's remarkable that you've such restraint. I don't know if I could keep a secret like that. And forever?"

She laughed. "It's easy enough. I like to take the money

and run. Though, I've had a change of heart after…well…"
She shrugged. "The divorce."

"Twenty years is a long time. You should be proud of the accomplishment."

"Yes, I'm an old lady. Been around the track a time or two. And have the baggage to prove it. And I've taken my punches. Now I'm trying to get back up on the proverbial horse and—I've run out of clichés. On another note, I'm celebrating my fiftieth birthday next week."

"I never would have guessed."

"You don't need to be kind."

"Fifty isn't old."

"I've never thought it was. Until I learned that my husband had been screwing women half my age."

"That's rough. I'm glad you had the courage to walk away from him. No woman should be treated as an afterthought."

She smirked. "I feel as though I brought it upon myself. There's a certain amount of guilt that comes from knowing I didn't try hard enough. An afterthought is exactly what I've accepted in my love life and my career. The woman no one pays any mind to. The one who does all the work and gets none of the credit. But enough moaning." Had she really spilled all that to him? Saralyn! Divert the point of view. Now. "How old are you?"

"Thirty-five."

"So your parents must be in their…fifties?" Mercy, they were closer to her age than he was.

Saralyn, what the hell? Drop all fantasies of an affair with a younger man right now!

"Mum is sixty, Dad a few years older."

Wasn't like she was considering doing anything with him anyway. Fantasies were fantasies for a reason. Because they couldn't, and shouldn't, become reality. She must stick to merely studying him as romance-hero material. Although, every time he stood near, her entire body seemed to reach for him. Desired a new plaything. And that she was even thinking of him as a plaything startled her. She was not that woman.

Was she? No.

Maybe.

He leaned closer and bent to catch her gaze. "I don't know where your thought process is taking you, but I will toss out the fact that age means nothing to me. I know people from your generation tend to look askance at couples separated by large age gaps. But really, my generation doesn't like to label or assign expected conditions."

"'Your generation'? 'Askance'? Oh, brother."

He chuckled. "Don't think about it too much, Saralyn. You are a beautiful woman. You intrigue me. I like a smart woman."

"Is that so?"

He nodded. "It's hard to find someone I can talk to."

"Maybe you're looking in the wrong places? I mean, there are literally billions of women out there. Of all ages."

"There are. And yet…" Standing, he snatched up the bag of coconuts and claimed the machete. "The crazy thing is the one who intrigues me most feels unattainable."

He swung the bag over a shoulder. "You know, you can take the meat out of that coconut and use it to cook. Maybe even—" he winked and it was such a cocky, charming move Saralyn felt it enter her heart like an arrow shot true "—make a coconut cream pie."

With that he wandered off, leaving her clutching the coconut to her chest as she watched his exit. His legs had a slight bow to them. His stride was confident and sure. The muscles across his back advertised an undulating landscape no woman could resist exploring. So alluring. A dashing specimen of man.

"So. Much. Man."

She thought about what he'd said. Was *she* the one who intrigued him? Words to make any woman's heart flutter. And swoon.

She didn't swoon. That was silly girl stuff. She was a grown woman who had been married, had gone through a devastating divorce and knew what it was she wanted and didn't want from a partner. She didn't want a creep who thought he could gaslight her and have women on the side. Nor did she want an inexperienced young pup who wasn't ready to settle. She did want...

What *did* she want in a man? Because she did crave a relationship. The divorce had not destroyed the part of her that enjoyed being a couple, having conversations and sharing life. She'd not gotten that from Brock. The craving had always been there, and it remained in an inaccessible chamber of her heart.

But she wasn't going to jump into happily-ever-after with a man she'd only just met. A man who knew one of her favorite television shows as well as she did. Sweet, people-pleasing Mary Ann had always had a thing for the handsome, smart professor...

She studied the coconut's innards, thinking if she were to scrape out the meat it would make a rather tiny pie. And how to make a crust? She'd never been much for baking. Frozen chocolate chip cookies popped in the oven were about her speed.

Would it please David if she did make a pie for him? Just like...

She tossed the coconut aside with a thrust. "What are you doing? You were going to stop being such a Mary Ann!"

The man had wriggled under her skin with his charming words and bedroom eyes. He'd even intimated that they might be... Well, he had only stated that age didn't mean a thing to him. He'd not implied they could have a thing. An affair. A tropical island tryst.

So why was she thinking about all those things and more?

CHAPTER FOUR

DAY THREE DELIVERED more island luxury. Following a swim, Saralyn lounged on the chaise, sunning herself. The sunshine here was ineffable. It was warm but not hot. Bright but not searing. Her pale skin did not burn and was tanning nicely. It was like someone had manufactured the perfect sun and hung it directly above her. Add in the barest of breezes that wafted the gorgeous scent of tropical flowers about her like perfume, and she was in heaven.

Yet the day could get more perfect. Currently, a half-clad hero wandered across the sand, having swam up from Atlantis. He smiled at her and waved a little.

Saralyn lifted her chin in acknowledgment. Couldn't appear too desperate for conversation. Though, in truth, she craved it more than she thought she should. Her life and job had been comprised of solitude. Save the weekly phone call to her mom. Divorce showed a person who their real friends were. Ninety-nine percent of them had sided with Brock and she hadn't heard from them since. That Martha from yoga had hoped Saralyn could introduce her to Brock's agent had only come out that last session at the yoga studio when Martha had told her she couldn't speak to her now that she'd dumped Brock. Juliane was her one bright light, and now she would be physically incommunicado for the next six months. The intrepid biologist had promised to FaceTime as soon as she got settled in her new chilly digs.

"Do you mind if I join you?" David asked as he approached the empty chaise but two feet from her.

"It's your island," she said dismissively.

Best to keep the fantasy just that, she told herself.

Don't fall into the story of a wild and crazy affair with the handsome young man. Heartbreak hurts.

With a tug to her wide-brimmed straw hat to shade her eyes, she tilted her head against the chaise.

"If that's not an encouraging invitation, I don't know what is." He settled next to her, his motion sweeping sand over her toes.

She wiggled those toes. Her body stirred at his closeness, once again vying to reach for him in an immaterial yet intense way. It had been a while since she'd sat alone with a man. It was never the same as sitting alongside a girlfriend. Men smelled better than perfume and cosmetics. They exuded a sense of presence, of being, that always intrigued her. A certain intimacy sparked. And it was never simple.

"I won't talk," he said. "One thing I do know about you is that you like your privacy. I just want to sit here and let the sun dry me off from the swim."

"Suit yourself."

And so began the most maddening ten minutes of her entire life.

Saralyn was not about to turn her head to see if he looked at her. Couldn't risk him flashing her that charismatic smile, knowing he'd made her look. Nor would she pull up her legs and wrap her arms around her knees to cover her stomach. She lay stretched out, arms hanging loosely and fingers digging into the sand at her sides. Any movement would surely call attention to the cellulite that jiggled on her thighs. And—she did subtly suck in her gut.

No!

Her conscience screamed so loudly she almost cast a glance to the side to make sure he hadn't heard.

Just relax. Be...normal. As normal as an introverted word-slinger can be. The man doesn't care what you look like.

Or he shouldn't. She was not on this island to have an affair with the sexiest, most gorgeous, best-smelling human she had seen, heard or inhaled in...

Ever.

Saralyn closed her eyes and sank into the presence of him. He smelled like the ocean, salty and crystalline. Yet a deeper undernote of rugged masculinity rose to curl across her skin, tickle into her senses, and tighten her nipples.

Shoot. Her bikini top was a wild riot of bright tropical flowers set against a deep green background. Difficult for anyone to see what was going on under the fabric. She hoped.

Chill, Saralyn. The more you react, the more he'll notice. Just...smell him. Savor him. Enjoy the temptation like you've never allowed yourself before.

Because she'd never been so tempted by a man.

One truth she had accepted following the divorce was that she'd lost herself in her marriage. After she'd stopped attending parties and screening events with Brock, she'd become very much a hermit. Life had revolved around research and writing. Only the occasional morning jog around the neighborhood to get her creative brain churning. Yet there had been that one neighbor... Sexy, tall, blond hair and blue eyes. He'd always smile at her and wave. Yet she'd never allowed herself to think about him when alone, to imagine, to fantasize. She had literally castrated herself from enjoying the sight of other men. Which wasn't right. Even in healthy, monogamous relationships, the couple looked at others. It was human nature.

But she'd wanted to be the good wife. The one Brock was

never ashamed to be seen with, or to talk about. The house-
wife who sent him off in the mornings with a mug of coffee
and a kiss and who had a meal waiting for him when he arrived home at night. Yet it had quickly become a function
performed by rote. The morning kiss. The late-night meal
that she'd sit and watch him eat because she had eaten hours
earlier at the normal dinnertime. They'd share a brief conversation about his day at work. She'd tell him how many
pages she'd written. The mention of an event might come
up. Brock would always leave her an out. "It's not really for
spouses, you can stay home." Or, "Me and a couple of the
guys from work are having a few drinks." And she would
nod and apologize for nothing she had done, and he'd wink
and say she was a good wife.

A good wife who hadn't been attentive enough.

A good wife who had been oblivious to her husband's
affairs.

Had he even attended some of those spouseless events?
Through a bit of detective work, she had learned he had not.
Brock had kept an apartment by the beach and had used it
often. The emotional carnage resulting from that research
had knocked her flat in bed for weeks. Going through with
the divorce had further stripped her of any dignity and self-
love she possessed.

Running to her mother's arms back in Iowa had felt as
if she was giving up everything, so she'd forced herself to
stay in her and Brock's home and insisted he vacate. At the
very least, she'd maintained her ground. Until the settlement had ruled in Brock's favor to keep the home he had
initially owned before they'd met. Fair enough. She would
never completely surface from the humiliation of her failed
marriage while still occupying the very place where it had
all happened.

It was sad to realize how much she had lost in her marriage. And when a tear jiggled at the corner of her eye, she quickly swiped it away and sat up. Enough of this feeling sorry for herself. She'd done that.

"Well," she stated. "You're rather quiet today."

David shifted on the chaise, bending up one leg. The sex appeal conferred in that one dark-haired leg was off the scale. "I didn't want to disturb you."

"I appreciate your discretion. But I'm a big girl. If I need privacy I can find it for myself."

"So you can. I have to say, though…" He turned and propped an elbow on the chaise arm, leaning his head against the back. He'd developed a five o'clock shadow that only enhanced his sexy appeal. "Sitting here alongside you and *not* talking? That was kind of cool. I mean, I've never simply shared the air with a person like this before. I closed my eyes and focused on the sounds of the waves and the birds."

Birds? There had been birds? Saralyn's focus had been entirely different, but well, people were weird like that. One person's point of view was never going to be the same as the one sitting next to them. Especially if the other person had rock-hard abs.

"Thank you," he said.

She shrugged. If he were privy to her thoughts, he may not be so appreciative. She hadn't moved to any sex fantasies. The man was safe from those shameless mind forays. For now.

Ah, heck, she didn't have to play the uptight matron. As well, she couldn't sit on the beach every day and pout over a big life decision. Time to start carving out her groove.

"So, tell me what a girl has to do to find a little fun on this island?" she announced. "I did check out the swings by the dock. I remember swinging so high when I was a kid and then jumping to land in the nearby sandbox."

"You can do the same with the swings here but you land in the ocean."

"I know. I did it." The confession tickled at her confidence. It had been a fun jump and in that moment she truly had felt like a kid again.

"There are kayaks in the storage shed."

That sounded like a fun challenge to the old dog who desperately needed to learn some new tricks. "I've never tried kayaking."

"It's pretty basic. I can teach you."

"Kayaks look like they might easily topple."

"They don't. And if they do, you know how to swim. Shall I go grab the kayaks?"

Spend an afternoon kayaking with a man whose every movement drew her attention as if some kind of rare being? A little adventure never hurt anyone. And she needed that balance between what could become two weeks of sulking, muddling over her failure of a life, and what to do next.

Time to start living her life.

"Let's do it."

When Saralyn decided to let go of whatever anxieties life had heaped on her, she shone.

It didn't take long for her to catch on to the balance and rowing skills, and soon they had kayaked the three-kilometer circumference of the island. The waters on the villa side of the island were so clear and icy blue they allowed one to marvel over the fish swimming beneath them. Sight of the swings had sparked Saralyn's soul-enlivening laughter as she sped ahead of him. The seats hung six to twelve inches above water, depending on the tides.

David hadn't paddled nearly as fast as he could. He had no desire to win this race because the prize for second place was a happy woman whose big brown eyes danced as she sought his approval. No, it wasn't necessarily approval; perhaps she was only looking to see if he shared her joy. He most definitely did. If he had landed on the island when it hadn't been booked, he would have been alone, and likely would have moped for days. This woman encouraged him to avoid that fruitless muddle. And he was thankful for that.

Reaching the swings, she shouted in triumph and pumped the air with a fist. He floated next to her and held her kayak securely as she got out to claim a swing. Hooking their kayaks to one of the big poles that supported the swing frame, he joined her on the other one.

"That was fun," she announced as she pumped her legs and splashed her feet across the water's surface.

More than she could know. Elation lightened his being. Surely it had been months since he had smiled.

Oh, that poor boy's smile. He had only lived six years... Don't think about that now!

With a nod, David pushed down the depressive thought. He'd initially expected to be consigned to the chef's cottage, but Saralyn was blossoming and opening up in a surprising manner, which in turn prompted him to do the same.

"This place makes me feel like a kid." She settled her swing to a modest sway beside him. "I want to kayak every day."

"Any day. Any time," he offered. "I'll keep them anchored here so they're available whenever you feel the urge."

"I think it's my charming teacher that made it so fun." She tilted her head aside the rope that suspended her swing seat. "Thanks for taking the time to show me how to kayak."

"I've got all the time in the world. No business meetings. Nothing to distract me. Save you. You know you're beautiful when you laugh."

She made a humming noise, considering it, then shrugged.

"Thanks. I even forgot that I was wearing a skimpy bikini and dove into the experience."

"What's wrong with your bikini? I love the wild riot of colors."

"Sure, it is pretty, but…well. You must know how we women are about our bodies."

"I don't understand why women are so self-conscious about their bodies. I mean, you're all beautiful in your own way. What I like the most is the uniqueness of us all. There's not one person who is the same as the other."

"Twins."

"I'll give you that. You do know it's not so much the package you're in as your personality and smarts that attracts most men?"

"Tell that to all of Hollywood. I've spent the last two decades in Los Angeles. The home of the nipped, tucked, plumped and Botoxed. It's a mindset."

"A terrible one."

She sighed heavily. This was not the way he wanted the conversation to go. She'd been so elated.

"Do the women you write about put themselves down about their looks?" he asked.

"Not always. I write smart, focused women. Women who don't need a man but learn that it's nice to have a man around."

"Yikes. As an accessory?"

"Not like that. I mean… I tend to incorporate some of *my* beliefs when creating a strong heroine. Smart women who may not need a man, but like having them in their lives. Men are good for the female heart. And useful. Some of us aren't afraid to admit we like it when a man cares for us."

"Are you one of those 'us'?"

"I am. And I'm not so put off on the entire species of men just because my marriage failed. I'm open to whatever comes next for me."

"That's encouraging, but I'm a little stuck on the word *useful*. Like how? Fixing things? Changing the lightbulbs? Painting the house? Slaying the dragons?"

"Exactly!"

Again, her laughter bubbled out and David found himself reaching for her hand. She didn't notice, still clutching the swing rope, so he let his hand drop into the water. So close to contact with her warm, effervescent...beingness. He surprised himself he'd even made such a move. Hand-holding always felt like a task. Like a *function* he should perform and not a natural motion.

Her laugh stopped abruptly. "What? Did I say something wrong?"

"Not at all. I like listening to you laugh."

"Well." Regaining some composure, she sat up straighter and kicked her legs to sway the swing. "That's just weird."

"Then, call me weird. I don't think I would have succeeded with Crown Corp if I didn't toe the weird line."

"Probably not. You're an inventor so you have to be creative. We weirdos are the creative ones. The ones who dream big."

"What's your biggest dream?"

"Hmm."

As she considered the question, he considered her. Turning fifty? She didn't look a day over, well, he wasn't good with ages, but he'd place her at a solid late thirties, early forties. Her skin was smooth with only the faintest of creases at the corners of her eyes. Her body was shapely and toned, and—what parts of her did she not like? He couldn't stop wondering what it would be like to touch her skin. To bury his nose in her hair. To lean in and kiss her.

Yes, he wanted to kiss her. Not because he was alone with her on an island and it seemed the thing to do, but because she had drawn him into her aura and it felt sticky in the best way. He didn't want to disentangle himself from the energy she put out. It called to him. Lured him...

"After I leave the island, I'd like to walk into a new life," she said.

David sat up straighter, realizing he'd leaned so close to her that the swing had wobbled. Caught in a dream? It had been a good one.

A new life? "And what does that life look like?"

"A new place to live. In a different state. Maybe Arizona or even Maine. I'm not sure yet. I'm from Iowa. Lived there until my early twenties."

"That place gets as cold as New York. As does Maine."

"Yes, and while I love the snow, I've become accustomed to sun and warmth. I don't foresee shoveling in my future."

"Sounds wise. And in your new life, will you still be writing?"

"Yes, but will I be writing for myself or as a ghost?"

"Right. What does your dream say about that?"

"My dream says I'll be writing under my own name, getting paid well, and having readers actually know who I am. Fame? I crave that recognition."

That was interesting. And it was the first flaw he'd seen in her. "Fame doesn't come in bits. It's usually big and bold and in-your-face."

"I'll take it."

David tilted his head. "That surprises me."

"As someone used to being alone all the time, it also surprises me. But I'm all about not being a ghost anymore. People need to know who Saralyn Martin is. Or rather, Saralyn Hayes. I'm going to take back my maiden name. It feels strange to keep using my ex's surname."

"I hope you get what you desire. So you've made the decision to write that story under your name instead of the ghostwritten one?"

"Well."

That she didn't expound meant her dream may remain a dream. He sensed that she needed to jump beyond the closeted, quiet life she had led so far. However, from what he knew about fame, he didn't wish that for her. Not for anyone.

"I suppose you've already achieved your dream, eh?" she asked.

"The company? Yes, Crown Corp's success is a dream."

"'Remarkable things to change the ordinary world,'" she recited the motto he'd told her. "I love that."

"Yes, but I never set out to make billions."

"You just wanted to help others with a blanket that would hug them. I haven't tried the blanket yet. It's so warm there's no need for it."

"Sometimes a person just needs a hug," he said. "It's always there for that."

"You must be a master hugger if that was your raison d'être for creating the blanket."

"Me?" The idea of a hug made him...yearn. "Nah. I've never..."

A nervous tickle crept up David's spine. It was never easy to explain he'd created the blanket because he hadn't been given hugs as a child. Had always desired one. So when he was finally capable he'd created his own hug. It was similar to holding hands. Hugs and handholds felt foreign to him. Unattainable. And yet, it was all that he desired. The comfort with another person to really let go and accept what he'd never been given.

Yet that manufactured hug had been sullied by the trial. Truly, could he continue to produce the blanket and still maintain his integrity?

"I'm hungry," he said. Distraction was his only move when it came to avoiding his truths. "Do you want to come over to my place for some dinner?"

Saralyn's mind-reading gaze scanned his face a few seconds before nodding. "Sure, but you know I've got those chef meals delivered daily. And they feed two. Why don't you come over to my place?"

"It's a date."

"Oh, it's…" She stood from the swing, the water level midthigh. With a lift of her shoulders she said, "Yes, a date. Just us. The two of us—I'm going to run ahead and take a shower and change. Give me an hour to get a meal ready?"

"Of course."

She wandered to the beach and looked back at him once. He waved as he made sure the kayaks were secure. A date? With the beautiful woman who had inspired him to attempt holding her hand. It hadn't been a success. But he had initiated that daring venture. And that felt like a win.

Had she been nervous about calling it a date? And then maybe a little excited?

Who was Saralyn Martin-soon-to-be-Hayes? And would he walk off this island the same man after getting to know her better? Did he want to be the same man?

No, no he did not.

CHAPTER FIVE

Was CHANGING INTO a lace-trimmed tank top and tying the silk scarf about her bikini-bottom-clad hips dressing up for a date? Yes, island style. And no, she did not allow herself to feel guilty about it. Having a little fun with the only other occupant here on the island? What was wrong with that? It was just dinner. Wasn't like she planned to seduce him, lure him into her world and then marry the guy.

Saralyn paused before the convection oven where the dinners heated, startled by her thoughts. Marry him? She'd just gotten out of a marriage that had been ten years too long. She would never marry again.

She shook her head. That was a lie. She had no qualms about falling in love and possibly marrying again. She liked being in a relationship. But it was far too early to start thinking long-term. First and foremost, she sought someone with whom she could walk through life. Hand in hand.

"It's just dinner," she admonished her flighty thoughts that tended to put her heroes and heroines together too quickly and then they were in love before the first third of the story ended. Never enough conflict. It was something she focused on and had learned to stretch that conflict out through the story.

She and David had no conflict. Save the fact he shouldn't even be here. That he was treading on her own private escape. And that he was fifteen years younger than her and too handsome for a simple, slightly pudgy ghost like her.

Sighing, she shook her head again. Think positive! "This will be fun."

As she took the meals out of the oven, David wandered in with a bottle of wine and— Shoot, he was wearing a shirt.

"Have a seat! You've got perfect timing. The food is ready."

"And so is the wine." He popped the cork and poured their goblets before sitting.

"I love the meal delivery system you offer here." Saralyn set a plate of grilled shrimp with a mango kiwi salsa before him. "For someone who hates to cook elaborate meals, I feel like a chef warming them up."

"It's a popular option, though half our guests do opt for the chef. Marcel LeDoux is a good friend of mine. He used to be our family chef and fed me every day I was growing up."

"That's remarkable that you hired him to work here for you."

"I spent a lot of time in the kitchen when I was a kid and learned a lot over the years observing Marcel and his wife. She was our housekeeper. They were so in love. Made me understand what love could really be like."

"Didn't you know?"

David bowed his head. That felt like a confession, and he appeared as though he hadn't expected those words to leave his mouth so easily. She could relate. The guarded hero.

He lifted his head and added, completely ignoring her curiosity, "Marcel is also an amazing drink master. Larger groups will keep him on for party nights. He may be pushing seventy, but the old man can assume DJ duties in a pinch. You know there's a sound system throughout the island?"

"I do, but I haven't tried it. So I could put on some tunes and dance my way around the beach?"

"Of course. Connect your phone to it and you're off to a beach tango."

"I'll give that a try next time I have my phone out. I like the box. Out of sight, out of mind. It's an essential part of the whole vacation milieu."

She sat next to him, very aware he'd dodged her question about love. Too soon, she admonished inwardly. This was a friendly dinner not a seduction.

Comfortable with his presence now, she couldn't imagine that she'd initially been upset over him being on the island. On the other hand, she had every right to protest a man trying to move in on her peace and quiet.

"I've never tried this dish, so here goes…" A bite melted on her tongue. Subtle lemon and a spice she couldn't name enhanced the flavor but didn't hide it. Add to that the sharp tang from the fruit. "This is amazing."

"Right? These are much tastier than the mackerel I made for you the other night. Entire schools of them swim around the mainland. They never seem to come close enough to the island, though, to spear them."

"Wait, you caught those fish with a spear?"

"How else to do it?"

"A fishing rod and bait?"

"Ha! That's cheating. I prefer the challenge of spearfishing."

"I get that about you. It's your inventor's brain that constantly needs the challenge. What other challenges do you enjoy? I suspect you travel the world adventuring and living the big life."

"I think you've mistaken me for one of your romance heroes."

His steady stare mimicked one of those heroes perfectly. *Oh, Saralyn, do not fall into that smolder.*

"I'm not so interesting," he said. "And I avoid the big life, as you put it. I do play water sports and the occasional game of billiards. And I travel. Have a home in Greece. But my life is small. I work very hard to keep it so."

"That's unexpected. I would think a man with unlimited income would live in a castle, drive a fleet of cars, wear expensive suits and, well…where's your girlfriend while you are hiding on a remote island?"

She'd done it. She'd snuck in that question. Because really, a man as handsome and rich as David Crown had to be taken. Yet she'd noticed he had made a move to hold her hand earlier. It had startled her so much all she could do was cling to the swing rope. Much as she would have enjoyed holding his hand, it had felt sudden. Even, daring. Like standing on the edge of a cliff and wondering if she could manage the fall. Because hand-holding led to dating. And much as they'd labeled this dinner a date, she hadn't dated in, oh, so long. However to begin again?

"No girlfriend," he said through a bite of pineapple. "Haven't dated in half a year. I've been too busy."

"With the thing that you said you had to get away from?"

"Yes, the lawsuit. About the blanket. I prefer not to talk about it. But it has consumed my time."

"Sounds like your tropical island escape was necessity."

"My shoulders have already dropped and my gut has stopped churning. But I'm going to give you some credit for that. Your laugh…" He forked in a bite of shrimp, then winked at her.

Saralyn sipped her wine to disguise her sigh. The compliment zoomed straight to her core and spun it about in a heady rise of desire. And no girlfriend? She had read and written far too many stranded-on-a-tropical-island romances to know how this could go. Yet those couples were always close in age and generally spent the entire three hundred pages having sex like bunnies.

They had, after all, made a movie about just that.

Her life had changed with the divorce. And her body had changed since menopause had landed. While she was glad to wave goodbye to monthly cramps, the uneasy feeling that she would dry up and lose all desire had settled in. Logically, she knew that wasn't true. She'd done the research. But illogically, there were days she felt like an old hag waiting for the village young'uns to come ask for her wise advice while she cackled at them.

How to even make the first step toward dating again? It had been over twenty years since she had dated or touched, kissed, and made love to anyone but Brock.

The very thought of dating flashed her back to those uncertain teenage-angst years. Yet at the same time, teenage fascination with all things to do with kissing, touching and even more hovered around the edges of that angst. Only this time the fascination had matured and knew what, where and how to get the satisfaction it craved. And that scared her more than a first kiss in the backseat of a cherry-red 1970s Camaro.

Out the corner of her eye she realized David had propped his hand against his chin. His gaze pinned her with an unthreatening curiosity. An invigorating flash of warmth bloomed in her chest. And she knew darn well it was not a hot flash.

"What?" she asked.

"There you go. Lost again. That writer thing?"

More like an unsure-woman thing. "It is."

"What plot are you concocting right now? A romance?" He waggled a brow, which wasn't so much silly as a devastating arrow right to her libido. "Or a murder mystery where the machete-wielding hero finds the heroine sprawled on the beach, drowned, but for the ligature marks around her neck?"

"Wow, you've given that one some thought. Do I need to be worried?"

"No. I watch far too much of the mystery channel. It's my white noise when I'm at home. Promise I won't strangle you."

"Whew! I'm safe from strangling, but what about drowning?"

He lifted a brow, giving her a moment of heart-stopping concern, then shook his head. "I don't want to kill you, Saralyn, I want to kiss you."

Her mouth dropped open. She had the thought that at the very least she hadn't had any food in it. *Like some kind of silly fumbling teenager.* With heartbeats thundering, she closed her mouth and handled his surprising announcement with as much tact as a woman who had been touch-and-love-starved for years could manage. By stalling.

"You want very much."

Inwardly wincing, she mentally kicked herself for that idiotic reply. Of course, a kiss was on the table! But she didn't know how to do this. Flirting. It had been far too long since she'd felt desirable in a man's eyes.

She set down her fork. "Sorry."

"What for? I do want a lot. You are an exquisite woman, Saralyn. You should require very much from a man. And I should have to meet those requirements and expectations if I'm even to have a chance."

"A chance at what?"

"That kiss."

One that would explode her world in so many ways. Good, bad and—no, not at all ugly. And not even bad. But a little unsure. She suddenly felt bouncy and giddy. Like that teenager sitting beside her crush, wondering if he did make a move, if she would know how to respond. How to kiss him? It had been so long since she'd had a good and proper kiss.

One that curled her toes. Colored her thoughts with poetic verse. Shot straight to her erogenous zones.

Here sat a man fifteen years younger than her asking to kiss her. Perhaps it was a test? To see if he liked kissing an older woman? Did he have a thing for older women? So, that was his game.

Should it matter? Probably not. Maybe? Oh!

"There she goes again." David took her finished plate and walked around to the sink to rinse them off. "I want to learn to navigate that industrious brain of yours."

No one had ever said a nicer thing to her. Because her brain was busy and industrious and constantly working. Sometimes to her detriment.

Just be in the moment, Saralyn.

"It's gotta be fascinating inside there," he added.

"Or maybe a madhouse populated with esoteric research, myriads of crazy characters, and only a few real dreams and desires."

He sat at the table again and met her gaze. Soft caring in those whiskey browns. And a certain daring. "I'm going to make learning your dreams and desires my goal. And I'm a man who is known for attaining his goals."

"You already know my dream."

"To have a lovely escape on a tropical island. You see? I'm halfway to the goal already. Now, for your desires." He tapped the plate on which sat a small chocolate truffle cake. "Dessert?"

Saralyn preferred kissing David as the dessert. But her heart tugged her back from that adventure. Slow and cautious. "Please."

She'd not answered his question about the kiss. But neither had she refused it. David had surprised himself by outright asking. Normally he was more suave when pursuing a woman. And that he had seamlessly gone from being cordial and friendly to the island guest who had requested privacy to wanting to kiss her didn't so much surprise him as warn him against making a misstep. He didn't want to push her away.

Because he would like that kiss. Saralyn was the most attractive woman he'd met in a long time. As much inside as outside. Even though her insides seemed to be a crazy mess of distracted thoughts about her work and self-effacing thoughts about her body.

He could make her comfortable. Or he'd try. He liked that she was a challenge, not like the women who were eager to jump into bed with him simply because—well, because he was rich or handsome. He could read those women like a book. And not a very interesting book. He liked the mystery of Saralyn. And he intended to savor every page of her story she allowed him to read.

"Let's take the rest of this bottle out onto the veranda." He grabbed the wine bottle.

Goblet in hand, Saralyn led him to the vast planked veranda that curved along the beach side of the villa. It offered ample seating and space for a party. Tiny fairy lights were strung across the entirety and the furniture was wide, abundant and cushy. A circular electric fireplace mastered the center. With a voice command, the fire ignited and flames danced atop the colored glass in shades of violet, blue and green. With another command, David set the tropical-themed instrumental music to a low volume.

Saralyn sat on the sofa beneath a palm frond and tugged up her legs beside her. That move of placing her legs tight to her body felt as if she was putting distance between them.

Fair enough. That wouldn't dissuade him from this evening's goal of a kiss.

David sat on the wood floor before the sofa, his back to the edge of the thick padded cushion and his shoulder but inches from her knee. Stretching out his legs he crossed his ankles. From the moment he stepped foot on the island, he never wore shoes. He'd done research on grounding and how the body's innate electrical system recharged by walking with bare feet on soil, grass or sand. Never did he feel so relaxed back home in Manhattan where his shoes tread concrete, carpeting and asphalt.

"Is that the same bird I asked about earlier?" she asked of the soft twittering in the trees behind them.

"It's different. There's a bird book inside. The bookshelf offers all kinds of books on tropical flora and fauna."

"I'm on it." She stepped down and he touched her leg.

"Leave it until morning?" he asked. "Or did I accidentally ignite your research mode?"

"You did." She sat again, this time her legs before her instead of tucked on the couch. "But it can wait. This is a beautiful evening. I don't think I've ever seen such clear turquoise water topped by a rose-gold sky. The view is like a photograph. Gorgeous."

He turned and propped an elbow on the sofa to look up at her. "I suspect your research mode is still active."

"Guilty. I'm recording every sunset, every wild plant and bird. The feel of the sand under my feet and the rush of the warm water as I swim through it. Okay, fine. I'll turn off the writer. Just enjoy the evening, Saralyn! I may not get back here in a long time."

"You are welcome on my island anytime."

"That's kind of you, but I am here on my friend's rather generous dime."

"I didn't expect that you would pay. Anytime you want this place for a week? Please let me know."

"I'm not sure what I've done to deserve such a generous offer, but… I'm no fool. I'll remember the offer."

"Smart woman." The whisk of wings overhead alerted

them to a flash of brilliant red, blue and emerald. "Parrot," he said. "I do know that one. Only because they can be feisty. Watch your hair if you're eating on the beach."

"Thanks for the warning. Shades of *The Birds* just popped into my brain." She shuddered.

"Do you mind if I join you?"

"Please do. You sitting down there like a puppy is a little disconcerting."

"Disconcerted, eh?" He sat next to her. "Is that a step up or down from aghast?"

"It is a step in the lesser direction from aghast."

"Then, it seems I'm growing on you." He stretched an arm across the back of the sofa, behind her shoulders, but didn't touch her. Slow and easy. She may flee at any moment. Though he sensed her relaxation as she settled against the cushions and smiled at him. "Let's do some get-to-know-each-other questions."

"Oh, please, no favorite colors or pastimes."

"What's wrong with turquoise?" he asked in mock protest.

"Nothing at all. But if we're going to get to know one another better, we need to do a deep dive. And I have the perfect first question."

"Hit me."

She wriggled on the couch, finding joy in her conspiratorial advancing of the plot. "What book are you currently reading?"

Really? Nice. "Well played. Not only do you learn a title from that question, but you also discern that I do actually have a current read. Which, I suspect, will please you."

"Immensely."

"Current read is nonfiction," he said. "I go back and forth between fiction and non. While I can't rattle off the title and author's name I can tell you it's about the Victorian internet."

"What? That's...not right?"

"Oh, it is," he said with a delightfully evil tone. "Or, that historical period's version of the internet. The book details the creation and spread of the first telegraph system across the world. It's something I'm interested in since the Crown family's fortune was built on investments in those very first underground cables that were laid for the telegraph system."

"Really? I guess it was a sort of internet back then. Connecting people through technology. And your family helped to create it?"

"My great-greats had a hand in furthering the communications industry. From the telegraph and Morse code to the telephone and now the internet. The Crowns have always invested in communications and information technology. Look out AI, we're on it! Which, I'll tell you right now, made me a trust fund baby. That's not news. The media is always putting that label before my name like it means something."

"It doesn't?"

"Eh. It means the money came easy to me. And people judge me by that. I've never rested on my guaranteed-income laurels. From my first lemonade stand to selling Marcel's amazing brownies to my classmates at lunch, to fixing their electronic devices and showing the girls how to adjust their privacy settings to keep out hackers, I had to make my own money."

"As a fellow creative soul, I understand the need to work and constantly learn, and to be self-sufficient."

"You get me."

"Some of you, anyway. I would never say no to a trust fund, though."

David laughed. "I've known nothing else. And I do understand I am privileged."

"You don't act like it. But even if you did, what matters is your interaction with others. You seem kind and genuinely interested in…well, people." She looked aside, pressing the wine goblet to her lips. Feeling a little flush? Yes, he was interested in her. And she had picked up on that. He wasn't fishing in uninterested waters. "That book sounds good. I'd like to read it."

"I'll text you the title if you send me your number."

"I'll do that next time I touch my phone."

"So what book are you currently reading?" he asked.

"I generally have three, four or more books going at one time," she said. "A couple fiction, a few nonfiction. Some hard copies, as well as digital. Always research books."

"Which one rises to the top lately?"

"I've discovered a new author who writes hilarious historical-adventure romances. Superfun stuff that reminds me of the old Dick Van Dyke movies with the crazy characters that burst into song and have special abilities. And the romantic banter is first-rate."

"A little *Mary Poppins*? A little *Chitty Chitty Bang Bang*?"

"I love that you are into the oldies but goodies. Every child should be raised on such wonderful stories."

"I watched them in French," he said. "Reading the subtitles. From Marcel's personal library. I spent a lot of time in the den staring at those old movies. I wanted to read Marcel's books, but alas, I may have picked up a few French words over the years, but I can't read or speak it."

"Oh, *désolée*," she said consolingly.

He recognized the word for *sorry*. "You speak French?"

"Not at all," she said on a chuckle. "I have an arsenal of about five words that I use, and not always correctly. Many of my heroes tend to be French. I mean, come on, that language is like music. So sexy."

"Tell me about some of the books you've written. Might I have read them?"

"The ghostwritten stories are off-limits. I can't reveal that information. Because if I did, I'd have to kill you."

"Right, I forgot about that. But have you written for major names? Celebrities?"

"Most likely."

"Oo, you are tight with the details. Okay, I won't push. Maybe. Well, I'm curious now. Have you written anything under your own name?"

"Two books when I first started writing. One was an over-the-top paranormal romance with vampires, ghosts and time travel, rock 'n' roll and major home renovations."

"And the kitchen sink?"

"I did have a kitchen-sink scene in there as well."

David laughed. And she joined him slapping a hand on his thigh, which he felt she didn't notice but he certainly did. The contact was instantly electrifying. The connection started at her fingertips, zinged along his thigh and inserted itself into his nervous system, whooshing all the way up to his cortex. Basically, it made him very aware of his sexual needs. And fast.

"The other was my attempt at a comedy romance," she said, completely unaware of his distraction. "I'm not so good with the one-liners and pratfalls. I'm best with drama and monsters. Toss in a good heist and I am all over that."

"I'd expect the opposite from what I know of you. You're light and so bright. What is it about monsters that attracts you?"

"I like vampires and werewolves because I can create their world and control them within it. And I know they're not real, so it's fun to play with the possibilities of situating them in the real world. Unlike the serial killer books that I avoid like the plague. I don't like being scared by reality."

Neither did he. He'd never been a fan of horror movies

and the serial killer stuff. Real life could be much scarier than fantasy.

A flash of light off in the ocean distracted his attention from her voice and his wandering libido. Locals from the mainland Jet Skiing? They never came too close to the island.

"Can I get a copy of those two books?"

"They're out of print."

"Well, since you can't reveal your ghostwriting oeuvre, you'll have to write another under your name so I can read it. Saralyn Hayes, right?"

"Yes, I'll put that request on my list."

"I think it's already on your list but you're afraid to make it reality."

"I think you presume too much about my capabilities in general."

"I doubt it."

He studied her profile. With her hair pulled back into a loose ponytail, her cheekbones glimmered under the glow of the lights strung along the veranda. This woman had not lived five decades. She was utter goddess material. On the other hand, she wore a certain wisdom, a confidence that could only come from walking through the years and learning and witnessing the world. She wasn't a flighty, selfish young thing that believed a person's actions only mattered if recorded and posted on a thirty-second video. If he never dated one of those sorts again, he'd be happier for it.

"Now who's slipped into a random brain freeze?" she teased.

"Guilty. I was thinking about that kiss again."

"Oh." Her entire body tensed. She rubbed a palm along her arm closest to him. However, she relaxed as quickly. "Were you?"

To sit here and discuss a kiss felt awkward, despite his

very alert desire. And yet to simply lean in and take one from her didn't feel right. Never had he been so conflicted about a kiss. It had to be right. It had to not offend, but also to even think such a thing spoiled whatever pleasure might be gained from it.

Saralyn set her goblet on the table beside the sofa. With a twist of her waist, she turned to face him. Her smile grew biggest in her eyes. Subtly seductive? Yes, please. With only the slightest hesitation, she ran her fingers through her hair and pushed it over a shoulder. The move teased at the nerve endings in David's body that were already ultrahoned for the slightest beckon. He could feel her all over him though they didn't touch. And she smelled like the flowers growing throughout the island, with a hint of the mango that had seasoned dinner.

"I'm not sure how to do this," he confessed. "I don't want to impose. I don't want to presume anything about…us. I don't want you to think I'm taking advantage of you."

"That's a lot of don'ts."

Yes, wasn't it? Not his style. Was he flustered by a woman? Get over it, man!

"But as well, you are like stars in the sky far from the city, Saralyn. It is a marvel to look at you, and I can't stop looking at you. And I want to get close, reach up and…"

She moved in closer. "And?"

A flash of light—too close—made them both look toward the beach.

"What is that?" she asked. "Some kind of speedboat?"

"Jet Skiers. I noticed them earlier. Looks like they are heading toward the dock. Probably tourists unaware of the island's boundaries." He stood, not happy to have decreased their proximity. "I'm going to talk to them. Inform them this is a private island." When he turned to see if she would respond, he noticed her catch a yawn against her wrist. "Getting late?"

"It's been an adventurous day. I think I am ready to turn in. Thank you for the date. It was a lovely evening."

A loud rev of the Jet Ski turned his focus back to the beach. "Sorry, I'll get them to leave. Good night, Saralyn. See you tomorrow?"

"I'll make breakfast if you're interested."

"Always!"

He marched away toward the beach with a glance to the sky speckled with copious stars. Tonight, he'd almost kissed a star.

CHAPTER SIX

THIS MORNING AS she was getting dressed, Saralyn blew her reflection a kiss. Both the bikinis she'd packed were currently getting a refresh in the dryer, so she donned a pair of linen shorts and a floaty camisole. She pulled her hair back into a ponytail, then decided against it and went with a loose chignon with some strands down around her face. A romantic look.

For a romantic mood.

She'd almost kissed David last night! Almost. Darn those Jet Skiers. Yet, also, whew!

In the moment when they'd been sitting so close and had been *this close* to a kiss, her nerves had zinged beneath her skin. She'd tried to act as though she had it all together. *Grown woman here. Totally in for the seduction, for the kiss.*

And she had been!

But when they'd gotten so close that it had almost happened, a voice inside her head had yelled, *What are you doing? Do you even know how to do this? Are you crazy? Thinking you can just make out with the handsome man? The* younger *man. The hero you don't deserve. Because you don't know how to keep a man, to make him so happy he won't look elsewhere.*

Saralyn sneered at her reflection. Stupid inner voice. She had every right to kiss any man she desired. And it was about time to start acting on her newly emerging beliefs.

Look at that woman in the mirror. Knocking on the door to her fiftieth birthday. Divorced. Squeezed through the emotional wringer. Not so sure of herself. And yet, she had almost kissed the sexy billionaire.

"You almost did," she said to her now-approving reflection. "And next time? You will."

Grabbing her sun hat, she strolled out to the kitchen and remembered she'd invited David for breakfast. The prepared meal was a quiche, so she popped that in the oven to warm, then mixed up a pitcher of sangria. White wine, a hit of rum, plenty of fresh pineapple, orange slices and cherries. Yes, she was drinking in the morning. Because she could.

Remembering the sound system, she retrieved her phone from the Faraday box and connected to the Wi-Fi. Clicking on her *Good Vibes* playlist, a soft melody drifted in from the veranda speakers. She adjusted the volume lower. If the island were wired throughout, she was probably entertaining the entire place.

All of a sudden David danced up onto the veranda, singing the uplifting chorus. "I love this song!" he called as he walked inside and bowed grandly before her. A knightly gesture offered her a huge purple flower blossom. "For you, my lady."

"That's gorgeous." She took it and sniffed the deep violet bloom. Definitely not one of the sweet-smelling blossoms that had been perfuming the air.

"What's wrong?" He leaned forward to sniff the flower she offered. "Nope. That's not good at all." He took it and tossed it outside onto the sand. "Sorry."

"No worries. It was the thought that counts. I made sangria. And the quiche should be warm."

They went through the motions of plating the food and pouring drinks, dancing around one another, but not quite touching. The air between them was different now. More sensually charged but also a little tense. Saralyn wondered if he'd try to kiss her. Should *she* try to kiss him? For as alive as being around him made her feel, she didn't want to push a good thing and risk destroying it. Best to play it by ear and follow his lead.

Was that really the way a woman who intended to own her life and take control acted? Shouldn't she be more in charge? Grasp hold of her destiny and shape it to her command?

I am woman! Hear me roar!

David's finger snap near her face startled her into the moment. "Did I do it again?" she asked.

"Yes. Has the hero slain the dragon yet?"

"No, but he has captured the heroine's interest. They have a lot of pages ahead of them before any dragon slaying can occur."

"Good to know. I'll make sure the hero keeps his sword sheathed for a while. Uh…" He smirked and shook his head.

Saralyn considered what he'd just said and how it could allude to something sexual. Awkward? No, actually kind of cute that he was playing along with her mental mind bursts.

"I'm sure the heroine will appreciate the knight's caution," she reassured. "Of course, anything can happen in a romance. There are always twists to be had."

He met her glass with a *ting*. The sangria was sweet. With a wince at the surprising alcohol content, he said through a gasp, "I also like a good twist." He broke into a twisting-hip dance move. "See what I did there?"

"You're absolutely hilarious."

"Not so much, but I appreciate the rousing endorsement. Want to learn how to spear fish today?"

"Can I take notes?"

"Only if you don't mind them getting soggy."

"I'll keep mental notes. As long as you clean and cook whatever we catch."

"If you manage to catch a fish, I will be happy to take care of the dirty work that follows. That is, if I survive this drink and don't spear my own foot in a drunken haze."

"Cheers!" She tinged his glass again and he took another swallow as she finished off her sangria.

Yes, she was feeling her oats this morning. Or something that resembled a flirty, fidgety, flustery need to get on with the shaping of her life—and to do that shaping alongside David.

Later, after David had retrieved a couple spears and a line with hooks for wrangling their catch, they waded out to his favorite fishing spot and plopped down on a car-sized flat rock that served as a makeshift dock. Swim trunks his only clothing, he dangled his bare feet in the azure water and explained the fish usually arrived not long after the sun reached its peak in the sky.

"You ever fish before?" He leaned his palms back on the rock and turned his face to the sun, closing his eyes. "When you were growing up in Iowa?"

Saralyn would never tire of marveling over his physique, the gleaming bronze muscles and those soft dark hairs that glittered with water droplets. Every movement shifted those muscles tectonically and created a new sculpture for her to admire.

What had he asked? Right. Focus!

"Dad used to take us ice fishing. That involved me and Mom shivering in the corner of the icehouse watching the little portable TV while Dad manned the fishing line. I was never much into winter activities. The snowshoe trip to the frozen lake was misery to me."

"Thus your reason for heading to sunny California?"

"Pretty much. But also, my girlfriend Juliane suggested I move in with her so she could afford the rent, and I liked the idea of being so close to the entertainment industry."

"Lots of book agents in Los Angeles?"

"Enough. More script agents and movie producers. I've never had the desire to write a screenplay. Well…until…"

David rolled onto his side to give her his complete attention. She'd not intended to let that slip. She was contracted with a gag order. Not even Brock had been aware of her connection to the movie. Thank goodness. That information had been kept out of the divorce settlement.

"That 'until' sounded so damn intriguing," David said. "I might risk you having to kill me because I need you to spill the beans."

If the man had been plain and perhaps her age, just another Joe in the world and not the superattractive charmer who made her insides dance like a teenager crushing hard, she may have easily brushed off his query. She'd been doing it for years. Friends often tried to guess at who she wrote as, or what celebrities' stories she had written. Her lips were always sealed. Yet, she had suggested Juliane choose this specific island as her vacation spot.

You have to see where that movie was filmed. It looked so romantic!

Juliane would never have known it was *the* island.

Only now. If ever she'd had a niggle of desire to reveal her great secret it blossomed to a tickle. And she'd never been good at surviving a proper tickle.

David waggled a brow. The move lured her gaze to his deep brown eyes which held a mischievous grin in the irises. That implied tickle made her wriggle within her clothes. She'd been a good girl all these years. Kept her mouth shut. In ways that had devastated her emotionally. Wasn't it time to let out the merest hint? To take back some of her independence?

"I won't press," he started, "because I'm sure it's in your contract, but—"

"Let's just say I've written a novel for a major author, whose publisher then optioned that story and it was made into a movie. Recently."

His approving nod fed her need for notice, to be seen. She wouldn't be human if she denied how good it might feel to see her name listed in the credits for a movie. Her words on the big screen! What author didn't want to claim as much?

"Anything I've seen?" he prompted.

Saralyn compressed her lips. She'd said too much. And if David ever let it slip... Well, what could they do to her? Wasn't like she was receiving royalties from the movie or the book. The worst the publisher could do was never buy from her again. And that would make her decision much easier.

"It was set on a tropical island," she blurted out.

A flip-flop in her gut warned her not to say more. Yet, there it was...*tickle, tickle*. Wasn't it time she received *some* credit for her work? If one person in the world could know... It wouldn't be fame, exactly, but it might give her a taste of the feeling she craved.

"And it was filmed on this island," she tossed in quickly.

David sat up, resting an arm on his knee. "*Sex on the Beach*? You wrote that?"

She scrunched up her face and made the slightest nod. She hadn't expected he'd guess it so quickly. Then again, he was the island's owner. Of course, the film company had dealt with him to make the movie.

"That movie was awesome. And I'm not saying that because it was filmed on my island and they paid me a sweet rental fee for the month of filming. Although...whew! It was steamy. You wrote all that sex?"

Suddenly defensive, she lifted her chin. "You don't think I'm capable?"

"Well, sure, but... Damn, Saralyn Hayes. That was one hot story."

His eyes drifted over her body from head to as far down as she dared follow his gaze. Considering her on completely new terms after learning she had written an erotic story? It didn't offend her so much as lift her confidence. Hell yes, she could write the sexy stuff. No research necessary, boys, she knew her subject. And it had been made into a major movie.

"Nice," he added.

"All right." She picked up the spear from the rock beside her and pointed the tip near his chest. "Now's the part where I have to kill you."

She was killing him with her easy sensuality. David felt sure she wasn't even aware of it. The soft glint in her brown eyes. The natural rose shimmer of her slightly curled lips. And that earthy chestnut hair that spilled in waves over her bare shoulders. Her movements, a glide of a bare leg along the other, a curl of her fingers about the back of her ear, were naturally sensual. When had a death threat ever felt so seductive?

He held up his hands in surrender. "Whatever you do, make it quick." He tapped his heart. "Right here."

The spear tip hit the water and she laughed. "I could never pull off a murder. Sure, your body may be washed away to sea, but if a billionaire mogul goes missing? Or your body floats onto shore on the mainland? I'd break down and confess the moment a detective asked me my name."

"Good to know I'm safe from murder today."

But as for her seductive sensuality he'd play victim to that every day, all day.

"I promise I won't reveal your secret about *Sex on the Beach*," he said. "I know how binding contracts can be. I think it's cool that you let me in on it. And to know you're the word master behind that movie? Neato."

"Neato? Here I thought I was the older one. Where'd you dig up that word? From the 1970s?"

"Maybe? Attribute to me watching all those old black-and-white television reruns when I was a kid. In addition to Gilligan, the Beaver and Andy Griffith were my babysitters."

"Oh." Her gaze fluttered up to his. And her mood suddenly changed. "I'm sorry. Were your parents not around that much?"

David shrugged it off. Because he sensed a rise of empathy that he wouldn't know how to accept. "No worries."

In truth, his childhood had shaped him in ways he was still struggling with and he wasn't a guy who put his troubles out there for the world to analyze. It was bad enough the trial had done so. He'd been his own worst enemy of late.

"Hey!" He pointed to the water near her feet. "We're in luck."

Saralyn noticed the fish swimming around her legs, their silvery scales glinting the closer they swam to the sun-shimmered surface. She leaned forward on the rock to study the shallow waters. Her hair spilled over a shoulder and David reached to touch...

"Oh, I don't know," she said. He pulled back. "They're so cute. How can I possibly spear one of them?"

"Well, you did eat one the other day."

She bit her lip. "Shoot, I did. And you guys were very delicious," she cooed to the fish shimmering in the water. "Okay, I'm over it." She picked up the spear. "This chick cannot survive on four-star chef meals alone. Let's do this!"

An hour later, David counted three fish on the line. He'd speared all of them. As soon as Saralyn had locked in a perfect aim, she'd pull back and mutter some excuse about the sun glinting on the surface. Understandable. It probably took a certain sanguine thrill to do the deed, and she was far from cold-blooded.

Rather hot-blooded, he suspected. That movie had certainly pushed its R rating to the limits. Whew! Any woman who could write sex like that was— What was he thinking? Writers made up things for a living. That didn't mean she was a sexual dominatrix or had tried all the different positions that had been featured in the movie.

He wasn't interested in sexual gymnastics with Saralyn. Well, sure, but. What really intrigued him was the connection they were forming. She had sunk under his skin and was taking hold in his very being. And he liked the feeling. A lot.

"I've let you down," she said with a gesture to the fish line.

"Not at all. Any more than this and we'd have too much for a meal. I hate to waste."

"You're very good with the spear. You give off caveman alpha-hunter vibes."

He straightened at the compliment. Yes, he was a hunter of food. A warrior who brought home dinner for his woman. Triumph!

"I know I could have speared that one fish," she added. "And it's not because I don't have the courage. I just…"

Her sigh felt uncomfortable in David's soul. It was heavy with something that he recognized. A need for something ineffable. And yet, he knew exactly what that need was. It was voicing it that would challenge his very bravery and being.

"I should be able to catch my own fish. Prepare my own meal," she said. "I want to not need a man, you know?"

"Thankfully," he bowed to catch her gaze, "we live in modern society and it isn't necessary for you to do such a thing. You can buy fish in a grocery store. Slashing a credit card is still considered fending for yourself."

"I suppose." She would not be convinced.

"So…" He sat next to her and dangled the line of fish in the water. One of the silver-scaled fish still wriggled. "You don't need a man? Because of your divorce? Didn't you say something about liking a man in your life?"

"I did and I do. But I've learned a few things about myself lately. I don't want to rely on a man for basic survival. I want to be able to support myself. To buy all my necessities and do things for myself, like small repairs and changing oil on a car."

"Even I take my car in for the oil change."

"Yes, but it's so simple. You just remove the oil cap, unscrew the oil plug, let the oil drain, then replace the plug and fill 'er up."

"You have done some research."

"It was for a celebrity bio. He was a former auto mechanic. I research heavily to understand my subject. Anyway, I'm not saying men are bad. I like men. You guys are nice to have around."

"*Useful*. Wasn't that the word you used?"

"Yes, but in the most complimentary manner."

"Good to know you've not given up on us all. Will you… tell me about the marriage? Living the Hollywood lifestyle. It must have been crazy. But if it's too personal…"

She pulled up her legs to her chest and wrapped her arms around them, propping her chin on her knees. A protective position. Perhaps he shouldn't have asked, but he was interested in learning anything she would give him. He couldn't step back now. That almost-kiss had changed things. It had made him realize that since that first day he'd walked up to her on the beach, he'd wanted to get to know everything he could about the beautiful woman in the bright bikini whose laughter woke up his soul.

"I told you my husband is an actor," she finally said. "He plays Cave Kendall on *Paradise Place*. One of the last remaining soap operas still on television."

"Cave? Seriously? Where do they get those names?"

"Right? I once named a character Stone. Geography-related names tend to be popular for alpha males."

"I'll keep that in mind. Perhaps I should name my first-born Valley? Or Granite!"

"Oh, I like Granite. Very commanding and stoic. I would call him Gran for short!"

She laughed and her body tilted against his, their shoulders nudging. The sweep of her hair teased him to touch it, which he did, unobtrusively. She didn't notice. And when she pressed her chin back onto her knees, he kept the tip of her hair between his fingers. A strand to connect them. A lifeline he wanted to breathe through.

"Anyway," she continued, "I was introduced to Brock, that's my ex-husband's name, at a book release party. I knew he was an actor, and with stars in my eyes, I fell for his practiced charm. Then, I never believed it was an act. He had a way of making me feel special, like I was the only woman in the room. That lasted for years. But now I know it was... Well." She turned her head to face him. "I can hope some of it was real."

Should he offer reassurance? Didn't feel right. Whatever she felt about that long relationship was valid and hers to own. So instead he twirled the tip of her hair about his finger and waited for her to continue.

"Our romance was whirlwind. After a month, he proposed. We married three months later. Initially, I accompanied him to all the parties, premieres and media junkets. I quickly learned that I was not comfortable with the attention. It was rather seamless, me slipping into the background and claiming a headache or writing deadline to get out of another party. He eventually stopped asking me to go along with him."

David had never married or had a relationship that lasted longer than six months, so he could not relate to the mechanics of such a union. Certainly, his parents had never been around often enough to model what a loving relationship could look like. All he knew was from what he'd witnessed by watching Marcel and his wife. But he had learned enough about Saralyn to understand her need for quiet and calm.

Yet hadn't she said something about *seeking* the spotlight? To be known? Perhaps she hadn't thought that far ahead. How could a woman who was a self-proclaimed ghost be comfortable with the delving and merciless media spotlight?

"When a publisher asked Brock to write his autobiography, he looked to me," she said. "My agent was gangbusters about how easy the job would be. I had already ghostwritten half a dozen autobiographies about celebrities."

"Doesn't the definition of *autobiography* mean it was written by the person it's about?"

"Yes, but you'd be surprised how many are ghostwritten. Just because you're a celebrity does not make you a writer. Though certainly I know of many self-written autobiographies that are excellent. So, I agreed and it was an easy write. In two months, I had drafted out the entire manuscript."

"Is that fast?"

"It is for me. Generally, I take nine months to a year to write an autobiography. That includes research time. I saved the research on Brock for after the draft so I would have an outline of research points. I'd planned to sit down with him one weekend and interview him about any outstanding items. But first, I verified my facts and details. A stupid part of me looked up some of his emails, thinking I could verify dates of some notable parties. I never dreamed I'd fall into a rabbit hole that would reveal his affairs."

She bowed her head against her knees. "I was able to put together dates and events. And… God help me, one night, I searched his phone calls. The fool never erased those from his phone or his texts. That confirmed my suspicions. I stopped counting after six women over an eight-year period. There could have been more. I know there were. He would never confirm that for me during the divorce proceedings."

"I'm so sorry, Saralyn."

"Me too." She sighed heavily. "But I brought it on myself by not accompanying him to the events and parties. I should have made more of an effort. I wasn't the woman my husband needed."

That she blamed herself angered him. "A wife shouldn't have to babysit her husband. A marriage should mean something. Vows are made to be kept. They are not guidelines."

"Right? I took my vows seriously. Well, it's over now." She tickled her fingers across the water's surface. "I've moved on. Or I will when I return home. I have to be out of the house by autumn."

"And you're not sure where you will land?"

"Nope. My girlfriend Mabel, who lives in my hometown in Iowa, offered me her extra room until I find a permanent place. But I don't want to do that. Especially not if it sees me staying through the winter. And my mom lives there as well. I would like to be close to her but again… Winter."

"The cold does tend to be cold." David could handle the New York winters for the reason that he rarely spent time outdoors. Running on an indoor track and walking from valet stand to the sidewalk did not challenge a man's physical endurance for extreme weather.

"I'll get my act together," she said. "I've been telling myself I'm fine and… I think I am. I'm forming new grooves."

"You're a strong woman, Saralyn. You can have any life you desire."

"Bold words coming from a man who doesn't have to worry about money."

He wasn't sure how that related to the topic but he understood how people viewed him. He had a lot of money.

He could literally have any life he desired. "I earned that money."

"I know you did. That was a rude thing to say. I'm just in a different financial situation from you. Don't worry. I'm not destitute. I'll be able to buy myself a home and set up a retirement account. Then, if I can keep selling my writing, I'll be set. But that's the dilemma. *Can* I sell under my own name? It would bring in more money than ghostwriting does. Whew! I can't believe I spilled all that to you."

"I'm glad you trusted me to do so. It's the real you speaking now. Stepping out of your ghostly raiment."

"That's very poetic."

"I have my moments." He caught her grin and winked.

"You are a charmer."

"I'll take it. But it doesn't come naturally."

"I'd guess differently. You have a stunning smolder."

"So I've been told."

"Well, keep it holstered. Right now I think we need to take care of those fish before they suffer too much. That one is still alive!"

Sensing she needed a subject change, David hopped off the rock and gestured she should lead the way. Together they waded back to the beach.

"Thank you," she said, twisting her toes into the fine sand. "For listening. I rarely talk about the divorce. Not even with my mom. It felt good to put it out there."

She made a move, lifting her arms to perhaps hug him. And like a lightning strike, the past echoed in David's brain. *You wretched thing!* Instinctually, he stepped back from Saralyn. The line of fish slapped against his calf. He immediately regretted the impulsive move. But he had no emotional structure with which to make it right.

"Oh," she said, dropping her arms. "Sorry. I was just going to hug you in thanks, but—"

"No worries," he rushed out. "I'm...not big on hugs."

She tilted her head. Obviously thinking, *the inventor of a blanket that hugs a person isn't big on hugs*? It was never a conversation he was comfortable having. So he jiggled the line of fish and started walking away, "I'll see you in a bit! White wine goes best with these fellas!"

He caught her wave as he turned and hastened his pace.

Idiot! He'd just made a wrong step. Metaphorically pushed her away when he had wanted to pull her in and...

But that pulling-in part always baffled him. Much like holding hands did. He knew how a hug worked. And that people utilized hugs as a means of thanks, of comfort, a way of acknowledging friendship, of signifying intimacy. He'd been hugged a few times in his life. Quickly. Awkwardly. It always made him stiffen up and wish he were anywhere else.

The one time he had tried to hug his mom—that had ended disastrously. *You wretched thing!*

How to move beyond that voice that arose every time he considered the act of hugging another person? That's all he'd ever wanted in his life. A hug.

CHAPTER SEVEN

WHILE THEY WERE eating grilled fish and honey-glazed pineapple, the rain started to pick up. David explained the tropical storms were infrequent but could sometimes grow windy and wild.

"We should close the windows and doors," he said as they finished drying the dishes.

"Batten down the hatches?"

"Aye, aye!"

Saralyn smiled to herself, even as her nerves took a leap. If she was going to be stormed in, she was thankful to have David here with her. Had she been alone on this island, and if anything had gone wrong, or the wind blew off the roof, she certainly wouldn't have known how to deal with it on her own. Another reason why she would never completely swear off having a good man in her life.

David rushed around the villa, securing each room, and returned clapping his hands in a job well done. "All battened, captain. No need to be distraught."

She laughed at his almost supernatural power at determining her mood. "I am relieved that you are here. I love thunderstorms but the wind scares me. Will you stick around until the storm stops?"

"What if it rains all night?"

She shrugged. "Slumber party, it is."

His face brightened. "I've never been invited to a slumber

party." He plopped onto the sofa, spreading his arms across the back, and put up his feet on the table, fashioned from a twisted tree trunk. "What's involved? Painting each other's nails? Secret confessions? Slam books?"

"Seriously? You know what a slam book is?" Saralyn retrieved a bottle of wine from the fridge. Red, this time. She wasn't big on white, but it had gone well with the meal. "I think those things are considered vintage now."

"Man, I really am getting old."

"Let's not talk about age." She handed him the bottle, a corkscrew, and set down the goblets on the table. "I hereby declare all occupants of this island are classified as ageless."

The cork popped. He poured her a glass. "Hear, hear. Age is just for driver's licenses and colonoscopies."

"Let's also not discuss all the medical procedures one must endure when one reaches a certain age. Here's to long life and ever-flowing wine. You know the resveratrol in the grapes is good for your health?"

"Then, we're drinking this whole bottle." He tilted his goblet to hers.

For a while, they sat listening to the rain, which pattered heavily on the roof and against the three stories of windows. The curved room was incredible. Three stories of windows to capture the beach, sky and tropical foliage. Above the half-circle sofa hung a huge chandelier spiked with foot-long quartz-crystal points that formed a constellation. Outside, the palm trees swished like cancan skirts. The sky darkened, but still a ribbon of rose glimmered through the streaks of rain. It was weirdly romantic, if a person could get beyond the fear of a hurricane.

Saralyn loved a good rainstorm but preferred a gentle one that allowed her to walk outside in raincoat and galoshes. Yet what better houseguest than the man who had walked off the pages of her unwritten romance novel.

Now to start a meaningful conversation. Favorite colors and foods were off the list. Who cared about that stuff? She'd lived enough years to know most people did not change much and that they were set in their ways. And those were the ways she wanted to suss out regarding David Crown.

"We started on important get-to-know-you questions the other day with my book-reading query," she said. "So what's the one question you'd ask a person to get to know them?"

"Ah, that's easy." He tipped his wineglass to hers with a *ting*. "What new thing have you learned today?"

Oh, she liked that one. "Spearfishing!" she announced. "I think it's a good idea to learn something new every day, if you can."

"Agreed. Life has been given to us to be lived. Don't let it get old and rusty."

"We can't avoid the getting-old part."

"I mean, don't let your experiences grow stale and old. Boring. Same old, same old. Learn something new every day."

"Always. Even if it's only on the page."

And by all means, avoid searching your husband's phone records.

She'd learned a tough but necessary lesson. So perhaps a smart woman would move forward with a more discerning idea of what entailed privacy.

"So, you don't have a girlfriend," she blurted. Why bother with small talk? They'd done enough of that. "Why is that? I know you explained about the stress you've been going through with the lawsuit. But I would think a woman in your life would ground you after a long day at the office or laboratory, distract you from the craziness of life."

"Is that how girlfriends are supposed to work? Grounding and distraction? I haven't found one with those particular qualities."

"Maybe you're looking in the wrong places?"

He shrugged. "Eh. I've dated many. They are all in for the big life and are let down when they realize I'm not about the glitz and jet-set lifestyle. I've just never found my person. You know? That one person you don't feel you can go a day without talking to."

"When you put it that way, I'm not sure my ex-husband was my person. We could go days without talking."

"Really? Sounds nightmarish."

"Or just me playing hermit and him living his life despite his marital vows."

"That you are smiling when you say that gives me some hope that you've picked yourself up, dusted yourself off, and—"

"Am getting on with it. Picked up. Dusted off. Now, what's next?"

He turned and tilted his head to study her face. They sat close, knees touching and bodies slouched against the back of the sofa. It was a precious intimacy that didn't scare Saralyn so much as invite her to the next level. Push her to take control of her life and seek her desires.

What *was* next? She was feeling the wine. Relaxing.

"Are you ready to date?" he asked. "I suspect all the single men in Los Angeles must be pounding down your door."

"It's not so easy to begin again," she said while suppressing a sigh. "I did try an online-dating service a month ago." She mocked a shudder.

"That bad?"

"Oh, my goodness, it creeped me out. You've never tried it? Wait, I know the answer. A man of your charm and sex appeal would never need a dating app."

"If you say so."

He knew she was right, so she'd let it go. "I swiftly learned the idea of making a connection with a face on a computer and a few lines of descriptive text doesn't work for me. And the few times I texted a potential guy, they moved quickly to wondering about my favorite sexual position or if I'd be willing to meet them at a hotel. Ugh."

"Hookups are not cool."

"Not at all, and they're not something I'd ever be comfortable with. Making love with a person means something to me. You have to know and trust a person before you… well." She glanced at him shyly now. He nodded, agreeing with her unspoken sentiment. "I mean, I'd love to date again. You men are imminently interesting. And it's not that I fear the next man will be a repeat of Brock. It's that I don't exist in a man-meeting environment. I work from home. Spend innumerable hours sitting before the computer. I don't go to parties. And I lost most of our shared friends with the divorce. So…how to meet a man?"

"How about random encounters while walking your dog and the leashes tangle about your legs?"

Saralyn laughed. "You really do like those older movies, don't you?"

"Love them. But I suspect you're not a dog person?"

"I've not had pets due to Brock's allergies. I hope to someday get a cat."

"Cats are independent, entitled and demanding, but incredibly cool. Perhaps for the great manhunt, you just need to find yourself alone on a tropical island with one of them?"

"Perhaps?" She sipped and lingered with her lips on the slick glass edge.

David's eyes danced in the dim light. And he smelled like rugged races up the side of a mountain only to take a plunge into a refreshing clear ocean. A kiss felt inevitable. But the cliché nudged at her. Forced together by a storm. Sitting together on the sofa. Sharing snippets of their lives with one another. The inevitable was naturally a kiss.

"Wow." He grabbed the bottle and refilled his glass then hers. "You and that wandering brain of yours."

"I know, it's a terrible habit."

"Tell me where you just were?"

Dare she? He probably wasn't aware of the romance tropes and how they played out on the page.

"I mean," he leaned closer, his breath hushing across her cheek "I could guess…"

"I was thinking we could try for that kiss again," she rushed out. "But."

"But?" A slight lift of his chin scored him a point on the seduction scale. Because the angle of his eyes looking down at her put her in a languorous inner sigh that wanted to stretch out and let him drink her in. Yet it was his deep, try-me voice, which spilled over her skin, that took it to the next level. "What's stopping you?"

"Honestly? The cliché of it."

"The…" He gaped. Then ruffled his fingers back through his thick, loose curls as he chuckled. "Is this what dating a writer is like?"

"We're not dating."

"Technically…" He lifted a finger. "We did claim dinner as a date. And right now we *are* flirting."

Saralyn tugged in her lower lip with a tooth. A smile was irresistible. Flirtation had never felt so easy. So natural. Maybe she could try a hand at this dating thing?

"All clichés aside," he said, "you fascinate me, Saralyn. There's always something going on in there." He touched the side of her head, then smoothed his fingers along her hair-line. A touch that skittered thrilling shivers over her skin, down her neck and to her breasts. "I want to dive in and swim through it all. Learn the universe of you."

"The universe of me?" Wow. That one did it for her. The man couldn't understand how his words touched all her erogenous zones. How his touch had stirred a warmth that overtook her entire body. And it wasn't a cozy-winter-night's-snuggle warmth but rather a sit-up-and-demand-more kind of touch.

Tempted by his deep voice and poetic sweet nothings, she leaned forward and tapped a finger on his knee. "You may see a vast universe before you, but I'll never be an open book."

She traced her finger along his thigh and up, over the shirt he rarely wore, and pressed her palm over his chest and beating heart. The heat of him seared her senses and she had to repress an audible sigh.

"I like that about you," he said. "Mysterious. Authentic."

"You think?"

"You are." Tucking his curled fingers under hers, he lifted them to kiss her knuckles.

Saralyn sucked in a gasp at the tender touch. When was the last time a man had ever given her such intense and focused attention? *Too long ago.* The moment felt vast. Truly like the universe. It tingled with promise. Like stars twinkling in the sky. Or the crystals overhead. Desire enveloped her as if an invisible fog overwhelming all.

"Let's be cliché," he whispered. A wink followed. "Just for the fun of it?"

Oh, yes, please.

Saralyn leaned closer, meeting him forehead to forehead. "I'm in."

Their breaths hushed, mingling as they slowly connected. For one ridiculous moment before their lips touched, Saralyn wondered if she should push him away. The answer was a definitive no. She wasn't a silly teenager. This woman knew what she wanted.

Their mouths melted against one another. The heat of him transferring to her and softening her entire being. He couldn't know that she wondered if he would think she was out of practice. It didn't matter because every motion went slowly, learning, allowing her time to rediscover a place she had never visited yet had written about so many times. The hero's kiss. The heroine's sigh. That first moment when finally they connected in a manner that words could never describe. Intense want and need and even a greedy desire seemed to overwhelm. And it felt immense and wondrous and...

Saralyn pulled back. They hadn't moved too quickly. Just the surprise that she liked it so much, startled her.

"That was..." she said. "I've forgotten how easy it is to get lost in a kiss."

"I'll take that as a good thing?"

"It is. Because once lost, then a person must begin to find themselves."

"I don't know if my kisses can do that for you, but..." He kissed her quickly. "Let's keep at it. You never know what can happen. Or what you'll find."

Like falling for a man fifteen years younger than her? Like allowing herself to get lost and then hoping upon hope that she actually could find something new and exciting in the adventure of David Crown? What if she chased him away as she had done to Brock?

No. They weren't married. They had no vows or commitment to one another.

Maybe she could allow whatever wanted to happen *to happen*. She had accepted this surprise vacation with a determination to return home having found her groove. This could be just the groove she needed.

"I'm in," she whispered.

They kissed, trying different head positions and with soft laughter as they teased fingers along arms, ribs and the smooth underside of a jaw that segued into dark stubble.

Eventually they found themselves lying on the sofa. David's hand roamed her body and she didn't protest the exploration. A thumb rubbing her nipple arched her back and she moaned against his hot and full lips. His hips hard against hers could not hide his erection, thick and heavy. She rocked against him but cautioned herself. Sex felt inevitable, but... far too fast. She had only been here a handful of days. And she had meant it earlier when she'd told him making love meant something to her.

Was there anything wrong with enjoying the slow discovery of one another?

When David pulled reluctantly away and studied her gaze beneath the glowing chandelier, she could read his thoughts. He wondered if they might move to the next step. His body certainly alluded that he was ready and willing.

"I'm not sure," she said. She touched his kiss-plump mouth and he kissed her fingers. Slowly. Reverently. "This is moving quickly."

"We can go slower." His lips brushed the base of her neck. A soft hush followed by the tip of his tongue made her gasp. "I'm in no hurry."

"Parts of you may disagree," she offered with a nudge of her hips upward.

"I do have some self-control. Another kiss and then we say goodnight?"

"Sounds like a perfect ending to a perfect evening."

CHAPTER EIGHT

IN THE MORNING, Saralyn decided to check her messages. She'd been here almost a week. And as suspected, her mom had texted her nearly every day despite Saralyn explaining she'd intended to turn off her phone while here.

Just checking in. Are you okay? I heard about a hurricane in the Atlantic Ocean! I hope you're all right.

She texted back that she was in a different ocean entirely and not to worry. Lots of sunshine, sand between her toes, and good story ideas.

She didn't explain that those story ideas involved a sexy, tall, dark-haired man who could kiss a woman back to her teenage years. Her mom would worry if she knew she was on an island alone with a strange man. Lifelong hippie that she was, Sienna Martin was cautious about everything, even walking her small-town main street. Her mom would love for her daughter to move back to Iowa, find a house a few blocks away from her and become settled. And while Saralyn felt some pull to be close to her mother as she aged— she was a vibrant, healthy seventy-five—she knew her mom had excellent health insurance and a boyfriend who doted on her and who was also into daily walking and keeping fit. As well, she owned a small online business selling crystals and yoga mats. Saralyn couldn't ask for a better life for her mom.

Now, to focus on her life. Which was beginning to feel lighter. And promising. Was it the make-out session with David that had her dancing around the kitchen this morning in a bikini as she poured fresh-squeezed orange juice and prepared a bowl of sliced mango and coconut shreds?

Yes. And just thinking that cautioned her. David may make her feel younger, sexy and boost her self-confidence, but a little romance could never be life-changing. Especially when she had a bit more than a week left here on the island.

Well, it *could* be life-changing, but only on the page. She'd been burned romantically, and while she didn't want the divorce to affect the way she viewed any future relationship, the burn marks would never fade.

"Just have fun," she coached herself. "Be yourself. Let loose. No one needs to know about this experiment with kissing a new man. You'll return home and life will go on."

So a fling it was? While Saralyn was not the fling sort of girl, she didn't want to let the opportunity for a connection between her and David slip from her fingers. So why not enjoy herself? David had so many great qualities. He was quiet yet strong. Smart, yet she felt as though they were intellectual equals, which was a refreshing change. They could converse and it didn't have to be light banter about whatever was trending on social media.

Yet there was something he hid from her. She sensed a guarded heart in David Crown. It was in the way he'd avoided a hug and holding hands. What sort of trauma did a person experience that taught them to avoid closeness while also allowing him to kiss and caress her? It was the personal intimacy of the hug that seemed to frighten him. So odd that he'd invented a blanket that did what he most feared.

Perhaps it made sense.

She glanced to the sofa where the blanket had been neatly strewn across one arm. It was too warm to require a blanket; she'd been sleeping with the linen sheets pushed to the end of the bed.

Curiosity prompted her to pick it up. The fabric was light and soft as kitten's fur. She'd expected it to be heavy like those weighted blankets. Wrapping it around her shoulders, she tugged it across her chest and...

"Oh."

The blanket actually did hug her. It conformed to her body. Lightly. Not enough to feel pressure but secure enough to notice the pleasant envelopment.

"Wow," she whispered. "This thing really works."

Easy now to understand how David had made a fortune with this blanket. And that he donated it to homeless shelters and children's hospitals? What a lovely thing to give a child who may be frightened, alone, or awaiting a scary surgery. The person who had invented this blanket possessed the largest heart.

Yet he dared not take a hug for himself.

"So curious."

She folded the blanket and replaced it on the sofa. At that moment, her phone buzzed. She'd forgotten to place it back in the Faraday box after texting her mom. It was a text from her agent.

Shall I accept the offer? The publisher is waiting!

Pressing the edge of the phone to her lips, Saralyn closed her eyes. She could use that money as she settled into a new life. And so what if she delayed writing her Great American Novel for another five or six months while she ghostwrote the other story?

Thing was, she'd been delaying her move to self-reliance for over a year. Using the divorce as a crutch to mope and feel sorry for herself. The historical-heist story had been on the back burner for years. Of course, ghostwriting another story was the responsible choice to take care of her financial concerns. But it no longer felt right. How could she ever step into her new skin if she continued to hide behind the pages of another author's name?

Turning off the phone without answering the text, she placed it in the box and grabbed her sun hat. When in doubt, go sit on the beach.

A text from his CEO paraphrased what the social media had been buzzing about him the past few days.

Did David Crown quit this world? Where is he? The reckless billionaire is rumored to have fled for his private island. Was he more guilty than the innocent verdict declared?

He tossed his phone aside and it landed on his wallet where he'd pulled out the photograph. He looked at it every day. The boy's face smiled at him. Why did the media have to brew everything into a crazy maelstrom of lies? The facts regarding the lawsuit were clear. The trial transcripts had been released to the press. And he had not *fled*. He'd simply been done. Done with it all.

But they wouldn't let it go. How long did he have to stay hidden away on an island before the media circus moved on to the next sensational human, emotional wreckage?

He stabbed the machete he'd picked up for a morning of coconut hunting point first into the wooden countertop. The handle wobbled from the intense energy he'd released into it. Squeezing his hands aside his temples, he pushed his fingers through his hair and growled. He'd been so close to touching some kind of peace.

Yet he knew that while the island atmosphere relaxed and put him in a new mindset, it wasn't a cure-all. He needed to talk to someone. To put his feelings out there. Have them examined and recycled back to him in a manner he could sort through them all. It had been ages since he'd talked to a therapist. He'd gone his teen years and it had helped him to not necessarily forgive his parents for their lackadaisical and dismissive behavior toward him but rather to understand it. They had been raised as he had—at a distance and with nannies. They knew no other way to parent their own child.

That hadn't relieved him of the trauma they had unknowingly embedded in him since childhood. Yet he wasn't one to play the victim by clinging to the traumatic label and insisting he be treated with delicacy. He was a grown man. He owned his actions, and while he knew some actions were inadvertently the direct reflection of his younger years, he made a concerted effort to consider new ways to approach any issue that should arise. It was the inventor in him that allowed him to utilize creativity in most aspects of his life.

David loved his parents. Always would. But he would never make excuses for their distant parenting skills.

As for others in his life? Friends were few. David had quickly learned that the more money a man tallied in his bank account the more people wanted to cling to him, befriend him, share his air. All for the wrong reasons. He'd not gained a new friend he could trust since he'd invented the blanket. A few good buddies at the company that he could have drinks with and discuss women. Every man needed those. And the last time he'd seen Shaun, his best friend from high school, Shaun had been talking about joining the army and traveling the world. He'd looked him up online and had tracked him to Bangladesh. Shaun was currently stationed there with his wife and three children.

One day, David intended to visit Shaun. He craved a reunion with someone who understood him. They'd met in Central Park one summer afternoon and had bonded over

David's drone. Shaun had helped to fix a faulty wire in the remote and David had invited him over. Raised in a middle-class family, Shaun hadn't been impressed by the penthouse of pink marble and Gucci everything, but he had been curious over David's entertainment room slash laboratory. Together, they'd spent days sketching ideas for fantastical devices, shared quotes from favorite movies, and had learned each enjoyed reading about science and natural history. Shaun, being particularly tuned-in to David's emotions, had been the one to suggest David make a blanket that could give him what he'd not gotten from his parents—a hug.

David had been so busy he hadn't texted him in months. He should do that. Right now. Because if he let it slide, he'd only slip deeper into the void.

Insulated, was how he felt at times. A man alone in a world that rushed busily around him, pointing and staring and marveling and accusing, but never crossing the line to real communication and trust.

Something about talking to Saralyn made him realize she toed that line into his emotional needs. Probably she'd even smudged part of it away, for he'd told her some things about himself he never shared with anyone. He felt safe talking to her. Like a normal person who wasn't measured by dollar signs or even charitable acts. He could be himself with her.

But was she herself? Was he getting into something with a woman who might pull on a new costume and completely change? That seemed to be her goal. He liked the Saralyn he knew right now. She was beautiful, smart and daring. Sensitive and kind. She liked to laugh and be quiet. He had seen into the pain that she thought she could hide and wanted to erase, but it didn't frighten him. He understood it in ways he wasn't able to vocalize. She grounded him.

Aren't girlfriends there to ground and distract you?

Huffing out a breath, he shook his head at his deep wonderings. The woman had gotten inside him. And there was nothing at all wrong with that.

Picking up his phone, he calculated the time difference between here and Bangladesh.

A knock on the door brought a grin to his face. He called for Saralyn to come in and pulled on the shirt he'd tucked in his back pocket.

"Oh, don't do that," she said as she bounced in. The brightly colored bikini was back, which he appreciated. It enhanced her curves and drew his eyes to her bouncy breasts. Her smile beamed. "I rather like the view. You don't want all your hard work obtaining those muscles to go unappreciated, do you?"

With a smirk, he dropped the shirt. Just swim trunks? His usual island attire. And her lingering gaze did not make him feel demeaned. Hell, her attention felt great. As did the way she'd touched him last night. She had explored his skin with delicate fingers that had quickly become confident and brave. What a perfect kiss. The make-out session had ended too soon, but he could respect her need to take things slowly. They both had their emotional boundaries.

He quickly tucked the photo away in his wallet before approaching her.

"What's up with you this morning?" he asked. "You're more sunny than usual. Did something go well with your plotting?"

"I suppose you could say that. But it's nothing to do with my writing. My inner mermaid has plotted to come and steal you away and carry you to the depths. You up for a swim?"

He winced. "You didn't make that sound very appealing. I'm not much for drowning."

She laughed. "Sorry. I would never tuck away a man in a coral reef. We both know we're not up for the fallout following murder."

He laughed at that. No stomach for murder their shared trait? Ha!

"I am in the mood for a race," she said. "Breaststroke used to be my best event in high school. What about you?"

"Same. A race, eh?"

She nodded.

"Winner takes all?"

"Absolutely."

That she hadn't asked what *all* implied left it open for so many asks after he won. David set aside his phone and followed her out to the beach, which quickly turned into a laughing dash for the water.

After a triumphant, yet leery win, Saralyn waded to the big flat rock shaded by a curvy palm tree and sat. David followed. She had won by two body lengths. But as elated as she felt, she suspected the guy with more muscles than she'd ever own had let her win. And that annoyed her.

"Congratulations." David leaned in to kiss her.

She tilted away from his wet splashes as he sat beside her. Her prerace giddiness had fled, to be replaced by exhausted huffs. And a muscle-deep understanding that fifty was definitely not thirty-five. "I can't accept that win."

"What? Why? You're an amazing swimmer, Saralyn. That was a close match."

"Oh, come on, you let me win. I don't need any man to condescend to me."

"I didn't— Seriously?"

"Please, David, you've more muscles in one arm than I do in my entire body. Not to mention zero body fat. You could have easily overtaken me and won by a mile."

He lay back on the rock and blew out a breath. "It's been a while since I've used the breaststroke. I'm rusty! But believe what you want. Either way, winner takes all. You get to name your prize."

"I don't want a prize." It would feel like a participation trophy. Everyone got one, no matter the talent. Oh, but her muscles would be sore tonight. Fool! That's what she got for pretending she still had it.

Saralyn stood and stepped off the rock. "I'm going to shower and read this afternoon."

"You have to name a prize. It's only fair, Saralyn," he called after her.

Fair? Not really. But as exasperated as she felt by his claims to being out of practice—and she knew it was a lack of exercise that was making her testy—she shouldn't be such a party pooper. And that reminded her that a party lingered in her immediate future.

She stopped walking and wondered what a good ask would be. Something he might be able to acquire—and if he did, that would prove something to the hapless heroine. And make up for the race he threw.

"I want a cake," she called back. "For my birthday in a couple days. And not standard chocolate. It's gotta be unique. Fabulous! Worthy of fifty freakin' years."

"I accept the challenge, fair lady!"

A glance over her shoulder saw he'd turned to his stomach and rested his chin on his fist. Like a sunbathing merman with the occasional tendency toward knight-in-shining-armor. Those biceps could have won that race. And yet, he was more a gentleman than she perhaps knew how to relate to.

And she wanted to walk away from him?

Yes. She needed to brush off this icky feeling that he wasn't being honest with her about the win. Because it was her issue, not his. A dishonest man keeping secrets from her? Ugh!

Hoping he would get the hint she wanted to be alone, she

wandered toward the villa. Regret tightened her mouth. She had been too quick with him. Too rude.

Why did a silly race bother her so much?

She wandered into the villa and veered into the bathroom, stripping off her swimsuit and hanging it on the rack to dry. Once under the warm shower stream, she pressed her palms to the glass-tiled wall.

She shouldn't have walked away from him like that. Her gut knew she could trust David. It was her heart, which had been ignored and bruised by her ex-husband, that had charged in and made a scene out there on the big flat rock. She didn't want to haul her baggage from a failed marriage into whatever was going on with David. He didn't need that. The man had enough emotional baggage himself.

Had she thrown up that wall to stall her blind stumble into a new life? That groove she knew she needed, but really, she was comfortable with her status quo?

"No, you're not comfortable," she muttered. "And, yes, you are stalling."

If she were going to move forward and find a solid position in this world, then she couldn't allow any preconceived emotions about romance to tarnish what she and David were creating. Because they were making something here on this beautiful island away from the world. And it felt too special to ruin.

If only for another week.

Twisting off the shower stream, she hastily dried off and squeezed the water from her hair. Dashing into the bedroom, she grabbed a floaty cream-linen sundress and pulled it over her still-moist skin. She couldn't be worried about what she looked like. There was a man out there who'd been hurt by her idiotic need to throw up a protective wall. Time to knock out some bricks.

Running outside, she spied David walking across the beach and called to him. He didn't stop walking. Fair enough.

She had just sort of won a hundred-yard breaststroke, and she was feeling every one of her fifty years, that was certain. Huffing up behind him, she called, "I'm sorry!"

He stopped immediately and turned to her. No smile on his face, but his expression did lighten as he took in her appearance. Saralyn tugged at her skirt hem, which she only now realized stuck to her wet thigh. She pushed a hank of hair from her face.

"I was reacting," she said. "I know you are kind and wouldn't do anything to hurt me. And even if you did let me win, it doesn't matter. I shouldn't have been so quick with you. I don't want you to think poorly of me. Things from…my past just sneak in and… And that's not fair to you. Past stuff is my stuff, not yours. Oh, I don't know how to say this properly."

He walked up and without a word kissed her. A heady, urgent, take-no-prisoners kind of kiss. The kind only heroes utilized to claim the heroine. To make her understand that she would have no other man but him kiss her. Tilting onto her tiptoes to keep it, Saralyn slid her hands up his bare chest and clutched gently at his shoulders, and then more urgently. He lifted her by the thighs and with a jump she wrapped her legs around his hips. They didn't break the kiss. If she'd felt depleted of energy on the run across the beach, now David's skin electrified every part of her being, invigorating her. His breath danced with hers. Their mouths knew one another. Heartbeats thundered a passionate timpani.

"Thank you," he said, setting her gently to the ground. "I felt bad that you didn't believe me. Maybe I didn't push myself as hard as I could. But I get it. I know you're dealing with some things."

"I don't want to bring those things into what's going on here. This island was supposed to be my safe space."

"Maybe you don't want me around? Would that make it easier to sit with your feelings and resolve them?"

"No." But what a generous and thoughtful offer. This island was also his safe space. And she wanted to respect that. "I don't want that weirdness between us. Can we…?"

She pressed a hand to his chest, measuring his pounding heartbeats against her palm.

Just be honest. Don't push away another man.

"I want you to kiss me again. And again. And then again. And after that…"

"Again?"

She plunged against his body and showed him exactly what she desired. One kiss. Then another. Until kisses become long streams of silent poetry shared between them, set to a cadence they created. It was giddying. So much so that Saralyn allowed the happiness that bubbled in her being to burst out in laughter. David joined her and they bumped shoulders and turned to walk.

They strolled along the shore. "I'm so glad you landed on my island," he said. "And that you chose the executive package and not the three-hour tour. We may have missed one another had you done so."

"The three-hour tour?" It had been a line in the theme song to the *Gilligan's Island* show; the castaways had only intended to be out for a few hours. "You seriously offer that?"

"Of course! It's sort of a joke, but some have taken it up. It's an afternoon of island fun and games. But don't worry, Mary Ann isn't expected to whip up any coconut cream pies."

"Coming from a former Mary Ann who is attempting to find herself, I thank you."

"You're far from Mary Ann. You are Saralyn. You are the universe."

"When you say that, it jars me out of every stupid judgment I've ever had about my body or my actions."

"Aren't we all the universe?" He nudged against her shoulder as they strolled, the warm sand sifting over their toes. "We're made of stardust and atoms and are electrical beings."

"Yes, and we're supposed to all be connected on a greater level. It's cool to think about."

"So, Miss Stardust, next time you feel lesser or affronted by a person or memories from the past, you need to remember how exquisite you are."

"Why is it so easy for you to be like this? So accepting. I thought you were here to escape your own troubles?"

"I am. But focusing on you slams the door on any troubles."

"Then you might never face them."

"I will. In my own time."

"Wise words coming from someone so young. I never would have thought I'd find myself attracted to a younger man."

He laughed. "You have a hang-up about the age thing."

"It's not so much a hang-up as…" What *was* it? He wasn't a floundering youth who couldn't relate to her on an emotional level. Nor was he an overzealous Lothario who only craved what he could get from her sexually. David was smart, self-made and had found his place in the world.

"The age thing is a dying cultural taboo," he provided, and when she began to protest, he rushed to add, "Hear me out. It used to be a shock to see couples of greatly differing ages. Now? Not so much. It's a generational thing. I don't see age when I'm dating. I see the person. You. What does it matter about age?"

"Well." What *did* it matter? A lot. At least, according to

her *generation*, as he'd put it. And cultural influence. "As I've mentioned, it's my Hollywood conditioning. The way the industry treats women is reprehensible. Expecting them to maintain flawless skin, sex appeal and acquiescence."

"And the men can get old, fat and rich."

"I think men age more gracefully."

"Depends on the man. Trust me, you don't look a day over thirty."

"I'll take that."

"No arguments? You really are stepping into yourself, Miss Stardust."

"I think I am."

"Just one question about the age issue," he said. "What is it about a younger man that puts you off?"

"A lack of life experience and wisdom, for one. Also, the younger generation seems to have a different perspective on respect and kindness. Some seem so...entitled. I honestly believe it's a social media thing. Younger generations are literally being raised by the screen. But you're not like that. You feel like my equal."

"That is an immense compliment." He kissed the top of her head.

They walked for a while, wandering in and out of the tide. Not hand in hand, as she preferred, but their shoulders brushed. It reminded Saralyn of a photo her mom kept in her wallet of her dad and mom when they were dating. After a trip to Walt Disney World, they'd detoured to the Weeki Wachee Springs to see the mermaids, and that is where they'd gotten engaged.

Memories of her parents were precious and—they reminded her of a strange discovery her mother made.

"I have something odd to ask you," she said.

"Go for it."

To their left the horizon dashed purple below subtle orange and gold and pink. The waters had darkened, yet she felt safe walking alongside David. Her mother often told her that was how she felt whenever her dad took her hand.

"Walking here on the beach makes me think about my parents. They were so in love. My dad died ten years ago from brain cancer."

"I'm so sorry."

"Thank you. He went quickly. Sometimes death feels like a relief when you counter it with the suffering a person went through. Anyway, they were married for forty years. And just when you think you know a person left, right, up and down, you can discover something new about them. Even after death."

"Really? Your dad left a secret to be discovered after his death?"

"It wasn't left purposefully. After my dad died, my mom went through the old family albums that Grandma—my dad's mom—had given them when they were married. Mom intended to scan the photos and give them to Grandma on a CD. Mom got through half of them and noticed a photo that had been folded in half. It featured dad on the left and on the right was Grandpa. Both were sitting before a table, and it looked like Grandpa was looking at something.

"So she pulled it out and unfolded it, only to find whoever had folded the photo had done so to conceal the person sitting in the middle. It was a girl about my dad's age and she was showing her hand to Grandpa. On the back was a note that read *Showing Dad their engagement ring.* My dad had been engaged before he met my mom. But Mom had never known that. Dad hadn't said anything the entire forty years they were married."

"That's incredible. Was your mom upset?"

"Not really. It was just a weird thing to discover. But it made her realize that you can never completely know a person. So the reason I'm telling you this is, and it's a question I ask when I'm creating my characters, what is something about you that no one knows and might only learn after you're dead?"

"Ah? That's interesting." David shoved his fingers through his hair as he thought about it. She loved that unconscious motion. It flexed his abs and pecs and, his gorgeous dark hair glinted with a few water droplets. "Okay, I got it. But you can't tell anyone because then I'd have to kill you."

"You can't imagine how much I love that we both have murder-worthy secrets to share."

"Yes, well, if this got out, I'd be laughed out of the Normal Club."

"There is such a thing?"

"Apparently there is. Pretty sure they have badges and drive electric vehicles."

"And you think *you're* in that club? I'm not so sure about that. I rather think it would be a boring club. But do tell?"

"I was in a band once."

Saralyn spun before him, stopping their walk. She playfully gaped at him.

David offered a sheepish shrug. "It was a band that I formed with two friends, Shaun and Clive. We were fifteen. Practiced in Shaun's parents' garage."

"Seriously? That sounds cool. Not deathbed-secret stuff. What kind of songs did you sing?"

"Here's where the deathbed-secret stuff gets involved. It was emo scream metal. Called ourselves The Wretched Things. We were incredibly not cool."

Saralyn wasn't aware of that genre of music, but to imagine it put black clothing and long bangs on David with lots of silver studs and abrasive, gut-mined screaming. Not an image she would have ever conjured for him. "You're right. That one's a take-it-to-the-grave secret. Were you the singer?"

"Oh, no, I played…" With a grand splay of his hand, and a bow at the waist as if on stage, he announced, "Synthesizer."

Saralyn dropped her jaw open.

He nodded. "I know, right? You are swooning right now. I was very talented with the keyboard."

"I'm not sure if it's a swoon or…" Laughter sat just at the tip of her tongue. "I don't know that I've ever heard emo scream metal. And with synth? Isn't that an eighties band sort of instrument?"

"Totally."

"Oh, my God, you have to sing one of your songs for me."

"Definitely not. The synth player never sang. He just mouthed the words and flipped his hair." David flipped back his hair dramatically. "I went to the salon and had it straightened. Wore the long bangs over my eyes. I embodied emo. All the girls swooned."

"I bet."

His laughter burst out. "Actually, we never played outside the garage. And I think we were together about three weeks. But I know there's a picture circulating somewhere. I'm sure Shaun has the original. One day, I will get it from him and burn it."

"Not if I find it first." She waggled her fingers before her. "My research skills are remarkably honed. If it's online, I can find it."

David clutched his chest in mock horror. "Would it dissuade you if I gave you my autograph?"

"Only a song will do. You must remember one of them?"

"I think we only had the one song. 'Cyber Chick.' Let's see…" He put out his hands and bent his fingers, then performed some piano-playing motions. *"Duh-dum-dee…*

Cyber Chick! You're so fine. Your bits and bytes turn me on." More air-synth playing. *"Nah, nah, nah, nah, nah!"*

Bursting into a fit of giggles, Saralyn tucked her head against David's shoulder. "Oh, you win. I'm swooning!"

He flipped his hair and leaned in to kiss her. "We rock stars get all the girls."

"You can have me."

David made a show of setting his imaginary synthesizer aside and then tugged her close with a hand to her hip, his eyes never leaving hers. "I do want you, Saralyn."

She'd actually said that he could have her. Had she meant sexually or in a more general sense of her attention and devotion? Both sounded great.

"I have a plan," he suddenly announced with a glance to the sky, which was rapidly losing its golden hue. "Full moon tonight. Will you meet me for a swim up top?"

"Up top?"

"Haven't you hiked the tiny mountain yet? There's an infinity pool up there along with a badminton court."

"I haven't, but now I'm intrigued. A midnight swim?"

"No racing allowed."

"I'm in!"

CHAPTER NINE

AN INFINITY POOL overlooked the west side of the island and was a fifty-stair meander from ground level. Pristine hedges surrounded potted palm trees along one edge, and the water was as blue as the ocean. A poolside bar was fully stocked and of course David had poured wine before Saralyn had shown up.

This was the longest he'd stayed on the island. And he couldn't blame that entirely on the fact there were important matters in his life he needed to sort out. He could have done that in a few days, then hopped a flight back to New York. And it wasn't even because he felt as though he were being stalked by the press. Hell, he was. The daily calls from his COO confirmed that.

No, it was the fascination with Saralyn that kept him here. And she hadn't asked him to leave, so he felt lucky about that. He knew he'd have to face the issue he'd come here to resolve. And quickly. But not on this beautiful moonlit night.

"I can't believe how big the moon is." Saralyn rested her elbows on the edge of the pool, where if viewed from a distance, it appeared to spill over and into the ocean. "I think it's called a supermoon when it's so big and orange. And so close, like I could reach out and touch it. I wonder what my horoscope says about it."

"Do you follow horoscopes?" David rested the back of his head against the edge, his body floating out before him.

From such a position, he couldn't see the moon behind him, but the soft glow on Saralyn's face mirrored its brightness. "What's your sign?"

"I am a Virgo. And yes, that means I like things done a certain way. Generally, I'm the only one who can do said thing the correct way it needs to be done. I'm methodical, but no, I'm not as frigid as we're made out to be."

"I've noticed your tendency toward warmth as opposed to cold." He cast her a wink. "I'm a Cancer."

"Birthday recently? I could have guessed that. You're very kind and put other people's feelings above your own. Sometimes to your detriment."

Nailed that one. It was always easier to let others do the emoting rather than himself.

"Happy belated birthday," she said, and tilted her wine goblet against his, which sat on a floating tray near them.

"Thank you. Thirty-five is an odd age. I'm not old but I'm not young. In the AI research-and-development world I'm considered an oldie, but in the finance-and-business-tech world I'm still a newbie. And we inventors can be any ol' age so long as we don't risk it by blowing ourselves up with our experiments. That's why I don't pay much attention to numbers. Who cares?"

"Sure, but you probably wouldn't date a seventy-year-old, would you?"

"Probably not. She'd be too wise to hang around someone like me."

"Are you saying I'm not wise? I like hanging around you. I don't feel as though we are so different age-wise. You get me. But you also don't make me feel like a matron. I'm your peer."

"You are my peer."

"Says the rock star with the emo bangs."

"You see? That sort of information gets out and I will never live it down. I trusted you."

"You still can trust me. I will never tell. And you know I'm a good secret keeper because I've ghostwritten more than twenty books and no one knows who they are for."

"Save the story filmed on this island."

She waggled an admonishing finger at him. "Just you, my partner in crime."

"Yes, yes. We have mutual blackmail material to hold over one another." He tilted back a double sip of wine and resumed a floating position. "You know I was thinking we never got to your confession regarding things one might only learn about you after you're dead. Give me something deep and dark that would surprise others."

She sighed and turned her head to rest against the pool edge alongside him, letting her body float and her arms sway out to the sides. David let his hand brush up against hers and she linked her pinkie finger with his. It wasn't quite holding hands. And it didn't make him uncomfortable. More of a means to anchor each other so they didn't drift away. A precursor to a real handhold? By all the desires he'd ever had, he hoped so.

"I'm not so sure I've ever touched deep and dark," she decided. "Hmm… Actually, it's something I think about a lot lately. Something that everyone expects from me. It's like they all know Saralyn will be fine because she does the being-alone thing so well."

David swept his body down and propped an arm along the pool edge. A moon goddess floated beside him. He could almost feel her heartbeats waver in the water around him. He wanted to touch her, to…hold her hand. To show some support, but… He wasn't sure it would be taken in the manner he hoped, so he kept his hand out, floating on the surface.

"After my death, people will be stunned to learn that I

actually never wanted to be alone," she finally said. "I've been there, done that. Surprisingly, I experienced it through a twenty-year marriage. I spent more time by myself than with my husband. Being a writer is a very insular thing. We writers don't drive off to an office to work and don't have office mates. We can't make friends over the watercooler. So, solitude is something I've grown into. Admittedly, I think I've done it well. But…"

A turn of her head searched his gaze. David swallowed. The conglomeration of stardust floating beside him radiated light, yet he could sense the darkness that shadowed that light.

"I'm afraid of being alone," she confessed. "It doesn't appeal to me anymore. I want the connection to people, to another person. I want a relationship."

"Like marriage?"

"I don't know about that. I became a virtual hermit in my marriage. No wonder he sought attention from other women."

"No, no, you're not going to blame yourself for Rock's indiscretions."

"Brock."

"Sorry. Rock. Brock. Stone. Granite. They're all a bunch of jerks."

"Hallelujah!" she cheered. Then she crimped her brow. "I just know 'alone' is no longer interesting to me."

Pulling her closer to his body, David bowed his forehead to hers. "You're safe with me, Saralyn. I would never do anything to hurt you."

"I know that."

"And you're not alone. You're with me."

Her hand slid down his neck and along his arm under the water. "Let's stop talking about my ex and focus on the romantic scenery. It's positively bookworthy. It makes me want to kiss you."

He kissed her. "I can't stop touching you or taking in your moon-kissed skin."

"Then don't."

After a heady yet splashy make-out session, they moved to lie on one of the luxurious wide chaises highlighted by the tumescent moon. They lay side by side, not in a hug. It didn't bother Saralyn. Okay, it bothered her a little. She loved to snuggle. She was actually snuggle-starved if she thought about the rare times she'd managed to wrangle her former husband into a moment of quiet caresses. But she wasn't going to press David for a need she had to accept he may never be comfortable fulfilling. And really, if she wasn't ready for sex, she mustn't test those boundaries and give him the wrong signals by suggesting they snuggle. That he'd stopped kissing her when she'd asked meant the world. This man was clued in to her emotional needs.

A surprising chill shivered over her skin as the palm fronds ruffled in the breeze. "Can you grab me a towel?" she asked.

He jumped up and retrieved one of the thick bamboo-colored towels from an open cupboard. Saralyn stood and wrapped it around her. She then kissed him, lingering at the corner of his mouth with a nip and a tease of tongue. His passionate growl did crazy things to her libido. And obliterated her nerves about making love. Toss the man down and have her way with him? The fantasy fit her mood. When she shivered, he rubbed his palms over her shoulders.

"Let's head back to the villa."

They strolled down the wide wood-and-tile steps. David's hair was drying slowly and his body gleamed in the moonlight. When she wanted to hold his hand, she remembered his aversion to doing that. As snuggle-starved as she, then. Neither of them really knew how to initiate what they both desperately wanted. Yet, weirdly, he had no qualms holding her close when they made out.

Was it that he needed the distraction of kissing to get him out of whatever mental trap his brain got caught in when approached by a hug? She was no psychologist. But she wouldn't let it rest. Now that the man had broken down her reluctance, she wanted to forge ahead and enjoy this slightly taboo affair with the sexy young billionaire.

Whew! A lot of new adventures for one day. And she didn't regret any of them.

CHAPTER TEN

LAST NIGHT, they'd fallen asleep on the couch after David had filled her head with all his fabulous and fascinating inventions in the works. They'd woke this morning, ate some fresh fruit, gone for a swim, and now he'd challenged her to a game.

"It's very odd that you have a badminton court in the center of the island." Saralyn selected a racket from the cabinet at court's edge. The infinity pool was on the other side of the changing rooms slash lounge lanai. "As opposed to the standard tennis court, I guess."

"Badminton is my jam." He tossed the white plastic bird into the air and caught it smartly. "Of course I'd put a court on my island. It was a no-brainer."

"Hand me that bird, Brainless. I get to serve first."

He clasped the bird to his chest. "What did you call this?"

She shrugged. "It's a bird or something, isn't it?"

"I am offended. You, the queen of research, don't know what *this* is called?"

"I've never played badminton. Only tennis. What is it?"

"Some call it a birdie, but the official name of this little projectile is a shuttlecock."

"A…" Saralyn covered a laugh with the back of her hand. Then she made an obvious glance down to his khaki shorts.

"Are you serious?" He waggled the plastic object before his face. "My shuttlecock is up here, you dirty-minded woman."

She swiped it from his hand. "My serve."

"You win again," Saralyn announced but not with any sign of disappointment. "As a man of your unparalleled talent should. But give me a few more years of practice and I'll give you a good challenge."

"I eagerly await the match."

David saw she put her arms up, moving in for a hug, and while his mind wanted to turn into her and boldly receive what she was offering, his body flinched and he moved against her with the side of his body, allowing her to wrap her arms across his back and chest for a weird embrace. The only kind he could manage without having a mental argument over the mechanics and emotional fortitude that was required of such an act. Much as he knew it must be awkward for her, it was ten times more awkward for him.

Yet also, meaningful. Her actions spoke volumes to him. The hug was received mentally far more deeply than any physical action.

She pulled back and twirled her racket. "You're not much for hugs, are you?"

"Woman, I can kiss you silent and make your body sing with a mere touch. Why so worried about a hug?"

"I'm not worried." Though her side-eye glance did judge a little. "It just seems like you pull away whenever I try to hug you. Side hugs are not real hugs. Honestly, it's kind of weird for a guy who invented a blanket that literally hugs a person."

"I believe I told you I'm not much for hugs." A lie. He just wasn't skilled at giving or receiving hugs. Because he'd never had the experience to learn how they really worked.

"I don't get that."

Her persistence could not be ignored. He'd love to pull Saralyn into a big hug. Hell, he'd love to make love with her. They were getting closer to that intimacy. He was all about taking his time with her. However, she had but a week left and if he didn't act soon he may never win her trust. It's what he desired from her along with sexual intimacy. So that meant he had to be honest with her.

"Hugs are...the ultimate intimacy," he said. "More so even than sex."

Saralyn set down the racket and leaned against the supply cabinet. She wore a flirty silk skirt over her bikini and her movement set the ruffles into a sensual flutter. "Really? Because sex and making love both seem pretty darn intimate."

"You differentiate?"

"Of course. Making love is emotional and heartfelt. Sex is not. I mean, sex is great, and it can involve emotion. Eh, it's the romance writer in me. Don't think about it too much."

"I do think about making love," he said, "with you."

That arching eyebrow of hers always alluded to something she was willing to consider. Perhaps work into the new groove of a life she was shaping.

"Same," she offered confidently. "But first, give me the details on you and hugs. Or is it another death surprise?"

That made him laugh. Not nearly so surprising as him having formed an emo band when he was a teenager. But it was deep. And emotional. And... To spill a part of him that really didn't require spilling? Or rather, no one needed to hear about his awkward family dynamic.

And yet, he wanted to give Saralyn a part of him because he trusted her.

He took the racket from her and hung it with the rest of the equipment at the edge of the court. "Let's walk."

The wooden path spiraled down from the court to the mainland. A stroll was the de rigueur pace for any destination on the island. One of the parrots swooped over their heads but not low enough to make him thrust up a protective arm to protect Saralyn. They weren't eating. They were safe.

About halfway down, David stopped and gestured they sit on the massive tree step that had been carved in situ to create a portion of the stairway. It was now or never.

"Okay, here's the deal about me and hugs," he stated. "I was never hugged as a kid."

She tilted a startled glance at him.

He scrubbed the back of his neck, then offered, "The Crown family is not close or demonstrative. No hugs or kisses. Not even a vocal validation or approval of a job well done. Remarkably, I didn't realize until I was around nine or ten how little my parents touched me."

"Oh, David, I'm so sorry."

"It's what I've known, so it wasn't something I thought about much."

For the most part. But naming one's garage band The Wretched Things?

"Mom and Dad were jetsetters, involved directly in the everyday operations of the Crown family foundation and charities. They were rarely around the penthouse."

"What did they do exactly? Or do they do? Do they still work?"

"Yes, but not in a standard nine-to-five job. I explained that my great-greats invested in the telegraphy cables that brought the telegram to the world. That's how we came to our wealth. Old money. Because of those wise investments, we've never had to work, but my parents are type As who need to. Or rather, be busy. Running foundations and charities *is* work."

"Sounds like the best kind."

"It is, in that it keeps them busy and their minds sharp. I know, they're not that old, but I want them to age gracefully, and if they can continue their work, that'll be the fountain of youth for them."

"You care about them."

"Of course I do," he said, but softened the last word so it didn't sound like he'd been as offended as that comment made him. He did love them. In his own way.

"I could have gone the same route as them," he continued, "assuming a position on the foundation board and delegating to others, but since childhood I've always been interested in science and how things work. I enjoy creating new things. And tearing things apart to see how they work. It excites me. And I quickly learned a good day's labor gave me a serotonin boost. I can't imagine not having a physical job to challenge my brain and body.

"Anyway, while my parents tended their lives, I was basically raised by nannies. A very cold nanny in particular. She was astute and to the point. She never rewarded good behavior, nor did she punish. She was…unemotional. I didn't have parents to demonstrate emotion to me."

"You said something about the chef and his wife teaching you so much?"

"Exactly. I do love the LeDouxes for their kindness and for allowing a lonely boy to peer into their lives to see what real love was."

"So, your parents… They didn't hug you?"

He exhaled. "When they were around? No. 'Mum and Dad are very busy, David. We love you.' And then they'd wave and rush out the door for another few weeks. I…did attempt a hug one time. I believe I was nine. Well, it's silly to recall."

Yet it had influenced him in ways that affected him even to the present.

Saralyn slid a hand along his upper arm and gave it a squeeze. "Tell me?"

"It was one day at school, and I'd seen the parents waiting to pick up my fellow classmates greet their child with a hug and a kiss. I always marveled over that ritual. The kid would run into their parent's arms. No kid ever walked away from a hug frowning. So one day I gave it a go. Mom had stopped to pick me up—a rarity, but she had a meeting with the school's headmistress—and I ran into her arms for the hug. She reacted with offense, pushing me away and fretting over her white clothing. 'You wretched thing,' she said. 'You've dirtied my skirt.'"

David swallowed at the memory. It lodged in his throat and stirred a sickly quaver in his body. He thought he'd gotten beyond the emotional letdown of that experience, so it always surprised him that memory could summon the feeling as if it were yesterday.

"The name of your band," she said softly.

Saralyn's hand slid down his arm, stopping at his wrist. In that moment, when his heart felt open and safe, he twisted up his hand and clasped hers with his. She gave his hand a squeeze. It worked to tighten his chest and loosen something behind his eyes.

He nodded. "Seemed appropriate for a metal band, eh?"

She tilted her head against his shoulder. The caress worked like the real hug he so desperately wanted. And with her hand in his? The moment was not so frightening as he thought it should be. Instead, it warmed his very soul.

"So you didn't know the physical intimacy you were missing until you started dating?"

"Exactly. And then, you know girls and guys. We want to get our hands all over one another. The first time a girl hugged me, I sort of flipped out. And then when I thought about it, I realized it could be nice. But it never happened again. I mean, teenagers don't spend a lot of time hugging, they get straight to the good stuff."

"I get that. But I believe hugs are also the good stuff."

"Probably." Though he hadn't an actual *experienced* example to prove it to himself.

"Anyway, that 'lacking intimacy' led to me obsessing about connection with other people. I could make conversation, be in groups, have friends, even have sex with a woman. But the intimacy of two bodies hugging, of being fully clothed and quiet, and simply sharing... That disturbed and excited me. I wanted the feeling, but it scared me. But I also *needed* that feeling. So the safest way to get it was to invent the blanket."

"I take it you've some technical skills that made that happen?"

"Yes, I spent six years in college. I've a master of science in artificial intelligence, a biotech science degree and also computer coding, and an associate in electrical engineering. Seems like a lot, but I breezed through my studies." He shrugged. "Learning comes easy for me. Anyway, I tried a few psychology courses, to add some variety to my education, but that bored me. I like tinkering and tech. Though the psych stuff did influence me. Do you know when a person receives or gives a hug oxytocin is released? A hug that lasts twenty seconds can reduce stress, lower your blood pressure, even your heart rate. There are studies that prove it can also boost your immune system."

"It's good for depression, yes?"

"You bet. And if you're feeling tired, a hug will give you a lift. It's utterly amazing what that simple yet impossible act can do for a person. After I learned all that, I had to invent the blanket. It was a no-brainer."

"I tried the blanket the other day. It really is marvelous."

"Thanks to a nudge from my best friend, Shaun, who possesses an uncanny ability to read people's emotions, I set out to help others," he said. "I knew it could be a good thing for kids in hospitals, elders in senior homes, some who are on the spectrum, anyone who was alone or unable to make a connection naturally."

"But just now you used the word *impossible* to describe a hug. The inventor of the most amazing blanket has never experienced a real hug? David, that makes me so sad. Makes me want to hug you right now. But don't worry, I won't. I think it has to come naturally for you."

"Thank you for understanding that. I want, more than anything, to hug you, Saralyn. But you're right, it has to feel…"

"I would never push you away," she said softly.

He nodded, thankful for her understanding. Then he lifted their clasped hands. "And look what you've accomplished. We're holding hands."

"I wasn't going to call attention to it."

"Did you think I'd be freaked?"

"Maybe."

"I was, which is why I kept talking as a means to distract myself." He studied their hands. "This feels…like we are putting our trust into action. In some synesthetic sort of manner I can actually see the trust. Do you think I'm a nut?"

"Not at all. Emotional synesthesia sounds cool. Yet I have to wonder, if your parents were never around, who was it that showed you how to be such a kind and generous man?"

"Oh, that's an easy one. Marcel, our chef!"

"Of course!"

"I spent a lot of time in the kitchen watching him prep and cook. He'd let me help him. But the reason I kept going back, despite the cuts to my fingers and the ridiculous inability to properly peel a potato, was that he talked to me like a real person. He was interested in whatever I had to say. He would encourage me when I told him about my latest crazy invention. And as a teen, I observed the love between Marcel and his wife. It was kind, respectful and a little fiery."

"I'm so happy you had that example to learn from. I wish you could have experienced the comfort of a hug growing up. But that lack pushed you to invent something that has helped so many."

"Yes, well…" Another text from his COO this morning had suggested it was time for him to return to New York City to face the press. "I'm thinking of pulling the plug on the whole thing. The lawsuit put a black mark on it all."

He didn't want to discuss the lawsuit. That was rife with emotions that he'd come here to sort out. On his own. "Let's go make something to eat."

She nodded, seeming to sense his need not to expound. Bless her for that. He'd opened a part of himself for her today. And their clasped hands proved he could trust her. But the dive had been deep, and right now he needed to come up for air.

CHAPTER ELEVEN

THE NEXT MORNING, as David was sweeping out the chef's cottage, his phone buzzed. He'd sent a text to Shaun ten minutes earlier.

How's it going, Crown?

Always well. But I miss you, buddy. It's been too long.

Feel the same. You're the one with all the cash. Fly in and spend a week with me sometime!

Let me know when and I'll be there.

Awesome. I'll check with the wife and get back to you. So, you at work?

On the island. With a woman.

Nice.

It's different. I respect her. And I want her at the same time.

Ah. Well, then, that's love.

David stared at those last two words. That was crazy. A pulsing red heart popped up on the screen. Now Shaun was just yanking his chain.

Love? It hadn't occurred to him that something so profound could be forming between him and Saralyn. Nah. Couldn't be. Love didn't happen so fast, did it?

Rationally, he knew it was possible. He'd read as much in his psychology studies and when he was researching for the blanket. And Marcel had always told him how he and his wife had experienced love at first sight.

Crazy, he texted back.

Whatever. Love sneaks up on a guy. Gotta go. My kid has soccer practice. Will text my schedule in a few days. Good to connect, Crown!

Same.

David turned off the phone and crossed his arms, leaning against the counter. Love? No, it couldn't possibly be.

And yet.

He'd never felt this way with a woman. The many women who had moved through his life had appealed to him on different levels, and he'd enjoyed their company, treating them well, taking them out, learning about their likes and dislikes, having sex with them.

Sex is different than making love.

That was true. All those relationships had ended because he hadn't felt them right, in a way he couldn't define. He hadn't felt an ineffable connection to the woman.

Like an atom clinging to stardust.

A broad grin grew. "Well, all right, then."

When checking her phone for texts from her mom, Saralyn saw that Juliane had called two hours earlier. She immediately returned the call and Juliane gave her the lowdown on her living conditions: sparse and cold but homey, with a bookshelf stocked with old mysteries and an amazing AI microscope that generated simulations geared toward her project. Her fellow biologists were all men save one other woman. The two women did not feel threatened; it felt like family. And the food: yuck.

"How's the island treating you?" Juliane asked. "Is it just like the movie?"

Fluffing out her hair that was almost dry after a morning shower, Saralyn plopped onto the curved couch under the constellation chandelier and ran a hand down her bare thigh. "Exactly the same. Blue sky. Blue water. Endless bliss. I've been living in a bikini. Eating gourmet meals. Swimming with the fishes. Spending far too much time sunbathing. And have learned the finer points of badminton."

"Sounds like a dream, but despite the nearly one-hundred-degree temperature difference in our locations, I still don't regret missing out. Wait. Badminton? Are you playing…by yourself?"

"No, I'm playing with the self-proclaimed badminton champion, David Crown."

"The *owner* of the island? What the— Why is he there? And what's going on that you two are engaging in extracurricular sports? And please tell me that *extracurricular* extends to the form of sport I have in mind."

Juliane did have a dirty mind. The woman was a wonder when it came to helping her brainstorm sex scenes.

"If kissing is extracurricular, then yes," Saralyn said. "David is here because apparently the fine print allows him to stay anytime, even if there are guests."

"The fine print? Who reads that?"

"Right? But no worries. We've gotten to know one another and…"

"And…?"

Saralyn's sigh settled her deeper into the sofa and the hug blanket flipped against her shoulder. She pressed it to her cheek. A truly kind person had invented this blanket. "I like him, Juliane. And the fifteen-year age difference doesn't bother me anymore."

"Ooh, Mrs. Robinson!"

"Oh, please, I am not some married older woman seducing a college student," she said, recalling the movie plot they both referred to. "David is not like any man I've ever known. He makes me believe that I can do this thing called *moving on*."

"Saralyn, I'm so glad to hear that. But now I need the sordid details. Please tell me there are details that can be labeled sordid?"

With a laugh, Saralyn filled her in on their kisses and growing intimacy. And how he made her feel seen and not at all worried that anything he did see might offend him.

"He's been a balm for my soul," she said.

"You don't need balm, Saralyn, you need straight-up sex. I know it's been a long time since you've been with anyone but The One We Will Not Name, but you are a mighty woman who has survived a nasty divorce. Now it's your turn to take what you want."

"Me thinks you simply want to live vicariously through my sexual antics."

"Well yeah! What do you think I'll be doing for the next six months up here with only a cell phone to talk to my boyfriend?"

They laughed and chatted about how one manages a twenty-yard walk outside in weather that hits minus double digits and if it might be possible to package up some tropical sunshine and ship it north.

When a soft tune started playing outside on the veranda,

Saralyn smiled to recognize it as a romantic Sinatra song. She spied David standing in the open doorway, shoulder casually propped against the door, and a bouquet of those smelly purple flowers in hand. He made show of sniffing it, wrinkled up a disgusted face, then tossed them over his shoulder.

"I have to go, Juliane. Something sordid just walked in."

With a hoot and a clap, Juliane sent her "love" and "good luck," even as Saralyn turned off the phone and tucked it away.

Still propped in the doorway, David winked at her. "My plans to seduce you with flowers have failed. I forgot how stinky they are."

She strolled up to him and pretended to look around him to the scatter of purple and white flowers on the veranda deck. She could smell them even at this distance. With a crook of her finger, she gestured he follow her inside. "Your plans may not be entirely lost."

With that, she turned and he caught her by the arms as he kissed her soundly.

"I've been thinking of you since I woke," he said. "Probably even in my dreams."

"Lucid dreaming is what I do well. It helps me to plot my stories."

"How's our story going so far?"

"The hero has unknowingly slain a few minor dragons that have annoyed the heroine over the years."

"Really?"

She nodded. "Kiss me again. And then…"

"And then?"

She turned and strolled toward the bedroom, untying the silk scarf from her hips as she did so. Glancing over her shoulder, she revealed her best Mrs. Robinson–flirtatious eyelash flutter. And then she blew him a kiss.

David caught the kiss and pressed his fingertips to his mouth. As he approached, she leaned against the doorframe. He took her hand and kissed the back of it.

"No plans to hike the island this morning?" he asked.

She shook her head. "The wind is starting to pick up. And you know how I dislike the wind."

"I do know that. You like to stay inside."

"And be protected by a big, strong, handsome man." She couldn't even wince inwardly at that one. Nothing was going to change her mind. Every inch of her skin wanted David's attention, his touch, his kisses. And it was time she listened to her body instead of her erratic writer's brain.

"I'm strong," he offered.

"And handsome." She tipped onto her toes and kissed him. "I want to make love?"

He smiled against her mouth, then met her gaze. "Was that a statement or a question?"

No place for nervous jitters now. Saralyn Hayes was in her groove.

She tugged him inside the bedroom by the waistband of his swim trunks. "A statement."

He closed the door behind him and pulled her into his arms as they tumbled onto the bed.

Saralyn lay in bed beside David. They'd made love. For hours. An orgasm here. A wander into the kitchen for refreshment. Luxuriously slow kisses and delicious touches. Another orgasm. Light chatter about their favorite positions and then performing them.

Now they lingered. The wind had softened and fluttered the curtain and a symphony of birdsong danced through the open window. David had drifted to sleep. A light afternoon nap. He deserved it after his vigorous performance. All afternoon. And she'd kept up with him. Her sexual stamina had not suffered because of divorce, aging or menopause. It was refreshing to know that. No old lady here!

Lying on her side, her hand resting on David's chest, she replayed their conversation about his inability to accept a hug. Not for lack of trying. What a cruel mother to have pushed him away like that. The distant parenting. It had obviously shaped him in ways both good and bad. The good was the invention of the blanket that helped so many. The bad, well. She just wanted to pull him into a hug and show him how much she cared. But she didn't want to frighten him.

It was odd that he was so comfortable with her in bed, sharing his body, licking over hers and lying against her, skin against skin. But it wasn't a hug. When they made love, they moved against one another, laughed, kissed and touched. Yet it wasn't a moment for quiet, listening to one another's heartbeats or simply hugging.

Snuggling beside his warm body, she stroked her fingers through his soft, dark chest hairs. He smelled like the sea, the foliage and earth, and her body coiled instinctively toward his strength. Safe here with him.

Could it last? Did she want it to last?

While the idea of making love to a man and then *not* starting a relationship seemed to be the norm in today's society, if she were honest with herself, she still clung to her ingrained beliefs. This intimate connection meant something to her. She never would have invited him into the bedroom if it hadn't. She didn't want it to be surface or discarded as a hookup. And she did not care to be alone anymore. Been there, done that throughout her twenty-year marriage. Creating a deep and lasting connection with a man was important to her.

Was David the man who could connect with her as she

navigated her way through this new chapter of her life? Was she jumping in too quickly?

She shouldn't think too far into this. Just enjoy the moments. It wasn't as though she had many days left on the island...

She'd come here to make some life decisions, not gain a lover or boyfriend. Once she set foot off this island, she had much to take care of. Moving. Writing. To ghostwrite or not? She still hadn't decided! And when calling Juliane, she'd seen another text from her agent.

It would be easiest to take the ghostwriting job. How long could she put off taking that big and scary step into independence?

"I will make a decision. Before I leave the island."

But for now, and perhaps the rest of the day, she intended to luxuriate in David Crown.

And so she did.

CHAPTER TWELVE

TODAY WAS HER fiftieth birthday.

And she was on a gorgeous tropical island and had acquired a younger lover. What a way to walk into that auspicious age!

A tango echoed softly from the speakers set at various places around the island. Saralyn could generally locate the area where the sound was coming from, but she'd yet to spy an actual speaker. Likely they were in the shape of a coconut. This song she recognized from one of her favorite movies about married assassins discovering they had been assigned to take the other out.

After rising this morning and making silly love in the shower, they'd shared a quick breakfast. But the insistent pings on David's phone could not be ignored. Apologizing, and insisting he keep all business away from the bliss they had begun to create, David had gone to the chef's cottage to make a few phone calls. She'd sensed the tension in his tone as he'd kissed her quickly and then wandered off. What he'd come here to escape had followed him. She certainly hoped he was able to overcome it.

She'd taken to picking flowers. These blooms smelled like candy and had interesting long stamens. Tiny birds flocked to them, sipping from deep within. She didn't pick many; it felt wrong to spoil the scenery and they were so big. Three vibrant pink blooms, each as big as a cat's head, would fill the villa with a heady scent.

The world felt lush and sensual. Her eyes viewed it anew without the tedious doldrums and disappointments of decades past. Had good sex done that? Yes!

Turning dramatically, she clutched the thick flower stems and performed a makeshift step to the music. She had no clue how to tango. Didn't matter. She felt free and unencumbered. Today was her birthday. And she intended to celebrate every molecule of it.

She hadn't mentioned the auspicious day to David over breakfast. If he remembered, great. If not, it didn't matter, because who really needed to be reminded by a handsome younger man that she was older?

Stop it, Saralyn!

She wasn't thinking like that anymore. Age meant nothing to David. And she was beginning to respect his point of view on that subject. She didn't have to subscribe to any preconceived expectations!

Shaking her hair to feel it dust her shoulders, she spun and performed a few steps across the sand. Swaying her hips, she surrendered to the sensual pull. When someone clapped from behind her, she spun and smiled through the bouquet. The urge to drop her shoulders, bow her head and make herself a ghost did not arise.

No longer would she stand behind a man.

Lifting her arms and infusing the air with the floral fragrance, she swiveled her hips and went off script with the tango and into her own sensual dance. It felt good to move her body to the rhythm of the nearby waves.

When she turned, David had squatted and rested his chin in hand, his attention completely on her. The hero enraptured? Silly romance. What mattered to her was that she felt safe to dance before him. And a little naughty.

With a wave of her hand and a shift of her hips, she embodied the music. Closing her eyes, she concentrated on the air that brushed her skin and sifted through her hair. Intoxicating fragrance spilled over her being. The regard of her lover as she danced before him felt tangible, soul deep.

No, she wasn't dancing for him. She danced for herself. For the woman she was determined to embrace, respect and honor. Saralyn Hayes was fifty years old, had a beautiful life, and could make any decision she wished to make. From this moment forward, it was all good.

"You seduce me with your confidence," he said.

"I think I've seduced myself." She dipped and handed him the flowers, then spun out into a fun twist and hip shimmy. "I've never danced for myself before!"

"Your beauty puts these flowers to shame."

She was about to counter that compliment when her heart rushed in and stopped her. *Just accept it!* So she did.

"You can join me if you like."

"Nope. This dance is all yours, Miss Stardust."

"Sounds like a lounge singer who croons into one of those old-fashioned microphones." She grabbed an imaginary microphone and announced, "And singing at the Galaxy Lounge tonight…ladies and gentlemen, Miss Stardust!"

David whistled and clapped and leaned back to catch his elbows in the sand, the flowers abandoned near his side. "Bravo!"

Saralyn performed a final spin, feeling every ounce of joy and happiness explode out of her in laughter. Turning, she dove next to David and kissed him.

He brushed the hair from her cheek and kissed her nose. "I hope that's not the last performance by Miss Stardust I get to watch."

"She only does private engagements. And I'm pretty sure only for men named David with the last name Crown."

"Eh, there could be quite of few of us in this world. I'm immediately jealous."

"I promise to reserve all seats only for those David Crowns who own tropical islands and who can spear a fish."

"I promise to show up for every performance. So what has compelled you to dance on the beach like a flower goddess summoning the sun?"

"The music tempted me, and all of a sudden, I…became myself."

"You inspire me, Saralyn. I hope someday I can dance by myself. Metaphorically, that is."

"You already do that. But I know something has sidelined you lately. Work stuff." And he didn't want to talk about it, so she would respect that. "But dancing with a partner is more fun." She climbed onto his lap, knees in the sand to either side of his hips and pushed her fingers through his oh-so-soft-and-curly hair, tilting his head up toward her. "You are one sexy man."

"Miss Stardust thinks I'm sexy? Nice." He rolled her to her back and the twosome made out on a fragrant crush of flowers.

But too quickly, Saralyn wriggled uncomfortably. "Sand in my bikini."

"Take it off."

"You think?" She glanced up and around.

"Don't worry, the professor and Mary Ann are on the other side of the island, and I know the rest of the gang are doing things on their own. We're alone."

"Yes, but the sand is moving into uncomfortable places. Let's take this inside, shall we?"

He stood and helped her up, grasping the crushed flowers as she did so. Displaying the pitiful bouquet, he pouted mockingly.

Saralyn grabbed the bouquet and took off running toward the villa. "Catch me if you can!"

They didn't make it to the bedroom. Once on the veranda, Saralyn turned and blew a kiss to David. He caught it and crushed it against his chest. And in a bold move, she slipped off her bikini top and tossed it at him.

They landed on the padded veranda sofa amid kisses, caresses and frenzied clothing removal. All the heroes she had ever designed for the page had stepped into her reality. But they didn't embody David Crown. He was his own man. Far above any fictional creation. He was real, genuine and felt like a piece of her she'd never known was missing until she touched it now.

They came together quickly, easily, sharing themselves and moving like a well-choreographed tango that took and gave, and insisted and then surrendered. For the first time in her life, Saralyn landed in her orgasm freely and without reserve. She shouted and gripped her lover's hair and moved her body as tight to him as she could and then she let go and floated. In his arms.

He came as quickly and loudly, settling next to her on the sofa and huffing soft breaths filled with levity and joy. "That's so good."

"I agree," she said on an effusive gasp.

They lay there under a canopy of palm fronds, tropical flowers and birdsong, clasping hands. If this moment might never end, Saralyn would take it, no questions asked. She'd never felt...

"Are you happy?" she suddenly asked her lover.

"Right now? Hell, yes. You make me happy."

As was she. But. "I mean, overall. With your life." She turned onto her side and spread her fingers through his fine chest hairs, taking a moment to study his fast heartbeats. But her curiosity would not be curtailed. "If you put aside this escape to the island to get away from whatever is troubling you, can you say that your life is generally happy?"

"Kind of an intense question for having just made love. I'm still flying on that orgasm."

"I promise you'll get to fly again. But I do believe you are more adept at avoiding uncomfortable questions than I am."

"Fine. I'll play." He threaded his fingers through hers and kissed her hand. "Despite the stuff going on with Crown Corp? Yes, I'd say I'm generally happy."

"How do you know that?"

"Because… I've never wanted for anything materially. And I feel…well, not mad, bad or indifferent."

"A lack of harsh feelings does not make for happiness. What about wanting for something emotionally?"

"You can try to convince me I'm an emotional wreck all you like, Miss Stardust, but trust me, I am very aware that life has treated me well and I am grateful for that and have no real reason to be unhappy. What about you? Are *you* happy? Setting the divorce aside."

"I am. I'm content." She rested her chin on their hands, which he held on his chest. "Maybe too content. Especially when it comes to living like a ghost and avoiding interaction with people. I'm also not mad, bad or indifferent. I just think happiness is an inside job. Like a person shouldn't rely on anyone else for that feeling. You said I make you happy." For how long? Their time together was growing shorter! "But what about when I'm not around?"

"A person's mood can lift and improve and you don't need to label it as *needing* that other person, like some sort of happiness parasite."

"Now I'm picturing what such a parasite must look like, with tentacles and bright pink eyes."

He kissed her. "Save that for a science fiction novel. Life treats me well. Most of the time. And for that, I am happy."

Saralyn closed her eyes. "I'm going to start truly living in my happiness. Embodying it. To genuinely not rely on others for a good mood or even a ruined moment. I want to take responsibility for everything I say or do. I will create my own life."

"Seems like you're doing it."

"It does, doesn't it?"

"You dancing before me was like watching confidence. I know you've the past clinging to you, but each day, you shake off a little more. I don't think it will happen like a snap of the fingers."

"Shaking it off is a good way to put it. I'll probably dance it off." She twirled a finger in one of his dark curls. "I like what's happening here. Between the two of us. Beyond the sex."

"Same."

"When I leave the island, will it all reset and go back to the way it was before I set foot on these gorgeous warm beaches?"

"I don't want it to."

Neither did she. But she didn't live in New York, where she could be close to him. In a few months, she wouldn't even have a home. Was starting something with David worth the challenge? Would he be receptive to her wanting a man in her life? Even if she didn't live in his city? It was too much to bring up. It felt like she was forcing him to commit.

And they were both naked. Weird time to talk about the big issues.

"We'll see what happens, eh?" she offered lightly. "I'm going for a walk around the island." She kissed him and sat up, searching for her swimsuit pieces.

"You've stopped holding your stomach in," he commented as he watched her dress.

"I…" She sucked in her stomach, then released it. "What?"

"You've been doing it since the first day we met. A woman thing. I noticed you've become more relaxed. More yourself."

She smoothed a hand over her belly. He was right. She had relaxed. She'd not even given it a thought yesterday during their all-day sex session. This soft belly was all hers. Time to own it!

She pushed out her stomach in an exaggerated bulge. David laughed. And she laughed with him. Leaning over the sofa, she kissed him. "Catch you later."

"I've some business to take care of, but yes, I will find you later, Miss Stardust."

Following a post-sex snack attack of pepper-spiced hummus and veggies, David finished the phone calls he'd started before he'd been distracted by the dancing lounge singer on the beach. Much as he had separated himself from work, work always knew where to find him. There were questions to answer, contracts to approve and a marketing plan that required his notations on a pdf slideshow.

And the looming decision. Apparently reporters had started to camp outside Crown Corp. His COO had sounded nervous. He'd taken it upon himself to get public relations to look at their options regarding cooling the media's curiosity. David was confident the man could handle it, but he couldn't ignore the call to duty. To his very honor. He had to return to New York, and soon.

But not yet.

After speaking to the home office, he made one more important call. The delivery would take a few hours to arrive. As he set down the phone his thoughts drifted to the only other person on the island. What was he feeling about Saralyn, aka Miss Stardust of the Galaxy Lounge? She had touched parts of his psyche he'd never thought available to others. He'd *held her hand.* That was an emotional connection on a completely different level than the amazing love-making they'd shared.

There was so much going on inside him emotionally, what with work and now this island experience, it was almost too much to sort out.

Yet his intention to get straight whether he should stop producing the hug blanket was set aside. He'd been too pre-occupied with the wondrous feeling of being near Saralyn. She made him forget all the bad stuff. And he knew, ratio-nally, that a person should never depend on anyone else for happiness. He had to feel happy before he could be with an-other person. But *did* he feel happy?

Yes, more than he had felt so in years. All his life? Pos-sible.

Shaun's words returned to him. *Love sneaks up on a guy.*

He was falling for Saralyn. And that felt like something he wasn't allowed to have, such as a hug. He had to overcome that reluctance. Because if he could not, then he risked los-ing the best thing that had ever danced into his life.

CHAPTER THIRTEEN

As far as fiftieth birthdays went, this one topped the charts. Saralyn was on a beautiful tropical island, currently floating in the azure waters like an abandoned blowup chaise. She had taken a lover. The most handsome, respectful, sexy, arousing man she knew. She had begun to embody herself, to really feel her bones and skin and enjoy simply being a woman. A person who deserved notice and respect! And she was *this close* to walking away from the ghostwriting offer. Everything felt right.

How to frame this moment and keep it forever?

Because soon enough, she'd have to return to reality. Leave behind David Crown and his sensual kisses and masterful lovemaking. Well, she didn't have to leave him behind. They could...

What *could* they do? Have a long-distance relationship? Saralyn wanted nothing to do with such an impossible arrangement. If she dated a man she wanted him close, in the same town. She didn't do sexting or the whole "distance makes the heart grow fonder."

It was all or nothing, baby.

Could she have it all from David?

All the attention. All his laughter. All his confident smiles and brazen stares. She wanted the wild and sensual sex with a younger man. The fiery shivers that his touches ignited throughout her being. The feeling of being so wanted, so desired, as if she were the only thing that mattered to him. She wanted to walk alongside him and notice when others glanced a bit too long.

What's that? She's so much older than him. And he's so young. Interesting.

Saralyn wanted that *interesting*. She wanted that attention. She wanted to be noticed!

Swishing her fingers to spin her body on the surface of the water, she closed her eyes and smiled to herself. If she and David took their affair off the island, she would be noticed. The man attracted the media's attention. Could she do that again with another man?

The real question was, could she stand *alongside* another man, holding his hand, and be his equal? As opposed to standing behind in the shadows, the supportive one, and being okay with that. The shadows had grown cold and uninviting. And when had Brock ever returned with support for her career?

Standing back and looking over her relationship with Brock now, it was much easier to see the manipulation on his part. Keeping her at home, writing and earning just enough to be satisfied but never to support herself. He had been a necessity, her provider. And she'd gotten stuck in that blind thinking.

And no, she wouldn't accept all the responsibility for her husband's wandering eye. She had tried. She had been there for him. That marriage, to that man, just hadn't been the right place for her. And she realized that now.

David felt like the right place. But would he want her by his side for all to see? This may very well be an island fling for him. Enjoy a few weeks together, then, "See ya later, Miss Stardust."

She had to ask him where his head was at with all this. She needed to know. And she would.

After she'd floated on this sunny tropical dream for a while longer.

At the sight of the motionless body floating near the dock, David dropped the two green coconuts he'd cut for an afternoon refreshment and burst into a run. It could only be Saralyn. And…she wasn't moving. Had she drowned? Her body floated to the surface?

His heart thundered. Every muscle tightened and made breathing difficult. She was an excellent swimmer, but anything was possible.

He raced across the dock and jumped into the water, landing beside her body with a splash. Gripping her by the shoulders he lifted her, and at the same time, she sputtered and slapped the water's surface.

David swore and released her. Dark thoughts gripped him. Flashes of sitting in a courtroom. *Viewing those terrible photos.*

"Saralyn, I thought you were dead."

"What? David, don't be silly. I was floating. You look like you've seen a ghost."

"I thought I had." He swore again under his breath, heaving in air and wincing as his lungs protested his flight to rescue. She was fine. Yet he'd thought the worst. And had seen…such achingly horrendous images. And oh, but one tragedy had been enough of late. "I don't need another death in my life."

He straightened and squeezed his eyes shut, tilting back his head. Every part of the trial revisited his thoughts. The detailed report given by the coroner. The heart-wrenching confession of the mother and then the father. It had been too terrible. And when he'd thought Saralyn dead, his heart had raced to the same dark place that squeezed his chest so tightly he still gasped to breathe.

"I'm fine," she said too brightly from behind him. "Want to go for a swim?"

He shook his head and stalked toward the shore. "I can't do this right now."

"What? David, what's wrong?"

"Need to be alone," he muttered. "Sorry. Feelings...conflicted. I need to get this figured out."

When his feet hit dry sand, he took off in a jog.

The day hadn't ended exactly as Saralyn had wished. Since David had tried to rescue her from floating in the ocean, she hadn't seen him. And after hearing him mutter something about not needing any more death in his life, she'd sensed in that frantic moment he'd gone to a dark place. He'd said he needed to be alone. To figure things out. So she'd respected that and given him his distance.

But it was late. The golden waning moon hung low in the evening sky. She sat on the veranda, wearing the fluttery red sundress she'd packed specifically for today. It represented her bold step into the next chapter. The urge to perform some sort of ritual to take back her power and confirm her commitment to moving forward niggled. But what to do? The day had been a leisurely and pleasurable venture into self-care. This entire vacation had been so!

What she really wanted was to spend the last few hours of her birthday with David. Dare she seek him out? She would apologize for giving him a fright. Maybe he'd talk about it with her. She wanted to see inside all those places he kept secret and closed. Because seriously? She wasn't the only one who had fled to this island to work things out. David wanted certain things as well. She had been too focused on herself to realize that until now. She must be more cognizant of his needs. And tonight that meant privacy.

Collecting two of the portable solar lanterns from the veranda—one in each hand, dangling at her sides—she walked out onto the beach, wandering for a while. Eventually she found herself at the big flat rock that provided the best seating for twilight sea-gazing. Placing a lantern to either side of her, she sat. Ribbons of pink and violet streaked the darkening sky. The air tasted salty and the musical chirps of tropical birds echoed out from the trees behind her.

Resting her elbows on the rock behind her, she stretched out her legs and could just splash her toes in the water. "Happy birthday to me."

It wasn't as though she hadn't spent many birthdays alone. Brock had tended to forget or to work late, or to grumble about getting a reservation at a trendy place at the last minute. After a few years, she'd given up on reminding him and had quickly learned to treat the day as any other day.

She had lessened herself so as not to outshine him. She knew that now. Never should she have completely extinguished her light.

"I will shine," she announced to the sky. And then whispered, "Like Miss Stardust."

Still. She felt…unsatisfied.

Growing older shouldn't have to be a buzzkill. In fact, it required creativity and engagement, even if she was all alone. She could make her own party. There was wine back at the villa…

Saralyn turned to see David walking toward her. He wore rumpled white linen pants and an unbuttoned white shirt that revealed his chest hair. In one hand, he held a wine bottle, and in the other, he balanced a plate on what looked like a computer tablet…

"Happy birthday!" He sat beside her. "Did you think I would forget?"

She had. A twinge teased at her eyes, threatening a tear, but she shook her head.

"I'm sorry about earlier," he said. "I shouldn't have yelled at you. Especially on your birthday."

"You didn't yell at me. And I feel sure you were panicked and not in the right place for the casual swim I'd suggested. You thought I had drowned. I didn't mean to give you such a shock."

He tilted his head against hers. "I'll explain. But not tonight. Now is for the birthday girl. That dress is…wow."

His inability to describe how he felt hit her just right. She'd dumbstruck the hero? Go, Birthday Girl!

He set down the bottle and tablet and then displayed the plate, which held a small, elaborately decorated cake. White fondant embellished with lacy pink curls and coils blossomed into red and violet flowers. It looked like the island's tropical blooms had landed on the cake. And it sparkled!

"That's amazing. How did you…?"

"You did request a cake. And I do have connections."

"Marcel?"

"He was thrilled to go wild with the flavors, which he said would be a surprise. But I forgot candles."

"That's probably best. We don't want an inferno spoiling the goods."

He handed her the plate, which she lifted to her nose to smell. Sugar city!

"Don't dig in yet." He picked up the tablet. "Tonight, the Galaxy Lounge is featuring the former synth player from The Wretched Things." He tapped the tablet screen and musical notes sounded.

"Oh, this is going to be good!"

"Happy birthday…" he sang. Another run of musical

notes emulated a synthesizer. *"Happy birthday to you."* He performed a head-banging move and then flipped back his bangs to smile at her. *"I don't know the words, so I'll just end with the grand finale..."*

An exaggerated performance filled the air with an array of notes that sounded like "Happy Birthday" with an emo metal edge to it. And then with the last note, which he held down to extend the tone, he announced, "Thank you, everyone! We're here all week. Be sure to give the birthday girl a big round of applause!"

Lifting his fingers from the keyboard, he clapped, cheered and even tossed in a wolf whistle before bowing his forehead to hers and kissing her on the nose. "Happy birthday, Saralyn." He tugged a fork from a pocket in his shirt. "Dig in."

She took the fork and paused to absorb what had happened. The man had serenaded her, and he'd exposed a part of himself that he'd tucked away hoping to never experience again. She could fall in love with David Crown.

What was stopping her?

"You going to eat that or count the calories?" he asked with a nudge to her arm.

"Calories don't count on one's birthday." She stabbed the center of a bright violet flower and claimed a piece. It was indelicately large, but she shoved it in her mouth and closed her eyes. Oh, mercy. Not too sweet, and deliciously creamy frosting. Tangy fruity flavors burst on her tongue. Perhaps yuzu or some tart/sweet citrus. Heavenly. Rich.

Saralyn moaned. Now *this* was real love.

"That good?"

"Hold that plate still." She stabbed for another bite. "I haven't had cake this delicious maybe ever. Did you grow up being served cake like this? My goodness, it's so gooey yet dense. I... Turn the plate. I want to taste that red flower."

While he held the plate, she forked in a few more bites. Then she had the consideration to offer him a taste.

"About time." He opened his mouth and she fed him. "Yep, that's Marcel's four-star work, for sure. Another."

With a bite of cake in his mouth, he leaned in to kiss her. Sharing the mushy, cake-y kiss made her giggle. When he dashed out his tongue to lick her upper lip she returned with a nip to the corner of his mouth. They made a mess of one another, but it was the best birthday cake she'd had in fifty years.

"How does it feel to be fifty?" Swiping his mouth clean with the side of his hand, David reached for the wine bottle and took a swig.

"No different. And...very different, actually. I feel lighter, if that's possible. Like I'm still floating. But also a little sad for the years behind me."

"Why is that?"

"I've been asking myself, were my married years a waste?"

"No time is ever wasted if you can rescue the good memories and learn from the bad."

"So philosophical."

"Eh. I think I read it on one of those inspirational wall posters in an office once."

Saralyn laughed and swiped a finger across a smear of frosting on the plate, which sat on her lap. "I don't feel old."

"You're not old."

"I honestly believe, in your eyes, I'm not."

"Old is a state of mind. But. Probably around eighty, a person can claim oldness. I mean, eight decades should constitute wisdom and knowledge and having the right to tell others what to do."

He handed her the wine bottle. Before sipping, she said, "I want to do this with you when we leave the island."

She heard his inhale through his nose, but he didn't reply.

So he didn't feel the same? Shoot, she'd guessed wrong about him. This was just a fling for him. "Or not. I mean, this is just a fling for you, so—"

The kiss wasn't meant to silence her but rather silently ask for time, or so she suspected. And hoped. He wasn't yet ready to go there.

"I want you to have everything you desire," David said. "You're beautiful in the moonlight. I want to make love to you."

He'd cleverly avoided answering her inquiry about this being a fling. But as he leaned over her, his eyes delving into her soul and his body reading hers without even asking, she surrendered to his atomic pull on her stardust. They made love on the rock under the waning moon. With the occasional bite of cake to fortify and fuel them with more energy.

CHAPTER FOURTEEN

THE DAY FOLLOWING her fiftieth birthday felt like just another day. No cosmic awakening. No stunning transformation in her body. Not even minions bowing and asking to fulfill her every desire.

Really. Was it too much to ask for one tiny minion?

Waking this morning with inspiration gnawing at her brain, Saralyn had foregone the swim that David suggested. His non-response to her asking about this being a fling still cautioned her. Placed a narrow crevice between them that he seemed not to notice. Sending him off with a kiss, she showered and wrapped a robe about her body. Maybe she was overthinking things. Had to be.

Most certainly she was.

With a glass of fresh-squeezed guava juice and a plate of eggs beside her, she typed away on her laptop. Yes, she'd dug the laptop out from the Faraday box. The characters she'd created for her historical heist insisted she pay attention to their troubles instead of her own. And that was as good excuse as any to avoid the tough emotional questions. Right now the youngest thief was questioning her ability to pull off the heist of the century—stealing the famous Marie Antoinette necklace—while the other thief just wanted to get back home. To her own time.

How Saralyn did love a twist!

Fingers flying and her muse slinging words top speed, she glanced to her now-cold eggs and then looked back to the screen. The *shush* of waves not seventy feet from where she sat on the veranda couldn't entice her away from the story. Nor did the bird chatter fluttering overhead. Sunshine warmed her bare legs—writing in a bathrobe was decidedly freeing—and even the throat-clearing sound of the world's sexiest island hero couldn't compel her fingers to halt.

"Writing?" David asked the obvious that tended to make all writers roll their eyes.

Saralyn didn't bother with the roll. "Yep."

"Got it. Had my swim. Thinking about spearing some fish. I'll check in with you later."

"Yep."

"But I'm taking these." The plate beside her disappeared. "Cold. But not terrible."

She allowed herself a moment to pause and follow his retreat off the veranda and across the beach. His swim trunks couldn't hide that nice tight—

"No sex scenes in this story," she said, remembering, and placed her fingers back on the keyboard. "Only in real life."

With a burst of a smile, she resumed her work.

David had no desire to disturb Saralyn when her concentration looked absolutely riveted. He knew that feeling of chasing an idea or a muse. Some of his best days were spent alone in the lab deeply immersed in creation. Those were the days he only surfaced after dark with a smile and a bounce to his stride. Good times.

As he wandered the beach, eating the cold eggs with a fork, he marveled over how writers could create entire novels, conjuring complete worlds from their imagination. It seemed an impossible task. He did love a good mystery or thriller. But to possess such skill as to put it all together?

Incredible. Of course, what he did was similar. He took an idea and brought it to fruition. Like his current project. The Body Tuner—based on the Solfeggio frequency to naturally heal—was a result of years of mental creation, followed by months of technical research and bringing it to reality. Every moment fueled by imagination and creativity.

Realizing he felt some sort of domestic peace at having seen Saralyn work, casually stealing her breakfast and then wandering off, his steps lightened. The woman captivated him. Everything about her interested him. From her shy smiles that quickly switched to a self-assured lift of her chin. To the quiet moments when her brain went on an inner trip to another world, despite her standing firmly in reality.

What a fool her husband was to have looked to other women to satisfy himself. Saralyn was exquisite. David would never dream of looking at another woman if she were his...

He paused and turned to look back at the villa. The plate was empty. His heart was full. He was aware he'd avoided her question last night. It had come as a surprise. And he wasn't good with surprises.

Could they do the dating thing? Having considered it in the quiet dark hours after they'd made love last night, he concluded that he'd like that very much. But how to do that when she lived in California and he in New York? He could fly to see her every weekend. The expense was nothing. But she did have plans to move. Could he entice her to settle in New York City? He'd gotten the impression that she preferred a smaller town, someplace cozy and far from the flash of paparazzi.

His life was generally paparazzi-free. Generally. The trial had shuffled the media out from their caves. There wasn't a day he could walk from his Manhattan penthouse to the coffee shop down the street without encountering one or half a dozen with microphones and recording devices in hand. He'd accepted that his being a billionaire and the owner of Crown Corp attracted media interest. He had no problem with their interest, because he could compartmentalize and set that aside as a work issue. But when they invaded his private life, it made dealing more difficult.

He wanted to return home and have life reset to before the trial. Everything fine. Crown Corp kept producing blankets and his new projects would be on track to begin production. But unless he stepped up and made a decision one way or another on the blanket, it might forever be polluted with the media's opinion and the intense inner turmoil that had settled into his very soul.

That poor child.

Gripping the plate and staring down at it, he shook his head. He'd come here to make a decision. Saralyn was busy working. Now he must focus on how to move forward.

Returning to the chef's cottage, he washed the plate and then grabbed his walking kit—a rucksack fitted with binoculars for bird-watching, scuba mask for diving, and a machete for interesting finds—and set out to the far side of the island opposite from the villa.

Writing through lunch and only coming up for air midafternoon was a writer's dream. Yet Saralyn could no longer ignore her rumbling stomach, so she heated up a delicious shakshuka and devoured it.

Wondering where David had gone, she figured he must be doing work stuff. The CEO of Crown Corp could hardly tuck his phone in a Faraday box. That he'd left her to write had been beyond thoughtful. She hadn't even had to roll her eyes at him!

It was rare that nonwriters understood the writing process. That when the muse struck, she must be followed, entertained, preened over, which meant sitting before the keyboard until your fingers bled. Not literally but metaphorically. Spill it all onto the page. Also, an author could be writing when simply sitting on the sofa, eyelids half-closed. How Saralyn's imagination wandered. And she'd been following it since she was a kid. That she could make a living using her imagination was a blessing.

But writing autobiographies for celebrities did not require imagination. And while the fiction she ghostwrote did require a cooperative muse, it still felt distant from her heart. This historical project flamed in her chest and wanted her attention. The characters were so interesting! It was such an incredible feeling.

Her phone pinged. She'd forgotten to tuck it away in the Faraday box after checking her emails. Her mom had sent birthday wishes and a gift card for Saralyn's favorite cookie shop. Always appreciated, even if one monstrous cookie tended to tip the scales at eight hundred calories.

She glanced to the phone and just caught the notification with her agent's name across the top of the screen. She knew what Leslie was calling for. And while she should ignore it, it was time to face the life-changing decision she'd come here to make. One she had moved toward since arriving.

Pressing the answer button and putting it on speaker, she said "Hi" to Leslie, who immediately sighed and began her spiel about how Saralyn was taking an inordinate amount of time deciding. What was wrong? Was it the divorce? When would she get over that? It was time to move on. She needed this money!

Actually, she had moved on. And she had *gotten over it*. And she didn't need the money as much as her reactionary gut wanted her to believe she did. She had the settlement, which would allow her some financial cushion as she explored her writing options.

It was time to stand on her own two feet and use her own name. To be herself.

"I'm going to pass on this contract." Saralyn felt her confidence rise, yet still her spine tingled with nerves. "It feels right. I've been working on the historical project I mentioned to you last time we talked."

"Saralyn, you can't sell under your own name."

"Why not? New authors sell every day."

She was aware she was contractually bound not to reveal who she wrote for to any publishers. When submitting under a different name, she could only say that she was a ghostwriter. So, yes, this would be like starting over as a new author.

"And I've realized a lot of my fear over trying to make a go under my own name is because Brock kept me in a position of feeling lesser, like I needed him to support me. I've thought about it," she said to Leslie. "I have to do this."

Another heavy sigh. "Well, then, I hate to do this but I believe we have to break ties. I've held up the other author's agent long enough on this. Had her convinced you would take the project. Saralyn, this is easy money. And you know the writer's style and voice so well. Is it the movie potential? I can see if I can get you a piece of the residuals."

That would be a nice bonus, but it wouldn't go anywhere near giving her the recognition or creative freedom she desired. It was too little, with no regard for her work.

"It's not that. I'm ready for a change. I want to write under my own name."

"Martin isn't even your name."

Writing under her maiden name as Saralyn Hayes suited her. It was just another change that felt right.

"I'm decided, Leslie. And if you feel you can no longer represent me…" She would never get Leslie's full support in representing the new work. The woman had once been a shark in the publishing world; now it seemed she'd slipped into the easy sales with established clients and editors who knew her. "I can accept that. I'm sorry. You've done so much for me over the years." Except the parts about wheedling her into ghostwriting forever and taking the sure jobs. And discouraging her from writing under her own name. "Thank you for everything."

"Saralyn, I can't believe you can walk away from this offer so easily."

"It's not easy. Life hasn't been easy these past few years. But it's turning around." She glanced out at the azure sky, tufted along the edges with emerald palm trees and frosted with white foam wavering back and forth on the pale sands. "I am happy with my decision. Please send me whatever paperwork needs to be done to finalize our working together. Is there anything else?"

A scoff suited Leslie; the woman was abrupt and to the point, sometimes painfully so. She'd get over it. She boasted a client list of many famous names. "You'll never sell," she finally said. "I'll forward the dissolution forms to you."

The phone clicked off. Not even a goodbye.

Saralyn set down the phone and realized her fingers were shaking. She'd done it. She'd taken the step that she hoped would be the right one.

But was it?

Self-doubt crashed against her newly gained courage and she heaved up a stuttering breath that blossomed to tears.

"What have I done?"

CHAPTER FIFTEEN

LAST NIGHT DAVID had returned to the villa to find Saralyn in a quiet mood. She'd said she didn't want to talk, only to make love. So they had, as the sun set and the noises of tropical birds and insects settled for the night. But this morning, David had snuck out of bed and wandered the beach, phone in hand. It was becoming almost impossible to ignore the demands of real life.

Crown Corp needed him. Ryan Wexley, the company's COO called. The press wanted a statement from David. If they didn't get one they planned to go ahead with the "cleared of wrongdoing in trial but still hiding secrets. Do you trust your safety to this man's blanket?" headline. It was a cruel way to get him to talk. The media had access to the trial transcripts. But David could no longer avoid his responsibilities to the company. A statement was necessary. And not one sent via Zoom or video. It had to be in person. David had to connect with the public through a press conference, Ryan had said.

Ryan transferred David to his secretary. She would book a flight from the mainland to New York and let him know when the boat would arrive to ferry him. Tomorrow, though. He needed one last day with Saralyn.

They'd begun something amazing that he didn't want to walk away from. And she had indicated she'd felt the same. But how to make it work?

He didn't want to throw money at her or put her up in an apartment. That wasn't his style or hers. But was he prepared for what he suspected was her style? A real relationship where the couple lived together, in a real home, with real lives and respect and trust in one another. It sounded like a dream his younger self had chased for so long. He'd finally skidded to the side of the track and sat down, gasping, knowing he'd never reach such an untouchable goal.

The only way he could move forward with Saralyn was to open up completely to her. And he didn't know how to do that.

It was Saralyn who suggested they go sailing. David took her out on the streamlined, small dinghy and when the wind caught the sails, they glided over the turquoise waters. Laughter bubbled up and, in the moment, she didn't think to take notes for her writing. Though now as they floated, the sail barely billowing, and she lying on the bow deck with her chin on her fist, she did make some mental notes on the adventure.

"Writing?" David asked as he joined her and sat near the mast, hand securely on the rope that controlled the wheel.

"I'm not always writing when I'm quiet," she protested.

"Liar."

"Fine. You win. I can't *not* make notes about new experiences. And this one was exhilarating. But the wind has died down. How will we get back to shore?"

They were about a quarter mile from the beach and the wind had disappeared.

"It'll pick up. And if not, we've got paddles stashed right there." He kicked the side of the boat. "In fact, we're going the paddle route to get back. More research for you, eh? That'll build your swimming muscles."

"I'm up for it." She turned to her side and flipped a hank

of hair over her shoulder. "I got a call from my agent yesterday. It's…well, it's why I didn't want to talk much last night."

"I understand. Sometimes sex is better than words."

"I completely agree. But now I need to talk about it. My
agent was not happy. Make that my former agent."

"What went down?"

"I told her I wasn't going to write the next ghost book. I
want to focus on my own stuff now."

"I'm proud of you."

"Yes. Well." She rolled to her back and spread out her
arms across the fiberglass deck. The sun warmed her skin
like a lover's caress. "Did I do the right thing? I'm having
second thoughts, David. What have I done?"

"Sounds like you've become Saralyn Hayes."

Closing her eyes, she smiled at that statement. He got her.
What a thrill to be involved with a man who could see into
her, interpret her and get it right. It was almost as thrilling
as making love with him. And yet that ingrained part of her
that sought safety and security niggled.

"I could have taken one last job. Used that money to live
on while I search for a place to put down some roots."

"You don't have any savings?"

"The divorce settlement gave me enough that I don't need
an immediate income, but… It's my survivor mentality. Hard
to shake."

He leaned over her and kissed her. Long, slow, delicious.
Rocking on some sudden waves, their bodies brushed, caressed, and glided sensually. "You did the right thing, Saralyn. Don't question it. You followed your heart. Now all you
have to do is keep following it."

"You make me believe I can do anything."

"Why can't you?"

"Selling under a new name will be the challenge."

"If the writing you've done for another author ended up

on the silver screen I'm going to guess you're a damned excellent writer. You'll find your groove."

She stroked her fingers alongside his face. "I have found it. Now I need to groove on into a nice little place to write while I'm moving. My mom offered to let me stay with her, but that's a big no."

"You and your mom don't get along?"

"I adore my mother. She's a hippie who never grew out of her macramé sweater and hip-hugging jeans. She's an entrepreneur. She sells essential oils, yoga stuff and little witchy spells online. Makes some good money doing it."

"She sounds interesting."

"And…she's got a boyfriend who adores her. At seventy-five years old, my mother is getting it more than I am."

"Wait a minute—"

"My mom *was* getting it more than me," she quickly corrected.

"I wouldn't want you to feel inferior to your mother. Now, are you ready to paddle?"

She slid her hand down his chest and to his swim trunks. "First…"

He waggled a brow at her. "Out here?"

"Not up for it, lover?"

"I am up for anything and everything as long as it's with you."

CHAPTER SIXTEEN

AFTER A LIFE-CHANGING filet mignon that had melted on her tongue, Saralyn had taken charge of the dishes. David had gotten yet another phone call and wandered out to the beach while talking. Setting the last dried dish in the cupboard, she wrapped the gauzy floral scarf about her hips and wandered outside.

She spied David sitting on one of the swings amid the turquoise water. Evening sun glimmered in silver slashes on the surface. He wasn't swinging. Just sitting there. First glance, she sensed he was thinking and decided to give him his space.

Yet her heart wouldn't allow her to walk by him. Once again, she had to remind herself that it wasn't all about her. This island was a refuge for tattered souls. And as far as she knew, David's soul was still torn around the edges. Had he solved the dilemma he'd come here to work on? The man was hurting, and she couldn't dismiss that. She cared about him. And he needed to know that. Because it seemed all his life he'd wondered if anyone did care about him. That his parents had been so distant crushed her. Thanks to a thoughtful chef employed in his childhood home he'd grown into a kind man who did so much for so many, but she knew deep inside he craved the attention he'd never been given.

"Just like me," she realized with new wonder.

They were two alike. Yet, the more she grew to know David, the less and less she desired attention. Fame. *Being noticed.* Yes, she wanted to write under her own name. But she didn't really want the spotlight or adulation. That felt like ego and so surface. Something was altering in her. Scales were tilting and finding a new balance. He had done that for her.

Wading into the water, she sloshed a little to alert him that she approached. "Okay if I join you?"

He nodded and tucked the wallet he'd been holding into his shirt pocket. Then he tilted his head against one of the swing ropes that suspended it from the framework.

Still he didn't face her. And he didn't say much more.

Saralyn slid onto the swing and tickled her toes across the water's surface. The man owned this island. He was a billionaire. He had everything he could ever desire. Save for an ineffable something she suspected could only come from within.

"Want to talk about it?" she tried. "Or is this one of those let's-be-quiet moments?"

He smirked. "I've been sitting here awhile so I've reached maximum quiet mode. I don't mind talking, especially to you. I need to talk. But it's heavy."

"Is it about the reason you fled here? Getting away from media and the lawsuit?"

"You really don't know about the lawsuit?"

More than ever, she wished she'd remembered to research him online so she could relate to what he was going through and perhaps make it easier for him so he wouldn't have to explain, but... "Sorry, but I don't. I only check in with the news about once a month."

"You are an anomaly. I can't believe you were married to an actor for so long and yet managed to avoid the press and news."

"It's a habit I developed over the years. After the divorce, I grew vigilant about it. Not being on social media helps a lot. And as a ghostwriter, I don't have to worry about putting on a public face and talking to fans online."

She reached out and slid her fingertips along his thigh, but he didn't make a move to hold her hand.

"Before I get into what's bugging me, I want to ask you something." He absently patted his shirt pocket. "Do you have children?"

"No."

"Do you want to have children?"

She chuckled softly. "Honestly? Yes, I did once. I had dreams of domesticity. But Brock didn't. So my dreams changed. Over the years, I realized I enjoy children, but I much prefer not having to care for them. As for having them now? Remember—" she splayed out her arms in dramatic declaration "—*menopause*! So even if I did feel the tug to procreate I'd be tough out of luck."

"Oh. Sure. Sorry, I didn't mean to intrude into your personal stuff."

"I think we've moved beyond the personal intrusion stage. Menopause isn't the big scary. The hot flashes are rare. I put on an extra ten pounds. I'm dealing. And I can have sex without contraception. That's a bonus, especially when my sexy younger lover is so demanding."

His smile was soft but genuine.

"But honestly, having a child. In my house. Twenty-four/seven. Having to mold them, teach them, protect them?" She sighed. "It's a huge job. I can barely take care of myself some days. What about you?"

"Me? Having kids?"

She nodded.

"I'm on the same page as you are. I love children but I wouldn't know how to take care of them. My parents didn't offer exemplary role models to learn from. I'd never want to raise a child in such an awkward distant relationship such as I experienced." He sighed heavily and took the wallet out from his pocket. He didn't open it. Just tapped it against his thigh. "I can't stop thinking about how children have no power or control over what the adults in their lives do with them. It's very sad. Because of that… I've decided to stop production on the blanket."

So that was what he'd come here to make a decision about? But he was stopping production on the blanket because…of his childhood? "Oh, David, that's…a huge decision."

"It is. The lawsuit was brought against Crown Corp," he said. "It was a wrongful-death suit."

She hadn't expected— Well, she hadn't conjured any expectation. "Oh."

He opened the wallet, pulled out a photograph and handed it to her without saying anything. It was a boy, perhaps five or six, smiling brightly to reveal a missing front tooth. His blond hair was tousled. His cheeks freckled. A relative? Someone he knew?

"This is what happened." David shifted on the swing but didn't turn to face her. "Crown Corp was charged in the death of that six-year-old boy you are looking at right now. Which comes down to me, personally. The plaintiffs stated the blanket had literally squeezed their child to death." He did turn his head to catch her open-mouthed and truly aghast. "That's impossible. We've had the blankets tested, certified. There's no possibility it could ever exert more than .010 of pressure. Like touching a baby's skin with a gentle nudge. I never would have put the blanket into production if there had been an inkling of a chance it could cause harm."

Saralyn held the photo carefully. The boy's smile hit her differently now. Right in the gut. "Then, how did it happen?"

David scrubbed his fingers back through his hair. Bit his

lip. His knee bounced lightly, creating waves in the water around his calves.

"I attended the trial every day. It went on for weeks. The plaintiff's lawyers were tough. Really knew how to tell a story. Appeal to the jury. I almost began to believe I *did* have a hand in the boy's death. But the coroner's reports told a very clear story. The child had fallen down a full run of metal-edged stairs. The impact killed him instantly. He'd landed on the blanket. The parents were...outside at the time. They didn't even hear him scream.

"An expert coroner confirmed a contusion to the head was the killing blow. The parents had genuinely believed he'd been wrapped in the blanket and it had caused the death, but as the coroner's details were revealed, they accepted the truth."

Saralyn's entire body had tightened to a tense knot. How awful!

"The jury found Crown Corp not guilty of any involvement in the boy's death. And blessedly, the judge dismissed a negligence charge against the parents."

The heavy breath that exited David filled the air with a sadness Saralyn could feel. He held out his hand and she placed the photo on it.

"His name was Charlie," he said. "I will never forget him. Ever."

Tucking the photo away, he lifted his shoulders. And when he gasped a shuddering breath and then sniffed, Saralyn couldn't bear it. She stepped off the swing and walked around in front of him. He looked up to her, tears in his eyes. Just before she said, "it's not the blanket's fault, you were cleared" she stopped herself. No words could erase the ugly pain that had been inflicted on that child, the family and, inadvertently, David.

"I can't imagine how terrible you must feel for that family," she said. "For that child. Keeping his picture with you is a lovely way to honor him."

Shaking his head and bowing it, his shoulders dropped. A deep emotion pushed up from his depths. The air between them grew heavy and it tugged at her heart. Her soul leaned forward, seeking his. Her body followed. She touched his arm and, with her other hand, caressed his jaw.

"I will always feel responsible," he managed.

"No, you mustn't. Oh, David."

"Logically, I know it wasn't the blanket," he said. "It was actually there to…cushion his landing. Not enough, though." He inhaled heavily. "Crown Corp was cleared of any wrongdoing. But I'm haunted by the trial. I was meant to be there. To stand as a witness for that child's unfortunate death. Saralyn, I have to pull the plug on the blanket. I can't put it out in public anymore. It's…tainted. Wrong."

While she knew the blanket was not at all tainted, she could have no idea what the media and consumers thought of it. Truly, she hadn't seen anything on the little news she'd watched. But there must have been a media sensation in New York City. Certainly, initially, David and his company may have been accused. Emotionally, he must have been a wreck.

"It feels like the right thing to do." His body shuddered minutely. "And yet, is it? I don't know. I thought I'd come here to find the answer. I've been so busy with…"

With her? Oh. That hurt her heart. And yet, if she had distracted him from those wretched feelings for a little while, she wanted to claim that as a victory. But that triumph felt selfish. This was about him. And while she didn't know how to help him with this pain, she could be there for him.

Saralyn wrapped her arms over his shoulders and bowed her head to the side of his. "I can't tell you what to do in this situation. But I can be here for you." She hugged against him, standing between his legs and fitting her body into an embrace that she sensed would make him skittish. No way not to do it, though. The compulsion felt right. "You can tell me anything, anytime," she added. "And you can let it out. I've got you."

And in that moment, his body melded against hers and his arms wrapped across her back. He pulled her in tightly, burying his face against her shoulder and hair. And he sobbed quietly.

The man had been witness to something terrible, but as he'd said, perhaps he'd been meant to be at that trial, to bear witness in the child's name. And as she pulled him in closer, so deeply she wanted to crush his soul against hers, tears fell down Saralyn's cheeks. David was that boy. Not given physical affection as a child and fighting his own way through the world, navigating it well, but ultimately, ever seeking.

When he pulled back and gave one of those self-conscious laughs people do when they've just exposed a private part of themselves, Saralyn brushed the hair from his cheek and kissed his forehead. "I care about you, David. Thank you for telling me that. I know it was difficult."

"I trust you. I feel safe in your arms. I… I just let you hug me," he said in a wondrous tone.

She nodded. "You did. And you can have another whenever you desire."

"Like…" He studied their loose embrace, marveling over the surprise of it. A smile overtook his sadness. "Right now…?"

"Most definitely."

Their embrace resumed. He held her close, easily yet firmly. If he never let her go, she would live with that. He could take whatever he needed from her. It was easy to give what she could to one she cared for so deeply.

"So this is a hug," he whispered, and gave her a quick,

tight squeeze before loosening to hold her gently. "It wasn't so difficult as I imagined."

"I think because it came to you at the moment you needed it most." She kissed his forehead and pushed away the hair from his eye. Her lovely man. Her precious hero who sought only to protect the innocent. "I know I just said I couldn't tell you what to do, but I do need to state what I believe. That blanket has helped so many people, David. It would be a shame if you were to cease its production. Maybe you should let the public decide if it's something they want?"

"I don't understand?"

"I've seen big corporations apologize to the public and then they allow consumers to either continue to purchase the product or not. If it fails, that's your answer. If it continues to sell, that means people still need it."

"A public apology. Yes, I need to do that. My lawyers said I shouldn't. That I should just ignore it and it would go away."

"That's lawyers for you. But I know you. And this pain eating away at you won't truly go away until you release it."

"My COO called again this morning. The press is chomping at the bit for a statement from me, and they've threatened to go with some damning headlines if I don't speak to them. In person."

"Maybe an apology might be the thing that helps you?"

He kissed her hand and pressed his cheek against her chest, holding her firmly. "You're very smart, Saralyn. Thank you."

She bowed her head to his and caressed his body against hers. It felt right to give him what he needed and she prayed that he could rise above the torment that haunted his soul. Strong, smart and empathetic, he most surely would.

CHAPTER SEVENTEEN

A WARM QUICHE sat on the table, along with a pitcher of sangria and a tropical flower stuck in a tiny vase near the single plate.

Saralyn frowned. She'd been in the shower, luxuriating under the hot stream for longer than usual. And in that time, David had made breakfast and then…disappeared. She scanned through all the windows and open doorways and didn't see him on the veranda. After they'd made love last night, he'd reminded her he needed to return to New York to make a statement. Surely, he wouldn't leave without saying goodbye to her—

Oh! Whew! There he was, walking on the beach. Talking to someone on the phone.

She sat and dished up a serving of quiche and sipped the sangria. "Wherever I land when I go back to the States I most definitely will always have sangria in my home."

It would remind her of this dreamy vacation, the warm tropical breezes and bright turquoise waters. And that a man she cared deeply for had been so kind to think of her before he returned to business duties.

It was more than that. Saralyn put down her fork and caught her chin in hand as she watched David pace in the distance, his arm gesturing as he spoke words she couldn't hear. Swim trunks again this morning, and nothing else.

He was an island man and could exist in trunks and bare feet if he had no pressing concerns or work to tend. He was so rich he could do just that. But his inventive nature and caring heart wouldn't allow him to sit back and get fat off his riches. She loved that about him. He cared so much the death of a child had cracked his heart and now made him question everything.

Perhaps he cared too much.

She didn't want him to stop producing the blanket. It helped so many and could continue to do so. But he had to come to terms with the whole lawsuit and the boy's horrendous death before he could move forward.

"I wish I could hold your hand and walk you through it," she said. "I love you."

Saralyn sat straight. The words had come out of her mouth. She hadn't thought about them; it had been a true and honest statement.

"I really do love him." Her heart had taken a wild ride these past days.

Could they do the couple thing?

"He's not *that* young," she reasoned now as she finished the quiche. "He's smart and responsible."

And it wasn't as though she were dating a man in his twenties. A youngster barely out of college and just finding his way in the world of business, career and family. A man who may be uncertain about his future and may look to an older woman for guidance. David Crown was her equal in most every way. Her charming hero and daring rescuer. Her quiet conversationalist. Her lover. Her confidante. Her backup musician in the Galaxy Lounge.

He made her feel like Miss Stardust, standing before an audience, milking the attention and thriving in it. And if she never sold another book, never made a name for herself and readers began to know her by her real name, she could care little. Because in David's eyes, she was a star.

He'd told her to remember how exquisite she was.

Yes, she was.

Dare she tell him she loved him?

"Why not?" she whispered. "This is my new chapter. It's time to live it. Take a chance, Miss Stardust. The worst he can do is reject you."

She'd hate that. But it would be another lesson learned.

She shook her head. No, rejection would gut her. She couldn't endure another man shoving her aside as if she had limited use.

"I can't risk it." Maybe?

Downing the sangria in one long swallow, she set down the glass. It wasn't the heavy alcohol content of the drink that made her nod her head. It was the new and improved Saralyn Hayes who bravely stood and decided to take what she wanted.

The moment her feet hit the veranda, David turned and jogged toward her.

"Now or never," she whispered. She had to tell him she loved him. From there, they'd figure things out.

"Just got a call from the office." He stepped onto the veranda and shook the sand from his bare feet. "The boat will be here in an hour to pick me up. PR is working on a speech they want me to give to the press this afternoon."

"A speech?" This afternoon was…but hours away.

He wandered over and kissed her. "Mmm, sangria." With a brush of his hands through her hair, he slid them down to her shoulders and eyed her carefully. "I told you last night I had to leave."

"Right."

Had she been ready to tell him something? It didn't matter now. The man was leaving. He had important business

to tend. And what did it matter if a silly writer had fallen
in love with him and wanted to spend the rest of her days
with him?

"You need to go. But David." She clasped his hand and
squeezed. "You're not seriously going to stop production of
the blanket, are you?"

He sighed heavily. "I honestly can't say. It's going to be
foremost in my thoughts the entire flight home." He kissed
her quickly on the forehead. "I have to gather my things.
I'll be back so we can say goodbye!" He took off across the
beach for the chef's cottage, waving as he did.

Saralyn's wave wilted faster than did her heart. Because
her heart was doing a slow melt and sat jiggling in her rib-
cage.

So this was how it would end?

A tear slipped down her cheek.

David gathered the few items of clothing he'd brought to
the island and shoved them in a duffel bag. No shoes. Those
would be waiting for him on the pickup boat. A few toilet-
ries. His laptop and phone. He wandered through the cottage,
closing windows and turning off any electrical devices. A
cleanup crew would arrive after Saralyn left the island, but
he could never leave the place a mess.

He grabbed his duffel and stepped outside, pulling the
door shut behind him. He'd donned a shirt but still wore
his swim trunks. He'd change on the jet. When he arrived
at JFK airport he'd head immediately to work. They were
waiting for him to go over the speech. Media outlets had
been invited to the press briefing.

This was all happening quickly. And while he was a master at shifting modes and tasks this was *the big one*. The one
where he must put his heart out there for all to see. It was

not going to be easy. He'd only just summoned the courage to reveal that part of his heart to one woman. And now to do it before the world?

He wished Saralyn could be there to hold his hand. Give him the hug he'd learned how to accept from her kind and comforting embrace.

"Saralyn," he muttered.

Was he to dash off and leave her behind? What kind of idiot was he? No fool would leave such a woman behind. Especially since she'd recently taken ownership of his heart. Shaun had called it. Love had snuck up on him.

Did he have time to fall to his knees and profess his undying love to Saralyn? It would feel rushed, disingenuous. And he knew if he attempted such a ruse she would feel that forced emotion. But there were no dragons to be slain in the half hour before his ride arrived. No way to win the heroine's heart.

How to do this and not lose the girl?

He didn't know how to tell a woman he loved her. He'd never done it before. Could he tap into that emotion while also focusing on the afternoon's important press conference? He was feeling everything right now. It was starting to blur and make him feel unsure.

No. He thrived on the challenge of juggling multiple tasks at work. Adding in a personal life task?

He picked up the duffle and started to walk. "You've got this, Crown. Go win the girl."

Never in his life had he felt more purposeful or determined. Not even the initial release of the hug blanket had set such a fire beneath his feet. He was going to win the girl!

Taking the walk to the villa swiftly, sand flew in his wake and the birds cawed as if cheering him on. He turned around the last palm tree before the beach and almost crashed right into Saralyn.

She stepped back with a big smile on her face and announced, "David!"

"Saralyn?" He eyed the suitcase at her side. "I was just…"

"I'm coming with you," she stated. "I know I have a few days left on my stay, but I won't take no for an answer. I want to be there for you when you tell the world how you stand behind your product. And when you step back from the podium and turn around, I'll give you the biggest and best hug ever. Because… David, I love you."

Mouth open in shock, David nodded. And then his smile burst and he pulled her into an embrace and spun her. Their laughter echoed. And their embrace turned into a long and soul-touching hug.

"I love you," he said to her. "So you'll come to New York with me? I…can't believe this is happening. I didn't even have to slay any dragons."

She quirked a brow.

"I was headed here to win you over. To slay the dragon and take you home with me."

"You did help me slay a dragon or two. I would never have had the confidence to invite myself into your life if it hadn't been for the love, kindness and respect you've shown me since I set foot on this island. Can we make this work?"

"It's already working." He kissed her. "You're my girl, Saralyn."

"And you are my knight in a soft blanket cape."

He made a superhero pose, arms stretched out as if flying, then snapped his arms to a muscle-pumping pose.

Saralyn's laugh filled the air. "My hero!"

He picked up her suitcase. Across the beach the pickup boat slowly glided up to dock. "Let's do this."

"Right behind you, lover."

He stopped and shook his head. "I don't want you behind me. I want you beside me, Saralyn."

A tear spilled down her cheek and slipped into her smile. "David Crown, I love you."

EPILOGUE

DAVID'S SPEECH TO the press went well. He spoke from the heart, explaining the details from the trial that were not too exploitative to put out to the public. And while he knew the blanket had not caused the death, he felt the immense responsibility for the safety of children. Crown Corp would continue to produce the blanket—all proceeds would go to Charlie's Care, a charity he would create to foot hospital bills for uninsured children.

When he'd stepped away from the press stand, he turned and walked right into Saralyn's arms. Their hug drowned out the cacophony of the camera flashes and shouting journalists. Saralyn could only feel David's heartbeat against hers.

And when finally David turned to answer the one question repeated most: "Who is she?" he'd answered with a smiling, "She's my girlfriend, Saralyn Hayes, a writer you'll want to read, and we're in love."

Days later, after a tour of Crown Corp, a few nights treated to the rich and luxurious five-star restaurants in New York City, and a leisurely afternoon spent strolling through Central Park, Saralyn sat on the floor of David's thirty-second floor penthouse that overlooked the massive city park. The two corner walls of the living room were floor-to-ceiling windows, and the city lights dazzled while they snuggled with a blanket and listened to Frank Sinatra crooning over the speakers.

The wine was chilled, the recently delivered Midnight Munchies cookies had been eaten, and they'd made love for the second time that day. Naked and giggling as they arranged themselves beneath the giant hug blanket, Saralyn sighed as the blanket embraced them gently.

"This is so amazing," she said. "But I like your hugs better."

"I intend to practice the fine art of hugging as much as possible. If that's okay with you?"

"Practice on me all you like. So what's up next for Crown Corp? You mentioned you're announcing a new product soon?"

"Yes, it's the Body Tuner. It's worn across the shoulders and resonates a healing frequency throughout the body. I'm hoping it'll be bigger than the blanket. And maybe it'll help erase some of the sadness I feel whenever I think about that boy."

"You're grieving, David. Don't rush it. Just go with the feelings. And the charity you've created is such a perfect way to honor Charlie. I love that the child has a kind heart to think about him."

"I could never stop thinking about him. Do you think the new product will be a good thing?"

"I know the power of resonate-frequency healing is real. And with you behind it, it'll conquer the world."

"Will you be by my side to watch that conquest?"

"If you'll have me. Though..." She winced and looked aside.

All was well. And yet, now that David had conquered his immediate emotional threats, she still had a few of her own. She intended to contact a Realtor to look for a home, but she still wasn't sure where she wanted to plant roots. David had already asked her to stay in New York with him. It felt...

"Plotting?" he asked.

She turned back and kissed him. "Thinking about where I'm going to land and when I'll find the time to finish the story I've decided to write."

"I kind of thought you'd stay here with me. You can get a lot of writing done while I'm at work."

"I could, and honestly? I don't want to leave you. But. I don't know. And please don't take this the wrong way, but New York doesn't feel quite right. It's big and bustling. Like Los Angeles was."

"I get it."

"You do?"

"I do. And here's how much I get it. While you're figuring out where to land with a forever home, what about packing up your laptop and taking your muse to Greece to write the story?"

Saralyn pressed both her hands to his cheeks to study his gaze. The man was dead serious. And those deep brown eyes never lied to her. "Greece?"

"Yes, it's a country in the Mediterranean."

"I know where Greece is, you teaser. But what do you mean? Another island adventure but this time to write? I'm not sure that's in my budget. I feel like I need to pay Juliane for the trip. It wasn't cheap."

"Your friend's credit charge has been refunded."

"What?"

He shrugged. "I wanted to do that for you. And for a friend who is so good to you that she gave you such a generous trip."

"Oh, David, that's too kind of you." She kissed him. "Thank you. Juliane will be so happy to hear that."

"As for paying for a trip to Greece, I'll let you pick up the airfare, strong independent woman that you are, but the stay is on me. I own a place in Mykonos. It's my winter home. I like to spend time there when I've ideas to brew in my brain.

Prelab ideas that usually barrel out of my gray matter like confetti bursting in a party. Would you accept?"

"A free stay in Greece? To write?"

But it was too generous. And what would he expect in return? Did she want to be beholden to another man?

No, she mustn't view it in such a manner. It was a gift, offered without strings, as only David Crown could do.

"What Mediterranean adventure is taking place inside that beautiful brain of yours right now?"

"The adventure of having all the time in the world to focus on a project that means the world to me. How long could I stay?"

"As long as you desire. And you should invite your mom and her boyfriend for a week or two. Of course, I did say it's my winter home. I may stop in in a few months."

"I'd be disappointed if you did not."

His smile grew. "Does that mean you'll accept?"

She nodded. "I'm no fool. The bustle of Manhattan offers nothing over blue waters and white sands."

"Fair enough. Would it be okay if I flew in to stay with you every weekend?"

"I'd be upset if you did not, lover. My mom will be over the moon for the trip."

"I'd love to meet her. And her boyfriend."

"Will I ever meet your parents?"

"Do you want to?"

"I do. I want us to be…family."

"Yeah? I like the sound of that."

"Really?"

"Really. I know we're taking it slow, but I can't imagine going slow with anyone else. Ever." He kissed her deeply against the backdrop of the brightly lit cityscape and they snuggled into the best and longest hug, which segued into passionate lovemaking.

Saralyn had found her groove. And the courage to start anew. And the common sense to confirm she wanted a man in her life. A companion to adventure with, dance with, kiss and laugh with. Would they marry? At the moment, it wasn't important. Simply being in love was an out-of-this-world experience the twosome would embrace and enjoy.

The Galaxy Lounge was now featuring the indomitable Miss Stardust accompanied by her warmhearted, sexy and huggable synth player.

* * * * *

*If you enjoyed this story,
check out these other great reads
from Michele Renae*

Consequence of Their Parisian Night
Cinderella's Billion-Dollar Invitation
Parisian Escape with the Billionaire
The CEO and the Single Dad

All available now!

COMING SOON!

We really hope you enjoyed reading this book.
If you're looking for more romance
be sure to head to the shops when
new books are available on

Thursday 24th
October

To see which titles are coming soon, please visit
millsandboon.co.uk/nextmonth

MILLS & BOON

MILLS & BOON®

Coming next month

THE BILLIONAIRE'S FESTIVE REUNION
Cara Colter

"FAITH CAMERON?"

It had been so long since anyone had called her that, that Faith felt faintly puzzled. Or maybe it was shock.

Who was she, again?

"Saint-John," she said, correcting her rescuer.

Her voice felt like it was far, far away, detached from her, coming from outside of herself. She was so cold. She had never been this cold in her entire life. She wondered, foggily, if maybe it went deeper than being cold.

Maybe she was dead.

There had been a moment out there in that icy water when she had resigned herself to fate. *This is it.* She had fully expected to die out there, the price to be paid for that foolish decision to go after the dog.

Not that it had felt like a decision.

She'd felt compelled, and had been out on the ice in an instant. It was as if her brain had turned off, and instinct had kicked in.

She mulled over the possibility that she might be dead. She had read stories—scoffed at the time—of people who had died and been unaware of it.

Maybe all the rest of it—that man coming on his belly across the ice—had been a fabrication of hope.

And Faith, of all people, should know the dangers that lay in hoping.

So, possibly, she was dead. Somehow, it seemed totally

unfair, that on death she would be greeted not by the husband she had spent thirty years with, Felix Saint-John, but by her first love.

Continue reading
THE BILLIONAIRE'S FESTIVE REUNION
Cara Colter

Available next month
millsandboon.co.uk

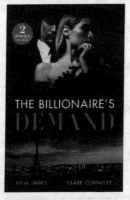
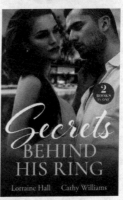

LET'S TALK
Romance

For exclusive extracts, competitions and special offers, find us online:

f MillsandBoon

X @MillsandBoon

O @MillsandBoonUK

♪ @MillsandBoonUK

Get in touch on 01413 063 232

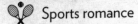
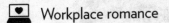

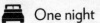